Rhyannon Byrd

DARK WOLF RETURNING

and

BLOOD WOLF DAWNING

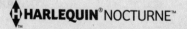

Recycling programs
for this product may
not exist in your area.

ISBN-13: 978-0-373-60978-9

Dark Wolf Returning and Blood Wolf Dawning

Copyright © 2014 by Harlequin Books S.A.

The publisher acknowledges the copyright holder
of the individual works as follows:

Dark Wolf Returning
Copyright © 2014 by Tabitha Bird

Blood Wolf Dawning
Copyright © 2014 by Tabitha Bird

Printed in U.S.A.

CONTENTS

DARK WOLF RETURNING

To the awesome readers who have given this series such wonderful support...

This one's for you!

Prologue

Love sucked. And it hurt. Like a bitch.

Carla Reyes believed this with every fiber of her being, because she'd learned it the hard way. By experience. She bore the internal scars to prove it.

But she wasn't alone. As far as tales of pain and betrayal and heartbreak went, she knew her specific story wasn't all that different from what had happened to thousands—make that millions—of other women around the world. At the emotional level, of course. Obviously, the fact that her mother was a werewolf, which made Carla a half-breed, added a certain edge to the situation. As did the fact that the object of her need was a male so completely and utterly alpha wolf, he'd once made other deadly Lycans literally scurry out of his path.

Now, from what she'd heard, he intimidated everyone he came across, no matter their species. Everyone but *her,* that is. She'd taught herself to feel nothing where Elijah Daniel Drake was concerned. And it had worked for a long time. Until her shields had been blasted to hell and back almost two weeks ago, when she'd been taken prisoner by a rival werewolf pack and overheard their battle plans before making her escape.

Now the time had come for him to make things right. Both for her…and for Eli's birth pack, the Maryland-based Silvercrest Lycans. Failure wasn't an option, because failure could mean the death of not only the pack, but also her friends and their loved ones. And her fellow Bloodrunners meant too much to her to sacrifice because of misplaced pride.

As Carla drove into the star-filled night, she was so tired she could almost taste the sweetness of sleep, but refused to give in. For two weeks, she'd had to struggle through injury and fatigue to find him. Tonight, he felt closer—within her reach—and she knew this was it. She was currently making her way across Louisiana, and within a mere matter of days, her search would finally be over.

Then she was going to do what she should have done the moment he'd abandoned her. She was going to end the pain once and for all. Break the connection, like a bone fracturing beneath the force of a brutal, crushing blow.

She was going to make him cut her loose…and be free.

After that, things would be…easier. She would get on with her life, and find a way to forget that she'd ever even known Eli Drake.

Were there risks with her plan? Of course. Weren't there always when it was something that mattered?

Her life as a Bloodrunner—a hunter of rogue wolves who had taken a liking for human flesh—was nothing but one continual risk after another. And now, thanks to Silvercrest enemies who were planning to attack the pack, which was already weakened after catastrophes it had suffered at the hands of Eli's own father, an inevitable war was on its way. A bloody battle on a scale she knew might very well wipe out every person she'd ever loved and cared about. Her band of brothers, in the truest sense of the word.

They needed Eli and his fellow mercenaries on their side. Needed the mercs' strength and expertise to help train the members of the pack who were willing to fight. But once he'd served his purpose, she was making this happen. Ripping him from her heart and her thoughts for the final time. For forever...

Even if it killed her.

Chapter 1

Two days later...

Eli Drake blinked his bleary eyes, unable to believe what he was seeing.

Shit. Had he drank so much he was hallucinating? If so, his pickled mind couldn't have come up with a more stunning, confounding vision. The hole-in-the-wall, small town Texas bar where he and his crew had landed for the night was a decent enough place to settle for a few hours while they tossed back some liquid therapy—and after the last assignment they'd taken, they'd definitely needed it. Hell, they could have drowned themselves in whiskey and beer for days on end, and it wouldn't have been enough to wipe out the horror of what they'd seen in that little South American village.

So, yeah, the woman who'd just walked into the bar *had* to be a by-product of his inebriation.

Only…as far as he could recall, he'd only had two whiskeys. For a man his size, even if he had been human, that wouldn't have been enough to make him start seeing…imagining… *Damn it.* He couldn't even get the words out within the privacy of his own mind.

Maybe it's a stress vision? I probably just need a break from my shitty day job.

Yeah, that was a better explanation than the alcohol, and extreme stress *had* been the riding theme of his life these past few weeks. Months. *Years.*

Squeezing his eyes shut, Eli focused on forcing the vision away. He didn't need crap like that screwing with his head. Sure, he was going to have to face her soon enough, considering he and his men were finally headed back to the mountains where he'd grown up, to his hometown of Shadow Peak, where the Silvercrest Lycans lived. But he wasn't ready for it now. Not tonight.

Facing Carla Reyes again after three years of banishment was something that would take battle armor and a heavy duty, steel-lined cup to protect his balls.

Fate, however, apparently didn't give a damn.

When the Lycan to his left softly swore under his breath, his deep voice rough with appreciation, Eli choked back a biting curse. Christ, he wasn't imagining things if others could see her, too. She was really there. In the flesh. Carla-Fucking-Reyes.

His next indrawn breath confirmed it, his dick hardening with ridiculous ease beneath the fly of his jeans. The soft, sleepy, feminine moan that followed made him look down, and he was momentarily surprised to find a woman straddling his lap, her face planted against his chest. He'd completely forgotten she was there, but then, it'd been a while since she'd spoken. He couldn't recall her name, but she wasn't in any shape to remind him.

She was out cold, a line of drool slipping from the corner of her pink lips.

Hmm... Classy chick.

With a jerk of his chin, he signaled Kyle Maddox, his second-in-command and the guy who'd spotted Carla, to deal with the comatose blonde. But it wasn't the woman on his lap that had Kyle's attention, his nostrils flaring as he pulled in the Runner's scent. Eli knew the moment his friend pegged her as a half-blood Lycan, his dark brows slowly rising on his forehead.

Eli gestured again to the blonde in his lap. "Take her."

Kyle snorted as he moved to his feet and lifted the woman into his arms. "And do what with her?"

Keeping his gaze locked on Carla, Eli said, "Just make sure she gets somewhere safe for the night. I don't want one of these assholes in here taking advantage of her."

"She's definitely a local girl, so I'll talk to the servers. Maybe one of them can take her home with them."

"Good," he muttered, impatient for Kyle to get the hell away from him before Carla reached the table. "Just do it."

Carla had spotted him in the crowd and was headed his way, her gaze sliding toward the nearby group of Lycans standing at the bar—Sam, James, and Lev—who were watching her with unmistakable interest. Even Kyle, who had moved over to join them with the blonde in his arms, had his full attention focused on Carla. She looked exhausted, but gorgeous. At five-six, she was just tall enough that she didn't look like a child when standing beside a man of Eli's height, but was still...petite. Lithely muscled and battle-scarred, but somehow still incredibly feminine. Big brown eyes flecked with green and framed by thick lashes. Slim, delicate nose. Waves of thick, silky hair the colors of sunshine and honey and gold, the soft bangs falling across her brow. She was, quite simply, stunning. The most perfect, alluring, sensual female he'd ever known.

And, Jesus, that mouth of hers had always been his undoing. Full, sexy, sweet. Velvety and pink, like the petals of a flower. He wanted to devour her. Kiss her until he drew blood, which wasn't surprising. From the moment she'd hit adulthood, this little half-breed had always drawn the hunger of both the man *and* the beast inside him. A hunger that was as visceral and dark as it was insatiable. How he'd fought it for so many years, when he'd been living with the pack, he didn't know. He should have been given a damn medal for not falling on her like a rabid, sex-starved animal the instant she came of age— but he'd somehow kept himself under tight control, his fears for her safety the only thing that had a chance in hell of keeping him in line.

He'd been a goddamn saint when it came to Reyes... until that last week before his banishment.

As if they were some kind of penance for his sins, the memories of her from that week still woke him in the dead of night in a sweat, filled with an aching need that was primal, savage, and raw. So powerful he could taste it in the back of his throat. Here he was, three years later, and he still dreamt about her every night he didn't drink himself into a stupor.

Studying her expression, Eli wondered if she was about to make him pay for the carnal things that had happened that week. Is that why she'd tracked him down? To tell him she'd rather see him dead before letting him return to the pack? Because that was definitely hatred he could see burning in her beautiful, narrowed eyes.

Shoving his emotional reaction to her presence to the back of his mind, he focused instead on simply watching her…waiting. Eating up the sight of her in the tight jeans and T-shirt and battered hiking boots.

At a quick glance, you would never guess she was a hunter of deadly werewolves. Certainly, the clueless humans in the bar, who had no idea they had shape-shifters in their midst, would have never guessed she was both battle and weapons trained. The Silvercrest Lycans would be surprised to know that much of that training had come from Eli himself, since it'd been in secret. Every aspect of their complicated "friendship" had been private and secret and forbidden.

God, he'd been so drawn to her. Though he was older than her, she hadn't been a typical giddy twenty-two-year-old when their relationship had developed. She'd been sweet, but reserved. Eager for friends, and yet, wary to trust. But she'd trusted him. Past tense.

Eli had never told a soul about them, and he could only assume that Carla had done the same. Though not for the same reasons.

He moved to his feet when she reached the table, fighting the powerful urge to pull her into his arms, and the next thing he knew her tiny fist was launching toward his mouth. *Whack!* Damn, she'd hit him so hard it jerked his head back, the coppery taste of his blood instantly filling his mouth.

Softly laughing under his breath, Eli lifted his hand and wiped the blood from the corner of his lip as he brought his gaze back to hers.

"What the hell is so funny?" Her soft words vibrated with fury.

"Nothing," he murmured, thinking he'd come close to getting what he wanted. Someone's blood had been drawn, just not hers. And not in the way he'd hoped for.

Contempt clouded her expression. "You never could just give an honest answer to a question, could you?"

"Insults and accusations already?" he drawled, sliding back into his chair. The worst thing in the world he could do was let her know how the sight of her affected him, especially when he could feel his own angry frustration with fate and life and her blatant hatred building inside him, desperate for release. "That didn't take long."

She drew in a sharp breath at his snide tone, the skin around her eyes tightening as she took the seat across from him and asked a passing server for a Scotch. It was clear from the look on her face that she hadn't meant to launch into the topic of their past. She was irritated with herself that she had, and seemed determined to get to the point of this strange, unexpected visit. "You know about your dad?"

"That he's dead?" He lifted a hand, rubbing his stubbled jaw. "Yeah, I heard about it."

As soon as the words left his mouth, a painful mix of emotions flashed through her eyes before she managed to bank them. "And you didn't think to come home?" she asked in a careful tone.

Brows drawn together, he tried to reason out why she thought the death of his psychotic father would herald his immediate return. Had the entire pack thought he would come crawling back the moment he learned that dear ol' daddy had staged a bloodthirsty coup that resulted in the death of the pack's entire governing body, the League of Elders? An attack that would have led to Stefan Drake's total control of the Silvercrest Lycans, if not for the help of the half-breeds his racist father had tried so hard to turn the pack against.

The League of Elders might have banished Eli for the unsanctioned kill he'd made on one of the rapists who'd attacked his sister three years ago...but they weren't the only reason he'd stayed away. Hell, they weren't even at the top of the list. No, his reasons for staying away had far more to do with... Well, with things he spent a lot of time trying not to think about. Things he was still trying to figure out how to deal with.

And every damn one of those things had to do with the woman sitting across from him.

Voice low, he finally responded to her question. "Once I heard that you and Eric and Elise were all right, I didn't see any reason to rush home. But I didn't plan on staying away forever, Rey. I was coming back."

"When?" she asked, as the server set her drink on the table.

"Now, if you can believe it. That's where we're headed."

"Bullshit." She gave a bitter laugh. "You know what I think? I think you were waiting for *me* to come to *you*. And here I am," she offered with a sharp smile, spreading her arms wide, and he couldn't help but notice the way the cotton shirt stretched tight across her mouthwatering breasts. Then she leaned forward, bracing her palms flat on the rickety little table with its scarred surface and dirty ashtray, and lowered her voice. "But I'm not here to beg for myself, Eli. I just need you and your ragtag little group to come back with me and do what you do best."

Hoping to rile her into hitting him again, like some kind of masochist—though he was pretty sure he just wanted to feel her hands on him—his lips curled in a cocky smirk. "You have no idea what I do best. You only got *part* of the show, if you'll recall."

"Not interested," she grunted in response to his silky, suggestive tone, before taking a drink of her Scotch. She winced as she swallowed the smoky alcohol, then wiped her mouth and shot his cocky expression right back at him. "And let's face it, Eli. The only thing you've ever done well is kill."

"Ouch, Reyes. If I didn't know better," he murmured, clucking his tongue, "I'd say you don't like me anymore."

She rolled her eyes. "Just get your band of Merry Men together and let's get out of here."

"Merry Men?" he snorted. "I'm no bloody Robin Hood."

She smirked. "Yeah, what was I thinking? The idea of giving something to the less fortunate is probably a little sappy for a guy like you."

"A guy like me?"

Lifting her brows, she said, "You know, the big bad mercenary who doesn't give a shit about anything or anyone, except for how much they can pay him. I hear you've cultivated the reputation well."

Irritation burned through his veins, not easy to hide. But he managed with a lazy grin and a slow drawl. "You shouldn't believe everything you hear. A lot of men will lie when it suits them."

"Oh, God." She suddenly started to laugh so hard it made him scowl. Wiping the tears from her glittering eyes, she finally managed to splutter, "D-don't I know it."

Hell, he'd walked right into that one.

A fraction of his control began to slip, his hands flexing as he fought the urge to reach out and grab her, yanking her into his lap. "You're pushing it, Reyes."

Her laughter faded, and she kept her gaze on the Scotch as she swirled it in her glass. "If you're uncomfortable with my attitude or reactions," she murmured, "then I gotta tell you that I don't really care. I'm not here to make you feel better, or to talk about the past." She stopped swirling her drink, her dark gaze lifting, locking with his. "I'm here because your family needs you. You do recall that you have a brother and sister, right? And I can only imagine they have a hell of a lot to say to you right now, considering you haven't been returning their calls." She pushed back from the table and gave him a look that would probably scare a lot of men into doing whatever the hell she wanted them to. "Now get off your ass and let's get out of here."

"No," he rasped. "Not until you answer a few of *my* questions."

"Like we have the time," she started to argue, but he cut her off.

"We have as much time as we need, because I'm not going anywhere until you fucking spill." He took a deep swallow of his whiskey, and waited for her to bring her chair back to the table, before asking, "You came here alone?"

"Of course." At the look on his face, she said, "What? You thought someone needed to come with me and hold my hand?"

His jaw got tighter. "Why now?"

She glared back at him as if she couldn't understand what his problem was. "War isn't enough of a reason?"

"From what I've understood from Eric's messages, the Silvercrest have been in trouble for a while now."

"With no help from you, huh?"

He narrowed his eyes. "Like I said, I was planning to head back."

"Right. How kind of you."

"Why *now*, Reyes? Why *you*? You didn't rush out and try to track me down months ago, when this all started. So tell me the truth. Why— Now?"

She held his stare, and he could tell she was planning on just waiting him out, until she let herself really look him in the eye. Whatever she saw there, whether it was anger or his sheer determination—it made her frown deepen. Forcing the words out between her quickening breaths, she told him, "It was the right time. I felt...raw. And I suddenly *knew* I could find you. When I was in danger, the bond started to pull at me—"

"So you feel it, too?" he cut in sharply, interrupting her explanation. His heart started trying to pound its way through his chest with hard, violent beats, and it was all he could do to stay in his damn chair in his relaxed pose, instead of surging to his feet and grabbing her shoulders, demanding she tell him *everything*.

Still scowling, she cast a wary look toward the hand still holding his glass, as if surprised it hadn't shattered in his brutal grip. Her chin lifted in assent.

"I've wondered about that." He tossed back his drink, slamming the empty glass onto the table, while his thoughts churned. He felt pain, frustration, loss. But mostly rage. A deep, seething rage for everything that had happened, and why.

He cleared his throat, his hooded gaze locked in hard and tight on her face, trying to read her expression. The bond should have enabled him to feel her emotions as easily as his own, but it didn't, because it was only half-formed. He'd realized that right from the start, though it'd taken time to sort out exactly how the partially formed bond would affect him. And it'd kept him up at nights, wondering if Carla was being affected in the same way.

When he couldn't get a damn thing from the look on her face, Eli lowered his gaze to the table and heard himself saying, "For what it's worth, I didn't even realize the bond had taken hold until almost a week after I left. By that time, I was already in South America."

When he looked up to see her reaction to his confession, she turned her head to the side and laughed again. The sound was hollow and heavy, sounding as exhausted as she looked. "Well," she murmured. "I guess it's good to know I'm not the only one stuck in this hell."

His jaw tightened, but he forced out a slow breath, not wanting to rise to her bait. And she was definitely baiting him, spoiling for a fight. Damn it, he was handling this all wrong, but it was like a train wreck he couldn't stop from happening right in front of him. He was pissed at how badly he wanted her. At how fucking sexy she looked. How angry she was at him.

Knowing he needed to change the subject, he asked, "What were you in danger from?"

Her mouth flattened with irritation, as if she hadn't meant to let that bit slip out either, her reluctance making him even more suspicious. He could feel it in his gut, the fact that there was something she didn't want to tell him. "I'll sit here all damn night and wait you out if I have to," he threatened in a low voice. "But you're going to answer that question."

She took a deep breath, her nostrils flaring a little, and he felt the pull down in his lower body get even tighter as he wondered if she could scent him the way he could scent her. Not just on a Lycan level, but one that went even deeper. And if she could, was it affecting her, making her hungry for something only *he* could give her?

Her head dropped back on her shoulders, then dropped forward, and he could have sworn he heard her give a soft growl. Then she lifted her head, looking right at him, and nervously licked her lips. "I know Eric's been leaving you messages at a number he had for you, asking you to come home. Didn't he tell you about Elise?"

Because he was so often in places where cell phone coverage was nonexistent, and hadn't had a permanent base since leaving the pack, Eli had used a couple of different messaging services for both work and his family. It was one of those numbers that Eric had been calling.

Answering her question, he said, "I haven't heard from Eric the last couple of weeks. He sounded pretty pissed off in his last message, because I hadn't returned any of his calls. But I wasn't in a situation where I could talk to him," he explained, which was only partially true. "What is it you think he should have told me about Elise? Is she all right?"

"Two weeks ago, Elise was kidnapped by Sebastian Claymore."

He shot forward to the edge of his seat. "Was she hurt? What the hell happened?"

From what he'd been able to piece together from Eric's messages, Eli knew that a Lycan named Roy Claymore had assumed control of the Whiteclaw pack, and Sebastian and Harris Claymore were his nephews. Eric's last message had mentioned something about Harris being under suspicion for hassling their sister, Elise, and that had been enough for Eli to know he needed to get his affairs in order so that he could head back, even though he'd known it would mean facing Carla. Elise had already been through too much not to have her brothers there looking out for her. He just hadn't realized the situation would escalate so quickly. Had thought he still had time to make it back, before he was needed.

"She's fine, Eli. She made it out of there that same day, and she wasn't...they didn't hurt her."

"Eric mentioned that the Runners were having trouble with the Whiteclaw, but said he'd go into more detail when I got in touch with him. What exactly did the Claymores want with her?"

"It's a long story, and not one for someplace this

crowded. She was scared, but she wasn't harmed. I made sure to give them a hard enough time that it kept them busy."

"You were with her?" he asked sharply, while the mother of all headaches started pounding in his temples.

"I was taken as well," she murmured, clearly not wanting to make a big deal out of it. "They were able to sneak up on us, and we were taken back to Hawkley together."

They'd taken his woman and his sister to Hawkley, the Whiteclaw pack's hometown? A place where they would have been surrounded by those bastards?

Oh, hell, those sons of bitches are gonna die.

There were about a million questions he wanted answers to, but Eli scraped out the most important one first: "Did they touch you?"

The idea of her in danger—a danger he hadn't been able to sense because of the weakness of their bond— was too much for him, making his inner beast seethe for release. His gums ached from the heavy weight of his fangs, the tips of his fingers burning as his claws prickled beneath his skin. He couldn't believe he was a fraction away from shifting in the middle of a goddamn human bar, but that's how this woman had always affected him, making him do things he'd never thought he would otherwise do.

Instead of tensing up and getting riled by his demanding tone, her posture had relaxed, one lightly muscled arm hooked over the back of her chair. "That isn't something that should concern you."

"Did they touch you?" he asked again, his voice now little more than a snarl.

Cocking her head a bit to the side, she studied him through her lashes. After a heavy silence, she finally said,

"I would have been raped if I hadn't managed to get free. As it was, I just got knocked around a bit."

He wanted to roar at how casual she sounded about that, when it made him want to go for the blood of every Lycan who'd hit her, gleefully ripping them apart, one painful piece at a time. "How did you get away?"

"I knew that when the Runners realized we were missing, Wyatt would—" She paused suddenly, giving him a strange look. "Uh, when Eric left you messages, did he happen to mention that Elise and Wyatt Pallaton are bonded now?"

"I didn't know it'd happened, but Eric thought it was headed that way."

He could tell she was trying to figure out how he felt about his sister permanently attaching herself to the male who was Carla's Bloodrunning partner, but he didn't know. Until he saw the two of them together, he wasn't forming an opinion. If Pallaton treated his sister right and made her happy, he'd have no issue with him. If he didn't, Eli was going to kick his ass. It was as simple as that.

Reaching for her glass again, she said, "Anyway, I knew Wyatt and the others were coming, but there was no way they would get to her if I didn't create a distraction. So that's what I did."

"And afterward?" he pressed, sensing that she was leaving out a hell of a lot. He had a strong suspicion her distraction had required her to put her own life at even greater risk to save his sister's, and it made him both grateful and viciously angry.

She downed the last of her drink, and set the glass back on the table. "While I was making my escape, I heard some things that compelled me to steal some money and a car and come after you."

"To drag me back home. For the pack."

She gave him a look that would have wilted a lesser man. "It sure as hell isn't because I want you there."

"What did you hear?" he demanded, noticing the discoloration on her cheekbone as she turned her head and the light caught it. It was a healing bruise, and based on how many days since she'd gotten it, he knew it must have initially been brutal. Lycans had accelerated healing abilities, and though she was only half wolf, her body healed much faster than a human's. Given the look of her face now, Eli imagined she'd been more than knocked around a little, and he was looking forward to paying back the ones who were responsible. In blood and pain and death.

"Before I left Hawkley," she finally replied, bringing that dark gaze back to his, "I overheard some of the Whiteclaw soldiers talking about their plans for the Silvercrest. They haven't managed to secure the number of soldiers they were hoping for from other packs, so they've come up with a new plan. One even deadlier than we'd feared. Since you said Eric didn't go into a lot of detail in his messages, it sounds like there's a lot you need to be brought up to speed on. But you can believe me when I say we need a miracle, Eli. Unfortunately, the only thing we've got on our side, other than my guys, is you."

He knew who she meant by her "guys." There were five men who made up the Silvercrest's Bloodrunning team: Mason Dillinger, Jeremy Burns, Brody Carter, Wyatt Pallaton, and Cian Hennessey. Actually, he needed to make that six men, since his brother Eric was now working as a Runner, though the last Eli had heard, his brother wasn't partnered up yet the way the others were.

At his silence, she added, "You were always rumored to be the most ruthless wolf the pack had ever seen. Jeremy told us you tore the male who attacked Elise into pieces. That's the kind of man we need."

For a moment, he was surprised that Jeremy knew what had happened, since his father had purposefully kept the Runners ignorant of Elise's attack. The only reason Carla had known was because Eli had told her. She wouldn't have been able to share that confidence with any of her fellow Bloodrunners without giving away their secret relationship, but that didn't mean that the truth hadn't eventually been leaked by someone else. For all he knew, Elise herself had been the one to finally share the horrific story. Or perhaps Eric, since he was now one of them.

Not that it mattered. Regardless of how Jeremy had learned what he'd done, what she'd said was true. Eli *had* ripped that bastard to pieces, and he didn't regret it. But it bothered him that Carla might think of him as some kind of monster, and he couldn't stop himself from asking her if that's what she'd meant.

"Are you calling me a monster?"

"No." She slowly arched her brows. "I'd only use that term if I was talking about your personality."

He let that slide, knowing she was willing to say anything to make the canyon between them even deeper.

"So how did you find me?"

She shifted a little uncomfortably in the chair, but she didn't refuse to explain. "It was like the thing with the Whiteclaw jolted me out of a fog, and I suddenly knew that it would work. That if I wanted to, I'd be able to pinpoint your location. So instead of making my way back home with the others, I stole a car. Grabbed a map from the glove box. Called Wyatt and told him I was coming after you."

Staring at her beautiful face, Eli felt a confusing wave of emotion sweep through him, piercing and sharp. He'd heard that in times of danger, a bonded mate could use the connection that created the bond to locate their other half.

And if the distance was too great, they could use a map to help feel the "pull" that would take them in the right direction. From the sound of it, it'd taken Carla several weeks to find him, which seemed longer than he would have expected. But, then, their bond wasn't complete, which meant it probably didn't pull as strongly as others.

He refused to acknowledge how much that little fact irritated him. He hadn't had any right forming a bond with her in the first place, much less to be angry that it wasn't as powerful as it should have been.

"You need to come back," she said, the quiet words breaking into his thoughts. "Your pack needs you, and Elise and Eric need you."

"And what about you? Do *you* need me?"

She didn't try to shy away from the question. Looking him right in the eye, she said, "Like I need a hole in the head."

There were so many things that he wanted to say to that. The anger that had initially risen up in the face of her own rage was fading, replaced by a raw, intense knot of regret that was making him break out in a sweat. "We have a lot we need to talk about, Rey."

"Like hell we do. All I need is your ass on that mountaintop, ready to do battle, and not a damn thing more."

Eli gave a frustrated shake of his head. "You really think we can fight together and not talk about the elephant here in the room with us?"

"That's exactly what I think, because I have a few conditions before I agree to *let* you come home."

"You came here for me," he pointed out, scowling as he picked up on one of his guys snickering under their breath. It sounded like Sam, and he knew the jackass was enjoying hearing him get his ass handed to him by a woman. "What do you want, Reyes?"

Voice little more than a whisper, she kept her gaze locked on his, and said, "I want the bond broken."

His muscles pulled so tight he was surprised he didn't shatter, a feeling of dread coiling through his insides that felt remarkably similar to fear. "It can't be done."

"It *can*."

"What the hell are you talking about?"

"Come home with me, Eli. Fight for your pack. And when the blood clears, you and I can erase what never should have happened in the first place." She leaned forward in her chair, her eyes bright. "We can finally end this nightmare, once and for all."

"You really think you can do it?" he scoffed. "Break an unbreakable bond?"

"Yes." She gave him a slow, determined smile. "I plan on breaking the hell out of it."

Chapter 2

Carla knew the instant he realized she wasn't bullshitting him, his belligerent expression slowly giving way to shock.

It was because of Eli's supercharged bloodline and her own powerful alpha genes that they'd ended up in this mess. At least that's what her friend Jillian believed had been the cause of her problems, landing her with a bond that was, but wasn't. One that was only partially fixed in place, thanks to the crappiest timing in the universe. Or…maybe the luckiest, depending on how you looked at it. In Carla's case, a partial bond was better than a full, *un*breakable one.

As it was, she'd been able to manage without him. Oh, her heart had been battered and bruised for…well, for a long time after he'd abandoned her. But she'd been able to go on, functioning without him.

The only thing she hadn't been able to do was crawl into bed with another man.

Eli, from the look of things when she'd walked into the bar and found him with a scantily clad blonde passed out in his lap, hadn't been suffering that particular symptom. And, God, did that tick her off.

After all, it wasn't like a guy who looked like him would have trouble getting any woman he wanted in his bed. A man too gorgeous to be real—and certainly for his own good. Chiseled, rugged, and massive. Tall and broad and ripped with muscle. Golden skin. Ice blue eyes rimmed with dark, stormy gray. Thick, inky black lashes. He'd always worn his hair short when she'd known him but it was shaggy now, curling around his neck and ears. Messy in that way that movie stars spent a fortune trying to achieve, while Eli probably just ran his hands through it and let it dry. Unfair, how beautiful he was. A dangerous, primal predator who could slay with nothing more than a sarcastic twist of that bold, sensual mouth.

He was so breathtakingly masculine, and so impossibly lethal. To the heart as well as the flesh. And she knew that lesson better than anyone.

Taking a deep breath, she tried to calm down, knowing he could no doubt sense her every emotion. But it was difficult when inside she was seething with rage. She hated feeling this out of control. It wasn't something she allowed, given her occupation. Anger made you stupid, and a hunter couldn't afford to make careless mistakes.

Neither could a woman.

The silence that had settled between them was just about to the point where she wanted to snap at him to say something already, when the tall guy she'd seen him sitting with earlier approached the table. Thankfully without the blonde Eli had dumped in his arms. "I hate to

interrupt, but we need to get out of here. They're closing soon."

Eli nodded, then moved to his feet in a rippling display
of muscle that his jeans and T-shirt did little to conceal.
As she stood, as well, the rest of the group who'd been
standing nearby at the bar joined them, looking between
her and Eli as if they were waiting for him to make the
introductions.

Sounding more than a little pissed off, Eli said, "Carla,
this is Kyle Maddox, Sam Harmon, James Bennett, and
Lev Slivkoff. Guys, this is Carla Reyes. I, uh, know her
from home."

Carla almost winced in sympathy for the gorgeous
jerk, since he'd sounded so awkward there at the end, as
if he didn't know what to say about her. He'd obviously
never mentioned her to any of his friends or coworkers or
whatever a badass Lycan called the other badass Lycan
mercenaries that he fought with. Something buried deep
inside her gave a stupidly pained cry at that fact, but she
refused to pay any attention to it. She wasn't going to
let a little hurt make her act like an idiot in front of him.

"It's nice to meet you," she murmured, shaking their
rough, battle-hardened hands. They were all tanned and
tall and dark, except for Lev, whose shoulder-length mane
was as golden as hers. And while the others had dark,
midnight-colored eyes that nearly drowned out their
ebony pupils, his were an interesting mix of green and
blue that could barely pass for human.

They were all pretty much stunningly attractive, oozing the kind of raw sex appeal that probably made most
women drool when they saw them—but Lev was definitely the best looking of the bunch, reminding her of a
badass Russian enforcer she'd once met during a hunt.
When he grabbed her hand, she almost laughed, think-

ing he was going to kiss the back of it, like something out of a movie. But he didn't. Instead, he turned it over and licked the inside of her wrist with a rough tongue, right over her pulse. Her startled gasp was drowned out by Eli's guttural snarl, and the next thing she knew Lev had released her hand and was stumbling into the guy named James, who had a wicked scar on his throat, because Eli had just given Lev a violent shove.

"Don't be a jackass," Eli growled.

"He loves me, really," the Lycan drawled, though there was something in his rich, masculine scent that told her he was more. They all were. She just didn't know what that *more* was, and there was no way in hell she was asking when she wasn't sure she wanted to know the answer.

Carla kept a careful eye on the group as they settled their bill at the bar, not quite sure what to expect from them. They were eyeing her with open looks of curiosity and friendly smiles, but she was still a bit wary. Not physically, but emotionally. The last thing she wanted was for one of them to blurt out a question about her relationship with Eli. And they looked nosey enough to do it.

"Since the men and I are heading back with you," Eli rumbled, "we should find a motel for the night, then hit the road first thing in the morning."

She'd just started to ask how quickly he thought they could reach Maryland, when the sound of screeching tires and loud voices came from the bar's front parking lot.

"What was that?" she asked, though no one was paying her any attention. They were all focused on the one named Sam, who had made his way over to one of the front windows and was peeking outside. "Shit," he muttered. "It looks like we've got a problem."

Eli grabbed her arm and jerked her behind him. "Who is it?"

"I can't tell yet," Sam replied, while the remaining customers, along with the staff, started pouring out the back entrance. It apparently wasn't the first time this place had seen this kind of "problem," and given the look of the clientele, Carla doubted it would be the last. "But we've got three pickups with beds full of armed bad guys," Sam was saying, "and they're stopping by our trucks. So my guess is that they're here for us."

"Were you followed here?" Lev asked her.

"What? No! Of course not."

"Then they're definitely here for us," the one named James murmured in a deep, gravelly voice.

"Don't be so sure," Eli muttered. "She has a knack for dragging trouble in her wake."

"I do not!" she snapped, poking him hard in the back of his shoulder.

Sam scratched his head as he sauntered back over to the group, a funny expression on his handsome face as he looked at Eli. "I've never seen him like this," he seemed to be saying to the other guys. "He's always so blasted nice to women. Why's he keep riling this little thing?"

James shrugged. "Beats me."

"All of you, mind your own damn business," Eli growled.

Kyle flashed a smile. "I don't know about you guys, but I'm starting to get a good idea of the problem."

Lev threw back his head and let out a lusty laugh. "This is gonna be priceless."

Eli slowly looked from one man to the next, his powerful frame drawn tight with tension. "Shut up about her," he said in a low voice, "or I'll break your heads before those idiots out there even get a chance."

As she moved back to his side, Carla thought he looked

and sounded more than ready to thrash the next guy who teased him, but they didn't seem to care.

"You don't have to get so testy," Sam drawled, his dark eyes shining with humor. "We like her."

"I'm afraid the feeling isn't mutual anymore," she muttered, reaching back and pulling the gun she'd stolen off one of the Whiteclaw soldiers from the waistband of her jeans.

"Oh, God," Lev murmured, clutching his heart when she opened the clip, checking her ammo. "I think I just fell in love."

At her startled look, Sam laughed. "Lev has a thing about women who can handle a weapon."

"Mmm. That I do."

Kyle snorted. "He has a thing about *all* women."

The blond arched his tawny brows at the grinning merc. "And you don't?"

Kyle winked and blew him a kiss. "Don't go sounding jealous, honey. You know I love you."

This time, Lev was the one who snorted. "You just like the way I fill out my jeans."

Carla looked at the four laughing idiots and wondered what on earth she'd gotten herself into. What was Eli doing with these clowns? She'd come here for warriors, damn it. Not a collection of frat boys who enjoyed ribbing each other.

Though, to be fair, these mercs didn't look anything like any frat boy she'd ever seen. They would have made even the college ball players look puny.

Ah, now I get it, she thought a few minutes later, after they'd decided how to handle the situation and she, Eli, and Kyle had made their way out the back entrance and around the left side of the building. The customers and staff had thankfully scattered, no doubt heading into one of the other bars farther down the road, since there wasn't much of anything else around. There'd been a small group of human thugs lying in wait for the mercenaries just outside the exit, but Lev, Sam, and James, who'd gone out first, had quickly taken care of them, before going right. Then the three mercs had engaged the armed gunmen causing havoc in the front parking lot, while Eli and Kyle stayed with her in the shadows.

These guys might act like a bunch of frat boys, but they sure as hell didn't fight like them. Relief swept through her in a warm rush as she watched them, making her breathe a bit easier. If she was going to have to endure the seven circles of hell by being close to Eli, she at least wanted to know it was for a good reason. And protecting the ones she loved was as good a reason as there was.

Wyatt was worried about her, and had tried talking her into coming back during each of their conversations since she'd started this journey. It was a testament to how much she meant to all the guys, since they knew Eli and his men were needed—but they apparently cared about her even more. She really was like the little sister none of them had, aside from Eric, and she should have realized how they would react to her heading off on her own. There was probably going to be hell to pay when she finally made it back to the Alley—the place that the Bloodrunners called home.

But at least it would have been worth it. These mercenaries might be even more of a joking, smartass group than the Runners, but they were seriously skilled when it came to combat. Bullets sprayed from the humans' guns as they scattered around the remaining cars in the lot and shot wildly into the night, unable to pinpoint the mercs' locations as the guys quickly took down one assailant after another. She could sense Eli and Kyle's need to join the fight and help their friends, but knew they were sticking close to her in order to provide protection.

Eli Drake had always been the most overprotective male she'd ever known, and that obviously hadn't changed. She knew he didn't want to leave her side, but when it looked like four of the thugs were going to slash the tires on the two shiny, badass black trucks she assumed belonged to the mercs, he told her to stay with Kyle, and headed off to deal with them.

"You know, we don't have to hide over here," she murmured, as soon as Eli had left. "I'm perfectly capable of helping in a fight."

"I'm sure you are, honey. But I think Eli would probably castrate me if I let anything happen to you. And I'm kinda partial to all my body parts."

That probably would have been the end of it, if another truckload of men hadn't come barreling into the lot. Someone must have called for reinforcements, and this time the truck stopped near the side of the building where she was waiting with Kyle. No longer willing to stand this one out when the mercs were so outnumbered, she lifted her weapon as she moved toward the cover of a nearby grove of pecan trees and started firing on the armed gunmen who were shooting into the parking lot.

Carla had managed to take out five of the humans, before she felt a sharp burn cut across her left side, just beneath the edge of her bra. It felt like acid had been poured onto her skin, but she kept firing, until the last gunman in the truck fell. Then she slumped against the thick tree trunk Kyle had pulled her behind, listening to the fighting still taking place out in the parking lot. There wasn't as much gunfire now, and she knew things were winding down. They needed to get out of there while they still could, before the cops showed up and things *really* got complicated.

"You're gonna be in so much trouble," Kyle predicted, his low voice holding the soft, melting edge of a Southern accent. "Eli told you to stay out of it."

"I didn't even get my claws out," she huffed. "All I did was fire some bullets."

"He's still gonna be pissed."

Ignoring him, she took another look around the side of the tree and watched as Lev finally caught one of the few remaining gunmen for questioning, his big hand fisted in the front of the guy's bloodied shirt as he pulled the Hispanic-looking male close to his face and spoke to him. The human was apparently being stubborn, because Lev gave him a frustrated shake that probably jarred the thug's brain loose. She could see his lips moving, and a moment later Lev tossed him aside, not even bothering to watch where the guy landed as he turned and started making his way over to where she stood with Kyle.

"What the hell is their problem?" Kyle asked, as soon as Lev was within hearing distance.

"They work for Julio Varga. Seems ol' Julio thinks Eli slept with his woman when we were staying down at their compound last month."

All this because Eli screwed the wrong woman? she thought, her lip curling in a disgusted sneer. "Why doesn't that surprise me?"

Kyle clucked his tongue at her in admonishment. "He didn't touch her, honey." Jerking his head toward a smirking Lev, he added, "It was this jackass who couldn't keep it in his pants."

Lev's grin got wider. "Not fair, man. She caught me when I wasn't wearing any."

"You could have tried a little self-control," Kyle muttered.

"I did," Lev protested. "But then she got on her knees and—"

"Enough!" Carla waved the hand still holding her empty gun, cutting him off. "I don't want to hear this."

Waggling his brows, the golden Adonis sent her a crooked smile. "You sure, pretty wolf? It's good stuff."

"Then maybe over a beer sometime," she relented, finding his boyish charm kind of endearing. He was like a big freaking teddy bear, once you got past the serious sex appeal. "But not in the middle of a fight."

Before either male could say another word, the gunfire abruptly ended, and Eli was suddenly standing right in front of her. His face and arms were spattered with blood, his shirt and hair damp with sweat, while all those acres of hard muscle flexed beneath his skin as he breathed in a harsh rhythm. And the expression on his face was as darkly furious as his tone. "What the fuck, Carla? Did you or did you not hear me tell you to stay out of it?"

"Oh, I heard you," she murmured, trying to ignore the fire in her side. "I just don't take orders from you."

His nostrils flared, and he fisted his massive hands at his sides. "If you had, then you wouldn't be bleeding."

"Shit! She got shot?" Kyle moved to get a better look at her, and his eyes went wide when he saw her blood-soaked left side. "Damn it, woman. Why didn't you tell me?"

"Because I'm fine. It's just a graze." She lifted her brows when she looked at Eli. "And I didn't know you found the sight of a little blood so upsetting."

One of the mercs choked off a laugh, though she couldn't tell which one. She was too busy keeping a care-

ful eye on Eli, since he looked like he wanted to throttle her.

"Come on," he finally muttered, gripping her right
arm and dragging her with him as he headed toward those
massive black trucks that sat on the far side of the lot.

"Wait, I need my car!" she yelled, looking toward the
little VW she'd picked up for almost nothing the week
before. It looked a little sad, but damn it, that car had
character. She couldn't just leave it there all by its lone-
some to turn into a rust bucket.

Eli flicked a dismissive look over the car. "That piece
of shit stays here."

"Oh, no, it doesn't!"

"It's not even yours," he argued, obviously noticing
the Georgia plates.

"Is too!" she shot back, wishing he wouldn't walk
quite so fast, since her head was starting to get a bit
woozy. "I bought it off a guy in Atlanta last week for a
hundred bucks."

He stopped and gave her a look that set her teeth on
edge, as if he thought she'd gone out of her mind. "You
bought a stolen car off some random guy?"

She clenched her teeth, having already figured that
part out for herself. No way the human would have sold
it to her for that amount if the transaction had been legit.
He'd probably just been looking for some quick money
to pay for his next fix. And it's not like they'd dealt with
any of the legal paperwork. She'd just needed to ditch the
car she'd stolen off the Whiteclaw and find something a
little more fuel efficient, since it'd become apparent that
tracking down her so-called "other half" was going to
take more time than she'd hoped.

So, yeah, the car was most likely hot. But she'd still
paid money for it!

"What if I take the keys inside and leave a note to let them know she's up for grabs?" James offered, speaking up for the first time since they'd come outside.

"Fine," she muttered, figuring it was better than nothing. "But please get my bag out of the trunk first."

James nodded as he took the keys she'd dug out of her pocket, the pain in her side burning like holy hell as she moved. But she refused to groan, not wanting to give Eli the satisfaction. Instead, she glared at him as he pulled a set of keys from his own pocket.

"Are you even sober enough to drive?" she asked with a scowl.

He wasn't looking at her, but she could swear he was rolling his eyes at the question. "We're not human, Rey. It would take a hell of a lot more than what any of us have had tonight to put us over the limit." Then, in a lower voice, he muttered, "And you should know I wouldn't put you at risk like that."

Five minutes later, she was sitting in the front seat of one truck, one of the guy's T-shirts balled up and pressed against her side, while Eli drove and Lev and Sam sat in the spacious backseat. Kyle and James had piled into the other truck, along with everyone's gear. Since Eli refused to stay in the town they'd just been attacked in, in case this Varga guy decided to send more men after them, they had to drive for nearly an hour before they found a cheap roadside motel that had enough rooms for them all. Unfortunately, she hadn't been paying close enough attention when they were checking in, the blood loss making her a little dizzy, because it wasn't until the keys were handed out that she realized they were one key short.

Which meant they had five rooms, instead of six.

Son of a freaking bitch!

"Eli," she started to growl, before stumbling and

nearly face planting against the cracked concrete walk-way that led to the rooms. *Damn it!* Her lack of decent sleep the last two weeks, combined with the stress of finally facing Eli again, not to mention the blood loss, was getting to her. She was thankful the other Runners weren't there to see her like this. They never would have let her live it down.

Kyle had grabbed her before she collapsed, his hold careful, as if he was afraid of hurting her. Did she really seem that fragile? "I think one of us should carry her," he said, glancing at the others over the top of her head. "She's looking a little pale."

"I've got her," Eli grunted, his heavy arm wrapping around her shoulders as he pulled her out of Kyle's hands and jerked her against his side.

"I don't know, boss man. You sure you don't need any help?" Kyle asked from behind them, sounding both concerned and like he was trying not to laugh his ass off. She wasn't sure what he found so freaking funny, but if it turned out to have anything to do with her, she was going to kick him. Hard.

"Kyle?" Eli muttered, as he opened the door to one of the rooms and all but shoved her inside.

"Yeah?" Kyle asked from the sidewalk.

"Piss off." Eli slammed the door in the merc's smirking face, then turned around and shoved a hand through his hair, his narrow gaze immediately connecting with hers. Carla had sat down on the foot of one of the beds, her left side now completely covered in blood. She'd felt a wave of relief when she'd seen that there were two beds in the room—but the look on Eli's face as he pinned her under his dark glare completely shredded it. He still looked like he wanted to throttle her, but there was something even darker than anger in his unusual eyes, and it had her pulse kicking up. She wasn't afraid of him, but that hungry, visceral look made her nervous as hell.

Needing a distraction, she said, "I could have paid for my own room, you know."

His response was dry. "My mistake. I wasn't aware you'd be flush with cash after escaping from a kidnapping."

She lifted her chin. "I didn't run empty-handed. I stole a wad of cash off the Whiteclaw. There's still enough left to pay for my rooms and my meals on our way back."

"Don't worry about it. We've got it covered," he murmured, slipping two packs she hadn't even noticed he was carrying off his shoulder. She was glad to see that one of the bags was hers. The blood on her skin was starting to get sticky, and she was trying to work up the energy to head to the shower so she could clean it off, when he set his bag down on the desk, opened it up, and pulled out a first-aid kit. He came over to the bed she was sitting on and started taking things out of the kit—antiseptic wipes and some ointment—setting them on the comforter.

Carla knew she should object when he grabbed the chair in front of the desk and dragged it over, sat down, then took a pair of scissors from the kit and started cutting her ruined shirt off. But she just couldn't find the energy. If he wanted to help her, fine. It didn't mean anything, and it sure as hell wasn't going to lead to anything.

"Your men, they seem pretty loyal to you," she said to break the uncomfortable silence. As well as to get her attention focused on something other than how freaking hot he looked. Eli had always worn the post-fight look well, and it looked even better on him now, with his shaggy hair and fierce expression. There were more little lines crinkling at the corners of his eyes than the last time she'd seen him, but they only added to his rugged appeal. It was one of those unfair imbalances in the universe, how things that made a woman look aged usually only a made a man look more attractive. And Eli wore that "lived in" look well.

She didn't think he was going to bother giving her any kind of response, but he surprised her when he tossed her ruined shirt aside and said, "They're a good bunch of guys. We've been through a lot together."

She didn't have time to be embarrassed about sitting there in nothing but her jeans and bra, because he opened one of the wipes and started cleaning the oozing wound. Her breath hissed through her teeth at the sharp sting of pain, but she forced it to the back of her mind and asked, "How did you all meet?"

He tossed the wipe into the nearby trashcan, and shot her a wry glance. "How about I tell you that story when you don't look like you're about to pass out?"

"I'm fine. I've had worse than this and survived." *Both physically...and emotionally.*

He frowned, as if he'd heard her thoughts. Or maybe he just didn't like the idea of her getting hurt. He never had liked her being a Runner, thinking it was too dangerous. But she'd never had any intention of leaving her job to make him happy. The way she'd seen it, if he'd truly cared about her, he would have learned to accept her and see her for who she really was: a woman *and* a warrior.

But, then, he'd never really cared about her, had he?

Trailing his rough fingertips just under the graze, he said, "You'll heal with rest, but the bra needs to come off or it's going to keep rubbing against the wound during the night."

Carla looked him right in the eye and gave him her best *as if* look. "Not—Happening."

"I wasn't asking, Rey."

Gritting teeth, she muttered, "You always were a bossy, manipulative jerk."

He snorted as he shoved the chair back and knelt in front of her, his big body so close she could feel his delicious heat like a physical touch against her chilled skin. "And yet you used to love spending time with me," he offered huskily, his mouthwatering scent settling on her tongue like a gift. "What do you think that says about you, princess?"

God, he was so damn good at pissing her off. "I'm *not* a princess."

His sensual lips curved in a way that would have made any other woman whose heart he hadn't shredded lightheaded with desire. "Sure you are, Rey. All those big bruisers in the Alley think of you as their little sister, which makes you the princess of the group."

"They think of me as their equal," she snarled, wondering why he was goading her on purpose. Then she felt her nipples tightening in the cool air, and realized he'd managed to cut her bra off while she'd been growling at him. *Argh!* She must be woozier than she'd thought if she hadn't caught on before he'd bared her to his dark, heavy-lidded gaze.

He was staring at her naked breasts, *hard,* and she blushed clear to the roots of her hair, trying to cover herself with her right arm, her blood nearly boiling when she caught the crooked smirk on his lips.

His hot gaze flicked up to hers. "After everything that happened between us that last night we were together, modesty is a little pointless now, don't you think?"

"It was dark in your room that night." Not to mention it was three years ago, and he'd been drunk off his ass.

"Yeah, but I'm a pure-blood. My night vision is even better than yours." He flicked his tongue over his teeth, and his lips twitched into a wicked grin. "My sense of taste, too."

Lust shot through her in a burst so primal and potent it made her shudder, and it took every ounce of strength she possessed not to pant...or throw herself at him. "I would have thought you were too wasted to remember anything from those particular *minutes,* Eli."

He slowly arched one of his dark brows. "That night wasn't the only time I had your taste in my mouth, Rey."

She blushed even hotter when she realized he was talking about the time he'd licked her juices from his fingers after they'd been inside her. He'd made her come with his hand during their last "sober" interaction together. It'd been two days before the drunken night at his house in Shadow Peak, and they'd met in the woods, as they so often had, carefully avoiding the prying eyes of the pack.

A bitter laugh sounded inside her head as she thought about that telling fact. She should have known then that she was nothing more than his dirty little secret. Something he was too ashamed to admit to. But she'd been blinded by love and faith and foolish dreams. Dreams that had lived inside her heart for too many years to fight them.

With perfect clarity, Carla could still remember the first time she'd ever set eyes on Eli Drake. She'd been no more than twelve, and he'd been...well, the most beautiful man she'd ever seen. He should have detested the sight of her, given his father's virulent hatred of humans and half-breeds, but he hadn't. Instead, he'd grinned at her that day that they'd passed on a small street in Shadow Peak—but it'd been years before they'd ever spoken to each other. Ten, to be exact. And she could still recall the details of that night as if it'd happened only yesterday.

Her mother had always had...issues. And she'd had dismal taste in men. After a string of abusive relationships with Lycan males, Nicole Cates had vowed to only date humans. But the relationships never lasted. The only lasting relationship Nicole had ever enjoyed was with a bottle.

Carla was the result of a short-term affair her mother had had with a human named Antonio Reyes, and he'd disappeared from her life as quickly as he'd entered it. To her family's surprise, and disgust, Nicole had decided to keep the child, thinking a baby might help her find some stability. But it was Carla who'd become the caretaker. Nicole's family had made it clear they wanted nothing to do with their pathetic daughter and her half-human offspring, and so the two of them had been on their own. Though she'd had the support of her fellow Bloodrunners when she'd gotten older, no one from the pack had ever helped her and her mother, until the night she'd first spoken to Eli, less than a week after she'd turned twenty-two.

She could still feel the hot slide of angry, frustrated tears slipping down her face as she'd struggled with her mother's limp body that night, the salty taste of them on her lips. She'd had a call that Nicole was passed out on a sidewalk outside one of Shadow Peak's bars. Too embarrassed to tell the other Runners, she'd left the Alley and gone up to town to handle it on her own. As she'd tried to get Nicole on her feet, shame had burned in her belly at the thought of the girls she'd gone to school with seeing her mother like this, knowing how horrible they would be. The derogatory names they would call them. The same names she'd heard her entire life.

And then, out of nowhere, Eli had walked out of the darkness and taken her mother from her arms, carrying her home while a stunned and wary Carla had walked beside him. She'd been amazed to realize that he not only knew her name and where her mother lived, but that she was Bloodrunning partners with Wyatt. Afterward, they'd talked out in her mother's backyard, and it had been the beginning. Of their friendship. Of her love. Of…of everything.

Eli Drake had been her hero that night, coming to her rescue at a time when she'd desperately needed him. But now he was her nightmare. The thing in the world that could hurt her most. That could break her.

Her mother had always warned her that a Lycan male would destroy her heart if she wasn't careful. How awful to learn that Nicole had been right.

Shattered by the memories flooding through her, Carla closed her eyes, determined to block them out—to block *him* out—hoping it would help her find some measure of control. *Huge mistake.* The sudden touch of his tongue to the sensitive skin over her ribs made her gasp, then whimper, and she flushed with mortification. God, she couldn't have sounded more needy if she'd tried, and his hands flexed against her hips, holding her tighter.

"What the hell do you think you're doing?" she choked out, when she felt the delicious rasp of his tongue gliding higher, until he was licking the flesh of her blood-smeared breast that she hadn't managed to cover with her arm. Her breath seized in her lungs, her eyes shocked wide as she stared down at him, too stunned to do anything more than shiver as she watched him lick another smear of blood off her tingling skin, taking the crimson fluid into his mouth, like it was his *right*.

"Christ," he groaned, the hungry sound vibrating deep in his chest. "Like I could ever forget that taste."

"Eli?"

* * *

Pulling his head back, Eli looked up at Carla's flushed face, and thought *To hell with it.* He needed this. No matter how dangerous it was to his sanity, he *needed* it. *Craved* it. Would have sold his damn soul for it.

Not giving himself time to change his mind, he leaned in close again, wanting her mouth this time, but she jerked back from him, turning her head to the side, her chest heaving. He started to tell her to stop acting like a fucking child and just give him what they both needed after being apart for so long, then stopped when he caught sight of the tears spilling over her pale cheek.

Shit.

"Rey," he breathed out, feeling like he'd just been gutted. In all the time that he'd known her, he couldn't ever recall seeing her cry. Not since the night that he'd helped her with Nicole.

Her throat worked as she swallowed. Then she turned her head to look at him and licked her lips. "From the moment we first realized there was something between us, you told me to wait, so I waited," she whispered unsteadily. "To give it time, so I did. And do you know what I got for it? *Nothing.* Except your lying ass disappearing without a single goddamn word."

He wanted to look away from those tear-soaked eyes that were making him feel like the biggest son of a bitch who had ever walked the planet, but couldn't. "I was banished," he heard himself scrape from his tight throat. "What did you expect me to do? What the hell would I have said?"

Years-old fury flamed beneath her tears, so bright it made him wince. "Maybe *Come with me*? Did that ever cross your pea-sized brain? If you ever meant a single damn word that you said to me, you would have asked—"

"I had no idea where I was going," he bit out, the familiar rise of frustration nearly strangling him. There'd been no goddamn right answer where she was concerned. No matter what he chose, what he did, she would have ended up hurt. He'd simply tried to choose the path that would be easiest for her. And...*fuck,* maybe easiest for him, as well—at least when it came to his emotions—which just made him sound like a coward. "I didn't have a home to offer you, Rey. No security or protection. How could I have asked you to give up everything you'd ever known for that kind of life? To leave your friends and family?"

"*You* were my family," she whispered, digging that knife even deeper. "At least I thought you were. Fool that I was. You just wanted to screw the girl who'd never bedded down with a Lycan, didn't you? Was it a bet between you and your friends? Did you all laugh about it behind my back before you left?"

"You know that's not true," he growled, wanting to shake her. "I didn't want anything to happen to you. I was trying to take care of you!"

She gave a bitter laugh. "And what a stellar job you did. I'd hate to know what it's like to be someone you *want* to hurt."

"Carla, I—"

"*Stop!*" she pleaded, wiping the tears from her cheeks with the back of her free hand. "Please, just...stop. I don't want to hear another lie from you. I just want you to leave me alone."

Shit! This is so screwed up.

Moving to his feet, Eli stared down at the top of her golden head, and wanted to roar with frustration. "I wish I could make you understand, but everything I've done... the reasons...it's complicated, Rey."

She didn't say anything. She just turned and crawled up over the bed, then curled into a ball on her side, telling him without words that she was done listening to his bullshit.

"Sleep fast," he muttered, moving to sit on the foot of the other bed. Elbows on his parted knees, he dropped his head into his hands, squeezing his skull, and kept talking. "We're getting an early start tomorrow. And I still have questions, so be ready to start answering them."

There was no response, but he hadn't expected one. He listened until her breathing evened out, then moved back to his feet and stripped down to his fitted boxers. He pulled the covers over her small, curled up form, forcing himself not to look at her too closely because he knew he'd never be able to stop once he did. Then he turned out the light.

Lying down on his bed, Eli put his hands behind his head and stared up at the watermarked ceiling, wondering what in God's name he'd been thinking. He'd actually thought he could get his head together before he and the guys reached Maryland and he had to face her again. What a jackass idea. Even if it'd taken months to get back, it still wouldn't have been enough time to sort out this messed-up situation.

And he could no longer say for certain if he was still trying to protect her...or if it was his own miserable hide he was worried about. Especially seeing as how she wanted rid of him. Wanted to break the tenuous bond that tied them together, severing that final connection.

Turning on his side, he stared at her delicate shape beneath the soft streams of moonlight filtering in through the blinds, and pulled in a deep breath of her warm, intoxicating scent. This woman had been under his skin for years, and he wasn't sure if staying away from her anymore was the right answer...or the wrong one.

All Eli knew was that it was killing him, not being in that bed with her, holding her against his body, where he wanted her.

And where she'd always belonged.

Chapter 3

After a horrible night's sleep, and a scalding shower that'd barely made her feel alive again, Carla had changed into one of her last clean pairs of jeans and a T-shirt. There was only so much cash she'd been willing to spend on clothes from the money she'd stolen off the White-claw, and so her wardrobe was limited at best. Life would have been a lot easier if she'd had her stupid wallet on her when she'd been kidnapped, but hey, at least she'd had her cell phone. And she'd thankfully had another bra and pair of panties in her pack for this morning, as well as a hairbrush. So while she wouldn't be winning any beauty contests at the moment, it was nice not to have bed head.

Eli had woken her up with a touch on her shoulder about thirty minutes ago, just after six a.m., and told her he would be waiting outside the room while she got ready. He didn't mention anything about their argument from the night before, and neither did she. In fact, she didn't even look at him. She could forgive herself for her momentary lapse last night, but that was her only pass. From now on she needed to stay sharply focused. She had her eye on the prize—being free of him once and for all—and she wasn't going to let her stupid hormones ruin it for her.

No matter how crazy desperate for him those little suckers turned out to be.

And I doubt going without will kill me, she thought dryly, running her brush through her hair. *If that were the case, I'd have dried up and died a long time ago.*

A glance in the mirror over the dresser showed that she was still sporting a few yellowish bruises, had dark circles under her eyes, and the tight pinch of fatigue in her facial muscles. She might be only twenty-eight, but she felt eighty. Damn near looked like it, too. But what the hell? It's not like she wanted him to be attracted to her. Zipping up her pack, she tossed it on her bed and joined him outside.

As they walked to the crowded diner next door, where they were meeting the others, he asked, "You ever hear from your mom?"

Nicole had finally given up on the pack a year before Eli's banishment and left Shadow Peak, claiming she needed to find a place where she could make a new life for herself. "No," Carla replied in a flat tone, wondering if her mother had ever managed to succeed with her dream. If so, she was obviously too content there to worry about contacting the daughter she'd left behind.

He didn't say anything more, and the guys kept the conversation light when they joined them for a quick breakfast. Afterward, they all headed back to the room she and Eli had shared to discuss the situation in private. Once everyone was settled, Eli explained to her what the men already knew: that his father had had a maniacal plan to take over the Silvercrest. A bloodthirsty plan that had resulted in a significant loss of life, had shattered the pack's sense of safety, and left an entire group of teens—as well as most of the residents in Shadow Peak—emotionally traumatized. As a result, the town had been left without its leaders, and the Bloodrunners were now handling all elements of security for the pack.

Since it was up to Carla to bring them up to speed on the rest, she explained everything that had happened with the Whiteclaw pack over the past weeks, starting with how Eli's brother, Eric Drake, had met Chelsea, the human he'd recently married, while she was searching for her younger sister, Perry. Making a bad choice, Perry had gone chasing after the wrong guy and ended up falling in with the Whiteclaw pack who lived to the south of the Silvercrest, and who were now controlled by a man named Roy Claymore. With the Runners' help, Eric had been able to prove that the Whiteclaw had partnered up with the Donovans, a corrupt local Lycan family, on a number of illegal activities, the most horrific being one that involved human girls. With the Donovans' support, the Whiteclaw had been drugging the girls and pimping them out for Lycan gang rapes. The drugs not only acted as an aphrodisiac on the girls, but also impaired their memories of the attacks. And Claymore was using tapes of the assaults to later blackmail the participants into aiding the Whiteclaw.

She then told them that the Runners had managed to close down a strip club in Wesley, a human town not far from the Silvercrest's territory. The Whiteclaw had been using the club to find the girls, and closing it down had only increased Roy Claymore's power hungry desire to destroy the Silvercrest and take their land. Something Claymore felt would be easy to accomplish, given the state the pack had been left in after Stefan Drake's failed bid for power.

Later, after an attack that some of the Whiteclaw and Donovan wolves had made on the Runners in the Alley, they learned that the Whiteclaw had also developed a "super soldier" drug that not only made them violently strong, but also camouflaged their scent. Which meant they were damn difficult to defeat.

The atmosphere in the room had been grim during her telling, but the group's tension only increased when she explained about the plans she'd overheard before making her escape after her and Elise's kidnapping.

"The Whiteclaw were hoping to blackmail the other packs in our region into helping them by providing foot soldiers. But they haven't secured the kind of numbers they were hoping for, so they came up with a new plan. They've used a sizable portion of the money they've made from the gang rapes to purchase help from someone in your line of work. A man named Jack Bartley."

"Son of a freaking bitch," Kyle muttered.

"You know him?" she asked.

"We've gone up against him before," the merc explained. "He's human, but he's a maniac. Has a small army under his command, and they'll do anything for the right price."

"He's human?" she murmured with surprise.

Kyle grimaced. "Well, most of him is. It's rumored he has shifter blood somewhere in his family tree, which is how he knows of our existence."

"You were right to be worried," Sam murmured. "Bartley and his men will spell bad news for your pack."

She wanted to argue that they weren't *her* pack, they were Eli's, but bit her tongue instead. She didn't need to make herself sound any bitterer about the pack's long-standing treatment of the Runners than she probably already had.

"When you went up against him, did you win?" she asked.

"Yeah," Eli muttered from his position against the wall, his muscular arms crossed over his chest. His dark brows were knitted with tension. "But it was at a cost. We lost one of our best men. A guy who would often come and work with us when he needed to earn extra money for his wife and kids. Bartley got his hands on him during the op, and by the time we found him, all that was left was a bloody pile of tissue and bone. They'd skinned him alive."

"Jesus."

Holding her worried gaze, he said, "He can be stopped, Rey. We just need to outthink him."

"Can you do that?"

He jerked his chin toward his men. "These guys can."

"So these different drugs—the ones they were giving the human girls and the ones that they use on themselves to improve their abilities—are still in production?" Kyle asked from his seat on the foot of the bed. Lev had positioned himself up by the pillows, his back braced against the cheap headboard, while Sam had his shoulders propped against the door and James sat in the desk chair. Carla sat on the foot of the other bed by herself.

Answering Kyle's question, she said, "As far as we know, production has been halted. We have a Fed named Monroe dealing with the drug labs out west, where it was all being made. Monroe's sister is married to one of the Silvercrest males, and the Fed is someone we consider a friend. But there's still the problem of the drugs they have stocked in Hawkley."

"Why did they target my sister?" The quietly spoken question had come from Eli, and she took a deep breath before turning her head to look at him again.

"They wanted to make a dig at the Runners, and saw Elise as an easy mark. We never should have let her stay up in town by herself, because it drew their attention."

He made a low sound of agreement, but she could tell he knew there was more to the story. Things she wasn't telling him. But he didn't push, and she wondered if he was dreading the explanation as much as she was dreading having to be the one who gave it.

"It's getting late," he suddenly muttered, pushing away from the wall. "We can talk things over some more when we stop for lunch, but right now we need to get on the road."

Fifteen minutes later, they had their gear stowed in the backseat of the truck James and Lev were driving, the rest of the group loaded into the other one, and were heading back down the highway.

With Sam and Kyle in the front seat of the truck she and Eli were in, Carla didn't speak to him during the journey, though she'd carried on some light conversation with the two mercs. For such ruthless badasses, they were nice guys who even managed to make her laugh a few times, while Eli glared out his window, lost in his own thoughts. The hours went by faster than she'd thought they would, and before she knew it they'd reached a little town the men had stayed in before, where they planned to stop for the night.

They ate together at a great little diner that made killer fried chicken, then grabbed rooms at a local motel. Six of them, at her insistence, which had caused the men to slide curious looks between her and Eli. He went off with Kyle to meet up with a local weapons dealer they'd done business with on several occasions, hoping to score a small arsenal that they could take back to the Alley with them, and refused to let her come along. So she was left sitting alone in her room, with nothing but her thoughts for company. It was still only nine and she was too wound up to sleep, so when Lev knocked on her door and asked if she wanted to grab a drink at the pool hall around the corner, she was glad for the distraction.

They ordered a pitcher of beer, picked out their cues, and before she knew it, she'd laughed her way through three games and they were starting on their fourth.

"No, no. You're going at that shot all wrong," Lev drawled, coming up behind her and leaning over her back. "You've got to move this hand here, and this one here," he told her, rearranging the placement of her fingers on the cue.

"Thanks," she said with a smile, when she made the shot. "That was—"

"Slivkoff!"

She jumped as Eli's guttural shout silenced the noisy pool hall, the back of her head connecting with Lev's chin. He swore as she quickly turned to apologize. "Sorry!"

"No problem," he murmured, casting a funny look over the top of her head. She couldn't tell if he was about to laugh…or run for cover.

Sensing Eli was close, she turned and found him rounding the pool table, heading right for her. Once again, the scowl on his gorgeous face matched his tone as he growled, "What the hell do you think you were doing?"

Huh. Was it just her, or did he ask that question *a lot?*

Squaring her shoulders, Carla slowly arched one of

her eyebrows. "What did it look like I was doing? Lev asked if I wanted to play some pool."

His nostrils flared as he stared her down. "And that meant you had to rub your little ass in his groin?"

Lev started to argue that point, but she lifted her hand to silence him. Setting her cue on the table, she took a deep breath, crossed her arms over her T-shirt covered chest, and tried not to let Eli see how furious he'd just made her as she carefully said, "Considering the bimbo blonde who was passed out in your lap last night, I don't think you can cast any judgments here, Eli."

He opened his mouth, then obviously changed his mind about whatever he was going to say, because he snapped it shut again. A muscle was starting to pulse at the edge of his jaw, his pupils were nearly blown, and his teeth were clenched so hard she was surprised they hadn't cracked. Carla recognized the signs of him struggling with his temper, and couldn't help but shake her head at his outrageous display of jealousy. After ditching her when he was banished, he didn't have any freaking right to get pissed about anything that she did!

"We're getting out of here," he finally muttered, jerking his head toward the door. "Now."

She could have argued with him, but since he'd already ruined her fun, she didn't see the point. Instead, she gave him her snarkiest smile and said, "Sure thing, *boss man*."

Lev was grinning like a jackass when she turned to tell him goodbye, so she socked him in the shoulder, which just made him laugh. Turning her back on the goofball, she wondered if he'd set this whole thing up just to make Eli jealous, and if so, why?

Whatever Lev's reasons were for asking her to play pool with him, it had definitely put Eli in a bad mood. Not that he'd been anything but irritable the entire day.

But now she could feel him seething behind her as she headed back to her room, his glare all but drilling holes in the back of her head. Not to mention her ass. When she reached her room, he managed to push his way in behind her before she could slam the door in his face, which had been her intention. After the way she'd broken down in front of him the night before, the last thing she wanted was to be alone with him.

Instead of moving deeper into the room, Carla leaned back against the door after she'd shut it, and crossed her arms over her chest again. The graze on her side from the bullet was no longer hurting, thanks to her healing abilities. It'd already scabbed over and probably would have been gone in a day or two, if she weren't so run-down at the moment.

"Did you get the guns?" she asked, watching him pace along the foot of her queen-size bed, his big hands braced on his hips. He was dressed like the badass mercenary he was, wearing black boots, a faded pair of jeans that perfectly molded his muscular thighs, and a black T-shirt, its short sleeves stretched tight around his powerful biceps. Wherever you looked, his tall body was hard and sinewed and ripped. Even his hair-dusted forearms were mouth-watering, with heavy veins and ridges of muscle pressing against his scarred, golden skin. Then there were his thick wrists. And those big, masculine hands…

"Yeah, we got them." He sounded distracted, and she could sense his agitation and his…*hunger.* She just couldn't tell who or what it was for. Her? Food? A fight? Or some woman she didn't even know? The bond wasn't strong enough to give her any definitive answers—just annoying enough to mess with her head.

Pushing her bangs out of her eyes, she went for the safest topic she could think of to take her mind off her nerves. "I noticed that both of the trucks were missing from the parking lot. Did the guys go out somewhere?"

"Yeah," he muttered without even looking in her direction. "They're out finding women."

"Ahh."

He stopped in the middle of the floor and shot her a piercing look, the lamp on her bedside table casting a soft spill of light over his right side, while his left was bathed in shadow. Voice low and rough, he asked, "Given their agenda for the night, why do you think Lev was here with *you?*"

"How would I know?" she snapped, throwing her arms out wide in a gesture of frustration. "Maybe he just liked the idea of spending time with a woman he knew wasn't going to have sex with him?"

He didn't make any verbal response to her outburst. He simply folded his arms over his broad chest, the black cotton stretching tight across his solid pecs, and glared at her.

"The truth is I don't know what he was thinking, Eli. I just know that you're acting like an ass."

Moving with the slow, predatory precision of a hunter, he lowered his arms and came toward her, his heavy-lidded gaze so hot she felt scorched. "You keep pushing me like this, Rey, and I'm gonna start thinking you want me to do something about it."

She shook her head. "Am I even meant to know what that means?"

He came even closer, until she had to tilt her head back in order to hold his gaze. "It means that if you think you can get my attention by flirting with my men, you're going to end up getting a hell of a lot more than you bargained for."

Pushing off from the door, she jabbed her finger in

the middle of his chest. "Back off. You have no claim on me, so stop the act. I'm not buying it."

"You think it's an act?" he rasped, the softness of his voice giving her chills.

"I know it is!"

He had her backed against the door before she even knew it was happening, pinning her there with his big, muscular body, his rigid erection pressed hard against her stomach. Cupping her jaw, he tilted her head back even more, and put his face right over hers, so close their noses were nearly touching. "This feel like an act to you, Rey?" he asked huskily, his warm breath coasting over her lips.

"Don't even think about it," she warned. Though the effect was kind of ruined by her quickening breaths and flushed cheeks.

His eyes were still angry and hot, but the corner of his mouth kicked up in one of those deliciously wicked, crooked grins that had always made her melt. "Baby, I can't seem to think about anything else."

"Try—harder," she sniped. "Because I'm seriously not interested in being your sloppy seconds, Eli."

It seemed to take him a moment to figure out what she was getting at, and then his expression darkened. "I didn't touch the blonde," he told her, biting out each word.

A harsh, humorless laugh jerked up from her chest. "Oh, really? So she just happened to pick your random lap to pass out in last night?"

That muscle started to pulse in his jaw again, the day's growth of stubble looking damn good on him. "What she was doing there isn't any of your business."

"Exactly!" she yelled, shoving hard at his shoulders. "So get the hell away from me!"

Catching her wrists, he pinned them against the door

on either side of her head, the tight tips of her breasts pushing into his muscular chest as he pressed even closer.

"Tell me you don't feel *this* the same way that I do," he said against her lips, rubbing them softly with his. "Tell me and I'll leave you alone, Rey."

"Damn you," she moaned.

He laughed roughly, the low sound deep and dark and sumptuous, like he was suddenly feeling happy and hungry all at the same time. "That's what I thought, baby."

And then, before she could blink or scream or draw her next breath, his mouth covered hers and his hands left her wrists, laying claim to her body. His touch was aggressive, *greedy,* as if he'd wanted the feel of her under his hands for too damn long to control himself, while his kisses were…mouthwatering. Slow, deep, and deliciously intimate, his tongue stroking and rubbing, while he ate at the shivery, needy sounds that she made. He'd only just started this…this…whatever *this* was, and she was already lost, sinking into the moment like a weighted body being pulled deeper and deeper into the sea. Drowning… no longer even trying to resist. She only wanted to fall deeper because she'd been just as desperately starved for the feel and touch and taste of him. She didn't even remember moving her hands when he released her wrists, but they were fisted in his shaggy hair, the silky strands so warm and thick against her fingers. She pulled him tighter against her, lost in the slick, explicit kiss that made her think of his powerful body moving and thrusting into hers. It was that intense. That raw and hungry and achingly erotic.

When he pulled his head back and suddenly buried his face against the side of her throat, Carla gulped at the cool air, her lungs starved. He was rolling his hips against hers, one hand shoved up under her shirt and bra, molding her heavy breast, his thumb and forefinger pinching the throbbing nipple, while his other hand gripped her hip, jerking her against him. She crawled up his hard, rugged body and wrapped her legs around his waist, giving him what he wanted. He notched the thick, heavy ridge of his erection against her jeans-covered sex and thrust against her, stroking her clit at just the right angle, and she cried out as her head shot back, hitting the door, the husky sound of her shout echoing off the room's dingy walls.

"Need it in my hand," he growled against her throat, breathing hard, his voice little more than an animal's primitive snarl. His mouth was directly over the place where he'd started to mark her all those years ago, and she wondered if he even realized. "I need it *now,* Rey."

In a distant part of her mind, she knew this was… wrong. Foolish. Dangerous. To her heart and her pride. She wasn't meant to fall into his arms…or crawl up his body, holding him as if she wanted to crawl right inside of him. Claim him. Keep him. *Forever.* She knew that, damn it, but it didn't matter. When he was touching her, the hot, drugging scent of him filling her head, his exquisite taste on her lips, nothing else mattered but him. Needing him. Wanting him. *Getting* him.

"Please," she heard herself beg, too desperate to even care that she was pleading with him. With the monster who had broken her heart. "God, Eli. *Please!*"

His lungs worked hard as he ripped at the buttons on her jeans, his mouth hot against her skin. His tongue stroked across her racing pulse point just as he shoved his hand into the front of her cotton panties, the fabric already drenched with her juices. His fingers delved, separating her slick folds, searching out the small, sensitive opening. He circled it, before pushing inside, working that long finger deep into her tender, clutching tissues while his thumb found the tiny knot of her clit and started playing it…stroking it…faster and faster. He pushed in a second finger, forcing her body to stretch and take it, and her hips rolled, needing them deeper. Needing to be full of him.

"Jesus, Rey. You're just as tight and soft as I remember," he groaned, each roughly spoken word laden with something, with some unnamed emotion, that made her want to scream at him for breaking her heart and destroying what they'd had. "I've fucking dreamed about this so many times."

"Eli," she gasped, sinking her nails into his shoulders, the pain in her heart momentarily forgotten as he used his fingers to drive her wild, thrusting them hard and deep, stretching her in a way that felt so good she could feel tears gathering at the corners of her eyes, her throat shaking. She needed him inside her. Not just his fingers, but the thick, engorged shaft she could feel him grinding against her hip. Needed him on top of her, his body hard and heavy and hot against hers, while he shoved all those brutal inches inside her until she was clenching around him, milking him, lost in the most mind-blowing climax of her life.

Her sex was creamy and swollen and ripe, ready for whatever he wanted to give her. Fingers. Tongue. Cock. She was aching and desperate for every part of him, same as she'd been every night that she'd dreamed of him since he'd left her. Even years before then, when she'd wanted nothing more than for him to make her his, always waiting…and waiting. But he was fighting it. She could tell. Resisting with everything that he had, and it frightened her to think of why. Why she wasn't enough

for him. Why he'd always struggled against their connection with such ferocity.

Fight back! Resist! Damn it, she should be tossing the
rejection she could feel coming right back in his face, but
she…she couldn't. As he touched her between her legs,
his rough fingers stroking through those slick, plump
folds with such perfect skill, making her gasp…arch…
shiver, the only thing she was willing to fight for was
more.

But as with everything else when it came to this man,
she was destined to lose.

One moment his fingers were buried deep, bringing
her to the cusp of a shattering orgasm, and in the next
she was empty, his palm pressed tight against her sex,
cupping her, holding her…and she could feel the smooth,
hot slide of his fangs against her vulnerable throat. *Ohmygod!* Did he want to bite her? What on earth was going
on with him?

His body was pressed so rigidly against hers, and
she sensed his…pain. A visceral, devastating, burning
agony. He cursed hoarsely, and she felt the first tremor
that rocked through him, followed quickly by a second,
until he was shaking so hard in her arms it made her
teeth chatter.

"E-Eli?" she stammered through lips that were salty
with her tears.

He quickly set her on her feet and pushed away from
her with a choked roar, his eyes hooded and bright as he
clenched his teeth. His dark brows were drawn with an
emotion she could have sworn was anguish. Something
had stopped him, but the bond was too weak and his
emotions were too intense for her to read him clearly.
Which was perhaps a good thing. Whatever had caused

him to pull away from her, she had a feeling she wasn't going to like it.

"What the hell, Eli? Are you—"

"Don't! Don't touch me!" he snarled, stumbling back from her when she started to reach for him. His gaze darted from side to side, reminding her of a trapped wolf desperate for escape.

She crossed her arms over her middle, determined to hold herself together. "What's wrong?"

"Nothing," he scraped out, sounding as if a brutal set of hands was crushing his throat. "Just...just go to bed, Carla. It's late."

"No. I want to know—"

"Just get in the damn bed!" he barked, brushing her aside so he could rip the door open. "And lock this damn thing behind me!"

He slammed out of the room then, and she reached out and slid the lock into place with a shaking hand, her thoughts reeling, and her body... *Oh, God*. Her body was vibrating...awakened. Misery crashed over her like a cold rain, and she shivered even harder, somehow making it to the bed. For the second night in a row, she crawled onto a lumpy mattress and curled into a ball, trying to block out everything until she was nothing more than molecules of air. Weightless. Floating. No pain or fear or emotions.

Carla tried to reach that feeling of nothingness with every ounce of her will, but it never came. As she lay there in the cold, depressing room, she just kept wanting and longing and aching...for things she would never have.

Chapter 4

Her life since setting off in search of Eli Drake had been the worst kind of hell, and Carla had never been so eager to return to the Alley as she was now.

She'd skipped breakfast that morning because, well, rejection apparently killed her appetite. Exhaustion weighed heavily on her shoulders, and while she knew it was unforgivably stupid to have let her body do the thinking instead of her head, she was simply too tired to beat herself up over what had happened with Eli. Learn, regroup, and move on. That needed to be her motto, because if it wasn't, she'd still be curled up in that crappy motel room bed, wishing for things that were useless. And oh so obviously bad for her.

As far as wake up calls went, the way Eli had walked out on her *again* had been a bruiser. But she was tough. She could take the hit and keep on going.

What she couldn't do was let him get too close to her

again. Work together? Fine, so long as she wasn't alone with him. But kissing? Touching? Losing her head over him because her body craved him like he was freaking manna from heaven? Uh, no. That was *not* a part of her game plan. She would give herself last night as a freak moment of insanity after missing him as badly as she had, but no more. That'd been her last freebie. There wouldn't be any others.

When they'd climbed into the truck that morning, both of them taking the backseat again, Eli had turned to her and asked, "Are you okay?" At her questioning look, he'd stiffly explained his concern. "I wasn't thinking about the bullet graze last night. Did I hurt you?"

"My side is fine," she'd murmured. He'd caused her pain, just not physically.

As if he'd read her mind, he'd said, "I wasn't rejecting you, Rey. I was—"

"It doesn't matter," she'd cut in, watching the clouds through her window as the wind blew them across the sky like puffs of dandelion seeds. "I don't care."

"That's a damn lie. If you didn't care, you wouldn't be hurt. And I'm sorry as hell that it happened, because I didn't mean to hurt you. Not last night, and not before. That was the last thing that I... *Damn it*, I was trying to pro—"

Her head had whipped to the side so quickly her hair smacked her in the face. "If you say you were trying to protect me, I will get out of this truck and I won't get back in it. Understood?"

"We need to talk about this," he'd argued.

"No, we don't need to do anything, because the time for talking was last night. Now you can just forget that anything ever happened."

He'd muttered something under his breath that she

didn't catch, but didn't say anything more when Kyle and Lev hopped in the front, the blond merc taking the first stint behind the wheel. She'd balled up a sweatshirt Kyle offered her, using it as a pillow, and slept.

Then, when they'd stopped for lunch a little while ago, she made sure to catch Eli alone before they entered the restaurant, and told him, "I don't know what your problem is, and I don't care. I just want you to know that what happened last night—that's it, Eli. It doesn't happen again. You don't get to keep making me feel like a fool."

She hadn't waited around to get his reaction, heading inside to join the others. He'd come in a few minutes later, and passed on ordering anything, which had garnered some interested looks from his friends. Lev had lifted his brows at her, as if to say *What'd you do to him?* She'd shrugged in a *I have no idea what his problem is* kind of way, but the merc didn't buy it, his sea-colored gaze filled with curiosity. Too drained to worry about any of it, she'd sucked down a few spoonfuls of soup and resumed her nap once they were all back on the road.

Or at least she'd tried to. Unfortunately, sleep eluded her for the second part of the day, and it wasn't just Eli's brooding presence that had her feeling so restless. It was the entire situation.

After so many days like this, cooped up in a vehicle, Carla was thankful her mother had never been the family vacation type. She was ready to chew her own arm off because she was so…so on edge. She felt trapped, like there wasn't enough air in the cab for her to get a deep enough breath. And what air there was smelled like Eli, which did nothing to help her relax.

Needing to eat more often than human males because of their high metabolisms, the guys decided to stop for a late afternoon snack once they crossed into Maryland.

They found a popular diner, and despite her foul mood, she bit back a grin at the reaction the mercs received as they walked to their table. The humans there might not know what the tall, good-looking mercenaries were, but they sensed there was something different about them, the way a vulnerable animal might sense the nearness of a beautiful, mesmerizing predator; the instinct to run battling against the desire to soak up the stunning view.

When they got back in the truck, Kyle said they needed fuel and pulled into a nearby gas station, while Sam pulled in behind him.

"I'm gonna grab some sodas for everyone to have on the road," Lev said, getting out just as Kyle started pumping the gas.

Sitting in the backseat with Eli again, she knew she needed to make use of their privacy. There were things she needed to tell him before they reached the Alley in a few hours, and now was the perfect time.

Turning toward him, she asked, "Are you nervous about tonight?"

He hadn't spoken to her since trying to explain himself that morning, remaining silent, his rugged jaw clenched tight, even when she'd stopped him outside the diner at lunch, telling him that last night would never have a repeat. He'd spent the day in a dark, dangerous mood, and now was no different. Keeping his gaze focused out his window, he responded to her question with nothing more than a slight shake of his head.

"I called Wyatt this morning, so they know to be expecting us at the Alley."

This time, he nodded, still not looking at her.

Carla sighed, forcing herself to just get to the point. "Listen, Eli, there's something I need to tell you before we get there, and now seems like the best time."

He must have picked up on something in her tone, because he finally turned toward her, his dark eyes difficult to read as they connected with hers.

Rubbing her damp palms across her jeans, she said, "It's about Elise, and I think you should know because… well, coming back is going to be hard enough for you as it is. I don't think you need any more shocking revelations thrown in your face."

His head cocked a bit to the side, his gaze sharpening. "What are you trying to tell me?"

She wet her lips, then slowly exhaled. "When Wyatt found El in Hawkley, he had a confrontation with Sebastian Claymore before he killed him. Wyatt told me that Sebastian admitted he was one of the wolves who raped Elise the night of her attack. It was him and Harris, and the one you killed—some guy named Danny. He was helping them make the gang rape drugs."

He was breathing hard by the time she was done, and he lifted one of his big hands, shoving it back through his dark hair as his gaze skittered from one thing to the next—the front window, side window, the inches of leather seat between them that felt more like miles—his thoughts seeming to shift just as rapidly. A flush covered his cheekbones, seeming brighter for the way he'd paled, his tanned skin bleached of color. He worked his jaw a couple of times, cleared his throat, and spoke in a voice so rough, she almost couldn't make out the quiet, guttural words. "Wyatt killed them?"

"Yeah. Well, he killed Sebastian. I think he said that Cian killed Harris. But there's more."

He kept his gaze locked on the back of the driver's seat as he waited, his profile rigid.

"It was Roy Claymore who planned the whole thing. He used Elise as a test run for the rape drugs, which is why she was conscious during the attack, but couldn't describe what they looked like to anyone. He, um, was also the last one to rape her."

His head finally turned her way again, his dark, deadly gaze locking her in its grip as strongly as any physical touch could have held her. "And no one gutted the bastard?"

Understanding his frustration, she said, "They couldn't get to him that day in Hawkley because of his security detail. But Wyatt put a bullet in Roy's head. It didn't kill him, but it would have caused him a lot of pain. With men like Eric and Wyatt gunning for his blood, he has to know his days are numbered."

His head went back and he shoved the heels of his hands against his eyes, the muscles in his arms bulging beneath his tight skin as he worked his jaw like he was grinding his anger between his molars. The seconds stretched out, heavy with the tension and fury she could feel pulsing off him. Then he scraped out, "They blame *me*," and she realized he was struggling with a hefty amount of guilt in addition to the blistering rage.

Not knowing what to say, she bit her lip, fighting the urge to reach out and stroke the broad, straining shoulder that was closest to her. He didn't deserve her comfort, damn it. But that didn't mean she wasn't dying to give it to him, fool that she was.

"Eric—he hasn't tried to contact me since the kidnapping." His expression was anguished when he looked at her, making her chest tighten. "What other reason would he have for that? They blame me for not coming back sooner and helping to keep those sick bastards away from her."

Unable to stop herself, hating this burning need inside her to try and make him feel better, she said, "They don't blame you, Eli."

"Like hell they don't," he growled, every ounce of his surly aggression directed at himself.

"I'm sure there's another explanation. Since Eric knew I was coming after you, I bet he was just afraid of letting it slip if he left you a new message."

His dark brows pulled together in an even deeper scowl. "Why would that matter?"

"Can't you guess?" A wry grin tugged at the corner of her mouth. "He was probably afraid you'd run at the sound of my name and never be found again."

He didn't smile at her lame attempt to lighten his mood. If anything, he looked even angrier. "Is that what you think I would have done? You think I would have *run* from you?"

She shrugged as she focused her attention back on the mundane scene outside her window, noticing that Lev and Kyle were finally paying the cashier inside the small convenience store. "It doesn't matter what I think. I just wanted you to know before we got there."

The guys were heading back to the truck, so they dropped the conversation. But Carla could feel him seething beside her, and knew Roy Claymore was going to have more than one pissed off Lycan coming after him when the war finally hit.

Lev took the wheel again for this last part of the journey, and Eli murmured directions to the merc when they finally neared the mountains. Following Eli's instructions, Lev turned off of the main highway, onto the two-lane private road that wound its way up the mountainside, leading to Shadow Peak. Tonight, though, Eli wouldn't be directing Lev up to the town. Instead, they would turn off the road before they reached Shadow Peak, taking the smaller dirt path that led to the Alley.

The radio was playing softly in the background, the sky lit with the burnished colors of a brilliant sunset, while the wind rushed through the thick forest that lined the road, rattling the trees' leafy branches. It was a stunning setting, and Carla was seeking comfort from the view outside her window, glad to almost be home, when one of the massive trees suddenly crashed across the road just ahead of them, blocking their way. A sick feeling of dread immediately settled in her stomach, her nerves strung as tight as a bowstring. Lurching forward in her seat, she gripped Kyle's headrest and peered through the front windshield.

"This is bad," she whispered. "We're about to be attacked. The rogues working with Eli's dad did the same thing to my friends last year. It's a freaking ambush."

"Well, this time it's not my fault," Lev rumbled, trying for a bit of levity to break the tension that was so thick you could barely breathe through it. "Because I haven't slept with *anyone* from around here. *Yet*."

Kyle shoved the blond merc in the arm while Eli said, "It's the Whiteclaw."

"I think you're right," Carla murmured. "We have scouting groups scouring the mountain, keeping a close eye on all the Silvercrest's borders and roads. But if they're taking the drugs that mask their scent, it's possible that they slipped by the scouts without detection. Especially this far away from the Alley and Shadow Peak. The patrol routes are tighter the higher you get up the mountain. But they're taking a risk by attacking this close to the main highway."

"You think this is because of Eli?" Kyle asked. "Because we're here to help with the war?"

"I don't know," she said. "They might have caught wind that he was returning. Or this might just be a random attack. Who knows what they're thinking?"

"There isn't time to call for backup from the Alley. By the time the guys get here, this'll be over," Eli muttered, his voice more guttural than she'd ever heard it, as if his wolf was prowling just beneath his surface. But it would be a while yet before he could take the complete shape of his inner beast. The moon had yet to rise, still hanging low in the sky, which meant they could manage only partial shifts, releasing their deadly fangs and claws while still retaining their human shapes. They would be stronger, but not as strong as they would be in their standing wolf forms. If the Whiteclaw were doped up on the "super soldier" drugs, she and the mercs were going to be in a shitload of trouble.

Eli rolled down his window and sniffed the fresh mountain air, while Kyle used his cell phone to connect with James and Sam, who had to be wondering what was going on as they waited behind them. "I can't pick up any scent," Eli said in a low voice. "There's no telling how many are out there."

"We're still too close to the main highway to use any of the guns," she added. "If the noise drew any state troopers up here, we'd have an even bigger problem on our hands."

"Carla's right," Kyle agreed, his Southern drawl more raw-edged than usual. He definitely sounded like a man who was more than ready to kick some Whiteclaw ass.

"We need to get out of the trucks," Lev said, all traces of humor gone, his gritty tone sharp with menace. "We're sitting ducks in here. They're probably waiting for us to try moving the tree. But something tells me they're not going to wait much longer."

"Come on," Eli grunted, grabbing her hand and pulling her out on his side of the vehicle. "You stay behind me."

"Eli—"

"They're coming," Kyle cut in with a quiet growl as he came around the front of the truck, his attention focused on the road. The truck's headlights illuminated the fallen tree and the dense woods that lined each side of the two-lane road. "I can see them coming out of the woods up ahead. Doesn't look like they're armed with guns. They want blood on their hands."

Still holding her hand, Eli yanked her closer and put his face right over hers, his rough breaths brushing over her skin. "I mean it, Carla. You stay behind me."

Hating that he'd never been able to see her for who she was, she gave him a slow, tight smile, releasing her claws and fangs just as he'd done. "Not—gonna—happen."

Before he could argue, the Whiteclaw reached them, coming in fast and hard from the front, as well as the sides. Even if Eli had wanted to shove her behind him, he was suddenly too busy fighting off three attackers at once. There was no doubt the Whiteclaw soldiers had taken the drugs, their blows feeling like a freaking truck was hitting her as Carla blocked and kicked to avoid getting cut by the two who had targeted her.

Then the strangest thing happened.

Without any planning or verbal direction, she and Eli went back to back and began working together, moving in perfect synchronization as they engaged the seemingly endless wave of assailants. They fought so well together, it was insane. If she kicked a Lycan away, Eli twisted and slashed the male with his claws. When he swept a soldier's legs out from under him, she swiped her own claws across the bastard's throat. It was a primitive and deadly dance, and yet, there was a kind of savage beauty to it that the Lycan part of her soul could only appreciate, despite her fear.

She might not be afraid of the Whiteclaw, but she was *terrified* by the connection she so obviously shared with the male fighting at her side. She didn't even share this level of intuition with Wyatt, and she and the Runner had been partners for seven years!

When she and the pure-blooded mercenary both turned in the opposite direction and dug their claws into one of the Whiteclaw, pinning the soldier between them as their claws pierced him front and back, Eli growled, "Reyes, what's happening here?"

"Don't know. Just go with it and worry later," she muttered, pulling her claws from the Lycan's chest. A second later, Eli grabbed the male's neck and twisted, then tossed his lifeless body to the ground.

"Are they here?" he grunted, strands of sweat-dampened hair sticking to his gorgeous face as he turned his head to the side and caught her gaze.

"Are who here?" she wheezed, more breathless from the surge of lust that had just slammed into her than she was from the fight. God, he'd never looked hotter than he did at that moment, with his fangs and claws dripping with blood, his tall body rippling with power as his hard muscles flexed beneath his skin, his sensual lips parted for his rough breaths.

"The ones who hurt you in Hawkley," he growled impatiently. "Are they here?"

Angry with herself for being so freaking mesmerized by him, she gave him a cold look. "Why? You want to compare stories? Because you've hurt me more than any of the Whiteclaw managed to."

He flinched, jerking back a bit, as if her sudden verbal blow had physically struck him. His face paled and he looked away from her as he cleared his throat. "I just wanted to know so I could kill them for you," he told her, his deep voice stiff, even huskier than it'd been before.

Oh. She swallowed thickly, her throat too tight to give him a response. She didn't know the bastards' names, but she would easily recognize their faces if she saw them. The fact that Eli wanted to kill them for her made her feel like an ass for being such a bitch to him, but damn it, what did he expect? That she'd just sweep three years' worth of heartache under the rug and crawl back into his bed until he grew bored and bailed on her again? Thanks, but no thanks. And, seriously, he was the one who'd walked out on her last night!

Sam and James were fighting a group of Whiteclaw to their left, Lev and Kyle on their right, as four more soldiers came out of the woods, heading straight for her and Eli. Despite the awkwardness of the words they'd just exchanged, they still fought just as well together as they had before, Carla's smaller size enabling her to get in shots that Eli and his men couldn't make because of their height. The scent of Whiteclaw blood filled the balmy air, but despite the mercs' savage skills, only a few of the enemy had fallen, their drug-enhanced bodies capable of sustaining even the most brutal of wounds—which meant that death by decapitation or the severing of their spinal columns was the only way to take them down and ensure they stayed there.

By attacking at twilight, before she and the mercs could fully shift into the stronger, deadlier shape of their beasts, the Whiteclaw's drugs had put their men at a distinct advantage.

"Stay sharp! We've got more coming!"

The shouted warning came from James, just as a fresh

wave of Whiteclaw soldiers emerged from the trees. She and Eli took on six of them at once, and though she could feel the moon rising, and knew it wouldn't be long before they could use its power, she feared it wouldn't be soon enough. There were simply too many of them.

Damn it, she couldn't fail. Not like this! Not when they were so close to the Alley they were practically on its doorstep. She used her upper arm to wipe the sweat from her eyes, and cast a desperate look at Eli, her emotions in chaos at the thought that they might die here tonight, together.

"More coming in at our backs!" Lev called out, heading around the front of the truck.

"Don't attack!" she shouted, her voice almost weak with relief from having caught the scent of the approaching group. "They're Silvercrest scouts. They'll help us!"

Over a dozen familiar-faced scouts joined them a handful of seconds later, her relief so sharp she wanted to freaking cry. With the numbers now in their favor, they were able to defeat those Lycans who didn't retreat, and the battle ended within moments.

Charles Decker, one of the scouts from Shadow Peak who Carla and Wyatt had been working closely with, came over to where she'd just leaned back against the side of the truck bed, her hands braced on her knees as she pulled in deep breaths of air. She'd retracted her claws and fangs as soon as the fighting was over, her fingertips and gums still burning with heat.

Retracting his own claws, Charles shoved his sandy hair back from his face and gave her a concerned frown. "That was brutal. We were heading back up to town after checking on the south border when we heard the fight. I'm sorry we didn't get here sooner, Reyes."

"No worries, Decker. You came just when you were needed."

"Everyone good here?" he asked, casting a worried look over the mercenaries as they each peeled their bloodied shirts off, then used them to wipe the sweat and blood from their arms and faces. She quickly pulled her gaze back to Charles, pretty sure her temperature had just risen from the sight of all those broad, muscular shoulders and chiseled abs. When it came to doing a body good, milk obviously didn't have anything on mercenary work. And the way Eli and his men had fought was beyond impressive. Though she'd handled herself well, it was clearly the mercs' incredible skill that had enabled them to survive.

Replying to Charles' question, she said, "We're a little scratched and bruised, but alive, thanks to you and the other scouts."

Charles jerked his chin at Eli as he came to stand beside her, but that was as far as the greeting went. If the scout recognized Eli, he didn't say, and she wondered, as she often had since she'd gone in search of him, about what kind of reaction Eli would receive from the Silvercrest. Eric and Elise had had a tough time of it after Stefan Drake's failed coup, since there were many who chose to blame them for the twisted things that had happened because of their father. Recently, though, it seemed that more of the townspeople were swaying in the Drake family's favor, since Eric and Elise were now so closely tied to the Bloodrunners, and it was the Runners who were working so hard to keep the pack alive.

Nothing like a little self-preservation to make even the most bigoted of idiots become accepting.

Still, there were many in the pack, like Charles, who had made the firm decision to give the Runners their full support simply because they respected them, and Carla was thankful as hell for each and every one of them.

"We'll take care of the bodies," Charles was saying, his words drawing her attention back to his friendly, freckled face. "You go and get on up to the Alley. I know Wyatt's been worried about you."

Fighting the urge to ogle Eli's mouthwatering chest from the corner of her eye, she managed to give the middle-aged scout a grateful smile. "Thanks, Charles. And say hi to your wife for me."

Charles said that he would, and left to give the scouts their orders. One of the wolves, a thirty-something Lycan named Mike who worked as a mechanic up in town and was hot as sin, smiled at her, showing his interest, but she simply gave him a brief nod and turned her attention back to the mercs. She didn't do wolves. Full stop. Other than Eli, the only men she'd ever been involved with were human ones, when she was younger. Nice enough guys who had had no idea she was only half their species, which had meant the relationships were doomed from the start, though a few had lasted for several months. Thanks to her upbringing and her mother, Carla had never trusted a Lycan male enough to get down and dirty with him. The one time she'd taken a chance, he'd left in the middle of the act and then disappeared from her life.

She didn't think she could ever forgive Eli for that. Even if he hadn't wanted to take her with him, he'd at least owed her a damn goodbye.

"Who the fuck is that?" Eli demanded in a low rasp, one of his big hands wrapping around her upper arm.

Her eyes shot wide as she turned her head to look at him. "Excuse me?"

He stared down at her with a scowl, looking ready to

commit murder. "The guy with the chick hair who was smiling at you. Who is he?"

"Ohmygod, are you serious?" she asked, laughing. "*Chick* hair?"

"Who. Is. He?" His voice was soft, but knife-sharp, his gaze storm-dark and hard.

Thinking he had this jealousy act down pretty well, she gave him a bland look. "That's just Mike. He's a mechanic in Shadow Peak. Don't you remember him?"

His gaze cut to Mike, then back to her again. "Yeah, I do now," he muttered, shaking his head as he dropped his hand from her arm. "That guy was always an asshole."

Tucking the windblown strands of her hair behind her ears, she shrugged. "Well, he's been nice enough to me."

He turned his head to the side, his chest expanding as he pulled in another deep breath and rubbed the back of his neck. Tension poured off his tight frame, his massive shoulders bunched, as if he carried the weight of the world on them. She was getting ready to open the door to the truck and grab a shirt from her bag so that she could wipe her own face and arms clean, when he growled, "You let him touch you, he's a dead man. We clear?"

She choked back another shocked burst of laughter, unable to believe his freaking audacity. "You are unbelievable, Eli."

He leaned in even closer, his incredible scent playing havoc with her senses as the tip of his nose nearly brushed hers. "He might not be able to scent my bond on you, but it's there, Carla. And that means that until something changes, you're *mine*."

"And you care about this *now?*"

His gaze burned so hotly it made her feel scorched, her skin misting with heat that had nothing to do with the warm evening air. "You're damned right I do," he snarled, sounding every bit like the possessive lover she'd always longed for him to be. Too bad it was only an act.

She licked her lips, studying him through narrowed eyes. "You'll understand how ridiculous I think that sounds, considering you haven't cared what I do, or who I do it with, for a long time now."

Frustration sharpened his bold, masculine features. "Just because I wasn't here doesn't mean I didn't care. I told you, my reasons for staying away were—"

"Yeah. Complicated," she scoffed, her lips curling in a bitter, humorless smile. "I heard that lame excuse the first time you spouted it. No need to repeat yourself."

"Christ, Carla. It's not an excuse."

"Well, it's sure as hell not an answer. Until you're ready to give me one, don't think you have any right to so much as even mention that *ridiculous* bond to me."

His nostrils flared as he sucked in a sharp breath, his shoulders so broad he damn near blocked out the glittering stars that were beginning to light the skies. The weather had started to warm since she'd gone off to find him, and as the wind whipped through the forest, it tousled his dark hair, making him look so damn sexy and… touchable. And, God, did she want to touch him. Despite her anger and resentment, she had a sickening feeling that she would go to her grave with this incessant ache for his scent and his heat and the hard weight of his powerful body covering her, holding her, trapping her against him as if he never meant to let her go, still plaguing her. It would be a longing she could never satisfy or kill, slowly eating away at her, until she was nothing more than an empty, desolate shell.

She was cursed, damn it, and the unfairness of it all made her throat shake, her eyes stinging as tears gathered.

He opened his mouth, the fury in his beautiful gaze dimming beneath what she could have sworn was stark concern when he spotted her glistening tears. But whatever he'd planned to say was drowned out by Kyle's deep voice shouting, "Yo, boss man! Should we start digging?"

He pulled in a deep, rasping breath, his eyes narrowing a fraction before he seemed to force himself to turn away from her. "They're going to deal with the bodies for us. As soon as we've moved that damn tree, we can get out of here," he called back, the muscles in his back flexing beneath his tanned skin as he headed toward the felled oak. With Charles and the other scouts helping, it didn't take the group long to shove the massive tree to the side of the road, and when Eli turned and started back toward her, he seemed determined to pick up where they'd left off. But she wasn't having it.

"Let's just get out of here," she murmured when he reached her, turning and opening the back door to the truck. "We can talk later. But you've kept your family waiting long enough."

Chapter 5

Carla knew, from her phone conversations with Wyatt, that extreme changes had been taking place both up in Shadow Peak, as well as in the Alley, since she'd left to find Eli. Fully aware that war was coming, the Runners had made the young and the elderly their first priority. They'd initially thought to bring everyone into the Alley itself, but when it became clear that there simply wasn't enough room, they'd used one of the nearby glades as a sort of base camp they were calling Alpha One.

Mobile accommodations had been purchased and brought up the mountainside with rented big rigs, and the security was top notch, thanks to the volunteer scouting patrols. Every willing Lycan was going through combat training with the Runners, as well as working the patrols in the woods, with extra patrols being run around the clock for Alpha One. In her mind, she pictured the clearing looking like some kind of survivalist camp from an apocalyptic zombie film, but knew that Wyatt and the guys would have created something that was not only safe, but also comfortable.

As for their loved ones, the Runners had brought them closer to home. In fact, many of the couples now had parents or grandparents staying with them, in addition to their siblings.

She'd explained all this to Eli and his men over one of their meals, as well as the fact that two of the empty cabins in the Alley had been set up for their use. Carla herself would be staying with Elise and Wyatt, in their spare bedroom, since she'd agreed to let the soon-to-be mothers from town, three of who were due any day now, to use her place. She wasn't exactly comfortable with the idea of people she didn't know that well staying there, but their safety was more important than her feelings. The four Lycan females with newborns were already staying in the last free cabin, so there'd been nowhere else for the women to go.

To say that things were going to be damn crowded was a serious understatement. But since they expected the brunt of the attack to come in Shadow Peak, no one was willing to risk leaving anyone there who couldn't fight.

A few minutes later, they reached the Alley, which had gotten its name from a pure-blooded Lycan who'd once referred to the Bloodrunners as nothing more than a bunch of "back-alley mongrels." But despite the negative connotations of its name, Bloodrunner Alley was a stunning place, built in a secluded, slightly sloping glade and surrounded by the wild, natural beauty of the forest. And thanks to some hard work, they had all the modern amenities, from power to hot water and high-speed Internet access, just like they did up in Shadow Peak. The mercenaries would be comfortable there, and accepted, though she wasn't holding her breath on how things would go for them with the pack up in town until she saw it for herself. Wyatt had told her that public opinion had started to take a dramatic swing in the Runners' favor since she'd been gone, and she was looking forward to witnessing the change.

Carla had called Wyatt when they'd finally climbed back into the trucks, debriefing him on the ambush so that no one would be shocked by their fresh-from-a-fight appearance. The mercs had all pulled on clean shirts before driving up, but they still looked like serious badasses who had just been in a brutal battle. Make that gorgeous badasses, and she almost snorted at the thought of so much testosterone descending upon the Alley as they parked and exited the vehicles. God only knew the place was already drenched in it, thanks to Wyatt and the guys. Now it would be practically swimming in the stuff, and she was thankful as hell to have the other women there with her. Carla knew she might not be the girliest of girls, but she treasured her female friends as dearly as she did her Bloodrunning brothers.

Standing back a little so that she could watch Eli's reunion with his family, her stomach tight with nerves, her eyes actually watered when she spotted Elise hurrying toward the group, the female Lycan's bright blue eyes focused on her brother.

"Eli!" she cried, running toward him, her red hair streaming behind her. She threw herself into his arms, burying her face against his shoulder. "You're home," she cried, hugging him tight as he wrapped his arms around her. "I can't believe it. I've missed you so much!"

"Hey, baby girl," he murmured against her hair, holding her with one arm so that he could throw the other around Eric, who had just joined them. He gave his brother a hard hug, slapping him on the back in that way that guys did.

Eric's deep voice was gruff with emotion. "It's great to see you, man, but I hate that you had to come back to this shit."

"I'm just glad to be home," he said in a low voice. "I stayed away for too damn long."

Though Elise was a redhead, and Eric and Eli were both dark-haired, there was no mistaking that they were all related. She'd never seen the three *dark wolves* together before in the same place, and it was a stunning sight to behold, if not a little intimidating. Created when two exceptionally pure-blooded Lycans produced offspring, a *dark wolf* bloodline was the most powerful that there was within their world. As well as the most deadly.

The Drake siblings were like werewolf royalty, their blood as blue as the original werewolf king himself. A fact that only solidified her belief that Eli had never planned on revealing their relationship to the pack. Royalty didn't marry from the lower classes. The partial bond between them was no doubt a result of lust and too much alcohol, and she was surprised he hadn't shown more enthusiasm about breaking it. When his fangs had touched her throat the night before in her motel room, he'd certainly run fast enough, as if the idea of completing the bond was something he abhorred.

Yeah, like I didn't see that one coming, she thought bitterly, trying to keep her emotions from showing on her face. If Wyatt was watching her from the growing crowd, he'd see right through her, and there were some things she'd rather keep to herself.

When Jillian came forward, pulling Carla into a crushing hug, she took a shocked breath as the happy news she'd just gleaned from her friend's scent crashed into her. "Jilly, you're pregnant!" she squealed, her troubles momentarily forgotten in the excitement.

"I know!" the beautiful blonde said with a bright smile as she pulled back to see Carla's face. "Don't be mad, but I made Wyatt promise not to tell you over the phone. I wanted it to be a surprise."

Carla knew that Jillian and Jeremy had started trying to conceive before she'd left, and had even started converting the spare room in their cabin into a nursery, and she couldn't have been happier for the couple. If anyone deserved to get everything they wanted out of life, it was those two. Their past had been as pain-filled as her and Eli's, but on a public scale, and there'd been a time when no one had believed they would ever reconcile. But all of the doubters had been proven wrong.

Jillian came from an extraordinary line of witches called Spirit Walkers, who had long-served the Silvercrest Lycans as their holy women, or healers. As witches, Jillian, her mother and her sister, Sayre, couldn't shape-shift like the rest of their pack. But they were formidable in other ways, their powers growing stronger as they aged. Which meant that if Jillian and Jeremy had a daughter, she was going to grow up to be a serious little ass-kicker, and Carla couldn't help but love that idea.

"I'm so excited for you, Jilly. You and Jeremy are going to be the best parents ever, and we're all going to spoil that little hellion like crazy."

Jillian laughed, obviously of the same mind that any child of Jeremy Burns would be a troublemaker. But an adorable one, without doubt.

Introductions were still being made all around them, thanks to Eli, and Carla figured she should make her way over to Wyatt, who she'd finally spotted standing near Brody. Her partner looked as if he was still trying to decide whether he wanted to hug her for making it back or strangle her for taking off without him in the first place. She couldn't even work up any attitude to throw back in his face because she knew she'd feel the same if the situation had been reversed. Wyatt wasn't upset because she was a woman and he didn't think she could handle herself. After all the years they'd worked together, he knew she was as capable as any of the male Runners. But they were like family to each other, and she hated that she'd worried him.

Jeremy came up and wrapped his arm around his wife's waist, and Carla was about to murmur that she needed to go and talk to Wyatt, when Jeremy muttered, "Well, this should be interesting."

"What should be?" Jillian asked, but Carla had already seen what had caught Jeremy's attention. Lev had come to stand on Carla's other side, his heavy-lidded gaze focused on Jillian's younger sister, Sayre, who was talking to her mother and Brody's wife, Michaela. The mercenary was eyeing Sayre like he'd just found something good he needed to taste, and Cian—a badass, gorgeous, womanizing Irishman and the only single Runner left besides herself—looked ready to kill.

Lev's interest she could understand. Sayre was an incredibly beautiful eighteen-year-old witch with blue-gray eyes and curly, strawberry-blond hair. So, yeah, it was understandable for men to get a little lust-eyed in her presence. What everyone in the Alley was still trying to figure out was why the Irishman kept getting so pissed off about it. And he was definitely pissed.

"What's his problem?" Lev murmured to their small group, when he noticed how Cian was watching him.

"He's a little, um, protective where she's concerned,"

Jillian explained a bit awkwardly, as if she didn't really know what to say.

Lev looked Cian over with a careful eye, then frowned. "Isn't he a little old for her?"

Jeremy snorted. "And you're not, Slivkoff?"

"I'm young where it counts," the merc rumbled, which made the women who'd heard him laugh. Lev smirked while Jeremy just shook his head.

"You're gonna be trouble, aren't you?" Jeremy muttered.

"Naw," Lev drawled, his blue-green eyes twinkling with mischief. "I've promised the boss man to be on my *best* behavior."

Carla snickered under her breath, thinking Lev's "best" was probably a far cry from anything that could be considered good.

"So what the hell happened down on the road?" The question came from Mason, who had walked over to join them just as Eli slipped in between her and Lev, the warm breeze whipping Mason's reddish-brown hair around the rugged angles of his handsome face. "I know Wyatt got a phone call, but I'd like to hear exactly how it went down."

While Eli gave a detailed account of the ambush, Carla stepped away from the group, needing to put some distance between her and the sexy merc. Wyatt must have been waiting for her to separate from the group, because he headed right for her, hugging her so tight that he lifted her clear off the ground. "So glad you made it back in one piece," he rumbled, ruffling her hair when he set her back on her feet.

"You're not getting rid of me that easily," she teased, trying not to let him see how emotional she was. But he always had been able to read her like a book.

His voice dropped, and his gaze sharpened. "I know

you didn't want to get into it over the phone, but now that you're back, we're having that talk."

"Sure thing, *Dad*," she drawled, rolling her eyes.

Wyatt shook his head and snorted. "It's good to see that your little road trip didn't kill your smart-ass streak."

"As if anything ever could."

He laughed, then snagged Elise's hand as she walked by him, pulling her into his side. The next thing Carla knew, they were surrounded by everyone, and Wyatt was shaking hands with Eli, who had resumed his place beside her. Jillian started talking to her again, and Carla turned to give her friend her full attention. She was still busily chatting away with Jillian a few minutes later, when she heard something off to her right that caught her attention.

"I'll stay with Carla," Lev had drawled, sliding her a sexy smile and a wink when she quickly turned her head to look at him. "She needs someone watching out for her."

The group had obviously started talking about the sleeping arrangements, and she wondered what Lev was up to, seeing as how she'd already told them where they would be staying.

"The hell you will," Eli muttered, looking ready to take Lev's head off.

"No one's staying with Carla because Carla's staying with me and Elise," Wyatt pointed out in a dry tone, shaking his head in a way that said he clearly thought they were all acting like children. "And until I know what's going on, neither of you are setting foot in our place."

Eli frowned, glaring at Wyatt, which just made her partner smirk. Pall, as she often called him, knew damn well he'd just made it more difficult for Eli to get her alone.

"Eli, come on," Eric murmured. "I'll show you and your men down to your cabins."

Eli turned his head, watching her with a hooded, smoldering gaze, and she sucked in a sharp breath, stunned that he was being so obvious. It was clear to everyone there that he didn't want to leave her. Idiot male wasn't even trying to hide that scalding burn of possession in his incredible, thick-lashed eyes. She could feel the curiosity and confusion among her friends ramping up until she wanted to scream.

"Come on," Eric repeated, placing his hand on his brother's shoulder. "This is not the time or place, man, to get into it." Confusion creased Eric's brow. "Whatever the hell *it* is," he added under his breath.

Though Eli remained silent, the other mercs told her they'd see her soon, their grins knowing and full of mischief, as if they were loving the tension between her and their friend. Then they headed toward the opposite end of the Alley, following along behind the Drake brothers. Carla wondered if the other women thought it was as impressive a sight as she did, the six tall, powerfully built men moving in ways that made it clear they were anything but human. The tense set of Eli's broad shoulders as he spoke with his brother drew her attention, and she bit her lip, wishing she could read his thoughts.

The moment they were out of earshot, all eyes turned to her. Her closest friends, the ones Carla considered her family, were waiting for an explanation. And they weren't exactly patient, their low voices crashing into each other like storm-tossed waves as they gathered around her, demanding to know what was going on. Only Jillian stayed silent, the look of concern in her brown eyes letting Carla know that her friend was worried about how she was handling everything.

Not well, Jilly, she tried to say with her eyes. *Not well at all.*

"Everyone be quiet," Wyatt finally cut in, placing his hand on her shoulder as he looked over the group. "This is between Carla and Eli. When she's ready to spill the story, she'll let you know. Until then, leave her alone about it."

She blinked, amazed by his loyalty, even though she should have become accustomed to it by now. They might fight like cats and dogs sometimes, but he'd always had her back when it counted.

"Yeah, I guess we should probably head home for the night," Jeremy drawled with a sheepish grin, after Jillian nudged him. "But it's good to have you back, Reyes."

"It's good to be," she replied, knowing she'd never meant it more than she did in that moment.

"I'd like to say good-night to Eli," Elise said, squeezing Wyatt's hand and giving Carla a brief smile before she headed toward the cabins at the far end of the glade. God only knew what Elise was making of this thing between her and Eli, but Carla trusted El not to go blabbing to him about the questions everyone had just bombarded her with.

There were hugs and murmurs of good-night as the others headed back to their respective cabins, and then Carla pulled her bag, which James had brought over for her, onto her shoulder. Listening to the crickets chirping all around them, while an owl hooted in the distance, she walked with Wyatt over to the cabin he shared with Elise. "If it's okay with you," she said around a yawn, after he'd shut the door behind them, "I'm going to head on back to your guest room and crash."

"The room is all set up for you," he murmured, "but you're not running off just yet."

Carla lifted her brows. "I'm not?"

Shaking his head, Wyatt folded his arms over his chest and sat on an arm of the brown leather sofa that was placed perpendicular to the fireplace. "I might not make you talk to the others right now, but you're not getting off *that* easy."

"Meaning you want the story tonight," she said dully.

His expression was concerned, but kind. "I can't help you if I don't know what's going on, Carla. You're going to have to trust me. We've been through too much together not to rely on each other when we need to."

She shot him a disgruntled look as she let her heavy bag slip to the floor. "You didn't trust me with the truth about Elise."

"Because I didn't think I could have her." His dark eyes were piercing as they studied the strain on her face. "The situation isn't the same."

"It doesn't matter whether I can have Eli or not. I don't want him."

With a snort, he said, "Come on, Reyes. Lying is just wasting our time."

She shoved her hands in her pockets and scowled. "Lie? Truth? None of it matters, Pall. We would be a disaster just waiting to happen."

"You sure that isn't your mother talking?"

Wyatt knew the story of how a sixteen-year-old Nicole Cates had been seduced by an older male who'd sold her lies about how he could feel a bond building between them, while maintaining she was still too young for him to claim with a mating bite. Too naïve to know any better, she'd fallen for his deception and had given him her virginity, only to learn that he'd been using her. And her luck hadn't improved as she moved on from one abusive Lycan lover to another, until she'd finally sworn off pack males for good, drowning her sorrows in cheap booze and clueless human lovers. A weekend-long affair in Annapolis had resulted in Nicole's pregnancy, though Nicole and the man were virtual strangers. All her mother could tell her was that he was Spanish and his name was Antonio Reyes. Carla had taken the name Reyes for herself once Nicole had made it clear that she cared more about her alcohol than her daughter.

Giving Wyatt the short version of her and Eli's history, she said, "We knew, before he left, that there was a life mate connection between us, and we…bonded. If he'd asked, I would have gone with him when he was banished. But he…" A wry, pain-edged smile tugged at the corner of her mouth, and she shook her head a little as she stared into the empty fireplace that was on her left. "Well, he obviously didn't. Instead, he crushed my heart into useless little pieces. So no matter what my body might want, I *can't* trust him." She brought her gaze back to her partner. "And if I can't trust him, what's the point?"

Wyatt worked his jaw, looking as though he wanted to put his fist through something. Something, say, like Eli's face. It was at times like these that Carla was reminded why she loved this guy so much. He was the freaking family she'd never really had. The one she could always count on.

"So he's the reason you never date anymore?" he asked.

She nodded, swallowing the bitterness in her throat. She hadn't dated anyone in the last six years. Half of that time she'd been completely mad over Eli, and the other half completely destroyed because he'd left her.

Wyatt looked curious, and more than a little confused. "I don't sense the mating bond on you. Why is that?"

"Because it didn't fully take." When his eyes went

wide, she gave a sharp laugh and held up a hand. "And no, I'm not explaining any more than that. Suffice it to say that there was an unexpected interruption. Then the next thing I knew, he'd been banished and was gone."

He winced. "Christ. Talk about shitty timing."

With another wry twitch of her lips, she murmured, "In case you hadn't noticed, that's pretty much the theme of this story."

"I didn't even know you knew Eli Drake."

Shaking her head again, she said, "I didn't while growing up. Just *of* him. We never spoke until he helped me with my mom one night after she'd gone on one of her benders and I got a call from town to come and collect her. She'd passed out on the sidewalk."

His dark brows drew together in a frown. "When was this?"

"I'd just turned twenty-two."

"Where the hell was I?"

"You had joined Jeremy and Mason on a hunt for a rogue that had traveled into our territory." She'd planned to leave it at that, only to hear herself adding, "But the truth is that it wouldn't have mattered if you were home that night, Pall. I was too embarrassed to have asked you for help."

A fresh wave of irritation darkened his rugged face, and then he sighed, looking resigned. He knew her too well to expect her to have acted any differently. "Did you know he was yours? I mean, six years ago, on the night that he helped you with your mom?"

"Yes. I realized then, but I...I didn't know that he felt the same. Not for a long time." Pushing her hair behind her ear, she stared into the empty hearth again and quietly said, "As lame as it sounds, we spent the next three years being 'secret' friends. We'd meet for runs...for walks...

to hunt or to train, and I'd...I'd have to bathe like crazy after every meeting so that none of you would be able to catch his scent on my clothes."

The memories of those bittersweet nights swept through her in a wrenching rush of emotion, and she dug her nails into her palms as hard as she could, needing that bite of pain to ground her. Keep her from falling apart. She'd never trusted easily, thanks to her upbringing. But she'd *wanted* to trust Eli. Wanted it so badly that she'd been shattered when he'd left without a word, confirming her fear that she'd never been anything more than a dirty little secret he'd used to amuse himself.

Getting back to her explanation, she looked at Wyatt and said, "I always worried that he was too embarrassed to let anyone in the pack know we were friends because of my bloodline." Her voice started to shake, so she took a deep breath and tried to steady it. "I know now that that's exactly how he felt. But at the time, I felt so right when I was with him, I just didn't care."

"You deserve better than that, Reyes."

Her throat worked as she gave a hard swallow. "I actually asked him about it a few weeks before he left, and he told me that it wasn't true. That he would never care about something like that. But it doesn't change the fact that he abandoned me. That after sharing a close friendship with me that he didn't want anyone to know about, then finally admitting that he wanted me and making a partial bond with me on the night before he was banished, he just walked away from me without a single word. Given all that, I can only assume he was lying when he said my bloodline didn't matter."

Stroking his jaw, Wyatt sighed. "Or maybe he wasn't, and there was another reason for his silence. I wish I could give you all the answers, but this is something the two of you need to work out for yourselves. Just know that Elise and I are *always* here for you. Eli might be her brother, but you're family to us, too. And that's never going to change."

She was mortified to feel the sting of tears burning behind her eyes. "Thanks," she scraped out, his show of support meaning more to her than he could ever guess.

"And a word of advice?"

She'd started to pick her bag up, but let it drop back down to the floor at his serious tone. "Do I have a choice?" she asked dryly, sliding him an exaggerated smirk.

Wearing the stoic expression he was so well-known for, he said, "If you want him, don't waste the time you've got with him blaming him for the past."

She couldn't hide her surprise when she gaped at him. "You think I should just forgive him? What the hell, Pall?"

"I'm not thinking about *him*," he said in a low voice, his dark eyes kind. "I'm thinking about you, honey. And if he's your mate, you're never going to be whole without him."

Her heart was pounding so hard that it hurt, and she pressed a trembling hand to her chest. "He won't even tell me why he didn't take me with him."

"Just give it some time."

"I *can't*," she muttered, panicked...and determined to do whatever it took to kill the pain inside her. If she didn't, she was terrified it would hollow her out, leaving nothing but hatred in its wake, the same as it'd done with her mother. "I've already given him too much. I'm done."

Wyatt looked at her as if she wasn't making any sense. "Carla, that isn't how these things work. You can't just turn them on and off."

"Not with a full bond. But that isn't what we have."

"And you think you can keep going like this?" he asked, his tone and expression making it clear that he thought she was on the ragged edge.

She shook her head. "No. And I won't have to. I've talked with Jillian, and she—"

Lifting one of his hands to stop her talking, he moved to his feet and said, "Wait a minute. Jillian knows about you and Eli?"

"Yes," she admitted, her voice tight. "She...suspected that something wasn't right with me, and after she moved to the Alley to live with Jeremy, she finally asked me about it. I told her the truth because I...I wanted her help."

His dark gaze looked wary. "Her help with what?"

"I want her to undo it."

He blinked, staring at her as if she'd lost her mind. "Christ, Reyes."

"Can you blame me?" she grumbled defensively.

The groove between his brows deepened. "What did Jillian say? Can it actually be done?"

Wetting her lips, she said, "She had to research it, but she finally found a way she thinks she can make it happen. But I needed Eli here for it."

"And does he know this is what you want?"

Exhaling a rough breath, she rubbed her arms as she turned her head to the side. "Yeah, I told him the night I found him."

His voice became eerily quiet. "And what's the cost?"

She shot him a surprised look from the corner of her eye, her heart still beating to a pounding, painful rhythm. "The cost? You know Jillian wouldn't charge me anything. There isn't any cost."

"I'm not talking about money," he muttered, taking a step toward her. "The whole idea of something for nothing—that's not how nature works. So what's the cost to *you?*"

"It doesn't matter," she shot back, narrowing her eyes. "It could be the greatest risk in the world, and I would still do it."

His own eyes went wide. "Jesus, Carla. You hate him *that* much?"

She opened her mouth, trying to force the words from her tight throat. But they wouldn't come. Shaking…shivering, she locked her watery gaze with Wyatt's compassionate one, and stopped trying to speak. It was too late anyway. She didn't need to say anything to make him understand.

The salty tears that suddenly spilled over her cheeks told him everything he needed to know.

Chapter 6

The moment Eli stepped into the kitchen the following morning, every set of eyes turned toward him. Kyle, Sam, James and Lev had already started in on plates of toast and eggs, but he could see that some had been set aside for him to eat when he joined them.

Leaning back in his chair, Sam gave him a slow once over. "I hate to say it, but you look like shit, boss man."

Yeah, and he felt like it, too. Ever since Carla had detailed for him and the others what the Runners had been dealing with here, he'd felt the sickening slide of guilt working its way through his system. There'd been so many times, since he'd caught news of his father's death, that he could have picked up a damn phone and called home to check on his family. But he never had, because there'd been a part of him that hadn't really wanted to know, so that he could keep going through the motions of living without giving a damn. Because giving a damn sucked.

But after seeing the relief on Eric's and Elise's faces last night, he felt more than guilt. He felt like a pathetic bastard who'd let his family down in the worst way. More than his skill in battle, they'd needed him there just to give them support, and he hadn't been. He'd failed.

When it came to the people he cared about, that was apparently the way he worked.

Which means I'm nothing more than an asshole, he muttered inside his head, grabbing his plate and mug and taking a seat at the table.

"We spoke with Mason and the other Runners earlier this morning," Kyle said, his arms crossed on the sturdy tabletop. "We would have dragged you out of bed to join us, but you were sleeping like the dead."

He choked back a curse as he took a hefty swallow of his coffee, irritated that he'd overslept. But after two sleepless nights and the fight against the Whiteclaw, his body had finally demanded some downtime. Setting his mug down, he looked at Kyle. "What did you learn?"

"They have it on word that at least fifty battle-trained Lycans could be coming from various packs, ready to fight beside the Whiteclaw soldiers. They reckon that total number could be anywhere between two hundred to two fifty. Then you have to add in the mercs that Bartley's brought with him."

"And how many do we have fighting for the Silver-crest?" he asked, taking a bite of his eggs.

"Currently trained? About half that."

Lev whistled under his breath. "And those are shit numbers."

"Could be worse, if the Whiteclaw were a larger pack," James offered in his gravelly voice. "They're thankfully on the small side. But they've spent time training their men to fight, which is why they have the higher number."

"Did you talk to any of the Runners about the day-shifting option?" During one of the meals they'd shared with Carla while they'd been on the road, she'd relayed the story of how his father had taught many of his followers the act of day-shifting. It was a skill that had previously only been known to those who sat on the League of Elders, but Stefan Drake had used it as a way to give his followers an advantage over the Runners, and now the Whiteclaw were attempting to do the same with their "super soldier" drugs.

"I talked to the one named Brody about it," Sam said, after taking a drink of his coffee. "He told me they'd had a meeting about it, since its whole purpose is to be used during times of war. But given how things went down with your old man, and the younger Lycans who are still trying to get their heads on right after all his brainwashing bullshit, they believe it's safer to avoid going that route."

Eli scrubbed a hand over his stubbled jaw. "Yeah, I can see where they're coming from. Sometimes the cure can be even deadlier than the poison."

The group sat in heavy silence for a moment, until he looked round at his men and asked, "So what's our play? That can't be the only thing you've come up with."

Kyle placed his hands behind his head and rocked his chair back on its hind legs. "We've been brainstorming some ideas that we'll run by you tonight, after you've had a chance to settle in."

He swallowed the bite he'd just taken and grimaced. "Why not just tell me now?"

"Because you look like you need a break at the moment, and we're still putting our heads together. Just take some time to get things sorted out today, and let us deal with crunching these ideas into something that might work. Then you can listen to everything we come up with and tell us it's all wrong tonight."

He laughed, which was what he knew Kyle had been going for. It sucked that he'd lost touch with his family for so long, but he had to admit that he was a lucky son of a bitch to have found these guys. They were like a second family to him, and he was going to miss them when all was said and done.

He couldn't say exactly what he'd be doing when this thing with the Whiteclaw was over, but if he survived it, Eli was determined to stick close to the ones he'd left behind.

Whether they want me here or not.

"When I spoke with Mason this morning," Sam added, "he asked if some of us can help with the training. They've been working with any volunteers they get from the pack on weapons training and combat skills."

"If they want our help, they've got it. But I think we need to be careful until we have a better bearing on how involved they want us. I don't want to step on any toes around here."

In a dry tone, Lev said, "You're not exactly Mr. Popular with this group, are you?"

"I don't have a great history with the Runners," he admitted with a grimace, "but I'm hoping it'll improve."

"It better, if you want to keep your little lady love," Sam murmured.

James shoved Sam in the shoulder so hard it nearly knocked the guy out of his chair. "Come on, Sam. Don't you remember us warning you that the boss man would be out of sorts this morning?"

Shaking his head, Eli couldn't help but smirk at their antics. "You're all a bunch of jackasses."

They laughed and gave him an even harder time as they finished off breakfast, then cleared the table, making plans to meet up again later that afternoon. After the guys headed out, Eli grabbed a quick shower, then threw on a pair of jeans, his boots, and a dark gray T-shirt, eager to get outside and find out what Carla was up to. As he headed out the front door of the cabin, he almost reached up and straightened his damp hair, then stopped himself with a scowl. Last thing he needed was to start primping for her. When it came to Carla Reyes, he became almost more animal than man. No sense really in putting out false advertising.

The instant he got her under his hands and mouth, everything inside him—man *and* beast—went straight into feral aggression mode. She was just too much. Her taste. Her scent. The silky feel of her skin. All of it was guaranteed to turn him into a slathering animal that wanted to do things to her that would make most women run for cover—which was why he needed to get a damn grip on himself.

The last time he'd touched her, in that motel room the other night, he'd forced himself to pull back because he'd been on the verge of losing it. If he wanted to touch her again—something he wanted more than anything—he was going to have to find a way to leash that visceral, primitive part of his hunger, or he'd be sinking his fangs deep into her tight flesh, completing their bond, before he even knew what hit him. And Carla would end up skinning him alive.

Not that he would blame her, with the way things currently stood between them. Hell, at this point he'd be happy just to have her look at him without that scathing burn of fury and suspicion in her beautiful eyes. Though it was the pain that really did him in. Made him feel like his insides had been flayed and dipped in lye.

Pulling in a deep breath of the pine-scented air, he started walking a bit faster across the bustling glade, needing to be with her, close to her, even if she didn't want him there. He wasn't really in the frame of mind to fully appreciate the beauty of his surroundings, but he would have had to be blind not to notice how in the bright morning sunlight the Alley looked like something out of a freaking fairy tale, even with all the activity going on. The grass seemed greener here than anywhere else in the world, thick and lush beneath his boots, the air so crisp and clean it damn near made him lightheaded. Then there were the tall, majestic trees, thick with leafy branches, lining the perimeter, the surrounding forest brimming with life.

And yet, despite the surreal beauty of the glade, there was an air of tension and expectancy in the air that hung over those who lived here like a dark, dense storm cloud. They were doing their best to enjoy each day as it came and to be thankful for what they had, while remaining constantly mindful of the fact that everything could change in a heartbeat. That this idyllic paradise could all too easily slip into hell if they weren't vigilant.

He nodded to his sister when he caught her coming out onto her front porch, then looked around again, trying to spot a familiar head of honey-gold hair. When Carla was nowhere to be seen, he forced a grin onto his lips and made his way over to Elise. "Hey, beautiful."

She was standing on the top step, which put her only slightly above his height. Reaching down, she ruffled his unruly hair. "God, I can't get used to how huge you are now."

"I don't look that different," he muttered, going a little hot around the ears. His hair was longer than he'd ever worn it, and he'd put on more muscle in the last three years, as well as added a few battle scars. But he hadn't thought the changes were enough for others to notice. He'd obviously been wrong.

"Are you kidding?" she asked with a playful snort. "You look like a wild man."

Eli rolled his eyes. "Thanks."

"Come on," she murmured, smiling as she took his hand and pulled him up the steps. "I'll get you some more coffee. You look like you need it."

Instead of taking offense, he took a moment to study her in the morning sunlight, before saying, "And you look happy, sis."

A gentle smile touched her lips. "I am."

Eli squeezed her hand. "Good. You deserve it."

They went into the kitchen, and he let his gaze wander over the beautiful, spacious interior of the cabin as she put the coffee on. Then he took a seat at the table, feeling both at ease and nervous at the same time, his brain churning as he tried to work out what he should say…and what he shouldn't. He'd honestly never seen Elise look so happy and confident, and he didn't want to screw that up by bringing up a painful topic. Then she brought it up for him.

"You know," she murmured, setting their steaming mugs on the table and taking the chair caddy corner to his, "I never really got the chance to thank you for what you did for me." Her dark gaze was soft with emotion.

Swallowing at the knot in his throat, he rumbled, "You told me." He'd called a few times after his banishment, whenever he'd been missing his siblings too much to resist. But his calls had become less frequent over time, as it became harder to hear about life in Shadow Peak going on without him.

And each time he'd talked to them, it had just about killed him inside to keep from asking about Carla. About how she was. If she hated him. Who she was dating.

"But I never thanked you in person," his sister said with a smile. "Over the phone doesn't count."

"You don't need to thank me, El. It was my responsibility to look out for you, and I'm sorry that I didn't come back sooner. I know I've let you and Eric down."

Frowning, she said, "Eli, that isn't true. Yes, we wanted you here because we've missed you, but neither one of us would have wanted you to have to live through Dad's madness. I can't even imagine how horrific that would have been for you, given how closely you worked with him."

"But after he was dead—after the League was gone—I should have come home. Damn it, El, I should have been here to protect you from the Whiteclaw."

Looking adorably frustrated, she shook her head and said, "That's ridiculous. I think it's great that you're here to help, because God knows we need it. But you've got to stop thinking it's your duty to keep bad things from happening to Eric and me. No one expects that of you."

"I love you both," he muttered gruffly, "which *makes* it my duty."

"Well, we feel the same way about you. So I guess we can all just look out for each other. Fair?"

Some of the tension in his chest started to ease as he realized she truly didn't hold a grudge against him, and he found himself giving her a lopsided grin. "So now that both you and Eric have gotten bonded, I guess we have two new members of the family, eh?"

She slowly arched a slender auburn brow. "And what about you?"

"What about me?" he hedged, sliding his gaze away from the knowing look in her deep blue eyes as he took a drink of his coffee.

Softly, she said, "You can play coy if you want, but you should know that Wyatt told me about you and Carla. Not everything, but enough for me to know that you're life mates. And that you've had a complicated relationship for the past six years, three of which you haven't even been around for."

He flicked her a guarded look, his fingers tightening on the mug. "I don't want to talk about it, El."

"I figured as much. I just want you to know that even though I don't understand why you didn't take her with you, or come back for her, I think she would be good for you. She's an amazing woman."

"Yeah," he agreed, his voice thick. "She's something, all right."

She took a sip of her coffee, then said, "Wyatt and I sat her down this morning and must have thanked her about a hundred times. Honestly, Eli, I don't think I would have made it out of Hawkley alive if she hadn't put herself at even greater risk to give Wyatt the chance to reach me. Even Eric came over this morning and gave her a big ol' hug." She shook her head a little and gave a hard swallow. "What she did, it was one of the bravest things I've ever seen. She did everything she could to keep their attention focused on her so that I didn't get hurt."

A slight smile ghosted his lips. "She must care about you a lot, El."

Her dark eyes twinkled. "Or maybe she was thinking about you."

He grunted, taking another drink from his mug.

"I'm really hoping you'll talk to me about her, Eli." The quiet words were rough with sincerity. "I want to be able to help you, but I can't do that if I don't understand what's going on."

Steering the conversation in a slightly different direction, he leaned back in his chair and said, "Speaking of the little Bloodrunner, where is she? I thought she might be here with Wyatt."

Elise gave him a disappointed look, then sighed and gave in. "She and Wyatt are out checking on some things down in Wesley. With all the tension in the pack right now, we think a few of the younger wolves who were caught up in Dad's craziness might have slipped back into old habits. There've been a few human disappearances around Wesley, and we want to make sure they aren't the work of any rogue wolves."

A deep scowl settled between his brows. "Why the hell did Carla have to go?"

Frowning again, she said, "She's just doing her job, Eli. Don't be an ass."

"She could get hurt, damn it."

His sister looked as if she was trying not to roll her eyes at him. "This is Carla we're talking about. I get that you're protective of her, but she's a serious little badass."

His nostrils flared as he pulled in a hard breath. "Did she or did she not end up kidnapped by those bastards?"

"That was different."

"Was it? Because no matter how you look at it, she managed to get herself into a situation that put her in grave danger."

"And she got herself out of it. Seriously, Eli, what is your problem?" she demanded as she crossed her arms, her slender brows pinched. "I love you like crazy, but you're acting like a jerk."

He grunted, knowing damn well that he sounded like an ass. But he didn't know how to make her understand. He'd always worried himself sick over Carla's job, his fears only growing more intense as their connection had deepened. Now that he was back, that worry was scraping him raw inside. Made him feel like she might be stolen from him before he even had the chance to get ahold of her.

If a bloody miracle happened and she eventually agreed to let him complete the bond, how would he cope with what she did for a living? *Could* he cope with it? Would she give him any consideration at all, or dig her heels in and turn a deaf ear to his concerns?

Damn it, it was always like a chess game with her, and he didn't know how to win. Didn't know which move would be the right one to land him his queen—or what the hell he'd do with her once he got her, considering everything that stood between them. She made him feel a thousand different things at once, and he was still too wound up by her sudden appearance back in his life to make heads or tails of any of it. All he knew was that he was done with…with *this*. With feeling like the gulf between them was growing wider with every second that went by.

Elise's gaze sharpened as she studied his scowling face. "You know," she murmured, "whatever is going on between you and Carla, it hasn't exactly put Wyatt and I in an easy situation. He's protective of her, and I'm protective of you. But I'm starting to wonder if I'm on the right side in this thing."

"Leave it alone, El. You and Wyatt don't need us causing problems for you."

"Nothing is coming between us," she said in a tone that was more confident than anything he'd ever heard from her before. "We're just worried, Eli. But I have a feeling there's a lot you need to fill me in on, whether you want to or not."

"No offense, sis, but it isn't any of your business."

She turned her head a bit to the side, staring out at the thick woods that lay just beyond the kitchen window, the look on her beautiful face making his insides tighten, as if he needed to brace for an emotional blow. Then she looked at him and said, "Did you ever wonder why mother named me Elise?"

Wondering where she was going with this, and wanting to talk about anything in the world besides their mother, he gave an uncomfortable shrug. "No idea, El. I'm assuming she just liked the name."

Her lips twitched with a brief smile. "It never struck you that it was a little *too* similar to your own?"

His tension cranked a notch higher, and he mirrored her pose, crossing his arms over his chest. "What are you getting at?"

Softly, she said, "One of my earliest memories of her is the day she explained it to me. She said that Eric was her little troublemaker, but you were her rock. Strong and proud and never afraid to stand up for what was important to you, even though you were just a child. And she wanted me to be like that. She said it was never easy for women in our world, and she wanted me to have every advantage going in, so she named me Elise because she wanted me to carry a part of you with me, wherever I went."

He scrubbed his hands over his face as her quiet words wound their way through his head, then placed his fists against the tabletop and took a sharp breath. *Christ,* if his mother only knew what kind of boy he'd become after she'd left. The things he'd done to keep as much of his father's attention focused on him as he could, and not on Eric or Elise, were far from noble. He'd often acted like a bully and a thug just to keep the old man happy, and that was a shame he'd carry with him for the rest of his life.

Despite the ruthless reputation he'd earned as a high-priced mercenary, the rumors of his greed were greatly exaggerated. Yeah, he'd made a ton of cash at times, but there'd also been a lot of jobs that hadn't even come with a paycheck. More than once, he and the other guys had helped villagers who barely had enough to feed themselves, ridding the area of the bloodthirsty drug cartels who destroyed their fields and way of life. Had rescued women and children who'd been sold into the horrific sex slave industry, returning them to their homes. But Eli knew that sometimes there simply weren't enough good deeds to erase the stains on your past. Which meant he was probably a bigger fool than he'd ever realized, since he just kept on trying.

"Eli?"

Feeling as if the gritty words were being torn out of him, he forced his gaze to Elise's and said, "Don't, El. Whatever you do, *don't* be like me."

Covering one of his big, scarred hands with her soft ones, she gave him a crooked smile. "I hate to burst your bubble, but I think you're pretty damn awesome. So you'll stay my hero whether you want to or not."

He shoved his free hand through his hair, and swallowed the lump of bitterness stuck in his throat. "Damn it, honey. If you only knew."

"Knew what?" she asked, tilting her head a bit as she studied him.

He debated, wanting to unload the heavy burden of his secret after all these years once and for all, the weight of it crushing him down, but still terrified of what it would mean. Would his sister hate him? Would Eric? Would he lose them now that he'd only just come back to them?

And was the fear of that happening just another part of why he'd opted to stay away for so long? Because as long as he wasn't with them, he didn't have to fight this constant battle to keep what he'd done inside?

Needing to get the hell out of there before he said something he would no doubt regret, he pushed back from the table and stood. "Thanks for the coffee, honey, but I have to go."

She reached out and caught his hand, squeezing it until he finally looked down at her. "Eli," she murmured with concern, "whatever it is, you know I'll still love you. Right?"

He nodded as he pulled his hand from hers, then turned and walked out, no doubt leaving her with a thousand questions.

And not a single answer.

Chapter 7

After suffering two days of hell, Eli was ready to howl. He was frustrated, exhausted, and so goddamn hungry for a certain little half-breed it was driving him mad. She was doing a damn good job of avoiding him, the glimpses he occasionally got of her twisting him into knots of tension and craving. There were so many things he needed to say to her, things he needed to make her understand, more of them building up inside him with every hour that went by, but she wasn't giving him the chance.

Hell, she wasn't even willing to be in the same room with him. Which made it damn difficult to give her the explanations she'd demanded of him.

Their relationship, whatever it was at this point, had turned into one hot, tangled mess of *should haves* and *shouldn't haves,* and all he wanted to do was to tie her sweet little ass down and make her listen. He finally understood that there was no way forward until he did that, and while he still didn't have everything figured out in his head, the one thing he knew beyond any doubt was that he didn't want her breaking their bond. Yeah, there were a thousand and one issues they needed to work through, but that was the one thing that was non-negotiable.

"Yo, boss man!" Kyle suddenly barked, jerking Eli from his thoughts. "You heard a word I've said?"

"Doubt it," Lev murmured. They were all sitting around the kitchen table in the cabin that Eli and Kyle were sharing. Grinning like a jackass, Lev lifted his coffee mug and added, "He's too busy mentally undressing the little Runner in his dirty daydreams."

"Lev, shut up," he muttered, before looking at his second-in-command. "Sorry, Kyle. Go on with what you were saying."

Kyle leaned back in his chair. "I was telling you that the guys and I have finally ironed out a plan."

"Great. Let's hear it." He'd been waiting two damn days for this.

"First, the way we see it, there are two basic problems that we have to deal with: the fact that they have more bodies than we do, and the fact that they control the timing of their attack. There's not much we can do about the first, but the second is one we can take away from them."

His brows lifted with interest. "And how do we do that?"

Sam gave him a slow smile. "That's where the plan comes in."

Twenty minutes later, Eli agreed that what they'd come up with was a brilliant idea that might actually succeed despite their limited numbers, and he told the guys to take it to Mason and the Runners. The five of them had been working closely with the Runners for the past few days, with the exception of Carla and Wyatt, who kept taking every "out of Alley" assignment that came up.

Thankfully, he and the guys were getting along great with the rest of the group, and the training sessions they'd been helping out with were progressing even more rapidly than they'd hoped. Everyone in the Alley was trying to keep a positive attitude, and the arrival of thirty Lycans from the Pennsylvania-based Blackstone pack, who were willing to help with security patrols, had been greatly appreciated. And there'd been a message from the Greywolf—who had actually threatened to move in on the Silvercrest's northern border in order to prevent the Whiteclaw from encroaching on their territory—that they were standing down. Apparently, the news that Eli and his group of ruthless mercenaries were now working with the Silvercrest had been enough to make the Greywolf rethink their position.

The rest of the morning was spent working out on the training fields, and then he and the guys worked with Mason and Brody to fortify defenses in the Alley. As the day wore on, he constantly searched for Carla's blond hair in the crowd of people moving around the glade, but she wasn't anywhere to be seen.

"Hey, Eli, wait up!" Kyle called out, just as Eli was climbing up the front steps of the cabin they were sharing. He didn't have the patience to deal with any more of his friend's ribbing at the moment, and was about to tell him to get lost, when Kyle said, "I thought you might want to know that she's back."

He turned so quickly he damn near took out James, who was climbing the porch steps behind him. "Sorry," he muttered, shoving past James and Lev as he hurried back down, scanning the glade. The instant he saw her on the far side, he took off.

"Carla!" he called, not caring if he looked like an idiot to those who were probably watching him.

She kept walking, and he nearly crashed into Brody and Cian, who were deep in conversation in front of Brody's cabin, as he ran across the Alley, trying to reach her before she disappeared inside Wyatt's place and locked the door again. She'd fucking done it twice already when he'd tried to get her alone.

"Stop, damn it!" he shouted, causing everyone around them to quit what they were doing and look at him. "We need to talk!"

Ignoring him, she started walking faster. Eli cursed, ready to knock the damn door down this time if he had to—and then he got the break he needed. One of the soon-to-be moms stepped out onto Carla's porch to ask her something about the thermostat in her cabin, and she was forced to stop and answer the woman's question. Breathing hard, Eli slowed down and positioned himself partially in front of her, his hungry gaze taking in every inch of her delectable form while she finished her conversation. She was dressed in a dirt-stained pair of jeans, tight black T-shirt, and black boots, her golden hair falling loose around her shoulders. It was her standard work look, and he could tell by the light sheen of sweat on her arms and face that she'd been doing something strenuous, her provocative scent even richer than normal, so good he could sense it like something warm and sweet on his tongue.

When her conversation was finished, she started to walk around him, but he grasped her arm, halting her in her tracks. She didn't even bother looking at him as she said, "Let me go, Eli."

"Not until you stop acting like a child and talk to me,"

he bit out, leaning in close and tightening his grip, while still being careful not to hurt her.

She pulled in a deep breath, then slowly turned her head and took a good, long look at him with those dark eyes. "I can see you're not going to be reasonable about this," she eventually murmured, forcing a note of boredom in her words that made him want to put her over his knee and spank her until she stopped acting like such a little brat. "So, fine. If you want to talk, then talk."

Eli stared down at her, lost in his hunger and craving, and suddenly couldn't think of a single goddamn thing to say. Instead, he wanted to take her down to the lush green grass, strip her bare, and make her come until she stopped being so damn mad at him. Until he'd found a way to turn her hatred into something that didn't make him feel like he was dying inside.

She crossed her arms over her chest the instant he lowered his hand, her foot tapping out an impatient rhythm against the grass, while his mind remained completely blank.

"Well?"

He ran his tongue over the front of his teeth, then got right in her face. "Why are you avoiding me?"

"It's not that hard to figure out. I told you what I wanted to hear. Until you're ready to be honest with me, which I seriously doubt is why you keep trying to do this, I have nothing to say to you."

He bit back a curse, wondering if anything he said at this point would make a difference to her. She was so damn bitter. So angry.

Sensing the curious stares coming their way, he grasped her elbow and drew her reluctant body to the side of the cabin, where they were out of view. Then he gave into the visceral urge to have her locked down, and backed her against the rustic cedar planks, caging her in with his arms as he planted his palms against the exterior wall. Holding her hostile glare, he asked, "Why did you bother to come after me, to bring me back to this place, if all you planned to do was ignore me once we got here?"

"You're seriously this upset because you think I've been ignoring you? Jesus, Eli. You ignored me for two entire days in the truck while we were driving here!"

He drew his head back in surprise. "I wasn't ignoring you."

"Like hell you weren't."

"Damn it, Rey. Why do you think I sat in the back seat for those entire two days? I hate not driving, but I wanted to be as close to you as I could be. Even if we weren't talking to each other."

"You wouldn't even look at me!" she snapped, her beautiful eyes glittering with emotion.

His voice turned guttural. "I was looking at you every goddamn time you closed your eyes or stared out your window. I just didn't want you to know it."

Taking another deep breath, she asked, "And what about at the motel? What the hell was *that?*"

"That was…complicated."

She made a sound that was half snarl, half scream, and he had to grab her again as she tried to duck under his arm.

"I was afraid of losing control!" he growled, holding her against the cabin with his big hands pressed to her shoulders. "You…you *push* me."

"Toward what?" she demanded, only to immediately shake her head in frustration. "Never mind. It doesn't matter. The only *pushing* I plan on doing is pushing you away from me, so your problems are solved."

He could feel a muscle beginning to pulse at the side

of his jaw, his heart pounding to a hard, brutal rhythm. "That's not what I want and you know it."

She kept her angry gaze locked tight with his as she licked her bottom lip. "You're wrong," she argued, her breaths quickening. "I don't know *anything* where you're concerned."

Biting back a groan, he begged her with his gaze to believe in him. "You would if you would just give me a chance."

She paled as her eyes slid closed, and then she dropped her head back against the cabin with a thud that made him wince. "I told you at that shitty bar in Texas that I wasn't bringing you back for me, Eli. I brought you back for Eric and Elise, and for the pack. But not for me."

"So that's it?" he asked quietly. "You have no interest in what I do?"

She lifted her head, then slowly opened her eyes, their brown depths filled with pain. "You'll do whatever you want, same as you always have. I've learned not to care."

He moved his sharp gaze over her beautiful face, using everything he had to read her...to see beneath her bitter words. "I call bullshit, Rey."

"What?"

Pulling in a deep breath of her warm, mouthwatering scent, he spoke in a hushed, gruff voice that was thick with hope. "I can smell the need on you. See your pulse racing at the base of your throat. Christ, baby. I can fucking *feel* how much you need this. How much you need *me*."

She glared up at him. "Unfortunately for you, my hormones don't make the decisions around here."

A low, deep laugh rumbled up from his chest, and he lowered his head, pressing his lips to the soft skin at the side of her throat. "Maybe you should let them," he murmured, licking across her hammering pulse. "Because I want nothing more than to make you addicted to me. To how I can make you feel."

Her hands settled against his shoulders, but she didn't push him away. Instead, she sank her short nails into him, that little bite of pain shooting straight to his groin. "A woman's head has to be in the game as much as her body for her to really enjoy herself, Eli."

"I know," he rasped, nipping her delicate earlobe. "And if you just give me the chance, I'll get them *both* to the right place." He lifted his head, looking her right in the eye. "Take me to your bed, Rey, and I swear I'll do everything I can to make it worth your while."

She stared back at him through her thick lashes. "I thought you wanted to talk, Eli. Not fuck."

He put his face right over hers, his big hands flexing against her shoulders. "The talking comes *after,* Rey. After I've spent hours just making you come. I'll bury my face between your sweet little thighs and lick you until you scream. I could keep my tongue busy down there for days, that's how *badly* I want you. I dream about getting you under my mouth. Feeling you beneath my lips. Drinking you in, over and over. There were too many damn things I never got the chance to do to you, and I *need* them, baby. I need them so badly it's killing me."

For an instant, he thought she was actually softening, her skin dewy and warm with color, making him want to press his mouth to those fever blushes so badly he could taste it. But then disappointment cut into him like a knife as he lifted his gaze back to her eyes. He could tell by the way they narrowed that she wasn't going to surrender so easily. "You didn't get them because you went from never touching me, to messing around with me against a freaking tree, to falling on top of me like a drunken idiot two nights later, and then leaving me!"

He ground his back teeth together, wanting so badly to argue, but what could he say? She'd spoken nothing more than the truth. After trying so hard to keep his hands to himself, only allowing a few brief kisses and touches, she'd caught him that last night when his control was shattered. He'd been hurting for Elise, for what had happened to her, filled with rage that he hadn't been able to find the other bastards who'd raped her. Had been worried about what the League would do to punish him for the kill he'd made, but unable to regret it. No, he would have done the same thing, in the same way, again...and again. But he'd drank more than he normally did that night, needing to dull the roar in his head, as well as the pain in his gut that made him ache for the feel of Carla in his arms. And then she'd knocked on his door, and his control had simply vanished, decimated beneath a crushing force of hunger so violent and savage he'd nearly taken her right there, on the hard wooden floor inside the doorway. Somehow, he'd managed to get her into his bedroom, but that was the only concession to her comfort he'd been able to make.

He'd simply needed her too badly.

At first, he'd been worried she would stop him that night, since she hadn't been happy with how he'd acted a few days before, when his control had first started to slip and he'd kissed her. Then put his hands all over her.

She'd been into the kissing...*and* the touching. Had loved it when he'd put his hand between her legs for the first time, her shirt pushed up under her chin. They'd been in the forest, surrounded by the trees and wind and rain, and he'd had her little nipple in his mouth while he'd thrust two fingers deep inside her tender sex, undone by the hot, wet feel of her. She'd been the tightest, sweetest thing he'd ever known, and when she'd pulsed around his fingers in orgasm, he'd wanted to throw his head back and howl. And once he'd finally pulled his fingers from between her silky thighs, he hadn't been able to stop himself from shoving them in his mouth, sucking off every drop of her cream. But she'd been furious at the way he'd pulled away from her when she'd reached for the button on *his* jeans, putting an end to the stolen, erotic moment, knowing damn well that if she'd put her hands on him, he'd have been inside her in an instant. Something he'd wanted more than anything, but had known he couldn't have.

So, yeah, he'd already been working on a hair trigger where she was concerned. And then, two nights later, she was there, in his house, and he hadn't been able to fight it. He'd stripped her, taken her to his bed, and shoved her thighs apart to make way for him, his chest heaving with his frantic breaths. Heart pumping, he'd worked himself inside her hot, fist-tight sheath, completely lost in the exquisite, breathtaking feel of her, and had just pierced her throat with the tips of his fangs, when his father had started banging on his front door. Terrified Stefan would realize she was there, he'd jerked away from her, leaving her in his bed with the promise to be back. He had no idea how long she'd waited, but when he'd returned from being told that the League was determining his punishment for the unsanctioned kill that he'd made, she'd been gone.

The banishment had been announced the following day, and he'd known, in that moment, that he would probably never see her again. That he'd lost everything that had ever mattered to him.

Forcing his mind back on the present and away from those gut-wrenching memories, he told her, "I wanted to finish it that night, Carla. You have no idea how *badly* I wanted that. But I tried to do the right thing."

"Which was what?" she snapped, curling her hands into fists and pressing them against his chest. "Protecting the little half-human from your big bad self? You didn't think I would have been able to handle you?"

He shook his head, hard. "I wasn't trying to protect you from me." Though he should have, considering how savage she'd made him feel. "I was trying to protect you from my father."

"Riiight." Her tone made it clear that she thought he'd just fed her the most pathetic excuse in the history of brush-offs.

Forcing his words through his clenched teeth, he said, "You *knew* him, Rey. Knew what he was capable of. I never let myself have anything that he could use as leverage against me. What do you think would have happened if he'd learned that we… That we were…"

"Jesus, Eli. Just spit it out."

His words punched from his mouth like bullets. "An item. Thing. Whatever the hell you want to call it."

A smirk curled her beautiful mouth, and she clucked her tongue. "Come on, Eli. Get real. There wasn't any chance of him ever thinking that, because I wasn't yours. Maybe nature screwed up and thought I should be, but we both know the truth. I was just the half-breed you kept pushing away. The one you were too ashamed to be seen with."

"Wrong," he bit out, shoving his fingers into her hair and holding her head in a firm grip as he pressed his forehead against hers. "You were my everything, Carla. Besides my brother and sister, the only goddamn person that mattered. The person that mattered *most*."

Before she could say anything else to piss him off,

he took her mouth and filled it with his tongue, rubbing it against hers, the taste of her so incredible it nearly broke him.

"Ask me to come with you," he panted against her soft lips, his body so hard and aching with the need to be inside her he would have gotten down on his damn knees if he weren't afraid she would run from him when he did. "Invite me to your room...to your bed. *Please,* Rey. I'm *begging* you."

"Never!" she cried, the single word cracking with emotion as she wrenched her head to the side.

Beyond frustrated, he exhaled a harsh breath, then turned away from her and paced a few yards away. Before he even knew what he was doing, he found himself smashing his fist into a towering tree trunk with so much force it would have broken his hand if he'd been human. He hit it against the rough bark, feeling his knuckles split and bleed, imagining it was his father's face since it was that bastard's fault he'd been too terrified to claim her like she'd deserved. And now, because of that, things were so screwed up, she wouldn't even give him the chance to make them right.

When he finally got himself under control and turned back around to face her, she was gone, which wasn't all that surprising. Still, a violent, guttural stream of curses burned at the back of his throat, and he braced his hands on his hips, struggling to catch his breath. What should he do now? Go after her? Follow her around like a pathetic puppy? Or the ol' tried-and-true coping mechanism of losing himself in the bottom of a bottle? If he went that route, at least he'd be able to dull this goddamn hollow feeling sucking at his insides for a short time.

Then again, given how badly he wanted her, there

probably wasn't enough alcohol in the world to ease this ache.

Forcing himself to move, he walked back out into the glade, and immediately spotted a worried-looking Eric headed his way. *Shit*. How much had his brother just seen?

From the look on his dark face, too much, and Eli knew he wasn't going to like what was coming. Eric didn't even give him the chance to try and deflect him with a bullshit excuse. His brother just jerked his chin toward Elise's cabin, where they knew she was working on a training schedule for the group, and growled, *"Now."*

Eric knocked on her front door after they'd climbed the porch steps, and the moment Elise opened up, she took one look at their scowls and frowned. "In the kitchen," she murmured, noticing the blood dripping from his battered knuckles. They followed her into the sunny kitchen, and Eli slumped down into one of the chairs at the table, offering a gruff, "Thanks," when Elise handed him a damp dishtowel. He wrapped the soft cotton around his hand, then surged back to his feet, unable to sit still as he started pacing from one side of the kitchen to the other. Elise had taken a seat at the table across from where he'd been sitting, while Eric leaned against the sink with his arms crossed over his chest. But neither of them was saying a damn thing, and he ground his jaw, keeping his narrowed gaze on the floor, knowing they were watching him, trying to figure out what his problem was.

Eric was the first to break the uncomfortable silence. "So about you and Reyes?"

Eli flicked him a shuttered look. "Just leave it, Eric. I need to figure this out on my own."

His brother's dark brows were knitted with concern. "I get that, and I'm trying to be patient. To give you time to settle in after being away for so long. But I need you to answer a question for me."

"I already know what you're going to ask," he ground out, "and the answer is *yes*. She's mine."

There was nothing for a moment but the heavy sound of his boots on the kitchen floor as he paced, and then Eric gave a tired sigh. "Yeah, we kinda already figured that out. What we're wondering is...well, everything else that goes along with that. Why didn't you ever tell us? What the hell is going on between the two of you *now?*"

"Christ," he muttered, lifting his good hand and pulling it down his face.

"Did you know?" Eric pressed, unwilling to let it go. "Did you know that she was yours before you left?"

Hell yes, he'd known. Though he hadn't admitted it to her, or even to himself, he'd known for *years* before they ever even spoke to one another on that fateful night when she'd been called up to town to collect Nicole. He'd started noticing Carla when she hit her teens. Had watched her, waiting for her to grow older. And then the day had come when he could no longer keep his distance, despite all the reasons why he should. Why it would have been better for them both.

He could have walked away that night, when he'd seen her struggling with Nicole on the street, but he hadn't had the willpower. She was an adult, she was beautiful, and she was *his*. Even if he couldn't claim her, he'd wanted to be close to her. To know her. Spend time with her. It'd been torture, but he'd soaked up every single second that he spent in her company—and he'd ached for her every single moment that they were apart. Even on those nights when she'd been in her cabin down in the Alley, and he'd been up in town, with another woman underneath him, trying to ease the pain of wanting her and not having her. Of course, the meaningless sexual encounters had never worked. How could a guy enjoy sex with another woman when he couldn't get the image of the one he craved out of his head? When he kept thinking about how he'd feel if he knew she was doing the same thing with another male? What her face would look like if she were there to see him?

"Eli?" Eric prompted in a low voice.

Coming to a stop in the middle of the kitchen floor, he gave a hard swallow, then forced out a quiet, "Yeah, I knew."

His brother's deep voice was rough with surprise. "And you left her anyway?"

Lifting his head, he locked his gaze with Eric's. "I knew she was mine, but I didn't know that the bond had formed. Or at least some of it."

"*Some* of it?" Eric asked, shaking his head. "How is that even possible?"

Elise gave a soft laugh, speaking up for the first time since she'd sat down. "It's not too crazy if you think about it. I mean, Eli *is* as alpha as a Lycan can get, not to mention as pure-blooded, which means he probably has supercharged sex hormones or whatever it is that causes the bonding."

Eric waved his arms wildly, looking ridiculous. "Shit, stop!" he said to El. "Don't talk about Eli's freaking super sperm when I'm in the same room with you. That is *not* something I want to hear about."

"I didn't say super sperm," Elise argued, rolling her eyes. "I said supercharged sex hormones."

Eli used his good hand to cover his eyes, his ears hot, and wondered how he could get them to just shut up.

"And then there's Carla," Elise went on to say, obviously not ready to let the subject drop. "She's as badass as a female can get. It's not surprising the bond managed to at least partially take when you think about how potent they both are."

Eric groaned. "New topic, *now,* you little imp."

"You're such a baby," she said with another laugh, and Eli lowered his hand just in time to catch her tossing a balled-up napkin at their brother.

Eric grimaced as he batted the napkin away. "I'm not a baby. I just don't like thinking about my brother's... potency."

"Back atcha," Eli grunted. He'd just started to head back over to the table to take a seat, when a deep male voice let out a guttural string of curses right outside the kitchen window, followed by an equally pissed off sounding voice that definitely belonged to a woman. "Who the hell is that?" he asked, looking from Eric to Elise.

She stood up and peered through the slanted blinds. "Holy shit," she gasped. "It's Cian and Sayre!"

Eric frowned. "Are they arguing again?"

"Let's just say that if looks could kill, I'm pretty sure the Irishman would be pushing up daisies right about now." Shaking her head, she turned away from the window and sat back down at the table. "She just stomped off into the woods, and he stormed around the back of the cabin, probably heading back over to his place."

"What's the deal with those two, anyway?" Eli asked the question as he sat down, glad to have the focus off him and Carla for the moment.

"Who the hell knows?" Eric muttered, pushing his hands in his front pockets as he shrugged his shoulders. "He won't touch her, but he won't let any other guy get close to her, either. If he wants her, and I'm thinking he does, then he probably thinks she's too young for him."

"Isn't she?"

"Probably," Eric said again. "But then, from what I understand from the other Runners, no one's really sure of the guy's *exact* age."

Eli lifted his brows. "Didn't he grow up with all of them?"

Eric shook his head. "He spent time here visiting when they were in their teens, but lived in Ireland most of the time. He didn't move to these mountains permanently until later."

"He can be such a smartass," Elise murmured, "but he's a gorgeous one. And that accent of his is downright sinful, which I'm sure hasn't escaped the girl's notice. But there are a lot of issues working against him, like her age, his reputation as a man-whore, and his whole 'my past is a secret' thing. And then there's the fact that her mother hates his guts. Woman turns red every time she sees him."

Eli snorted. "I wouldn't think Hennessey would let a mother get in his way."

"You know what Constance is like," Eric said with a low laugh. "That's one extremely wicked witch when she sets her mind to it."

"True," he agreed, recalling the times when she'd scared the crap out of him and his friends when he was younger and she'd caught them doing something they shouldn't be. "But Hennessey has never struck me as the kind of guy who would let something like that get to him."

"Yeah. Constance Murphy is a pain in his ass, but despite all of it, the fact is that *he's* the one making his life hard at the moment."

Nodding, Eli said, "The guy's stubborn."

Eric's voice was dry. "Sounds like someone else I know."

He shot his brother a dark look. "Different situations."

"Are they? If I had to bet, I'd say Cian's afraid of putting the girl in a dangerous situation, though no one knows what that is. But he's no doubt trying to protect her."

"Then maybe you should give the guy a break," he shot back.

"I will," Eric muttered, "just as soon as he's manned up."

Despite his foul mood, Eli couldn't help but bark out a gritty laugh. "I have a feeling Hennessey would have your damn balls if he heard you say that."

Though frustration still burned in his hard gaze, Eric's lips twitched with a grin. "He could *try*."

Glancing at the clock on the wall, Elise said, "I hate to break this up, but Wyatt will be home soon. Do you guys want to stay for dinner?"

"Chelsea's making lasagna," Eric said, pushing away from the sink, "but why don't you guys come over and join us? I know she'd love to have you over."

"That would be fun," she said with a smile.

Eric's gray gaze returned to his. "Eli?"

Thinking that Carla might come along with his sister and Wyatt, he moved back to his feet and said, "Yeah, I can make it. I just need to head over to the cabin and grab a shower."

"I'll head out with you, then," Eric said. "I need a smoke."

They hugged Elise goodbye, leaving her to get ready, then walked out onto the front porch. He started to tell Eric he'd see him later, when his brother said, "I have one more question before you run off."

He sighed, propping his shoulder against one of the wooden posts that supported the porch's roof, and watched as Eric lit the cigarette he'd taken from the pack in his pocket. He'd have wagered every penny to his name that Eric's question was about Carla, his suspicions confirmed when his brother looked him in the eye and asked, "Is she the reason you've stayed away? I mean, once you heard that Dad and the League were dead and realized you could come back home? Is she the reason why you didn't?"

"Yeah," he rasped, taking the easy way out with that oversimplified response.

Eric's pale gaze searched his with piercing intensity. "And do you love her?"

A hollow laugh punched from his chest, and he started to shove his hands in his pockets, before realizing he still had the dishtowel wrapped around his shredded knuckles.

Exhaling a silvery stream of smoke, Eric frowned. "That's not an answer, man."

He rubbed his good hand over his mouth, then gave another heavy sigh. "I've been trying to figure out how I feel about her ever since she walked back into my life and punched me in the mouth."

His brother laughed. "That sounds like Carla."

Lips twitching with a wry smile, he said, "Yeah, she's definitely got a temper on her."

"So you gonna answer the question?" Eric pressed, taking another deep drag on his cigarette.

Eli shifted his gaze over Eric's shoulder, staring out at the forest, the heavy tree limbs swaying like giant beasts in the wind, and struggled to put his thoughts in some kind of order that made sense. A few moments later, he drew in a deep breath of the fresh mountain air, and gave his brother the truth. "Yeah, I love her," he said in a low voice that thrummed with emotion. "I loved her when I left, and despite all the bullshit I started to tell myself over the years, trying to stay away, I never stopped loving her." Looking away from the sky, he took another deep breath as he settled his gaze back on Eric. "Somehow, I love her even more now. So much that it's scaring the hell out of me."

Eric's dark brows were drawn with concern. "Because you're worried you'll lose her?"

"I'm worried about all of it," he admitted gruffly, scrubbing his hand down his face. "Her safety is part of it. I hate the danger she puts herself in, like she's got some kind of death wish. But then there's the fact that she keeps claiming to want her freedom. Not to mention the strong chance that she might never be able to forgive me for leaving her or learn to love me back. That she might get tired of it all and walk away for good." *Destroying our bond and leaving me with...nothing.*

With a sharp exhale, his brother said, "I get what you're saying, Eli. I really do. But you need to stop and take a long hard look at what Carla's capable of. She's not like our mother was. She's not...fragile."

He frowned, thinking the topic of his mother was the *last* thing he wanted to come up right now.

"And secondly," Eric was saying, "do you know what I remember most from when we were younger?"

He shook his head, eyeing his brother with a careful gaze.

Jerking his chin toward him, Eric said, "The way you never gave up, man, no matter what you were up against."

"This is different," he grunted.

"Oh, yeah?" Eric murmured, lifting his brows with a challenging look. "How?"

Grimacing, he crossed his arms back over his chest and said, "I can't *make* her forgive me, Eric. I can't force her to give me a second chance."

"And have you asked for one? For a second chance?"

He rubbed the back of his neck and cursed, realizing that all he'd actually told her was that he was sorry for hurting her…and that he wanted in her bed. He'd never really gotten around to explaining what he wanted *after* that, but then, she hadn't exactly given him the opportunity to.

"Eli, if you want her, let her know. Be honest with her. You'll never know what could have been if you aren't, and you'll end up regretting it till the day you die."

"I just don't kn…" He trailed off when he suddenly caught sight of a worried-looking Sayre running back into the Alley, her pale face flushed with color and her blue-gray eyes wide with panic.

"Jeremy!" she shouted, cupping her hands around her mouth as she stood just off to the side of Elise and Wyatt's porch.

Eric tossed his cigarette aside and raced down the steps with Eli right behind him. "Sayre, what's going on?" his brother asked the girl.

She turned toward them, grabbing Eric's arm as she started talking in a rush. "There's been a…a…damn it, I don't know what to call it."

"Just take a deep breath and tell us what happened," Eric said, while the hairs on the back of Eli's neck lifted as something inside him twisted with fear.

"A woman," Sayre panted, her knuckles turning white as she gripped Eric's arm even tighter. "A Whiteclaw female…she escaped from Hawkley and came to us for help. But she wasn't alone. She was followed here by one of their soldiers."

"Jesus," Eric hissed. "Is she all right? Is everyone okay?"

"She'll be fine. Jillian is with her in the woods. Everyone's fine. But that man…he tried to kill her…and Carla… *Ohmygod*, she was so amazing!"

Eli's head jerked back as if he'd just been clipped on the chin. "Carla? What the hell was she doing there?"

"She must have shown up just before I did. I think we were both looking for Jillian, and Carla saved her. She saved them both," Sayre told them, her big eyes shining with shock as she looked from one to the other. "She put herself between them and that maniac—"

"She *what?*" Eli roared, making the young witch flinch.

"She saved the woman and Jillian. The woman was clinging to my sister for help, and he would have killed them both, but she saved them. It was the most incredible thing I've ever seen. I would have helped her, but by the time I realized what was happening, he was already going down."

"Sayre," he croaked, a cold sweat breaking out over his face, "where is the man now?"

She brought her wide eyes back to his, and blinked up at him. "He's dead."

"Dead?"

Voice soft with awe, she nodded and said, "Carla killed him."

Chapter 8

They'd brought the woman, who appeared to be in her early thirties and was named Rachel, back to Jeremy and Jillian's cabin. All the Runners were gathered in the couple's living room, along with Eli's men, ready to hear the full story.

Sayre had offered the woman a damp washcloth, which she was using to wipe the dirt and smears of blood from her bruised, tear-streaked face as she sat in a chair that'd been placed in front of the empty fireplace. Her eyes were wide with apprehension, moving from one person to another. She looked overwhelmed and more than a little frightened, but there was also a fierce sense of determination in her dark gaze that made Eli think she just might be the real deal, instead of a spy sent to infiltrate their ranks.

Of course, that didn't make him feel any calmer about what Carla had done.

Eli had managed to plant himself right at the little Bloodrunner's side the moment she'd entered the cabin, and he was still seething with fury. The Whiteclaw she'd taken down had been a goddamn behemoth. At least six-six, with probably more than a hundred pounds on her. He didn't know what the hell she'd been thinking.

While everyone was still getting situated, he kept his narrowed gaze focused on the woman as he spoke to Carla. "Do you have any idea what that asshole could have done to you?"

He'd kept his voice low, barely above a whisper, but knew she'd heard him from the stiffening of her posture. Then she asked, "Does it matter? Fighting him was a risk I was willing to take. Do you honestly think I would have just left Jillian there to deal with him herself?"

"She's powerful. She could have handled it."

"She's also *pregnant,* you ass. And like family to me. I would *never* turn my back on someone I cared about, no matter how dangerous the situation was."

He ground his back teeth together, ready to grab her arm and drag her to someplace private where they could talk. Yeah, it was a caveman move, but he was desperate enough to use it.

"Whatever you're thinking," said a deep voice on his other side, "I wouldn't try it."

He turned his head and found Wyatt watching him with a hard, steady gaze. Before he could tell the Runner to mind his own damn business, Wyatt said, "The two of you need to sort this out later. Right now, we need to hear what this woman has to say."

He jerked his chin in agreement, knowing it was the right move, but still too pissed off to be civil about it. A few moments later, the room finally settled down, quieting, and he realized Rachel's dark gaze was focused intently on Carla. The woman lowered the washcloth to her lap, her fingers clenched around the damp cotton, and swallowed hard before saying, "You're the female Runner, aren't you?"

From the corner of his eye, Eli watched Carla give the woman a wary nod.

Tears glistened in Rachel's eyes as she whispered a heartfelt, "Thank you. Thank you so much."

At Carla's uncertain look, the woman lifted her chin and said, "You gave me the courage to fight back and escape. We all—the other women and I—we all heard about the half-human female who bested the Whiteclaw soldiers in Hawkley and got away. It...you...what you did, it inspired us."

"Oh, um, that's...wonderful," Carla managed to get out, though he could tell by the huskiness of her voice that she'd been floored by what the woman had just said.

Sitting beside his wife, Torrance, on the arm of one of the leather sofas, Mason said, "Rachel, what is it that you want? Is there someplace you're trying to reach?"

Strands of short black hair stuck to her battered face as she shook her head, her watery gaze shifting to the tall Runner. "I...I want to stay here. I'm seeking sanctuary," she told him. "And I'm not the only one. There are others. They just...they don't know how to get away."

"But you did?"

More tears spilled over her pale cheeks as she shook her head again. "I would have brought them with me, but I...I didn't have a plan. I just saw the opportunity, and I took it. I knew that if I didn't, I might never get another one."

"How do we know you're for real?"

"Eric, don't," Chelsea murmured at his brother's side, grasping his hand in hers. Eli had only spoken to his brother's human life mate a few times, but he liked her. She was a beautiful woman, but more than that, she was…real. And as head over heels in love with his brother as Pallaton was with his sister.

"No, it's okay," Rachel murmured, taking a deep breath. "I understand why you would be concerned, given everything that my pack has done. But I can prove that I'm for real. I can…I can give you information."

Brody spoke up for the first time from his position against the far wall, between his wife and his Bloodrunning partner, Cian. "What kind of information?"

The woman wet her lips, then said, "I know where they've stored the drugs. The ones they take to make them stronger and mask their scents."

In a soft, lilting burr, Cian asked, "And why would you help us?"

A shudder worked its way through her narrow frame, making Eli wonder just what this woman had lived through with her pack. She cleared her throat, her gaze lowered to her lap as she scraped out, "Because of Roy's greed. It's…it's like a sickness. His arrogance is spreading, and the men are…they're out of control." Pulling in another deep, ragged breath, she lifted her head and locked her shattered gaze with Carla's, as if seeking strength as she quietly added, "They…they do whatever they want, to the ones like me. With the way things are now, any female who is unmated is considered…fair game."

"Christ," Jeremy muttered, dropping his chin on top of Jillian's head, his arms wrapped around her waist as they stood together with her back to his front.

Sayre, who was staying close to the woman's side in case she was needed, said, "The man who was chasing you. Who was he?"

"My cousin," she whispered thickly, turning her head to look at Sayre. "And a bastard."

"Will they come looking for him?" Carla asked, no doubt wondering what kind of fallout they might be facing from the kill that she'd made. Everyone in the room knew that it'd been justified, considering the Lycan had been ready to kill whoever got in his way—but Eli knew Carla would blame herself if anyone ended up hurt because of what she'd done.

Answering Carla's question, Rachel said, "I…I don't think so. He worked for Roy, monitoring the pack's stock of drugs, along with a few other Lycans. That's how I know where they're stored." Her shoulders shook as she explained, "When he drinks, he talks. Or…I mean, he *did*. But he's not so important that they would waste time trying to find him. Not with everything else they have going on."

"These stocks you mentioned," Mason said, drawing her attention back to him. "What can you tell us about them?"

"They're running low on the drugs they use on the girls—the human ones. But they have a large supply of the stuff that the soldiers take, because Roy bought so much when it was first created."

Recalling how Carla had mentioned the Fed who was working to destroy the labs where the gang-rape drugs were being produced, Eli assumed that was why they were running low. But the fact that they still had a strong supply of the "super soldier" drugs was troubling.

"And what about the drug that Sebastian took?" Eric asked.

She looked confused. "Which one is that?"

Eli had heard about the drug that Sebastian Claymore had taken the day he'd kidnapped Elise and Carla. It had enabled the Lycan to shift more of his body during the daytime than was normal, as well as increased his size and strength. At the time, Sebastian had claimed to be working on an additional drug that would allow him to completely day-shift, and either drug could prove catastrophic for the Silvercrest if they were produced in mass quantities.

With his arm around Elise's shoulders, Wyatt answered the woman's question. "It's a drug that allowed him to shift more completely during the day. Not a complete shift, but enough that it was noticeable."

She shook her head. "I don't even know about that one."

"That's good," Brody rumbled. "Hopefully his personal supply was limited."

"Rachel," Eli murmured, drawing her attention to where he stood. "Could you draw a map that leads to the exact location where the drugs are stored?"

Nodding, she said, "Yes. I just need a pen and paper."

"I'll get it," Sayre murmured, heading out of the room, and Eli looked over at his men, who were standing together against the far wall, where they'd been quietly listening. Their expressions were hard with outrage, and each one jerked their chin in assent to his silent question. He nodded, then looked round at the Runners. "We're heading out."

Carla's slender fingers bit into his arm. "Now?" she asked, staring up at him with wide eyes as he turned his head to look at her. "Where the hell are you going?"

"If we're going to make full use of the intel, then we've got to move quickly, before they shift the drugs to a new location."

Her slender brows knitted together. "Then we'll make a plan."

"There's no time," he argued. "It might take them a while to realize that Rachel and her cousin are missing, but once they do, we've lost our window of opportunity. We've got to go now, before they can move their stock."

Determination hardened her gaze. "Then I'm going with you."

Over my dead body, he thought, hating that he had to pull his arm from her grip, now that she was finally touching him. But it'd be a cold day in hell before he ever let her set foot anywhere near that godforsaken town again. She'd been lucky to make it out alive the first time, and there wasn't going to be a second one.

Wondering just how angry he was about to make her, he said, "That's not gonna happen, Reyes. The guys and I are going in alone."

"The hell you are," Eric muttered, while the other Runners seconded him.

Looking around the room, Eli frowned. "This isn't personal. It's basic logic. The guys and I are trained for this kind of op, and we're used to pulling them off alone. Mixing things up at this point is only going to make it more dangerous."

His brother's scowl deepened. "That doesn't mean we're going to let you and your men fight our battles for us, Eli. That's not how this works."

"We're not trying to fight anyone's battles," he growled, hating that they were having this argument in front of a roomful of people. "I understand what you're saying, but the reason the guys and I are here is so that the Runners don't have to do everything on their own anymore. So don't be a stubborn jackass about this. Just stand down and let us get this done before it's too late."

Eric cursed under his breath, his metallic gray eyes molten with frustration. But he didn't shove another argument back in Eli's face. Instead, he exhaled a rough breath, and muttered, "Don't think I'll let you pull this shit again. This is your one pass. You get in, you get out, and then you get the hell back here."

Eli nodded at his brother, then cut his gaze back to Carla. She stared up at him with a dazed look on her pale face, as if she was still trying to figure out how this had happened. Fighting the urge to reach out and yank her into his arms, he turned away from her and told Rachel he'd be back for the map, then followed his guys out of the cabin.

Carla stared at the front door, after Eli and his men had left, and blinked like someone coming out of a long, deep sleep. She felt like she'd been hit over the head, her thoughts disordered, her pulse roaring in her ears like an engine that'd been revved too high.

No matter how hard she'd been trying to put him from her mind, avoiding him as she worked herself into exhaustion, her dreams had been plagued by his irresistible presence. Deliciously raw, erotic dreams of the night they'd bonded. Of their hot, sweat-misted skin sliding together as he'd kissed and licked every inch of her he could reach, while rubbing his hard, heavy erection between her thighs, against the slick cushion of her sex. His dark voice whispering things so intimate and wicked, she'd been ready to come before he'd even started to push inside her. He'd been so big, so broad and long, she'd barely been able to take him. But she'd wanted to. She'd wanted to take…and take…until he'd emptied himself into her. Until she'd taken everything he had to give. All the hunger and passion and emotion burning inside him.

Emotion she'd so foolishly hoped was love.

Only, she'd been wrong. He hadn't loved her, and she'd

had to accept that. But that didn't mean she didn't care about him. That she wasn't worried for his safety, especially when *she* was the one who'd brought him to the Alley.

Unable to just stand there and let him leave her, she hurried from the room, aware of the curious way the others were watching her, and ran after him. From the height of the porch, she looked across the glade, watching as he and Kyle climbed the porch steps of the cabin they were staying in, while the other three mercs went into the other one. She knew they would be collecting their gear, and she started running as fast as she could, determined to reach Eli before he could leave the privacy of his room. The things she needed to say to him were preferably done without an audience.

Without even bothering to knock, she let herself into the cabin and hurried across the living room, down the hallway. She had no idea which room he was using, but she tracked his mouthwatering scent to the second doorway on the left. Opening the door, she quickly stepped into the room and pressed her back against the door as it closed, then reached back and flipped the lock. He was standing by a dresser that sat against the far wall, the dishtowel that had been wrapped around his battered knuckles earlier nowhere to be seen as he checked the clip on a heavy handgun—but his attention was no longer focused on the weapon. He'd looked up the second she'd opened the door, his narrowed gaze now locked in hard and tight on her own.

Pulling her lower lip through her teeth, she took a deep, shuddering breath and said, "Are you sure about this? About what you're doing?"

He looked away from her as he tucked the gun into the back of his jeans, then grabbed a thick, complicated watch off the dresser, hooking it around his powerful wrist. "Why wouldn't I be?"

"Damn it, it could all be a setup. She could be lying!"

"My gut tells me she isn't, but either way, we're good at what we do," he said in a low voice, still not looking at her as he turned and grabbed a set of keys off the bed-side table. "They're not even going to know we're there."

Frustration, and no small amount of fear, made her want to scream as she asked, "How the hell do you know that?"

He turned his head, his dark gaze locking hard on hers again with a sharp, drilling intensity, and she could physically see the satisfaction building within him, burning in those incredible blue and gray eyes. "You're actually worried about me, aren't you?"

"No!" she snapped. But it was impossible to hide the way she was shaking…trembling…her damn heart pounding so swiftly it was making her dizzy.

Looking too impossibly gorgeous to be real, he fisted his big hands at his sides and started coming toward her, around the foot of the bed, each step making her breath come just that little bit faster, until she was panting. "If you don't give a shit about me, Rey, then why do you look so terrified?"

"Don't be so damn cocky! I brought you here to help us win. Not to go off taking ridiculous chances with your life!"

"And here I was thinking you didn't care if I lived or died." He stopped right in front of her, his heavy-lidded eyes burning with molten heat as he lowered his rugged face directly over hers. To her horror, her head went back in an embarrassing sign of submission for a female wolf, seeing as how it left her throat exposed and vulnerable, and it wasn't the first time that it'd happened with him.

Before he could call her on the telling action, she growled, "Shut up," and grabbed him behind the neck, yanking his head down as she rose up on her toes, crushing her mouth against his.

With her pulse still roaring in her ears, Carla kissed him like she wanted to crawl inside him. The way he growled deep in his chest and gripped her hips with his big hands, jerking her against his hard, muscular body, only made her more desperate. It took him no more than a heartbeat to claim control of the kiss, his tongue sinking into her mouth like he owned it, stroking and rubbing, tasting every slick part of her he could reach. It was so perfect, so freaking *right,* that she wanted to push him down to the floor, rip his jeans open, and take him. She needed to take him as deep as he could go, until she was packed full of him—until she owned him completely—which was nothing more than madness, considering she didn't own him at all. Not his body or his hunger...and sure as hell not his heart, and the pain of that knowledge was enough to make her want to curl into a ball on the floor and cry like a freaking baby.

God, what am I doing? she thought, as a jolting, searing wave of panic stormed through her, constricting her lungs so tightly she almost whimpered. On the verge of a meltdown, she ripped her mouth from his and shoved hard against the same broad shoulders she'd been digging her nails into only seconds before. She only managed to move him back a few inches, but it was enough of a gap for her to wrench her body to the side, out from between him and the door.

She'd made it maybe a foot when he grabbed her arm, hauling her close again, his color high and his lips parted for the harsh, erratic rhythm of his breaths. "Where do you think you're going?"

"I...I need out of here."

"What the hell, Carla?" Instead of fury, there was something burning in his eyes that looked too much like pain, and she blinked in shock as he growled, "You don't get to kiss me like you're fucking my mouth and then just walk away."

Sucking in a sharp breath, she said, "You walked away from me first. Then again at that damn motel!"

"And I've already said I was sorry!" he roared loud enough for them to hear on the other side of the Alley. "You have no idea how much. I just...I needed to get my shit together. And I have. God knows I'm not going to let myself ruin this a second time."

She shook her head, hating the damn tears she could feel building behind her eyes. "I wish I could believe you, but I *can't.*"

"Don't," he rasped when she tried to pull her arm from his hold. "Please, Carla. *Christ,* don't walk away from me."

"Eli—"

"Please, just stay here with me for a minute," he said as he slowly reached for her other arm.

"What do you want from me?" she whispered, closing her eyes as he pressed her against the wall, covering her front with the breathtaking feel of his body. He was hard and hot and so blasted perfect it made her want to cry.

"I just want to make you feel good," he groaned against her temple, reaching between them and ripping at the button on her jeans, then sliding down the zipper. "I just need to be close to you, Rey, 'cause I've missed you so damn much."

"No," she gasped the instant his hot fingertips grazed the waistband of her panties.

He instantly stilled. "No?"

"I...I don't know." The husky, breathless words had been spoken in a needy voice she didn't even recognize as her own. "Damn it, I can't think straight when you're touching me."

He pressed his mouth to the corner of her eyebrow, the rush of his breath against her skin striking her as deliciously intimate. "Tell me to stop, baby, and I'll stop. But if you don't, I'm going to put my fingers in your sweet little body again and make you come so hard you scream."

Knowing damn well that she couldn't resist him, even when there was every chance this was going to be something she regretted, she dug her fingers into his thick hair and pulled his mouth back to hers, kissing him with every ounce of visceral emotion that was raging inside her. With every bit of passion and fury and heartbreak he'd ever made her feel, and he made a hard, thick sound deep in his chest, his tall body shuddering against her. He gripped the back of her neck, holding her in place for his marauding mouth, and the next thing she knew the hand between her legs was inside her panties, the heat of his palm making her moan. Then his fingers separated her, sliding between the slippery folds, before two of them circled the tender opening there and pushed hard inside her. They were big enough to make her breath hitch, her body still unused to a man's touch after so many years of being alone. Long and wickedly skilled, they filled her perfectly, stretching her open as he started to plunge them in and out of her in a greedy, driving rhythm that made her breathless and achy for more. She was so wet the movement of his fingers was making slick, moist sounds in the quiet stillness of the room, but she was too lost in the way it felt to be embarrassed.

Pressing his forehead against hers, he growled, "You feel so damn perfect, it's unreal, Rey."

Then the callused pad of his thumb settled against her swollen clit, rubbing the sensitive bundle of nerves with a firm, steady pressure, and that was it. He might have left her hanging in that motel room the other night—but not this time. With a hoarse cry on her lips, she crashed into a sizzling, searing orgasm, the shattering pulses of pleasure exploding through her like an unstoppable force of nature, filling her with heat. Her head shot back as her thighs trembled, her body completely open and vulnerable to him. To whatever he wanted to give her...take from her.

He lowered his head and nipped at the side of her throat, licking his tongue over her thrashing pulse, his big hand still buried between her legs, and he kept shoving his fingers into her drenched, clutching tissues until she was gripping them so tightly he could barely move them. "God, baby, that was the hottest thing I've ever felt," he said against her shoulder, his soft hair tickling her jaw. "Only thing that could be better is feeling you do that when I'm buried inside you."

Her lips twitched with a grin that she couldn't hold back, loving the way he talked to her. The way he wasn't shy about letting her know how he felt and what he wanted—at least when it came to sex.

Still feeling languid and drowsy with pleasure, she was sad when she felt him carefully work his fingers free, then pull his hand from between her legs. Needing to see his face—to see if he looked even half as shattered as she felt—she managed to crack her eyes open just in time to catch him putting those two glistening fingers in his mouth. They were drenched in her juices, and she thought it was the most erotic thing she'd ever seen, watching him swallow her flavor down his throat, while a thick, purely male sound of appreciation rumbled up from deep in his chest.

"Christ, that's incredible," he groaned, licking between his knuckles after he'd pulled his fingers free. "Like warm, salted caramel and cream. Rich and sweet and fucking delicious." His heavy-lidded gaze burned with hunger, and he placed his damp hand against the side of her face as he said, "I would drown in you right now if I had the time."

She blinked, too steeped in residual pulses of pleasure to understand what he meant. "Time?" *Why doesn't he have the time?*

His cock was a rigid, throbbing, impossibly thick ridge behind the fly of his jeans, and he pressed even harder against her, before giving a rough groan and taking a step back, pulling away from her. "I bloody hate it, Rey, but I've got to go. If I don't, Kyle's gonna come back here looking for me."

"Oh, God." She gasped for breath, feeling like she'd just had a bucket of ice-cold water thrown in her face. Frantically trying to sort out her jeans, she hissed, "I don't believe this! They're going to know what we were doing!"

He scowled as he crossed his arms over his wide chest, pinning her with a sharp, penetrating stare. "And what's so wrong about that?"

"Everything. Everything is wrong!" She covered her face with her hands, trying to get control, her emotions in chaos. "Damn it, I came back here to talk some sense into you. Not to…to…" Lowering her hands, she reached out and fisted them in the front of his shirt. "Please…you can't do this, Eli. It's too dangerous."

His scowl softened, but the look in his eyes remained hard and determined. Taking hold of her wrists, he said,

"This is what you brought me here to do, Rey. To make a difference."

"But I didn't expect you to go waltzing into the middle of their freaking town! And in broad daylight!"

"I'm not waltzing into the middle of it. Odds are good they'll never even know we're there, and if they do, we'll handle it."

His calm, even tone just made her want to howl with frustration. "I can't do this," she said unsteadily, her throat shaking. "You have me so confused."

"Don't," he growled, sounding like a man who'd just been shoved to the end of his patience. "You don't get to give me *that*—what just happened between us—and then rip it away."

"Eli—"

The next thing she knew, his hands were gripping the sides of her head and he was taking her mouth again, ravaging it, his tongue sliding against hers in an explicit show of hunger that damn near melted her down into an embarrassing puddle of need and lust and tears on the floor.

Lifting his head, he locked his hard, narrowed gaze with hers, and said, "When I get back, we're finishing that."

"No. We—"

"It's happening, Carla." He opened the door and went into the hallway, then turned his head and cut her a smoldering, devastating look over his shoulder. "So be ready."

Chapter 9

Hours later, Eli returned to the Alley just in time to change into a clean shirt and head over to the clearing where the ceremony was taking place that night. No way in hell did he want to miss this.

He'd gotten a call from Mason on his way back from Hawkley, letting him know that there'd been a meeting. Given how things were escalating, the Runners had gone ahead and asked Max Doucet and Elliot Connors to take their Bloodrunning vows early, before their official training took place. Max, a human who'd been turned Lycan, was Brody's brother-in-law, while Elliot was a Silvercrest Lycan who'd been befriended by Max and the Runners after getting caught up in some serious trouble with Stefan's followers.

Though Eric could have had his own ceremony weeks ago, he'd decided to wait and take his oath at the same time as his friends. Elise had told him that Eric was close to both of the young men, and they'd been honored that he wanted to share their ceremony with them.

And now that ceremony would be taking place in a few minutes, in a clearing not far from the Alley.

Though the Bloodrunning Laws were no longer considered in effect, the Runners had decided that it was important to uphold tradition and mark the occasion with the proper respect, and Eli couldn't help but agree with their thinking. The Runners' oath wasn't about pack law, but about pledging one's self to the responsibilities of the job and the friends who would always have your back, no matter the circumstances, as they'd proven time and again. Though he'd never had much interaction with the Runners before, the recent days he'd spent there in the Alley had shown him that they were everything Carla had always believed them to be, and while he still hated the danger that came with her job, he was glad that she'd always had this close-knit group to look out for her. To be there for her.

God only knew her mother had never done that.

And as much as it pained him to admit it, neither had he.

As he reached the edge of the clearing, he was glad to see that the area had been lit with torches, making it easier to search for that familiar golden head of hair. Looking out over the crowd, he spotted Carla almost immediately and headed her way, surprised by how many people were there. His men were still back at the Alley, cleaning up before they came over, and he wondered what they were going to make of this. If they'd be as surprised as he was, or if they'd just take it all in stride, same as they'd been doing since their arrival. In a lot of ways, he felt that they were more comfortable there than he was—which was no one's fault but his own. Instead of the scorn he'd pre-

pared himself to deal with from both the Bloodrunners
and his pack, he'd received nothing but friendly accep-
tance. A fact he was still trying to wrap his head around.

Moving through the crowd, he was stopped by several of the Runners and their wives, who wanted to tell
him they were glad to see he'd made it back in one piece.
Thankfully, the trip he and his men had taken to Hawkley had been a success. A bloody one, it turned out, but
well worth the trouble. With some well-placed explo-
sives, they'd managed to destroy the storage building
where the drugs were being kept, and made it out of the
town without any injuries to their group, though they'd
had to face off against two units of Whiteclaw soldiers
as they made their escape.

Once they'd made it back to the Alley, Eli had been so
eager to see Carla again, he hadn't even taken the time
to shower. The memory of what they'd done against his
bedroom wall before he'd left was burned into his brain
like a brand, and he wanted her so badly it was damn near
impossible to function. He'd never had such a pathetic
lack of control, and he had to choke back a deep rumble
of laughter and shake his head at himself, seeing as how
she'd managed to make him feel like a randy teenage boy
drowning in hormones when he was anything but. Hell,
he'd be pushing forty in just a few years.

When he finally reached her side, he pulled in a hungry breath, just letting her warm scent soak into his system, and deliberately didn't say anything, hoping she'd be
the one to speak first, so that he could gauge her mood.
But aside from a slight flaring of her nostrils, she didn't
so much as bat a lash at his arrival. Then someone shoved
between him and the person standing on his left, and
the little Runner stiffened as he was forced to press up
against her side, the touch of her arm against his making

him have to fight for control. But her reaction… *Shit*. He had to choke back a frustrated curse, because it was suddenly obvious as to what *she* was going to do. That she was going to keep fighting him, doing her best to resist the powerful, make-him-ache-for-her-down-in-his-bones attraction that kept pulling them together.

He could react the way he usually did, and get pissy with her. Or…he could try to play it cool for once, and see if maybe she wasn't just feeling a bit unsure after what had happened before he'd left.

Leaning down, he put his mouth close to her ear, and murmured, "Stay close to me."

"What?" She turned her head, and their faces were so close she nearly hit him in the nose. "Why?"

The corner of his mouth kicked up at the sight of her disgruntled expression. God, he really did have it bad when the woman's scowl started to strike him as adorable. Answering her question, he said, "First, because I like having you there, which shouldn't come as a surprise. And second, I believe in being cautious."

She didn't say anything more as she turned her attention back to the center of the circle that'd been marked in the ground, where Mason was standing with Eric, Max and Elliot. He didn't know if her silence meant that she'd agreed with him, or if she simply didn't want to bother with an argument, but he was glad she didn't try to storm off, and he moved to stand behind her as the crowd pressed in around them, using his body to keep her back protected.

The Lycans who were currently working as scouts with the Runners, as well as those who'd volunteered for training, had been invited tonight, and from the size of the crowd, it looked as though most of them had come. There was also a large group of teenagers there, and he recalled Jeremy explaining to him over a beer the other night that both Max and Elliot had been working with the teens who were left traumatized by the brainwashing bullshit his father had tried to pull.

Running his gaze over the gathering, it was as if he could physically *see* the bridge between the Alley and Shadow Peak being built right before his eyes. The Runners were no longer regarded as the dirty little secret that the pack needed, but didn't want to think about. Instead, they were now the soldiers who were going to lead the Silvercrest Lycans to victory or die trying, and the presence of so many pure-bloods tonight was an unmistakable show of respect that Eli was damn glad to witness.

In the face of war, it truly seemed that the pack was starting to heal the wounds that had been caused by so many years of racism, and he almost wished his old man could have been there to see it. That Stefan could have been there to witness how instead of destroying the Runners, his actions had only made them more powerful.

Mason's deep voice asking everyone for their attention drew his focus back to the circle, and he watched as Eric, Max and Elliot knelt in the grass before the tall Runner. Eli was more than a little curious about what exactly the ceremony would entail, listening with interest as Mason asked the three males to recite their Bloodrunning oaths. There was an almost dreamy, hypnotic feeling to the event, and he swayed forward just as Carla swayed back, their bodies coming together and staying that way as they watched and listened. With each of his slow, deep breaths, he was pulling more of her addictive scent into his lungs, and he couldn't stop himself from settling his hands on her narrow waist. She jolted a little at the contact, then settled, and he had to force himself not to hold her too tightly, lest he scare her away. She was as skittish as a colt when it came to letting him get close to her, and he was going to be damned before he did anything to ruin this peaceful moment.

He lowered his gaze for a few seconds, his height allowing him a breathtaking view of the front of her body, the tightness of her nipples against the cotton shirt that she wore making his mouth water, while most of the blood in his body started heading south. Knowing damn well that he was playing with fire, he forced himself to look away, shifting his attention back to the ceremony. His eyes shot wide open when he spotted Mason sliding a lethal-looking blade over his palm, blood instantly welling from the wound.

What the hell?

Before he could ask Carla what was happening, she'd pulled away from him and was walking into the circle, toward the others. He was on the verge of going after her, until he realized *all* the Runners were moving into the circle with her. One by one, they flanked Mason, then cut their palms as the blade was passed between them. He winced in sympathy for her hand, knowing that had to have hurt, though you wouldn't have known it by looking at her. She stood with her head high and her shoulders back, a proud smile on her beautiful mouth as the knife was passed to Eric. His brother used the crimson blade that'd been stained with each Runner's blood to slice his own palm, before passing it to Max, who cut his palm and then passed the blade on to Elliot, who did the same.

When the blade was offered back to Mason, he signaled for the three newly appointed Bloodrunners to stand, then announced that the ceremony had been completed. Everyone cheered until the noise could probably be heard all the way up in Shadow Peak, and then the crowd slowly began to disperse. Eli made his way through the crush as quickly as he could, heading toward Carla and his brother, and he couldn't help but notice that the women were all smiling at him as he passed by them, while the men jerked their chins in greeting, and an unfamiliar sense of rightness swept through him.

He didn't know *why* he felt at home here, but he was starting to realize that he did. He'd never been friendly with the Runners. Hell, his old man would have died before allowing it. But Eli had always held a respect for the half-breeds that he kept carefully hidden. Just as he'd done with almost every other real emotion he'd ever felt when he'd been forced to live under Stefan Drake's thumb. Which, when he thought about it, just made him a pathetic jackass who hadn't been able to make the hard choice and off the sick bastard when he'd had the chance, the way he should have done.

Instead, he'd run when given the opening, and he hadn't looked back. Not even when he realized that without him there, his father would be left to wreak havoc over the pack, and there would be no one to stop him. Eric had never truly been allowed into that inner circle of evil, so he hadn't known just how twisted Stefan had become, and Elise had simply avoided their father as much as possible. And as awful as it sounded, in the beginning, it hadn't bothered him. Hell, for the first time in his life, he'd been able to take a deep breath without feeling as if he was sucking in his father's foul spirit with every inhalation. But the feeling hadn't lasted long. As the days flowed into weeks, he'd felt more than just his abandonment of Reyes. He'd felt the pain of being cut off from his brother and sister…and yeah, even his pack. Had felt the separation from the land that had rooted its way into his blood and sweat and bones as he'd grown into a man. And yet, despite all the years he'd lived in

Shadow Peak, he could honestly say that he'd never felt as connected to the town as he did to the Alley and the men and women who lived there.

Though he was as pure-blooded as a Lycan could be, he'd never truly made a place for himself in the pack. He'd been an insider on the innermost circle of pack power, thanks to his father—but an outsider all the same. Maybe that was why he fit *here,* with the rest of his rough group of friends. They were each outcasts, and yet, he would have bet anything on the fact that Kyle and the guys felt a draw to this place that was similar to his own.

Reaching the Runners, he immediately pulled Eric into a bone-crushing hug that made everyone around them laugh, including Carla, who was wrapping a strip of cloth around her wounded hand. "Congratulations, little brother. I'm damn proud of you."

"Thanks," Eric grunted, hugging him back just as hard. "That means a lot to me."

They slapped each other on the back, then stepped apart. He turned to congratulate Max and Elliot, who were both all smiles and excitement, and found Carla standing with his brother and sister when he turned back around. Pushing his hands in his pockets, he stayed back and watched her talk with his siblings, and realized that while he was gaining perspective about *his* place in the pack, when it came to the sexy little Runner, he was still…lost. But he wasn't going to let it hold him back.

He hadn't been lying when he'd told Eric that he loved her, and he knew it was a goddamn miracle that she hadn't found anyone to replace him in the last three years—that the bond had tied her to him even when he wasn't there to fight for his place by her side. If she didn't still feel something for him, he didn't think it would have worked out like this. But it had, and she was still his for the taking if he could only convince her to give him another chance.

Christ, it would probably be the most difficult, painful thing he'd ever done. But he was determined to do whatever it took.

Even if it means baring my soul to her.

Looking around this close-knit group, he could see the intimacy of the connections between the Runners and their mates. These men were rough and rugged and ruthless, and probably at one point as opposed to making themselves vulnerable as Eli was. But they'd done it. They'd been brave enough to be honest with their women, and by God, he was determined to do the same.

If the choices were between having a shot at her and losing her forever, then he'd tell her whatever she wanted to know. The good, the bad, and the ugly—though the good would definitely be in short supply. And the sooner he did it, the better, because he'd already wasted too many years. Too many damn nights spent cold and alone, when she should have been in his arms, where she belonged. Now he didn't want to lose another minute of the time they had with each other.

Moving to stand beside her again, he looked down into her beautiful eyes and asked, "Walk back with me?"

To his surprise, she nodded, and he grabbed her uninjured hand before she could pull it away, his tight hold letting her know that he wasn't going to just let her go. She sighed, but didn't drag her feet as he set off through the moonlit woods.

"I see you made it back in one piece," she murmured.

Moving a low hanging branch out of their way, he said, "We ran into a few foot soldiers on our way out, after destroying the storage facility, but they were easy to deal with." He squeezed her hand, sliding her a playful wink when she looked his way. "I promise all your favorite pieces are still in good working order."

She gave a feminine snort as she shook her head. "Nice one."

"It made you smile. That's all I was after."

"Well, then, you're an easy man to please."

He shot her a wicked look. "When it comes to you I am."

She responded with something under her breath that was lost in the wind as it swept through the trees, rustling the leaves on their branches. It was a warm night, the stars glittering in the velvety blackness of the skies like diamonds that'd been scattered across its surface, while crickets chirped in the underbrush. With each breath that he took, Eli could scent the surrounding forest, a melting blend of pine and loam and musk, and it settled him enough that he trusted himself to walk beside her without taking her to the fertile ground and claiming her then and there.

But he'd have been lying through his teeth if he'd said he wasn't thinking about it.

Coughing to clear the knot of lust in his throat, he asked, "Do you want to hit the celebration?"

"I was actually planning on just heading back to Wyatt and El's. I'm pretty beat after today."

Hearing the tiredness in her soft voice, he gave her hand another gentle squeeze. "Then I'll walk you over."

A few minutes later, they'd skirted the outside of the Alley, avoiding most of the crowd, and were climbing the front porch steps to Wyatt and Elise's cabin. Hating that it was time to say goodbye, he was surprised when she turned to him and asked, "Do you, um, want to come inside for a while? I'm sure Wyatt and Elise will spend some time celebrating with the others. Or were you planning on going for Eric?"

"He's not expecting to see me there," he said in a low voice, searching her face for signs of what she was thinking. "But I have to be honest with you, Rey. If I come inside, I won't be able to keep my hands off you."

Her eyes widened a little, then darkened, but she didn't say anything. So he didn't know what the hell to expect when she pulled her hand from his, took her keys from her pocket, and used the one Wyatt had given her to unlock the door. She stepped inside, then turned to face him. "I don't want you to leave," she told him, flicking her tongue across her plump lower lip in an endearing sign of her nerves. "But you should know that I'm not ready to have sex with you. Despite what you said before you left about finishing what we'd started, that's not what this is."

Stepping into the house, he took a deep breath as he shut the door, then slowly exhaled. Holding her dark gaze, he said, "It's killing me that you feel that way, but I'm not going to argue with you. If you need me to be patient, then I can be patient."

She started to respond, but he cut her off as he stepped forward, closing the distance between them. There was a lot he needed to say, but she didn't look like a woman who needed to have her ear talked off at the moment. No, she looked like a woman who needed to have her man take care of her, pleasuring her until she was boneless and as soft as sun-warmed taffy. And that was something he could definitely give her.

Her head tilted back as he looked down into her beautiful face, and he was glad to see the color in her cheeks as he said, "But no more pushing me away, Carla."

She swallowed, her chest rising as she pulled in a slow breath.

Cupping the side of her face in one hand, he ran his thumb over the smooth surface of her lower lip, and quietly said, "Not from this mouth." His other hand slid down her side, and then he reached between her legs, cupping her there. "And not from *this*. I'll find a way to keep some measure of control tonight, but this time I'm tasting you or I'll die."

She pulled her lower lip away from his thumb, dragging it through her teeth. "You never tried to do that before," she said in a voice that was so soft and sexy, he could literally *feel* all the blood in his body rushing south, settling thickly in his groin.

Scooping her up into his arms, Eli kept his eyes on hers as he carried her across the living room, toward the hallway. "I'd waited too long to finally get my hands on you," he explained in a rough, gravelly rumble. "Once I did, all I could think about was getting inside you and staying there. But it was always something I wanted, Rey. The first time I saw you after you'd turned eighteen, I knew *exactly* what I wanted to do to you."

Her pupils were dilated, breaths falling soft and fast from her parted lips as she pointed to the door of her room. He carried her inside, then closed it with his booted foot and asked her to turn the lock. There was a soft spill of light coming from the bathroom, falling across the bed, and his goddamn hands were shaking by the time he laid her down there, in the midst of the rumpled bedding that carried her sumptuous scent. He came down over her, caging her beneath his body, his weight braced on his forearms as he settled his hips between her open legs, pressing against her. His breath hissed through his teeth, and he ground his jaw, forcing himself to pull back, knowing damn well he was tempting fate. By some miracle, he'd managed to rein his beast in when he'd touched her that afternoon—but he knew his hold on the animal was tenuous at best. He prayed it was smart enough to know that if ever there was a time to behave itself, it was now. She wanted him, but she was skittish…and unsure… and still as angry and hurt and suspicious as she'd been since the moment she'd walked back into his life.

So tonight was going to be about making her feel good—and then tomorrow he'd go back to battle for her heart and her forgiveness and the future that he wanted so badly he could taste it.

"You're so incredibly beautiful," he whispered, lowering his head and pressing his lips against the tender base of her throat, where her pulse was fluttering madly. He groaned with pleasure when her hands dug their way into his hair, clutching at the strands. "Is your palm okay?" he asked, worried that she was in pain.

"What palm?" she murmured, making him smile as his lips coasted over her collarbone.

Ignoring the ache throbbing low in his body, he knelt between her legs and reached for the hem of her shirt, shoving it up under her chin. In the next second, he had the cups of her bra pulled down, the soft light spilling over her lush, pink-tipped breasts, and with a thick sound of hunger, he covered one of the pretty nipples with his mouth, sucking hard enough to arch her back.

"Eli… *Oh, God*," she moaned, shivering, her hands tangling in his hair as she held him to her even tighter, pushing herself against his face. Breathing hard and fast, he pulled back, releasing the swollen nipple with a wet pop, and quickly moved to the other one, lashing it with his tongue, before sucking it between his lips and hungrily working it against the roof of his mouth.

"Next time I'm doing that for hours," he groaned when he finally pulled away, kissing his way down her trembling stomach, while his hands ripped at the button on her jeans, damn near destroying the zipper as he fought to get it down. She was panting, her eyes heavy with need as she stared at him, and he almost ripped the legs of her jeans as he yanked them down and off, needing to get to her so badly he was shaking. The tiny white panties keeping him from what he wanted tore off with a sibilant hiss as he ripped them apart, and then he was *there,* and *oh, shit,* he was going to completely lose it because she was so damned *perfect.*

Unable to wait, he shoved her thighs wider, opened her with his thumbs as he leaned down, and covered her with his open mouth, a thick sound of raw pleasure burning at the back of his throat the instant his tongue touched her drenched, silky flesh. He shuddered, unable to believe it was even better than he'd imagined it would be, his greed for her like a physical thing inside him, keeping company with his wolf. He loved the way she felt against his lips and tongue, so tender and soft. Was already addicted to her taste, it was so warm and lush and sweet. He wanted to feel her come undone against his face more than he'd ever wanted any goddamn thing in his entire life, and he wasn't shy about making it happen, shoving his tongue inside that tiny opening as deep as he could go. His mouth was nothing short of ravenous as he went completely wild on her, his fingers biting into her firm thighs as he shoved her legs even farther apart, needing her completely open to him.

"What are you doing?" she gasped moments later, when he pushed up on one arm, staring hard at her flushed face as she slowly came down from a wrenching, devastating orgasm that had pulsed against his tongue like a heartbeat, her taste so intoxicating he knew he wouldn't ever be able to get enough of it. "Eli?"

His voice was low, and as guttural as a growl. "I'm watching you come undone for me, Rey."

When he pushed two thick fingers inside that narrow, slippery opening, she gasped, "It's too much."

"Like hell it is," he shot back, licking his wet lips. "It's not nearly enough."

Before she could argue, he'd lowered his head again, his open mouth covering her hot, slick folds, while his tongue rubbed her hard little clit, then plunged back inside her. Deep, dark, hungry. He was consuming her. Making her melt into thick, honeyed liquid, which just made him feast on her even more savagely, until his low, guttural groans were drowning out the sounds of the celebration taking place outside the cabin.

He could have kept his mouth on her forever. She was that perfect. That sweet. That goddamn *necessary* to him.

She came again, even harder this time, her cries deliciously hoarse as her body pulsed and pulsed, coming completely undone for him. He gentled his mouth, licking her with soft, careful strokes, while his own body hardened to the point where he feared he might burst, his blood pumping so fast through his veins he could hear it roaring in his ears.

He hoped to God that she'd changed her mind about intercourse, because if he didn't get inside her soon, there was every chance it was going to break him. Turn him into the mindless, instinctual beast that lived at his core in a transformation that could never be undone, the reason of the man lost forever beneath that primal force of madness. He'd heard of it happening to Lycans who'd been pushed to the ends of their sanity, and God only

knew he could feel that point nearing, drawing closer…
and closer.

"Carla," he breathed out in a harsh rasp, resting his
forehead against her sleek thigh. "I *need* you."

He flinched when he felt her stiffen, instead of melting in surrender. She quickly scrambled out from beneath
him, leaving him kneeling in the middle of the bed while
she huddled against the headboard, her golden hair a wild
tangle around her flushed face, her pleasure-hazy eyes
shocked wide with panic.

"I…I can't," she whispered, shaking her head. "I told
you…I'm not ready. Not for…that. Not with everything
still so…so…"

He pulled in a deep breath as he gripped the back of
his neck with one hand, struggling to think through the
fog of hunger and craving and searing emotion that was
clouding his brain. "Don't you feel it?" The next words
spilling from his lips stunned him even more than they
did her. "Don't you want me anymore?"

"Of course I do. Of course I feel it! But that doesn't
mean I have to give into it."

"Why, Rey? Why the hell do you keep fighting it?"
He moved off the bed and back to his feet, standing at the
side of the mattress as he stared down at her. "I've said
I was sorry, and I meant it. I screwed up and it's killing
me inside. But I never meant to hurt you, and for that I
am so damn *sorry*."

"It doesn't change anything, Eli."

"It could, if you would let it," he grunted, shoving a
hand back through his hair in frustration.

"Look," she said after she'd taken a careful breath,
seeming to brace herself. "I…I don't want to be one of
those women who bitches and moans about how upset she
is, but never has the guts to just say what the problem is."

He waited, alert, heart practically climbing its way up the back of his throat. "I'm listening," he scraped out.

Pulling the sheet around her body, she moved off the other side of the bed, staring back at him over the mattress. A mere distance of feet that could have been miles for the way it felt to him. "When it comes right down to it," she told him, "I don't trust you. You…you completely *shattered* me when you left. And it was so…so toxic, because I had to hold it all inside, since no one even knew about you…about us, because you'd made it pretty clear you didn't want anyone to know. Jillian figured it out… but that wasn't until much later. There was no one I could turn to. No one to hold me when I cried myself to sleep every night. It just…it ate away at me. Changed me."

"Rey—"

"No," she whispered, holding up her hand when he started to head around the foot of the bed. "Just let me get this done."

He nodded as he forced himself to stand still, his throat so tight he could barely swallow.

She wet her lips, blinked a few times, then went on. "Now you're back, and you've suddenly started talking like you want more—a second chance. And messing around is one thing. Basic biology says that we're desperate for each other because we haven't been able to scratch this itch in three years, while the bond is doing everything it can to try and pull us together. So it's obvious why we're so hot for each other. But we have nothing, no reason whatsoever, to keep going with this thing on an emotional level."

"You're wrong," he growled, hating that she felt that way. That she was even *thinking* that way, her words ripping his insides to shreds.

"Eli—"

"You want a reason, Rey? Because I have one for you. The fact that I'm falling *in love* with you all over again is a hell of a good reason."

She paled so quickly she looked like she was bleeding out. "No…that's not true. It can't be."

Unable to stop the words now that they'd finally broken free, he said, "Or maybe rediscovering is a better word. I never fell out of love with you. Not for one moment, Rey. I just buried it. Hid from it." He took a few more steps that brought him closer, hating that he wasn't holding her. "And now you're going to try to hide from it, too, because you're scared. But you should trust me when I tell you that it won't work, baby. It won't work for shit."

She lowered her head, her shoulders shaking, and he quickly made his way around the bed, desperate to reach her. But when he placed his fingers under her chin and lifted her precious face to his, the sight of the tears spilling from her eyes made him feel like acid had been poured into his veins. "Christ, don't do that," he groaned, swiping at the tears with his thumb. "Please, Rey. It's breaking my heart."

"Why? Why are you d-doing this to me?" she cried, shaking so hard her teeth were chattering. "If I'd thought you were g-going to…to do this… *Damn it*, I never would have gone after you!"

Pushing her hair back from her face, he said, "I would have come back, anyway, Rey. That wasn't a lie. And I'm so damn sorry. For everything."

She squeezed her eyes shut, forcing more tears to spill down her cheeks. "Just tell me what you want."

Roughly, he said, "I want you to forgive me."

"Eli—"

He cut her off, his voice even rougher than before.

"Because I meant it when I said that I love you, Carla. I loved you before, and I love you even more now."

"Oh, God," she breathed, her face white as she opened her eyes and stepped away from him, stumbling back. "I just…I need you to go, Eli. Please, just go."

Frustration filled him so quickly he was surprised he didn't burst with it. "That's not going to solve anything. Stop pushing me away."

She sniffed, swiping at her tears. "I'm not pushing. I just…I need some time to think."

He opened his mouth, then clamped it shut, knowing that shouting at her would solve nothing. And that's exactly what he wanted to do at that moment, his beast as angry and frustrated as the man, prowling beneath his skin; a visceral, possessive creature that wanted to break free and claim what it damn well knew belonged to them.

Jesus, maybe I do need to get out of here.

"Please, Eli. If you mean it," she whispered unsteadily, "and you want me to be able to deal with this, then you have to give me the chance to think it through. *Please.*"

It went against every single natural instinct he possessed, but he knew she was right. Staying right now wasn't going to make anything better for either one of them. Not when the only thing he could think about was completing the bond and permanently marking her little ass as *his*.

Hating the brutal knife being twisted in his chest—the knife he understood all too well that *he'd* put there—he gave her what she'd asked for, and walked out the door.

Chapter 10

Climbing out of the truck, Eli squinted against the bright rays of afternoon sunlight and looked for Carla in the crowd that had gathered to meet him and his men, as well as Brody and Cian, who had come along with them this time.

Thanks to Rachel, who was currently staying with Eric and Chelsea, their mission that afternoon had been a success. With her help and knowledge of the area and its back roads, they'd been able to pinpoint the location of a weapons stockpile in Hawkley that Roy had been putting together and form a plan for going after them. It'd been a long shot, and while they knew that what they'd found wasn't the pack's entire supply, they'd managed to drive away with a hell of a lot of guns that would now be used to protect Silvercrest lives, rather than destroy them.

Though the building they'd targeted had been on the outskirts of the town, Eli had hoped to catch a glimpse of some of the women and children who lived there, ready to take them back with them if that's what they wanted, but it was just as Rachel had said. The Whiteclaw were cocky enough to leave their munitions poorly protected, but they had the female residents of the town on lock-down, refusing to let them outdoors.

And if Bartley and his men had already arrived, then they were keeping a low profile, because they hadn't seen a single one of the mercenaries during the two ops that they'd pulled off.

"Jeremy!" he called out as soon as he caught sight of the blond Runner coming across the glade to meet them. "We need Jillian! Lev took a bullet in the shoulder!"

"On it!" the Runner called back, changing direction as he headed back toward his cabin. "Just get him over to our place!" he threw over his shoulder.

James was helping Lev out of the backseat, the blond merc murmuring something about how it must be his lucky day, seeing as how he was finally being allowed near the pretty little witches.

"By the way," Brody murmured as Lev walked past him holding a wad of cloth against his wounded shoulder. "You flirt with either Jillian or Sayre, and Jeremy's liable to kill you."

Lev's white teeth flashed in a grin. "No worries, man. I'll be an absolute angel."

Kyle snorted. "Seeing as how that's impossible, I should probably say goodbye to you now, Slivkoff."

Everyone laughed, easing some of the tension that had settled over the group when they'd learned of Lev's injury, and Eli's skin prickled with awareness when Carla finally approached him, just as he was shoving his keys into the front pocket of his jeans.

"How'd it go?" she asked, a slight flush on her cheeks

as she pushed her hands in her pockets. This was the first time they'd been relatively alone since last night, the others all heading off in different directions, and he wondered if she was embarrassed about what had happened between them in her bedroom, or if that flush had something to do with what he'd told her. Or, hell, maybe she was just warm. For all he knew, she hadn't even thought about his emotional confession after he'd left her and headed back to his cabin—which had been one of the hardest goddamn things he'd ever had to do.

But as much as he wanted to be pissed at her for reacting that way, he knew that wasn't fair. Like she'd told him last night, the things he'd done in the past had killed her trust, and if he wanted her—and if he ever wanted to hear a similar declaration of love come from her own lips—then he had to be willing to put in the time and effort to rebuild it.

It wasn't something that was going to come overnight, no matter how badly he wished it could be like that, because this wasn't a damn fairy tale. But it was something he'd fight for until he'd drawn his last breath. He wasn't going to give up.

Not now. Not ever.

Shoving a hand back through his windblown hair, he held her dark gaze as he answered her question. "We got some of the weapons, but it can't be their entire stock. They've probably already distributed the heavy-duty stuff to their soldiers."

With a nod, she asked, "Is Lev going to be all right?"

A grin tugged at the corner of his mouth. "Didn't you hear him?"

She gave a soft, feminine snort. "Yeah, but from what I can tell, he *always* sounds like that."

"Don't worry about him," he murmured. "He'll be fine."

"So about the weapons. You know this kind of thing is just gonna piss them off, right?"

"I sure as hell hope it does. We're going to have our plans ready to go in the next day or two, and after learning what's happening in that town, the sooner we can give those women the chance to escape, the better."

"I agree with all that," she told him, as they both started to walk across the glade, "but was it really necessary to take such a risk? I mean, you went in broad daylight again, just the day after you destroyed their drugs supply."

"We chose the time they would least expect it," he rumbled, wondering exactly where they were headed. Not that it mattered. He'd follow her wherever she wanted to go, until she told him to get lost. And even then, he'd trail after her from behind, determined not to let her out of his sight.

She sounded more than a little peeved. "So then it's okay for you to repeatedly put your life in danger, but I'm not even meant to do my job? Do you have any idea how backward that is, Eli?"

She was obviously still pissed about their earlier argument, but he wouldn't have done a damn thing differently. She'd wanted to come with him and the guys, and he wouldn't hear of it, which hadn't exactly gone over well.

Breathing out a tired sigh, he said, "Rey, I'm covered in sweat and more than a little of Lev's blood. Can I just take a pass for a little while and argue with you about this after I've had a shower and grabbed a beer?"

"Fine."

He caught her arm as she started to walk away from him, and smiled down into her adorably disgruntled face.

"You want to join me?" he asked. Just because he didn't want to fight with her didn't mean he didn't want her with him. Hell, he'd keep her glued to his side if she'd allow it. Except, of course, for when it was dangerous.

She shook her head, tugging her arm free. He expected her to stomp off, but she didn't. Instead, she made an odd little movement with her shoulder, and said, "By the way, you had a visitor while you were gone."

At the odd edge to her voice, dread settled in his gut like a dead weight. "Who the hell would visit me?" He hadn't left any friends behind when he'd been banished. Not trusting his old man, he'd never associated with any of the pack Lycans except for those who'd served his father, and he wouldn't have wanted anything to do with them now, if they'd managed to survive. Eric and Elise had been the only ones who had ever mattered to him, until Carla had come along.

"I didn't get her name," she murmured, staring off to his right instead of looking him in the eye. "But Eric confirmed that she was one of your old flames."

Oh, hell no. He wasn't letting this screw up the small amount of progress he'd managed to make. Curving his hands over her shoulders, he waited until she finally gave in and looked at him, then said, "I did *not* invite anyone to come down here, okay? I haven't even spoken to anyone in town."

"Well, you can sort that out with her."

"Are you telling me she's still here?" he asked, his tone grim.

"No. Elise got rid of her." Her mouth twisted with a smirk. "But I have a feeling she'll be back. She seemed like the tenacious sort."

"Then I'll tell her she's not welcome here."

Her brows lifted with surprise. "You don't even know who it was."

"I don't care who it was. Not. At. All."

For a split second, he was staring down into the most stunning, breathtaking look of hope on her face that he'd ever seen, before she quickly snuffed it out. "You know, I get that you're trying to say the right things here, Eli. But you could save us both the trouble and just go ahead and sleep with her."

"That's not going to happen," he ground out. "I don't even want her."

"Is that right? Because from the sound of it, you certainly wanted her before. She said the two of you were *really* close, right up until the time you left."

Christ, he just couldn't catch a break, could he? Rubbing the back of his neck, he said, "Then she was lying, Rey. I don't even know who this woman could be, which tells you how much she meant to me. But if we're going to have this conversation, let's at least take it inside."

"Fine," she said for the second time, and he clenched his jaw. He was really starting to hate that freaking word.

She followed him over to his cabin, and he was relieved they weren't going to have to do this in front of his sister and Wyatt. Once they were in the bedroom he'd taken, he turned and locked the door behind him, then leaned back against it and folded his arms over his chest.

When she finally stopped pacing at the foot of his bed and turned to look at him, he said, "Do you want to go first or should I?"

She frowned, but jerked her chin for him to start.

"Okay, then, here it is. I don't want any woman other than you, Carla. I haven't for a long time. And I would think that was fairly obvious, seeing as how I keep getting my hand down your pants every chance I get and pouring my heart out to you like a lovesick sap. Does that sound like a man looking to screw his way through the pack?"

When her frown deepened, but she didn't say anything, he asked her again. "Does it?"

"No," she muttered.

"Well, at least you're willing to admit that much to me."

"What exactly do you want out of this?" she suddenly snapped, glaring.

"Not much," he snapped back. "Just *you*."

Her voice started to rise. "You really want a half-breed? Is that what you expect me to believe?"

He drew his head back, stunned. "Where the hell did *that* come from?"

"Isn't that what this has been about right from the start? You were ashamed of me, weren't you? That's why we were always a secret!"

"That's bullshit!" Fisting his hands at his sides, he stalked toward her. "You're just grasping at straws now, Rey," he said in a voice that was low and guttural. "I expected better from you."

"You are such an ass!"

"Because I screwed up? Yeah, I did. I know that. But I'm back and I want another chance. I bloody well *deserve* one after what I gave up for you!"

"What you gave up?" she wheezed, shaking her head. "For *me?* You're not making any sense! I didn't banish you."

"You, Rey. I gave up *you*. Don't expect me to do it again."

She blinked, staring at him as if she thought he was crazy.

"And don't ever think that I would feel the way my old

man did. Yeah, I followed him. I followed him so that I could keep an eye on that bastard, and keep him away from my family as much as possible. Which included my mother. I even..." The gritty words trailed off and he shook his head, backing up a step, unable to believe he'd almost told her.

"You even what?" she asked, her voice slightly softer now, as if she sensed that something in the argument had just shifted.

He opened his mouth, but his lungs were working so hard he couldn't get anything out.

"What, Eli? What is it?"

He squeezed his eyes shut, his hands fisting and flexing at his sides, while his chest heaved like a friggin' bellows.

"Eli?"

"I was the oldest, which meant I was the one she ran to," he heard himself saying in a voice that didn't even sound like his own. "Always. Whenever he lost his shit with her, I put myself between them. I don't think Eric and Elise even remember. I tried to keep them away from it. But I knew, I *knew* he would end up killing her if she didn't get out."

"I thought your mother ran off with another man. A human one."

Wetting his lips, he finally opened his eyes, looked at her, and said, "She did."

Her slender brows pulled into a V over the delicate bridge of her nose. "I don't understand."

"I would help her sneak off sometimes, so that she could get away from it all. I guess they met during one of her trips away from the mountain. I don't know anything about him, except that he made her happy. When she told me she wanted to run away with him, I wasn't surprised."

"Oh, no," she whispered, looking heartbroken for the little boy that he'd been. "What about you and El and Eric? How could she…just leave you like that?"

He gave a small, bitter laugh that tasted like crap in his mouth. "I think by that time she saw us as more of an extension of my old man than of herself. She knew she'd never make it if she tried to take us with her. The League of Elders would have given him full permission to come after us with every resource the pack possessed. But it didn't matter. As wrong as it sounds, I was…I was *glad* she wanted to go."

Quietly, she said, "Eli, you have nothing to feel guilty for."

The sound that ripped up from his throat was deep and sarcastic. "Don't I? When she told me what she wanted, *I* got her out, because I was trying to save her. Told her to never come back, because I knew he would kill her if she did. But I didn't realize what it would mean for everyone else. Her leaving him…it just pushed him even deeper into his hate-colored madness."

"But you couldn't have known that. You were only a child."

Another bitter laugh jerked past his lips. "That's what the older pack members would always say about us. They would talk about how sad it was that we'd lost our mother when we were so young. And, Elise, yeah. She was just a little thing. But Eric and I…we were hardly little kids. He'd forced us to grow up long before we were adults."

"Do Eric and Elise know that you helped her escape?"

His eyes widened, and he could feel the blood draining from his face. "Hell no. They'd never forgive me." He took a step toward her, his breaths still coming hard and fast as he said, "And you know what the worst part is? The worst part is that I should have had the balls to end it and kill him, but I didn't, because she made me *promise* that I wouldn't hurt him. So I kept thinking someone else would do it for me, but his disease, his hatred, it spread like a damn plague. And after I was banished, I left the rest of you here to deal with it!"

Closing the distance between them, he curled his fingers around her upper arms as he leaned over her, getting right in her face as her head went back and she stared up at him with solemn eyes. "You want to know why I never told anyone about us?" he asked, forcing the words through his gritted teeth. "Because I was *afraid,* Rey. Afraid of letting myself love you. Of what my father might do to you if he found out. Of the kind of man I had become because of him. I followed him so Eric wouldn't have to, but I hated every second of it. Hated the goddamn gut-wrenching terror of what he would do to you if he found out you were *mine.*

"And the night I finally took you to my bed, he'd already been pissed because of what I'd done. Because I'd jeopardized my position in the pack by killing El's rapist. She was his own daughter, Rey. He hated her, and she was a *part* of him. So what do you think he would have done about *you?*

"From where I was standing, the banishment was a twisted kind of blessing when it happened, because there's no way in hell that I would have been able to stay away from you after finally getting my hands on you. And he would have tried to kill you for it. Then I would have killed him, which would have turned everyone who followed him against us. We would have been marked for death the second he stopped breathing. So my banishment saved your life!" he ended on a stifled roar.

"If that was true, you would have come back when you heard he was dead. Or better yet, taken me with you!" Her voice cracked, and he winced at the pain he could see filling her glistening eyes. "God, Eli. You could have at least come to me and told me goodbye."

"I *did*." His throat was so tight he could barely force the words out. "I went to the Alley that night, Rey. I parked a mile out and walked in. No one even noticed because you guys were having some kind of birthday celebration for Jeremy. I stood out there in the damn trees and I watched you with them. With your friends. And I *knew* that as much as I loved you, and as much as I hated the goddamn danger your job put you in, the right thing to do was to let you stay with them. With your family."

"Oh, God," she sobbed, breaking away from him. With her arms wrapped around her body, she hunched forward, crying, "You had no right to make that decision for me. You were wrong!"

He swallowed, his own eyes stinging as he watched her completely fall apart. "I...I'm starting to see that. I should...have talked to you. I know that now."

She straightened and glared at him, her thick lashes drenched with tears. "You don't really love me," she said through her trembling lips. "I...I don't believe that. Either you're lying...or it's the stupid bond screwing with your emotions—with your head—now that you're back. I spent a long time thinking about it last night, and that's...that's the only explanation that makes any sense."

Feeling as if he'd been slashed open inside, he asked, "Why is it so hard for you to just believe me?"

"Why?" Her chest shook with a small, wretched laugh. "Because if you loved me, Eli, the truth is that you would have come back for me a long time ago."

At first, he couldn't get out the words he needed to say,

everything jammed up inside him, locking him down. He took a deep, rattling breath, struggling for his damn voice, and somehow managed to tell her, "I was afraid it was too late." Pulling a shaky hand down his face, he stepped close to her again, wanting so damn badly to take her into his arms and crush her against his body. "Christ, I was so afraid you wouldn't want me anymore. Makes me sound like a pussy, but it's the truth. I didn't know if you were feeling the same pull. Was afraid of what I would do when I saw you. What if you'd found someone else? I was always too worried to ask about you whenever I talked to Eric or Elise. I talked to them less and less over the years, not wanting to know. I swear I've lived with that same cold burn of fear every goddamn day since you became a woman and I realized how badly I wanted you, and it was even worse after I left.

"And maybe..." He shoved a hand back through his hair again, then shook his head. "Hell, maybe I felt like I had to protect you from me. From all the things I'd done for that bastard. Even with him dead, I would have still been the same person."

"You really think I would have cared?" she asked in that tear-drenched voice that was killing him.

Working his jaw, he said, "You *should*."

Her chin went up, a rush of angry color burning in her cheeks. "Well, I wouldn't have, because you survived him, Eli. You didn't let him break you. You might have acted like his thug, but you survived him and became the man you are today. A man I could have loved if you hadn't already broken my heart."

"Rey," he groaned, reaching for her.

"Don't," she snapped, stumbling back from him. "Don't touch me. I can't think when you do that."

"And I can't *not* touch you," he rasped, catching her

with one arm wrapped around her waist, the other lifting as he pushed her hair back from her face, "because you're the only thing in this world that I want."

"Eli—"

"Christ, Carla. *Listen* to me. What I told you last night, it was the truth."

She started to shake her head, but he gripped the back of it, holding her still.

Pressing his forehead against hers, he said, "If you won't believe my words, then trust what your body is telling you. Because *sex* doesn't feel like this. Sometimes it feels good, sometimes even fun—but it doesn't feel goddamn *necessary*."

"It's the bond," she cried.

Lifting his head, he stared deep into her beautiful eyes, and said, "Bullshit. It's your heart, Rey. And I want it so badly it's killing me."

She blinked, and then, without any warning, she suddenly grabbed him like she had in this same room yesterday, and crushed her mouth against his. He took her with him as he stumbled back, falling onto the bed, and she straddled his hips, rubbing herself against his already hardening body. Hunger rolled up his spine in a thick, searing wave, and he cursed the layers of clothing separating them. Breaking away from the kiss, he sucked in air, ready to beg her for what he wanted, but the words dried up on his tongue when she scooted back and shoved up his shirt, kissing the center of his chest, right over the thundering beat of his heart. He pulled in a sharp breath as he ripped the shirt over his head, and every muscle in his body tensed with anticipation as her mouth traveled lower, trailing biting kisses across his torso, around his navel, until she was nuzzling his happy trail with her nose and ripping at the buttons on his fly, the worn denim straining over the heavy bulk of his erection.

"What?" he gasped, half convinced he must have hit his head somehow and was imagining this. "What are you doing?"

"You're always touching me," she panted, kneeing his thighs apart as she tugged down his boxers and jeans. Wrapping her hand around the thick base of his cock, she looked up at him through her lashes, her voice even huskier as she said, "You're always making it about me. About my pleasure. But this time, it's going to be about you, Eli."

Bracing his booted feet on the bed, he reached down and shoved his boxers and jeans a little lower, his face so friggin' hot he knew he had to have turned bright red. But he had Carla's feminine little hand wrapped as far as it could go around his massive hard-on, her lush mouth hovering over the slick, swollen head, and he was pretty sure his heart was getting ready to pound its way right out of his chest. He looked too brutal to ever go inside that perfect mouth of hers—but then, he had a strong feeling he was going to look right there, too. As if it was where he belonged, his body close to hers, letting her do whatever the hell she wanted to him.

Then she took him between her lips, inside the moist heat of her mouth, stroking him with her tongue, and the sensation was so shockingly intense that he shouted.

Needing to see every carnal, mind-shattering second of this, Eli let his knees fall open and braced himself on an elbow, his other hand gripping her hair and lifting it away so that he had an unobstructed view of her going down on him. Of that hot little mouth hungrily sucking him deep, damn near sending his eyes rolling back in his head.

"I'm going over," he growled just moments later, warning her, but she didn't move away. Moaning around his aching shaft, she sucked him even deeper, and he fell back to the bed with another guttural, visceral shout on his lips as the climax ripped through him, so explosive his back literally arched off the mattress. He shoved his fingers into her soft hair, holding her to him as it went on and on, the sexy sounds she made only driving him further over the edge, until he was shaking and cursing and willing to bet everything he owned on the fact that she'd almost killed him with the pleasure.

Son of a bitch, he thought, throwing his arm over his eyes as he tried to catch his breath. If he'd come that fast when he was younger, he'd have been embarrassed as hell. But this was Carla, the woman who turned him inside out, who turned him on like no other had ever even come close to doing, and he figured he was lucky he'd actually lasted as long as he had.

While he lay there trying to make sure he wasn't in the middle of a heart attack, she pulled her head back, releasing him from the hot, wet suction of her mouth, and rested her forehead against his lower abdomen. Her body shook with a fine vibration, her shoulders lifting and falling with her rapid breaths.

"Carla, that was unreal. I didn't even know it was possible to come that hard. Or that it could feel that friggin' incredible."

He felt a smile curl her lips. "That's because I lo—"

She instantly froze, whatever she'd been about to say choked off before he could catch it, her breaths coming so quickly he worried she was going to hyperventilate.

"Rey?"

"I…I need to go," she whispered, the soft words unsteady as she scrambled off the side of the bed.

"What?" He knew he sounded out of it, but he was still groggy as hell from the violence of his release. "What are you talking about?"

Pushing her hair back from her face, she turned toward the door. "I'm sorry, but I just realized that Wyatt's, um, waiting for me. He said he needed to talk to me."

"Wait!" he growled, jerking into a sitting position. "Jesus, Carla, just stop for a second and look at me!"

She whipped her head to the side as she flicked open the lock on the door, glancing at him over her shoulder, and he felt like he'd been punched in the gut.

He could see the fear on her beautiful face as clearly as if it'd been lit up like a neon sign.

"Damn it, don't do this," he choked out. "Don't run out on me again."

"I've never run out on you," she argued, twisting the handle. "I might have asked you to stop, or to leave, but I've never run away. And I'm not running now. I just... I have...I have to go," she said in a carefully controlled tone, before hurrying out of the room.

By the time he'd yanked his jeans over his hips and made it onto the front porch, she was already halfway across the Alley. He ran after her, not caring what he looked like—just a crazy half-dressed man with wild hair who was cursing a blue streak. But he forced himself to stop when she ran inside Elise and Wyatt's cabin, knowing damn well they were at home. He could see the colored lights from their TV flashing across the living room window. Yeah, he could force his way inside, but where was that going to get him? In an argument with Wyatt? The usually easygoing Runner had already made it perfectly clear how protective he was when it came to the woman he thought of as a sister. The only person who meant more to him was Eli's own sister, and he scowled, not wanting to make this situation any more difficult for Elise.

Shit. He would have to get to Carla another way. Maybe wait until everyone went to sleep that night and sneak in through her bedroom window, the way he'd considered doing before. But what if Wyatt set an alarm? He didn't care if he made a jackass of himself by setting it off, but Carla would probably want to kill him if he ended up putting everyone in a panic.

Figuring he'd just keep calling her cell phone until she picked up, he turned and headed back to his cabin. Just as he was about to climb the porch steps, he caught the raised voices coming from the side of the cabin, and went back down to take a look and make sure everything was okay. But the instant he walked around the corner, he realized it was the Irishman and the little witch who seemed to be driving the guy crazy.

"You go off on a walk with that guy again, Sayre, and there won't be enough of him left to bury," the Runner was snarling in a low voice, the rough words vibrating with fury.

"Why are you doing this?" she hissed, sounding on the verge of tears. "What the hell is it to you who I go out with?"

"He's got a reputation. All he's interested in is getting between your legs."

Eli didn't know who they were talking about, but he hoped to God it wasn't one of his guys. The last thing they needed was trouble with any of the Runners—especially this one.

"Hah!" she shouted, stomping her foot against the grass. "That sounds like *you* and pretty much every woman you ever come across!"

"Don't," Hennessey growled, grabbing her by her upper arms. "This isn't about me. It's about—"

"Oh, just shut up," she snapped, cutting him off as she jerked away from him. "And stay away from me, Cian. I mean it. I'm tired of this stupid mind game you keep playing. You don't want me, but you don't want anyone else to want me, either? It's sick! Just leave me alone!"

She stormed off around the back of the neighboring cabin, and the Runner stared after her, his big hands fisted at his sides. He looked like a man who was having to physically restrain himself from doing something that he knew he shouldn't, and then he suddenly turned around, stalking forward with his head down, while a guttural string of curses fell from his lips.

"You've got a problem on your hands with that one," Eli said, before the guy could mow him down.

Drawing to a stop, Cian's head shot up, his grim expression twisting into an even darker scowl. "And you don't?" he muttered, obviously talking about Carla.

Scrubbing his jaw, he said, "Reyes is just being stubborn."

The Runner slowly arched one of his ebony brows. "Is that what you call a woman willing to risk her life to end her bond with you?"

He flinched at those softly spoken words, feeling as if he'd just been kicked in the stomach. "What did you say?"

Pulling a pack of cigarettes from his pocket, the Irishman took one out as he murmured, "There aren't many secrets here in the Alley, Drake. You'd do well to remember that."

Eli took an aggressive step forward, his hands curling into fists. "Why the hell did you say she was willing to risk her life?"

Lighting his cigarette, Cian took a long drag, then

slowly exhaled as he locked his shuttered gaze with Eli's. "You know how our world works," he said in a low, lilting rasp. "How nature works. One rarely gets something for nothing. There's always a risk, and some are greater than others. What matters is what we're willing to gamble with to get what we want."

"Are you telling me her life would be in danger if Jillian breaks the bond?" he growled, feeling a muscle begin to pulse at the side of his jaw.

Cian slid him a chilling look. "I'm saying it might damn well kill her."

He swallowed as he locked his jaw, thinking *Christ. Oh, Christ.* How desperate must Carla be if she was willing to take that kind of risk?

As desperate as my mother was?

He flinched again, that particular thought striking his body like a physical blow. It was *that* jarring and painful. He wanted so badly to quiet the voices in his head, but it was impossible to stop the destructive train of his thoughts. Because if she was willing to go that far, was there anything he could do, anything at all he could say, that would ever get through to her?

Wasn't that what kept me away from her these past months? The fear that she'd already scarred me from her heart?

Damn it, he needed out of this place. And he needed a bottle.

Turning away from the Irishman, Eli figured it was time that he finally made his way back home.

Chapter 11

Twenty-four hours later, Eli still hadn't returned from wherever he'd run off to. After their argument, Carla had stood at the window in Wyatt and Elise's guest room and watched him drive one of the mercs' big black trucks out of the Alley. And he hadn't been back since.

I should be relieved. It's what I wanted.

True. The only problem was that relief was the last thing she was feeling.

She hadn't wanted to run out on him, after sharing something so incredible, but she'd panicked when the word "love" had almost slipped from her lips. She might have finally come to terms with the fact that she was madly, desperately in love with him, but that didn't mean she was ready to tell him. Just because he'd said the words to her didn't mean it was smart to say them back. Not until she understood *why* he'd said them…and was sure of his feelings.

Because she really did fear that it might have more to do with the bond than it did with his heart.

But what about the things he said about his mom and his dad and how he felt about me?

Then again, am I just meant to forget that he supposedly decided to leave me behind for my own good, without even giving me the choice? Without even talking to me about it or telling me goodbye?

Damn it, she didn't know how to process everything that was churning round and round in her head, and the result was a cracking headache that she hadn't been able to shake for hours now. She wanted to crawl into bed and sleep for a week, the session she'd worked with Wyatt that day on the training fields making her as physically exhausted as she was mentally, but she was due over at Jillian's in twenty minutes for dinner, and she still needed to freshen up. So a nap was unfortunately not in the picture.

Fifteen minutes later, she'd managed to grab a quick shower, throw on a pair of leather sandals, clean jeans, and a slouchy gray top, as well as put on a little blush and lip gloss. Wyatt and Elise were over at her cabin, having dinner with the women who were living there at the moment, so she pulled her keys from her pocket as she stepped out onto the porch, intending to lock the door behind her. But she froze the minute she looked up and realized she wasn't alone.

They were all there, the Runners and their mates, standing around the front of the cabin, watching her with careful gazes, as if this was some kind of intervention. A wild burst of laughter almost rumbled up with that thought, and she wondered when her life had become like a crazy TV sitcom.

"Did I suddenly become insanely popular," she murmured, arching her brows, "or did you guys need something?"

Eric climbed up the porch steps, his handsome face set in a chilling expression of anger. "Go. Get. Him," he said in a low, guttural voice. "Now."

"What?"

"Eli went up to Shadow Peak yesterday, and spent the night at my place, where he apparently decided it was a good idea to get shit-faced. I want you to get your ass up there and bring him back."

Her eyes narrowed, and she could feel her own temper simmering at his tone. "Why me?"

"Because you're the one who put him there," Eric growled, and she was a little surprised that no one, not even Wyatt, took exception to the Runner's tone. Jesus, did they all blame her? Were they all on Eli's side?

Crossing her arms over her chest, she said, "You can't put this on me, Eric. That isn't fair."

"Why shouldn't I? He's done nothing but follow you around since he got back, trying to get you to give him the time of day, and all you do is make him feel like shit. Accuse him of stuff he hasn't even done. If I thought there was a chance in hell he could find someone else, I'd tell him to get out there and do it. But he's hung up on you, because the two of you friggin' belong with each other. So fix it and get him back down here!"

"Eric," his wife murmured, sounding concerned.

"Not now, Chelse. I've been patient, but this is getting ridiculous." He got right in Carla's face, and lowered his voice. "I watched him go through shit with my old man while growing up, doing everything he could to keep that bastard happy, never getting anything back for it. I won't watch him go through the same thing with you."

She flinched, reeling on the inside as Eric's harsh

words worked their way through her system. Was he seriously comparing her to their crazy psycho father? What the hell?

And why was she even bothering to argue with him about this when she actually *wanted* to go up to town and check on Eli? She'd have been lying if she'd said she wasn't worried about him. But then, she was also worried about what she might find when she got there.

"Are you sure he doesn't have company?"

Eric gave her a stunned look, then laughed. Shaking his head, he said, "God, I wish I could tell you that he had a woman with him. It would serve you right, Reyes. But he's at my place, and he's alone."

She'd known that Eric still had his house up in Shadow Peak, though he and Chelsea never stayed there. When she'd asked Elise about it, his sister had said that the couple was thinking of selling the house once things had settled down. But this was hardly the time to be worrying about real estate.

Since Carla was already dressed and had her keys with her, she left Eric and the others standing around the cabin after murmuring a few words to them and headed straight for her car. The short drive to Shadow Peak took forever, thanks to the security checkpoints she had to go through. She knew it was just her imagination, but she felt like she was being judged by every single person she came into contact with, as if she were walking around with a scarlet RB on her forehead that apparently stood for Raving Bitch. It hardly seemed fair, seeing as how none of these Lycans knew the full story, but such was the nature of gossip.

She was familiar with where Eric lived, and was parking on the curb in front of the attractive two-story just a few minutes after reaching the town. Her gaze flicked to where the black truck was parked in the driveway as she turned off the engine, telling her Eli was definitely there. Curling her hands around the steering wheel, she lowered her head, banging her forehead against the leather wheel, then stopped and raised her head again, looking around. There were so many scouts posted now, there was no telling who was watching her from the thickening darkness. Were they waiting to see if he slammed the door in her face? At the moment, she was feeling a bit as if it might be deserved, which made her scowl.

Forcing herself out of the car, she shut the door and headed up to the house, climbing the porch steps and then knocking on the door. The powerful, smoky scent of whiskey was the first thing that hit her nose when he ripped the door open, followed immediately by the richer, deeper scent that was completely his. A heady, erotic blend of soap and salt and the wild outdoors. Wearing nothing more than a faded pair of jeans, he stared down at her through hooded eyes that were thankfully focused, despite the scent of the alcohol. His jaw worked a few times, and then he muttered, "What are you doing here, Reyes?"

"Thanks to your brother," she murmured, "I've been sent to collect you."

"Ah. Of course you have. God knows you wouldn't have come after me on your own." He turned and headed back into the living room, leaving her to walk in and shut the door herself.

After glancing at the disheveled room, the coffee table littered with bottles and a blanket hanging halfway off the sofa, she looked at him and arched one of her brows. "Been having fun up here?"

He slid her a shuttered look as he sat on the arm of the sofa, his muscular arms folded over his broad, beautiful chest, the golden skin gleaming beneath the soft glow of the track lighting. "You'd like to think that, wouldn't you?" he replied, his tone flat. "To have something that would give you even more of a reason to hate me."

She stiffened, something in his tone setting her even further on edge. "I don't hate you, Eli."

"Sure you don't," he drawled with a mocking smile on his sensual lips.

She rubbed her forehead, wondering what his problem was. As well as hers. She couldn't seem to get close to him without saying whatever she could think of to piss him off.

"Believe it or not, Rey, no one's been here but me." At the look she cut him, he said, "Use your nose, little wolf. Come over here and sniff the blanket I've been sleeping under. Sniff any friggin' surface in the house you want. You won't find what you're looking for."

"Why?" she asked softly, blurting the question out before she had the sense to stop herself.

His gaze narrowed in on her face, the long lashes making it difficult to read the look in his eyes. "Are you asking me why I haven't been busy screwing my way through the pack?"

Her response was simple and to the point. "Yes."

She couldn't help but watch the way his biceps bulged as he lifted an arm, hooking his hand around the back of his neck. His breath left his lungs on a rough exhalation, and he said, "I haven't had sex with anyone because the woman I want hasn't been on the top of this bloody mountain with me." Lowering his arm, he held her gaze like he never meant to let it go, and continued speaking through his gritted teeth. "I haven't had another woman, Carla. Not since you. Hell, I haven't had one since long before that night we were together."

For a few dizzying seconds, all she could do was stare at him in shock, unable to believe he was actually trying this with her. God, did he think she was a fool? A naïve little idiot who would believe anything he told her, if it was what he thought she wanted to hear? "Don't. Even. Try. It," she seethed, so angry she was shaking.

He rolled one of those hard, muscular shoulders as he moved to his feet and turned away from her. He walked to the front window, bracing a hand against the top of the frame as he stared out into the starless night. "Get pissed, Rey. It doesn't matter what you do or what you believe. You can't change the truth."

"I'll never believe you."

"Christ, that's almost funny." His head dropped back on those mouthwatering shoulders as he laughed. "You believe everything that *isn't* true, but not what is."

"Fine, then answer me this. What about the blonde in the dive bar when I found you?"

The hand he had braced on the top of the window frame curled into a fist. She listened as he took a few hard, deep breaths, watching the muscles in his sleek back flex with the movement, and then he said, "She'd dropped into my lap, trying to flirt, when she passed out in my arms. Since I couldn't have cared less about her, I let her sleep there."

"You actually expect me to believe that nonsense?"

He turned around as he pushed his hands in his pockets, the masculine pose making him look like something that women would plaster all over their bedroom walls and drool over. Tall, dark, and outrageously delicious, with his piercing eyes and that wild hair, a dark covering of stubble shadowing the hard angle of his jaw. Taking a step toward her, he growled, "Would it make you believe me if I completely humiliate myself for you? What would you think if I told you that I was desperate for even that small, pathetic bit of comfort, after so many years of missing you until I felt like my insides had been scraped raw? That I'd sat there, drinking my whiskey, trying like hell to pretend that it was *you* I was holding?"

"I don't...I can't..."

With his gruff words drowning in frustration, he took another step closer to her and muttered, "I don't know why you think this would affect me any differently than it would you. How eager have you been to find some other male to rut between your legs?"

Her chest shook with a hollow, heavy laugh. "I was so angry with you that I *wanted* to. I wanted to find someone."

"Don't." His nostrils flared as he took a sharp breath, his deep voice little more than a snarl. "I don't want to hear it."

As quickly as her anger had come, it vanished, leaving her feeling deflated, like a balloon that had sprung a leak. "It...it doesn't matter. I couldn't go through with it. No one...I just...there was no one after you," she finished lamely, her voice so small it made her cringe.

For a moment, she thought he was going to close the distance between them and take her into his arms. But then he turned around again and stalked back to the window, his tall body hard with tension. "It was the same for me," he said quietly.

"I find that so hard to believe," she whispered. "I mean, you could have had any woman you wanted."

Seconds ticked by as he stood there before the large window, staring out at the darkened street, while she fought the urge to go to him and wrap her arms around him, pressing her cheek against his warm back...simply holding him as tightly as she could. Pretending, just for a moment, that she wasn't broken inside and the past had never happened. That they could start fresh, without any of the pain and fear and resentment.

Finally, he broke the silence, his deep voice rough with emotion. "There were a few times, when I was lonely, that I thought it might help to find another woman. Times when I tried damn hard to put you out of my mind. Wishing I could just rip you out for good.

"When I left here, I told myself that when the time came that I wanted sex again, I would approach it with the sense of detachment it deserved. A bodily function that had to be fed, nothing more. And when it was done, I would move on, wiping it from my mind. I wouldn't think about what I'd lost. And I sure as hell wouldn't waste time wishing for things that could never be mine."

He turned a little to the side as he slumped against the edge of the window frame, his profile so stark it could have been carved out of granite. "But I could never go through with it. I would find a woman, talk to her, drink with her. But when it came time to get down to it, not only were my body and heart unwilling, all I could think about was the look that would be on your face if you saw me touching someone else." Shaking his head, he gave a bitter laugh. "Guess that was stupid, though, seeing as how you already hated my guts. It's not like falling into bed with some woman I didn't even want could have made you hate me more."

She knew she needed to address this idea he had that she hated him, but she was still too stunned by the realization that was slowly sinking into her. "My God, you're serious, aren't you?"

Turning around, he crossed his arms over his chest, his gaze becoming darker as it locked with hers. "Why do you think my friends are always laughing at me, giving me a hard time about you? They've never seen me act like this over a woman."

She shook her head a little, still trying to wrap her brain around it. "The night I found you, in that bar, Sam said you were always so freaking *nice* to women."

The look he slid her was equal parts exasperation and fury. "Nice to them, Rey. As in wanting them to be safe, but not giving a shit about them beyond that." He scrubbed a hand over his face as a gruff laugh jerked from his lips. "But it was all a pathetic joke, wasn't it? Because we both know you don't really give a shit about what I do or who I do it with. Why would you, when deep down inside you can't stand me?"

"Why do you keep saying that? I thought you believed that I was madly in love with you? That we belonged together?"

His gaze lowered, dropping to the floor, while he drew in a deep breath of air that shuddered on his exhale. Then he said three simple words: "Cian told me."

Feeling more than a little confused, she asked, "He told you what?"

His dark gaze shot back to hers, burning with emotion. "About the bond breaking. About how dangerous it is for the one who's seeking it."

She wheezed as she took a step back, everything suddenly snapping into place with a lot of noise and reverberation, like a series of gunshots going off in her head. "Is that...is that why you're here?"

He rubbed his eyes with his thumb and forefinger, lips parted for breaths that were getting rougher by the second. "Yeah. I just needed...to think."

Carla heard the catch in his deep voice, and felt as if something dark and heavy was falling over her, like a cold rain. She honestly hadn't thought it would matter to him one way or another, or maybe she just hadn't let herself consider how he would feel about the risk she would be taking. Either way, it was clear to her now that her willingness to endanger her own life to destroy their bond was something that had hurt him deeply. Was *still* hurting him.

"Eli," she whispered, so confused she couldn't make heads or tails of any of the powerful emotions tearing through her. Moving like someone in a dream, she felt her feet covering the distance between them, and then she was standing right in front of him, her head going back so that she could keep her eyes on his beautiful face. Wetting her lower lip, she said, "I'm not doing this to hurt you."

He stared so hard and deep into her watery gaze, she felt like he was seeing right inside her. "I'm sorry, Rey. So fucking sorry, for everything, for all of it." The sincerity in his rough voice made her ache. "I never wanted to hurt you. That was the *last* goddamn thing that I wanted."

Her throat shook, melting, and she found herself lifting her hands to his face, her thumbs stroking over his flushed cheekbones. "It's really true," she murmured, an unmistakable note of awe in her voice that she didn't even try to hide. "You haven't been with anyone. I can see the truth in your eyes."

"It's about damn time you can see something," he groaned, and she didn't know if she was the one who lifted up or if he was the one who leaned down, but their mouths were suddenly crashing against each other and they were kissing as if they needed the other's taste to breathe…live…survive. He tasted sumptuous, like whiskey and hot, addicting male. A taste she knew she'd never be able to get enough of. That she'd go to her grave craving, no matter how many years she ended up having on this earth.

And then the raw, aggressive tenor of the kiss changed, their mouths gentling as it melted into something soft and lush and heartbreakingly poignant. Every stroke of his tongue was conveying something so much deeper than pleasure, as if he was pouring his very soul into the touch of his mouth against hers. His hands threaded through her hair, holding the sides of her head as he slanted his mouth over hers, stroking and licking and nipping, his warm breaths pelting against her lips as they shared the same air.

"You drive me so damn crazy," he rasped, wrapping one arm around her lower back as he drew her up against him, his body already hard and thick with need. Pressing his lips to the side of her throat, he said, "No one else has ever had the power to make me so angry, and yet, I've never been as happy as I am when I'm with you, Rey. Even when you're snapping at me, all I can think about is holding you and getting inside you and making you come, again and again, until you're steeped in so much pleasure all you can do is melt and shiver and smile up at me."

She gave a soft laugh, loving the feel of him under her hands as she stroked his shoulders, the muscles so firm and hard beneath his hot skin. "Not that it doesn't sound fun, but I swear you don't have to go to that much trouble just for a smile."

"Feels like it," he muttered, kissing his way up to her ear and then nipping at the delicate lobe, while his hands settled on her hips, holding her against him.

"Am I really that crabby?" she asked, grimacing on the inside.

"Just with me. You're all smiles with your friends. And hell, you smile all the time at mine, as well." His head suddenly shot up, a worried look on his gorgeous face as he said, "Has Lev been flirting with you since I came up here?"

"What? No," she murmured, running her fingers through his soft, thick hair, loving that she was able to touch him. "There's no need to be jealous, Eli. I'm not attracted to Lev. He's just a big ol' teddy bear. To be honest, he kinda reminds me of Brody."

"A teddy bear?" he choked out, sounding skeptical. "That's not how most women view Slivkoff."

Her eyebrows slowly lifted. "Well, I'm not most women."

He leaned back and let his hot gaze roam down her body, before giving a low, rumbling groan. "Don't I know it."

She smiled at that—one of those soft, beautiful smiles that made him want to throw her over his shoulder and keep her forever—and Eli could feel the fever inside him rising even higher. As if she could tell just how much power she had over him, she flattened her hands against his abs and started pushing him across the room, until his back hit the front wall of the house, to the right of the window. His heart started pounding like a friggin' jackhammer as she smoothed her soft little hands over his heaving chest, the smile on her lips becoming downright wicked as she leaned forward and pressed her parted lips against his left nipple, flicking the pebbled flesh with her tongue. His breath sucked in on a gasp, and her smile got bigger as she trailed her lips lower, her hands reaching for the top button on his jeans.

"Damn it, baby, don't," he groaned, gripping her wrists and drawing them away from his body, his cock so achingly hard he was surprised he hadn't burst through the zipper.

She pulled her head back and looked up at him, that succulent lower lip—the one he wanted to devote hours to tasting—caught in her teeth. "What? You didn't like the way I give head?"

A stunned laugh jerked up from his chest. "Not like it? I friggin' loved it."

"Then why are you stopping me?" she asked, pulling a little at her captured wrists. The wolf in him gave a low, aggressive growl, loving the sight of her caught and trapped, and he mentally shoved the animal back, determined to keep it under tight control. No way was he giving it an inch, knowing it would have its fangs buried deep in her slender throat the first chance it got, and they were nowhere near that point yet. Not when she was still thinking to sever their connection in an act that could very well end her life.

His heart stuttered at the thought, and he forced it from his mind, since it was only going to twist him up inside and lead to another argument. And there would be plenty of time for that later, when she wasn't looking at him in a way she hadn't looked at him since she'd walked back into his life and punched him in the mouth, her eyes soft and warm and full of desire.

Moving his hands from her wrists to her ass, he lifted her off the floor, her body locked against his as her legs wrapped around his waist. "I stopped you because as much as I loved what you did to me," he said in response to her question, turning so that she was the one pressed against the wall, "I didn't get my fix last night."

"Your fix?" she said with a smirk. "That makes you sound like an addict."

"For you I am. That's what I feel like when it comes to your body and the way it tastes."

She snuffled a soft, shy laugh, and he smiled, loving that happy sound on her lips.

"God, I can't get enough of you," he muttered against her mouth, kissing each corner, before touching his tongue to hers. "Not these lips…not any part of you, Rey. I want to lay you down, strip you bare, and lick every beautiful inch of you for hours on end."

"Will I get the chance to do the same to you?" she whispered, curling a hand around the back of his neck.

"God, yes," he breathed out. "As long as you want, baby."

He took her mouth then with every bit of emotion burning inside him, pouring everything he felt for her into the lush, drugging kiss. It was hot and wet and blisteringly perfect, her tender mouth moving against his, and he was in heaven until she suddenly started pushing at his shoulders. The instant he lifted his mouth, she turned her head to the side, and he gnashed his teeth in frustration, his beast surging up inside him, wanting to throw back its head and howl. She was doing it again—pushing him away—and he set her back on her feet before jerking away from her. Lifting his arms, he clasped his hands together behind his neck and clenched his jaw, not trusting what might come out of his mouth at that moment. Then he heard the noises out on the street, and realized *that* was the problem—the reason why she'd pushed him away. "Christ," he scraped out, shaking his head. "I don't believe this. No one's luck can be this shit."

"Eli, what's going on?"

"I don't know," he muttered, lowering his arms as he headed toward the front door. "But I might kill someone if it doesn't turn out to be the end of the world."

Stepping out onto the front porch, he looked over the group of Lycans running down the street, heading toward the woods at the far end. He recognized Charles Decker, the Lycan who'd been leading the scouting party that had helped them during the ambush, at the back of the group.

"What is it?" Carla asked, coming out onto the porch with him.

"Not sure." Sliding her a careful look, he said, "Will you wait for me here if I go talk to Decker?"

"I'm not helpless, Eli," she said with a sigh, shaking her head a little. "I could just go with you and we could find out *together*."

Shoving his hair back from his face, he held her gaze and tried not to sound like an overbearing jackass. "I know you're tough as hell, Rey. But until I know what's happened—what we're dealing with—I'd feel better if you'd stay near the house."

She looked like she wanted to argue—but then her gaze slid away from his and she casually shrugged her shoulders. "You'd better hurry," she murmured, jerking her chin toward the street, which was empty, the Lycans all gathered at the far end now, just at the thick edge of the trees.

With a silent, frustrated string of curses on his lips, he turned away from her and headed down the porch steps, knowing there was little to no chance she was still going to be there when he got back. Hoping like hell for a miracle and that she'd actually stay, even if it was only so they could talk, he jogged down to the end of the street, where Charles was listening to a report from two red-faced scouts. The younger men were hunched over with their hands on their knees, trying to catch their breath as they spoke.

"What's going on?" Eli asked as he joined the group.

Charles jerked his chin toward the trees, and Eli followed behind him as they walked about ten yards or so into the woods, until they reached a small clearing, where another group of scouts was busy discussing what sounded like a possible infringement on Silvercrest pack land by several Whiteclaw soldiers.

"We think it's a false alarm," Charles told him. "Sounds like it might have been a couple of Whiteclaw teenage boys meeting up in the woods with a few Silvercrest girls. But we have to double-check every part of the border now to make sure it wasn't a ploy meant to draw our attention away from something more sinister."

"Have you called in help from the Alley yet?"

With a nod, Charles said, "I just got off the phone with Mason a few minutes ago. He's already mobilized five different scouting groups and put them on it."

"Do you need any help?" he asked, thinking he could call his men up and they could join the scouting parties, but Charles shook his head.

"You and your guys have been going non-stop since you got here," the Lycan said, giving him a friendly clap on the shoulder. "This is one you can sit out for now. But I'm sure Mason will call you if it turns out to be something more than we're expecting."

He talked with the Lycan for a few more moments, satisfied that they had the situation under control, then turned to head back. When he emerged from the woods and looked down the street, toward Eric's house, he wasn't surprised at what he saw. Carla had run. But he didn't think it was because she didn't want him. Climbing up the porch steps, Eli gripped the back of his neck, and struggled to grasp on to the hope that it just might be because she *did*. That she'd run because she was finally starting to see that he was for real. That they had a chance, if she would just make the choice to fight for it.

He might have lost her tonight, but tomorrow was a new day, and he was going to do everything he could to get this right.

If he wanted to land his queen in this backbreaking game of emotional chess being played between them, then he needed to rethink his strategy. And he needed to do it fast, before he ran out of time and she slipped from his grasp. Not just for a day…or a month…or another three miserable godforsaken years.

But forever.

Chapter 12

After spending the day with Wyatt at the training camps, Carla wanted nothing more than to soak her tired body in a hot bath and enjoy a glass of wine. Then she wanted to drag her aching muscles to bed early, and sleep so deeply that she didn't even dream.

Lately, dreams had become a dangerous playing field for her mind. As treacherous a landscape as her memories of the night Eli had forged the tenuous bond that linked them. She kept thinking of how deeply she'd been able to feel his need that night, as well as the pain he felt for what had happened to his sister. His fury for the ones responsible, and for the one he'd killed so viciously. He'd needed comfort. Had needed *her*.

She'd felt that same need pouring from him last night, when he'd taken her into his arms and held her so tightly, his powerful body tremoring with desire. Was she just a fool, doomed to fall prey to a man who had brought her so much pain? Or was the fool the one who turned a blind eye to her own heart? Who never learned to forgive?

She didn't know. All she knew was that she fell further under his spell each time he touched her, which was the last thing that she needed.

Determined to distract her mind from thinking about him, she mentally worked through her day as she made her way on foot through the heavily secured woods, and found her frown only deepening. She and Wyatt, who had been a pain and tried to talk to her about Eli the entire damn day, had worked with a group of women who wanted to learn combat skills that could be used when the Whiteclaw finally mounted their attack—but the female Lycans had been woefully uneducated when it came to even the most basic fighting techniques. She hated the idea of telling them they couldn't fight, and yet, it wasn't right to send them up against soldiers who fought as dirty and deadly as the Whiteclaw did. So there were definitely going to be some hard decisions to make in that regard.

Reaching the edge of the trees, she came into the Alley behind Jeremy and Jillian's cabin, and headed around the side, toward the open glade. The instant she rounded their front porch, she caught sight of a tall male talking to Eric on the far side of the Alley, and immediately recognized those broad shoulders and the dark, shaggy hair as Eli's. She knew there was a part of her that had been hoping he would return, and yet, there was an equally strong part that had been terrified of that very thing.

As if he could feel the sensual weight of her stare, he slowly turned around, found her with his gaze, and started walking toward her. Mere heartbeats later, he was right in front of her, and she could only stare back at him, a little in awe. He looked so gorgeous, standing there with the falling sun burning at his back, his hands shoved deep in his pockets, as if he were afraid he might reach for her if he didn't keep them hidden. "I've moved back into the cabin."

"Why?"

He cocked his head a bit to the side at her simple question, his gaze deep and piercing as he stared down at her, making her feel as though he was trying to read her. Read her more intimately than any other person ever had. Then he quietly said, "Because I don't want to be that far away from you."

She shivered and pressed her trembling lips together, almost afraid of what might slip from her mouth in response.

Lowering his lashes a little, he asked, "So why did you run off last night?"

Squinting against the glimmering rays of sunshine, her face warm from the heat and the intense way he was watching her, she said, "I texted Wyatt and he told me what was going on. I thought I should get back in case I was needed, and I...I guess I just figured that the moment was...um, gone."

"Yeah, I guess it kind of was," he admitted with a slight nod, his dark hair blowing in the breeze. "But I still would have liked to have you there, even if it was just to talk, Rey. Hell, I'd have been happy just to chill in front of the TV with you or to go to sleep. Whatever you would've wanted."

She wet her lips with a nervous flick of her tongue, her pulse rushing. "I...I should have said goodbye."

He lifted his hand, tucking a windblown strand of her hair behind her ear, but didn't say anything.

"Eli, I...I know we need to talk. About a lot of things. But I'm exhausted. I...I didn't sleep much last night, after

I left you, and it's been a long day. Do we have to do this now?"

"No," he said in that low, delicious voice that always made her melt, his blue eyes locked on her so tightly she couldn't have looked away from him to save her life. "I just wanted to tell you that I'll do it."

"What?" she mouthed, blinking up at him in shock. It was the last thing that she'd expected him to say, and though he'd been vague, she knew *exactly* what he was talking about.

His eyes gleamed. "If Jillian promises to do every-thing in her power to make it safe for you, and you're still sure that it's what you want, then after the battle, I'll do it. I'll cut you loose."

She drew an unsteady breath, amazed at the burning sensation in her chest, as if he'd just stabbed her there with a lethal blade. If he truly felt like he'd *claimed* to feel about her, why would he give in? Did this mean she'd been right? Or that she'd merely succeeded in destroying something that should have been unbelievably beautiful?

Knowing she needed to say something, she somehow managed to murmur, "Th-thank you."

"Please, don't do that." His voice was still soft, but with a hard edge of raw emotion that made her breath freeze in her lungs. "It's ripping my goddamn heart out, Rey. So whatever you do, don't thank me."

She swallowed, unsure of what to do as she watched him shove one of those big hands back through his di-sheveled hair. Then he gave a hard sigh and braced both his hands on his lean hips as he turned his head, staring off to the side, into the distant line of trees.

Forcing the words up from the burning depths of her chest, she finally managed to ask, "What changed your mind?"

He took a deep breath, then slowly let it out. "If it's what you want, I don't want to disappoint you. Not again. I've already done enough of that to last a lifetime."

She licked her lips again, unable to tell if she was flushed or pale, her body both hot and cold at the same time. "Thank you," she repeated, even though he'd asked her not to, and hating the way the words tasted on her tongue. Or maybe she simply hated what she was thanking him for.

But I can't complain, can I? Not when I'm the one who asked for this.

Bringing his head forward again, he trapped her in the place where she stood with nothing more than a look. "But you should know I'm staying close."

She blinked, understanding there was a hell of a lot more to those words than their surface value. "What do you mean?"

His hooded gaze burned with primal, visceral determination. "I'll do it. But only on the grounds that until this thing is over, I'm your shadow."

Blinking up at him, she said, "I...I can live with that."

He seemed a little surprised, and maybe even wary, that she'd agreed without an argument. But it didn't stop him from saying, "There's more."

She nodded, waiting, unable to look away.

Crossing his arms over his chest, he looked her right in the eye, and said, "You should know up front that I'm going to do everything in my power to change your mind. About...about a lot of things."

Eli watched the slight shiver that moved over Carla's slender frame, her soft lips parting on a gasp, but she didn't say anything. Her throat worked as she swallowed again, then gave him a nearly imperceptible nod. He'd been expecting a hell of an argument when he put those words out there, and couldn't help but breathe a sigh of relief that she wasn't going to get into it with him now.

From the dark smudges under her eyes, he could see how tired she was. He felt the same, the previous night spent lying on Eric's sofa and staring up at the ceiling, lost in his thoughts. He hadn't been able to shake the tension grinding through his muscles ever since she'd left him, but it was currently easing with each second that passed by. Now that he was with her, he could finally take a deep breath again, and he savored the way her scent filled his lungs, unable to get enough of it, the heat only making it more wild and lush.

Lowering his arms to his sides, he held her gaze as he asked, "Will you let me help you tonight?"

She slid him a wary look. "Help me how?"

"You're just as beautiful as you always are," he murmured, while a wry grin tugged at the corner of his mouth. "But, honey, you look about ready to fall on your face any second now. Let me bring you back to my cabin."

She looked stunned, and more than a little tempted. But her tone was still cautious as she said, "And do what?"

He pushed his hands in his pockets again and tried like hell to look innocent, when he was fairly positive he'd never looked that way a day in his life. "Run you a bath. Feed you dinner. I'll pamper you all night long if you'll let me. I just want to spend time with you, Rey."

"Won't Kyle be there?"

He shook his head. "He's gone until tomorrow morning. He and Lev have headed into Virginia to meet up with one of our East Coast suppliers about securing another batch of weapons."

Aside from the scare last night, things had been strangely quiet in regards to the Whiteclaw—especially considering the raids they'd made against their drugs and their weapons—and Eli and the others couldn't help but assume that things were going to happen sooner rather than later.

He could tell she was torn about what to do, but he gave her the time to come to the decision on her own, wanting her to choose him tonight over being alone. *Needing* her to do that.

"All right," she finally murmured, the soft words making him smile.

"No need to look so wary, Rey. I'll be golden, I promise. Scout's honor."

She snuffled a quiet laugh under her breath. "I know damn well you were never a scout."

Eli grinned. "Wasn't for lack of trying. One of my friend's dads put together a troop when we were little, thinking it would be good for us, and he ended up kicking me out. Said I wasn't good at playing with others."

She shook her head as she smirked. "I'll bet."

"Hey, be nice. I was crushed. They got to go on all these kickass fieldtrips to places like DC and the beach, while I was left at home, cutting the grass."

Her eyes glinted with humor, and maybe even a little bit of sadness. "Aw. Now I *am* feeling sorry for you. Cutting grass sucks."

He laughed, then jerked his chin toward the cabin he and Kyle were sharing. "Come on. I promised you some pampering."

True to his word, Eli told her to sit on his bed and wait while he ran her a hot, steaming bath. The cabin had been furnished and stocked when they'd arrived, and he was glad to find some aromatherapy bath gel under the sink, a thick foam building up on the surface of the water as he poured a healthy amount under the tap.

"It's all yours," he told her when he came back into the bedroom, catching her holding one of his worn T-shirts against her upper chest. He arched a brow at her, and she blushed at being caught with his shirt so close to her face, as if she'd been sniffing it before he'd come in, searching for his scent.

Coughing to clear the lump of lust in his throat, he rubbed the back of his neck and said, "I'll just go, um, get some food on while you relax in your bath." Then he got the hell out of there, not trusting himself to stay and watch her undress, knowing it would be too much for him and shatter his control. And he was determined to do this right. To make it through one night with her, just enjoying her company, without everything falling apart on them.

He wasn't much of a cook, but he put some frozen pizzas into the oven while she took her bath, doing his best to keep his mind on his task…and not on what she looked like in all those bubbles, her beautiful body slick and wet and warm.

"Get a grip, jackass," he muttered under his breath. "It's gonna be a long night. You can't screw this up."

She grinned when she came into the kitchen dressed in one of his big T-shirts and saw the freshly baked pizzas he'd just set out on the table, between the two place settings he'd put together. A flush covered her smooth cheeks as she took a seat at the table, and he would have given anything to know if she was just warm from the bath, or if her reaction had something to do with the hungry sideways glances she kept stealing at his bare chest. The oven had made the kitchen warm, and he'd ditched his shirt, boots and socks in an attempt to cool off a little.

"You still like pizza, right?" he asked, forcing himself not to stare at the way his shirt had ridden up on her bare thighs when she'd sat down. Christ, was she wearing anything underneath it? He stole a quick peek at her chest and had to choke back a low, appreciative growl at the sight of her hard little nipples pressing against the soft cotton. Yeah, definitely no bra.

How the hell am I going to make it through this without lunging across the table and ripping that shirt right off her?

Before he could come up with an answer, she said, "I love it."

Sounding more than a little distracted, he asked, "What?"

She tucked her damp hair behind her ears, looking so much like the girl he'd first talked to all those years ago. "You asked if I still like pizza, and I said that I love it."

"Ah, right. Good," he rumbled, turning toward the fridge. He took two bottles of beer out, twisted the caps off, and placed them on the table as he sat down.

"So if Kyle's with Lev," she said, grabbing one of the slices of pepperoni and cheese and putting it on her plate, "where are the other guys tonight?"

He took three slices of the spicy beef, saying, "They're up in Shadow Peak with Brody and Cian, double checking all the security checkpoints we have set up around the town."

She took a sip of her beer, then picked up her pizza, her cheeks still flushed with that lovely warmth that made him want to kiss her until she forgot her own name. "They've been awesome at helping," she murmured. "You all have. I don't know what we would have done without you."

"Yeah, they're a good bunch of guys."

She finished chewing the bite she'd taken, then said, "You know, you never have told me how you all ended up together."

Carla watched as he finished off his first slice, then washed it down with a hefty swallow of beer. When he set the bottle back down on the table, he leaned back in his chair and locked his beautiful gaze with hers. "When I left, I didn't have a friggin' clue what to do or where to go. I was sitting in this dive bar down in Wesley, getting drunk, when this news program came on the TV, talking about how skilled soldiers could make a lot of money working as mercenaries down in South America." His lips twitched with a wry grin. "It was one of those journalistic exposés meant to showcase how dangerous the area was becoming, but all I saw was an opportunity. So I bought a plane ticket and headed down."

Grabbing the beer again, he tilted the bottle up to his lips, then went on with his story while she listened and ate. "And they were right about the money, as well as the danger. But I was feeling so reckless at that point that I just didn't care. I was on my third job when I ran into Kyle, Sam and James. They'd had some trouble with their packs and had decided to do the same thing I'd done. So we started working together, and a month later, we'd recruited Lev, who was living in Colombia at the time. The five of us have been working together ever since."

"You got lucky, all of you, to find each other the way that you did."

Fiddling with the label on his bottle, he said, "Yeah, I've never really thought about it like that, but I guess you're right." He took a deep breath, then slowly let it out as he lifted his gaze back to hers. "If I had to be away from here, I was damn lucky to have those guys watching my back."

"They look up to you."

"Don't know why," he drawled, setting the bottle down and reaching for another slice of pizza. "I think it's just that I'm the oldest."

"No. You're a natural leader, Eli. You always have been. You just never had a chance to do anything about it when you were here before."

He shrugged, then took a bite of his pizza, looking uncomfortable with the praise as he chewed.

"So you and the guys started your new life as mercs," she murmured, before taking another sip of her beer. "Was it hard?"

"Hell, yeah," he said with a grin. "But there were times when we made damn good money at it. And then, if it was something we believed needed to be done, there were times when we didn't make a penny."

"So I was right!" She smirked in response to his curious look. "You know, the whole Merry Men thing. I had you pegged!"

He arched a brow. "You got a thing about men in tights, Rey?"

"Maybe," she murmured, teasing him. She didn't really, though she was fairly certain she'd find Eli hot in *anything* he wore, even if it was hosiery.

They shared a quiet laugh, then settled into a comfortable silence while they finished off the pizza, and he went to the fridge to get them both another beer. When he sat back down, twisted the cap off her bottle, and handed it to her, she leaned back in her chair and said, "So the guys...they're different, aren't they? I mean, I sense that they're Lycans. But...there's more, isn't there?"

He leaned back and tilted his bottle to his lips, then

gave a rough sigh. Holding her gaze, he said, "I don't ever want to keep anything from you, Rey, but I'm afraid that's not my secret to tell."

She nodded, respecting that, since it meant he was a good friend. After a moment, she asked, "Were you ever close to dying? I mean, when you were out on a job?"

"Just once. Last year. We got caught up in a nasty turf war between two rival cartels, and I still can't believe we made it out alive. James and Sam took bullets in the arms and legs, and I got caught with a god-awful machete blade across my back."

She lurched forward in her seat so quickly she nearly spilled her beer all over the place. "Jesus Christ, Eli. Let me see."

He pushed back from the table and turned in his chair, showing her the left side of his back. She blinked, unable to believe she hadn't noticed it before, the long, raised scar cutting from the top of his shoulder blade down to the lower edge of his ribs. In that heartbreaking moment, she realized just how lucky she was to have found him in that shitty Texas bar that night. He could have so easily been lost to her over the past three years. Stolen away from her before she ever had the chance to get to know him again…or fall into love and lust with him even deeper than she'd been before.

There were some things she wasn't willing to leave this world without experiencing, and having this man, taking him into her body again and feeling him become a part of her, was one of them.

He watched her with a sharp, heavy-lidded gaze as she pushed her chair back and moved to her feet, coming around the side of the table. When she knelt on the floor beside him, he inhaled with a sharp breath that turned into a raw, guttural growl the instant she leaned forward and pressed a tender kiss against the middle of the scar. "Eli?" she whispered against his hot skin.

"Yeah?" he grated, his deep voice rough and low and deliciously husky.

She pressed her lips an inch higher. "Take me to bed?"

He went so still he wasn't even breathing. "You mean that?"

"Yes," she told him, leaning back and looking up at his hard, beautiful face. "In fact, I don't think I've ever meant anything more."

Credit Union
Pembroke
(910) 521-8881
There is a Difference!

CD 04/10/2015 17:23
PD 04/10/2015 00126 P002

Deposit   **$183.88**
CHK XXXXXXXXXXXXX8299

Current Balance   1,397.67

489

Chapter 13

The next thing Carla knew, she was in Eli's arms and his long legs were rapidly covering the distance between the kitchen and the bedroom. He kicked the bedroom door shut behind him, then quickly walked to the bed and practically tossed her into the center. She bounced with a startled gasp, glaring when she caught sight of his wicked grin. Then she realized his hot gaze had moved lower, to where her legs had parted and his shirt had ridden up, the pink, already slick folds between her legs completely exposed.

"Jesus," he rasped, his eyes gleaming with a hot, hungry glow as he started to reach for her.

"No, wait!" she blurted, propping herself up on her elbows. "If this is gonna happen, I want to see you. All of you, Eli. I want to watch you get naked for me."

His eyes widened a bit with surprise. "You want to watch me strip?"

When she bit her lower lip and nodded, he said, "I will if you will."

She slowly arched her brows as she drew her knees up, but didn't pull them together, leaving herself open to him. "I think you're already seeing everything there is to see."

The slow, provocative smile that curved his mouth was almost too beautiful to be real. "Lose the shirt, Rey. I don't want a single thing covering you but me."

Breathless with lust, she sat up and drew the shirt over her head, tossing it to the foot of the bed. Her breasts felt heavy and full, her nipples almost painfully tight, and she loved the way he consumed her with that searing, heavy-lidded gaze as he pulled in a deep, ragged breath of air.

"God, that's beautiful," he groaned, his breath hissing through his teeth as he exhaled.

She jerked her chin at him. "Lose the jeans, Eli."

When he bit his lower lip and undid his top button, revealing more of the taut, hair-dusted skin of his abdomen, it was so freaking sexy she almost forgot how to breathe. She watched with rapt attention as he slowly undid the fly and started shoving the jeans down to his thighs, each glimpse of skin making it obvious he wasn't wearing anything underneath. He shot her a smoldering look through his lashes as he pushed the jeans completely off, kicking them free. Then he stood before her completely bare, with his hands fisted at his sides, his chest rising and falling with each of his harsh, heavy breaths.

Carla had never had the chance to visually soak him in and look her fill before, so she was doing it now. "Don't move," she whispered, holding up her hand when he would have drawn nearer. "Stand still. Let me look at you."

A hard tremor shot through him, and he tightened his fists until thick veins popped up beneath his skin on the

backs of his wrists and his masculine forearms. "I'll...
try," he muttered in a tone so low and rough it made her
smile.

Catching her lower lip in her teeth, she swept her
greedy gaze over him, undone by the broad shoulders
and hard chest. The muscular arms and legs, and the
ridged, mouthwatering abdomen. The dark trail of hair
that swirled around his navel, then led down to that thick,
beautiful, brutal-looking cock...and below that, the dusky
testicles, heavy and weighted, drawn tight with need. He
made a low, thick sound as she stared at them, her hot
gaze sliding up again, to the broad root nestled in that
dark, curling hair. She followed every heavy inch of his
fully erect shaft, the width and length of him enough to
make her wonder how he ever managed to get it inside
a woman.

Lifting her gaze back to his dark, scorching one, she
said, "Okay, you can move now," and he was on her before she could so much as gasp, his powerful body pushing her back to the bed. His head lowered over her full
breasts, his big hands holding them up in offering, and
he breathed on one pink, swollen tip, the warmth of his
breath making her crazy.

"I've needed these in my mouth again so badly," he
groaned, squeezing her breasts together, her nipples so
pink they were almost red. With a guttural sound rumbling up from his chest, he closed his mouth over one,
and the blistering heat and wetness, the hungry strokes of
his tongue, it all made her cry out from an intense wave
of pleasure. She was holding his shaggy hair so tightly
it had to hurt, pulling him even harder against her, while
his mouth did things to her nipple that could all too easily make her orgasm. Just from his mouth on her breast,
which seemed so...impossible.

She trembled, trying to think…to reason, but she knew she couldn't blame her stunning reaction on the partial bond that they shared. Yes, it was there, pulsing and throbbing between them like a living, breathing thing, but there was *more* to it than that. More emotion…more need. Was this what the other couples in the Alley felt? If so, she was amazed they ever managed to crawl out of bed and get anything done.

When he pushed her legs wider with his knee and settled in the cradle of her thighs, rubbing that hot, textured shaft against the sensitive folds of her sex, he lifted his head, looked her right in the eye, and quietly asked, "Are you giving in because you think it will get rid of me?"

"Do you really think that?" she murmured, sinking her nails into his shoulders as she pulled him against her, wanting to feel his weight pressing down on her, surrounding her.

"No," he rasped, bracing himself on his elbows, "but I'd take you anyway. I'll take you any way I can—*oh, hell*."

Her eyes went wide. "What? What's wrong?"

"I don't have any condoms," he groaned, closing his eyes as he winced. "They're still in my bag, and I took it up to town with me. Damn thing is still out in the truck."

A frown started to work its way onto her mouth. "You were carrying around condoms?"

His eyes snapped open at her tone, and he shook his head once, hard. "For *you*. It's a new pack, Rey. Hasn't even been opened yet."

Her breath whooshed out of her lungs in a sharp burst of relief, and he shook his head a little again as he smirked, reading her like an open book.

"Wait right here for me, okay?" he whispered, leaning down and pressing a tender kiss to her lips. "I'll run out to the truck and get them."

"You don't have to," she said, running her fingers through his thick hair. "I'm covered as far as birth control goes. So we're, um, good. You know, if you want to…to just—"

"Hell, yes, I want to," he said so forcefully it made her dissolve into a girlish burst of giggles.

Eli closed his eyes again, taking a moment to simply soak in that beautiful sound. God, he hadn't heard her laugh nearly enough in the time that he'd known her, and he vowed to himself then and there that if she would just take a chance on him, he'd spend the rest of his life doing everything in his power to make her happy. To make her smile and laugh just like this.

But right now, he needed to make her moan.

Unable to wait a second longer, he opened his eyes and reached down, positioning the head of his rigid shaft at her warm, tender entrance. Then he started to push inside, thinking he'd be able to sink in all the way, so desperate to feel her clasping him in her wet heat that he was shaking with the need. But he froze almost immediately, his body caught in the hold of a terrible tension.

"What's wrong?" she gasped, gripping his biceps as she blinked up at him.

"I don't want to hurt you," he said in a raw voice, struggling so hard to keep control that he could barely get the words out. "Christ. You're *tighter* than a virgin, Rey."

The color in her face started to get brighter, and she wet her lips with a nervous swipe of her tongue. "It's, um, been…a long time for me. You know…other than the one time we were together."

He sucked in a sharp breath, his gaze locked tight on hers. "How long?"

She turned pink, her breaths quickening as she lowered her heavy gaze to his chin and whispered, "Since before that first night when we talked six years ago. The night you helped me with Nicole."

His eyes shot wide, his pulse rocketing.

Voice as strained as her expression, she said, "I… couldn't. There was no one…no one who…" The words trailed off, and she lifted her troubled gaze back to his. "You obviously didn't have the same problem."

No, he'd tried for months after that night to screw her out of his system with the pack females who were always ready to welcome him between their thighs. But he'd felt nothing with them. Not a goddamn thing.

"It didn't work. I might have gone to bed with those other women…but I didn't feel them, Rey. Didn't see them." He dropped his forehead against hers, and closed his eyes, determined to keep his focus for the moment on his words and not on how incredible she felt, her plush sheath holding the first few inches of his cock in a way that promised to blow his friggin' mind when he was buried deep inside her. Gritting his teeth, he said, "I stopped sleeping around when I finally accepted that it didn't matter a damn to me, who was under me. All I could see or hear or think about was you. I never touched another pack female from that night on."

"When was that?" she asked in a voice so soft he could barely hear her.

He pulled in a deep breath, and forced himself to pull his head back and look her in the eye as he said, "Nine months before I left."

She stiffened beneath him, the tips of her nails digging into his skin a little in her surprise. "And while you were gone?" she asked huskily.

Brushing his lips against her soft ones, he whispered, "You know the answer to that already."

"Eli, I—"

He cut her off, saying, "I'll answer any damn question you want, Rey. Just later, *please*." A trickle of sweat slipped down the side of his face, his muscles trembling under his hot skin as he fought to keep still and not pound himself into her, deep and hard and thick. "Because if I don't get inside you soon, I'm pretty sure my heart is gonna stop."

"You're the one who quit moving." Her grip on his shoulders gentled, a deep groan vibrating in his chest when she swept those soft fingertips down his rigid arms, his biceps bulging beneath his skin. "I didn't ask you to."

"Trying. To be. Considerate here," he bit out between his rough breaths, unable to hold back any longer. His hips rolled forward, pushing him another inch deeper into that hot, slick heaven, and he swore under his breath at how incredible it felt, her soft gasp making him need to thrust and thrust, working against her resistance until he'd hit the end of her. "And it isn't easy," he growled, fisting the sheets in his hands as he shook the sweat from his eyes, "seeing as how I was ready to lose it the second I got inside you."

She suddenly pushed against his shoulders, her legs moving against his, and the next thing he knew he was on his back and she was straddling him, pushing down on him with steady pressure, her eyes dark and hot as she bit her lip, and he went deep...*deeper,* as she took him inch by inch, until not even a sliver of space existed between them. She made a soft, provocative sound that was insanely sexy, the look on her face as she leaned forward and braced her hands against his chest, her head back, nearly making him come then and there.

"Oh, Christ," he groaned, holding her hips in a death grip. "You're gonna turn me inside out, aren't you?"

She stared down at him, her beautiful mouth curving with a small, sensual smile. "Could I?"

"You could do anything you wanted. Any damn thing you wanted, and I'd be at your mercy."

With that gorgeous smile still on her lips, she held his blistering gaze and started to move, the voluptuous pulse of her hips as she rose and fell on him so good he didn't know how he'd ever survived without it. Her mouthwatering scent was rising with the heat of her beautiful little body, her lithe muscles working beneath her silky skin as she broke him down with pleasure, taking him apart piece by piece. He felt his gums burn with heat as his fangs started to drop, his beast prowling beneath his surface. His knees drew up as his back arched off the bed, his grip on her hips so tight he worried he would leave marks, and he gnashed his teeth, determined to keep from ruining the best goddamn moment of his life.

"You're destroying me," he ground out, falling so completely into her shimmering gaze he didn't think he would ever climb back out again. "I don't know how much longer I can hold myself back, Rey."

She gave a soft siren's laugh that only made his blood pump harder. "Then just let go."

"You're already so swollen, and I don't want to make it worse. Don't want to make you...Damn it, I want you to *love* it with me, Rey." His voice was so guttural it barely sounded human. "I want you coming back for *more*, addicted to it. I don't want to hurt you."

"You won't. You won't hurt me," she breathed out,

leaning over him and nipping his lower lip with her teeth. "I'm not that breakable, Eli."

He growled, undone, swiftly rolling until he had her trapped beneath him again, his body buried hard and thick inside her. With his damp face right over hers, he watched her eyes glitter with a dark, possessive, primitive hunger that matched his own as he drew back and then gave her a hard, hammering thrust that shoved him even deeper than he'd been before. He loved the way she held him so tightly, but he needed her soft and melting with pleasure if he wanted to be able to ride her the way he craved. And God only knew he could never get enough of her mouthwatering taste. So he forced himself to pull out, knelt between her sprawled thighs, and lifted her hips as he lowered his head between her legs.

She gasped as he shoved his face against her drenched flesh, eating at her plump sex with all the raw, gnawing hunger that was burning inside him. She was so soft and sweet and deliciously slick, the tight clench of her sheath around his tongue as it plunged inside her making him growl like an animal. He heard a throaty cry break from her throat as she crashed, coming so hard he could feel the breathtaking power of the climax as it tore through her. He pressed his face even harder against her as she pulsed and quivered, the sounds she made driving him wild, while he went at her like a man who'd been starved for her taste for a lifetime, until he couldn't wait a moment more.

"Again," he growled, bracing himself on his arms and slamming his cock inside her so hard it drove her up the bed. "I need you to come again, Rey. I need to feel it on me."

She gripped his bunched shoulders and arched beneath him, pressing her breasts against his sweat-covered chest as he came down over her and started thrusting in hard, powerful lunges that were getting faster...and faster, taking her the way he'd been dying to for so many heart-breaking years.

"Oh, God, Eli. I'm there!" she cried, her silky sex clutching him like a hot, wet mouth, milking him as she came.

"That's it," he growled, throwing his head back as his own release thundered through him with the stunning force of a storm, completely destroying him as he pulsed and pulsed, pouring himself inside her until he started to wonder if it was ever going to end. Not that he wanted it to. What he wanted was to keep thrusting inside her while he buried his face against the smooth, tender curve of her shoulder, but he didn't dare, knowing he couldn't risk letting his fangs get anywhere close to her throat.

"Damn, baby, I think you killed me," he groaned, when he could finally find his voice again. His hips were still gently rocking against hers, his arms shaking as he hung his head forward, trying to catch his breath.

"Mmm...sorry about that," she practically purred, and he felt a grin tugging at the corner of his mouth. She sounded like a woman who'd been well and thoroughly taken, and he knew there was only one thing that could have made it better. Something he hoped like hell they were closer to now that they'd shared something so incredible.

"Don't ever be sorry," he told her, finally lowering his mouth so that he could kiss her soft, pink lips as he carefully pulled himself from her tight clasp. "I'll happily die again and again if it means getting more of this."

Touching her as gently as he could, he lifted her bone-less body up higher on the bed, until her head was resting on the pillows, then moved onto his side and reached down for the quilt, pulling it over her.

"You don't want more now?" she asked, looking a little surprised. And maybe even a bit disappointed.

"I *always* want you, Rey. But I can wait," he told her, reaching out and pushing her hair back from her flushed face. "I don't want to make you too sore."

She smirked up at him. "You're not worried about making me sore, just not *too* sore?"

"Hey, I'm a guy," he said huskily, leaning down again and brushing his lips across her smiling ones. "I love the thought of you walking around tomorrow, feeling how hard I took you every time you take a step."

"Barbarian," she teased, making him grin as she playfully smacked him on the shoulder.

Your barbarian, he thought. *Always yours…*

He could feel his body stirring, already hardening again, and knew he needed to put some space between them while he still could. Rolling into a sitting position on the far side of the bed, he grabbed a pillow and the afghan that was tangled up in the bottom of the quilt, then laid them on the floor, switched off the bedside light, and forced himself to lie down. A second later, her beautiful face peeked over the edge of the mattress, her bright eyes shining with laughter in the silvery wash of moonlight streaming in through the window. "You got something against the bed? Or is it me?"

Putting his hands behind his head so he wouldn't be tempted to reach up and grab her, pulling her down there to join him, he said, "I'm not sleeping in a bed with you until things between us are completely settled."

Her golden hair fell over the side of the mattress as she cocked her head a bit to the side, her expression curious. "Why?"

Because he was afraid that he would wake up, hazy with sleep, and reach for her. His need for her was so intense that he didn't trust what he would do in those foggy moments of consciousness. Sink his fangs into her and complete the bond, once and for all? It was so damn tempting, and yet, he knew it would be the kiss of death for any chances they might have of a future together, if he did it before she was ready.

Watching her carefully, he said, "When you're ready to give me what I want, you won't be able to keep me from sleeping beside you."

She blinked, and he could see the exact moment when she understood what he was saying. With a quick breath, and a flick of her tongue over her lower lip, she said, "You don't trust yourself, do you? You don't trust yourself not to bite me."

"I've told you what I want, Rey."

He had…and more than once. But as she stared down at him with that soft, shell-shocked expression on her lovely face, the look in her eyes a mesmerizing blend of emotions, Eli realized that for the first time, the little Runner was *finally* starting to believe that he meant it.

Chapter 14

God, I've been such a fool.

That was the painful, embarrassing thought that kept spinning its way through Carla's head as she sat in Mason and Torrance's living room the following morning, trying to listen to the plans being made. She'd meant to stay smart and focused on what was good for her—but her lust and lovesick heart had finally gotten the better of her, and now her disappointment was crushing.

Was what happened between us all for this? Was he just trying to get things to work out the way he wanted them to? To make me so crazy over him, I'd do whatever he wanted?

As if he knew she'd be feeling skittish after waking in his bed, Eli had already left the cabin by the time she'd blinked her eyes open, a little stunned to realize what she'd done. That she'd given in to her desire and made love to him. And it had definitely been making love.

She'd had sex before, and while nice, it didn't come anywhere close to what had taken place between her and the manipulative, gorgeous, too-freaking-sexy-for-his-own-good alpha.

Had she honestly thought she had a good idea of what truly emotional, hunger-driven mating would be like? Hah! She hadn't had a clue.

She didn't know if all Lycan males were like that, like *him*. He was the only one she'd ever allowed to get close to her in a physical way—the only one she'd ever wanted. But she'd have been lying through her teeth if she'd said she hadn't loved it. His strength. His aggression. The raw, primal savagery of his sexual hunger. A hunger he kept telling her was only for her. For her…and no other. And, God, how badly she'd wanted to believe him.

But now, after what he'd just said, and in front of everyone? She shook her head, wondering if she would always be nothing more than a fool when it came to this man.

When she'd climbed out of his bed, terrified by the warm glow of happiness burning in the center of her chest, she'd been desperate for the time to stand beneath a hot shower and make sense of her buzzing, complicated emotions, but there hadn't been any. Dressing in her clothes from the day before, she'd hurried over to Wyatt and Elise's, only to have her partner catch her coming in through the door. Instead of teasing her about her night out, he'd told her they were late for a meeting at Mason's. The next thing she knew, she was standing in a roomful of friends, her emotions still on edge. And the sight of Eli standing on the other side of the room had made her heart pound so hard that it hurt. He'd looked up, locking that intense, smoldering gaze on her face, and though the set of his mouth had been a little grim, it was still so beautiful that she'd wanted to kiss him until he was all she could taste and hear and see. She'd flushed, and he'd just kept staring, the fiend, even when everyone had started to notice.

She'd already known that their night together wouldn't be a secret. That kind of news traveled fast in the Alley, but that didn't mean he'd had to be so blatant about it. The way he'd stared at her—so hard and possessive—had made his thoughts clear to everyone around them, and she'd felt herself blushing all the way to the roots of her hair.

When she'd caught Wyatt smirking at her, she'd stomped on his toes with her booted foot, enjoying the low grunt of pain that'd slipped past his lips. "You're mean," he'd grumbled.

"Don't forget it," she'd muttered in response, determined not to look in Eli's direction again. But it hadn't mattered. She'd still felt the weight of his searing, possessive gaze on her, and damn it, it'd felt good. So perfect and right that she couldn't help remembering the dream she'd had during the night, when she'd been cuddled up in his sheets, his mouthwatering scent surrounding her.

She'd dreamed about their wedding day, of all things. Of a day when they would stand before their family and friends and pledge their love to one another. A day she'd been an idiot to even think about, considering the words that had left his lips when he'd looked at Mason a moment ago and said, "Before we get started, I want to say what I'm sure a lot of you are thinking, but haven't felt right about bringing up. So I'm doing it now. I know we need as many bodies going into battle as we can get, but I feel pretty strongly about the fact that the women shouldn't fight. Not just the ones who are only just learning some combat skills, but *any* of them. After seeing firsthand

what the Whiteclaw are capable of, it's just too dangerous." Without looking at her, he'd crossed his arms over
his chest and gruffly added, "And before anyone argues
that there are women in this room who are more than
capable of going into battle, that might be. But it still
doesn't mean that they should."

Her jaw had dropped as she'd stared at him, unable
to believe those words had actually just come from his
mouth. And she was so staggered by them, her heart feeling like it was being crushed in her chest, that it'd taken
her a moment to realize the meeting was still going on
around her.

Fighting hard to concentrate, she narrowed her burning gaze on Mason, and tried to listen. He was saying
something about how they needed to be prepared for the
fact that some of the Whiteclaw might have their own
supplies of the "super soldier" drugs, which they would
undoubtedly be saving for the attack, but she was only
half hearing him. The majority of her brain was still focused on what Eli had said, and what it meant for them.
He'd never made it a secret, how he felt about her job.
Now his words had confirmed that he didn't want her
fighting alongside the men she'd been fighting beside her
entire adult life, which was exactly where she belonged.

If he couldn't see that, then he didn't actually know
her at all. So where the hell did that leave them?

It was obvious that important plans were being made,
but she didn't have a clue what they were, unable to get
past the shock of hearing Eli say what he had in front of
everyone. In front of the men she'd worked with for so
long. She couldn't have been more insulted if he'd stood
there and told them all that he thought she was a pathetic
weakling who couldn't be trusted to do her job. Because
that's what it'd felt like, and she felt so betrayed she was

terrified she was going to burst into tears before she could get out of there.

The instant Mason called an end to the meeting, she shoved past Wyatt, who was trying to say something to her, and ran like she had the devil on her ass. It took her only moments to reach Wyatt and El's cabin, and she stormed through the living room, down the hall, ready to slam the door behind her when she reached the guest room—only to find that Eli was right behind her as she turned.

"Get out!" she snarled, shoving hard at his chest as she tried to push him back into the hallway. But the bastard didn't budge.

"I'm not going anywhere until we've talked," he said in a low, calm tone that grated on her nerves so badly she wanted to scream. Spinning away from him, she paced at the foot of the bed, breathing hard and fast, glaring at him from the corner of her eye as he shut the door, then leaned back against it, watching her with a hooded, cautious gaze.

Finally, she stopped pacing and braced her hands on her hips as she turned to face him. "What the hell was that in there?" she demanded, flinging the words at him.

Crossing his arms over his chest, he worked his jaw a few times before he answered the question. "I was only saying what I thought needed to be said."

"Ohmygod! Are you honestly that stupid?" she seethed, so angry she wanted to cry. But she was going to be damned before she spilled any more tears in front of him. "Or maybe you're just too blind to see what an ass you're being. Is that it?"

His lips pressed together in a hard, grim line, but his eyes gave him away. He didn't regret what he'd said. Not even a little. He actually believed that crap!

Breathing in rough, uneven bursts, she said, "You're always trying to protect me. But guess what? I don't need your protection, Eli. What I've always needed was your love. I needed you to stand by me. To fight for me. And you didn't. You ran. You didn't stand by me before, and you're *still* not standing by me. So I'm done!"

Eyes burning with a raw, molten gleam, he growled, "I did love you, damn it."

She shook her head. "If that's true, then you didn't love me enough."

"Christ, woman. I've said I'm sorry for leaving so many times," he ground out, lowering his arms to his sides as he pushed away from the door. "I've told you that I'm more in love with you now than ever, and I already loved you more than I ever imagined was possible. What more do you want from me, Rey?"

"I want something I can obviously never have!" she shouted, completely losing control. Of everything. Her emotions. Her fears. The entire goddamn situation. "So I'll take being free, instead. I want to tear you out!"

He took another step forward, and a muscle started to pulse in his cheek with a rhythmic, telling tic. "You didn't feel like that last night."

"That was sex," she snapped. "You of all people should know the difference."

"I know it was the best, most incredible sex I've ever had," he shot back, and she could see his wolf burning in his eyes, the icy blue now as dark and turbulent as a storm. "There isn't even a close second."

She glared, thinking he might literally drive her mad.

"I know I want it again. I haven't—" He broke off, seeming to struggle with what to say, then growled, "I'm—not—done. I'll *never* be done."

Fighting the urge to stomp her foot like a child, she

screamed, "God, Eli! You can make me so angry! No one's ever made me as angry as you do." She lifted her arms, pressing the insides of her wrists to her temples, her voice breaking with emotion. "I *hate* it. Hate feeling like that about you, but you need to listen to me. Please. Just listen." Pressing one of her hands over her pounding heart, she said, "I *love* what I do. It's not just a job to me. It's a part of who I am, and that's never going to change. If you loved me like you say you do, then you would understand that. Which means more than the fact that you don't love me. You don't even *know* me."

"That's not true."

"Are you saying you wouldn't want me to quit? That if we completed the bond, you'd be supportive of what I do?"

He opened his mouth, then snapped it shut again, his nostrils flaring as he pulled in a deep breath. Then he muttered, "I need to go and meet with Elliot and Max. In a few hours, we'll know whether or not it's a go tonight."

"That soon?" she gasped.

His dark brows drew together in a scowl. "Weren't you listening at the meeting?"

She shook her head. "No. I was too upset."

His scowl deepened, and he said, "If Max and Elliot have gotten the rumor mill going at full speed, then it looks like we'll be putting the plan into action not long after sundown."

She nodded, thinking that part of the mercs' plan was brilliant. In fact, the entire plan was genius. And who better to spread gossip than a bunch of gabbing teenage girls who were still in contact with other Whiteclaw teens? But how the hell had she managed not to hear that they might be going to war in a mere matter of hours?

"There must be a thousand things to do," she said distractedly, her thoughts spinning as she lowered her gaze. And there clearly wasn't any time for anger or arguments at the moment. Not when there was so much to get done and to organize. And despite what anyone else might say or think, she *was* going to be in that town fighting beside her Bloodrunning brothers. It would take more than Eli Drake to stop her. It'd take a freaking act of God, and even then she'd fight tooth and nail to make sure she was there when she was needed. "We can finish this later," she added, careful to keep her expression neutral as she lifted her gaze back to his. "You need to go, and I should go and find Wyatt."

Instead of turning and leaving, he stepped even closer, locking her in his hard, penetrating stare, and quietly said, "When we go to war—whether it's tonight or to-morrow or the night after that—I'm *begging* you, Rey, please don't fight in town. Please stay here and help look after the others."

Tears burned at the backs of her eyes, but she refused to let them fall. "Why?" she whispered, her chest heav-ing with emotion. "Why do you think I'm so weak?"

"God, Rey. I don't think you're weak," he groaned, lifting a hand to the side of her face and stroking her skin with his thumb. "I just…I don't want to lose you. Is it so wrong to want to protect something I care about more than I care about my own life?"

Clutching his powerful wrist in her hands, she stared up at him and said, "It is when you keep comparing her to something she's not. I'm not your mother, Eli. I don't need your protection. I just need your love. And your faith."

"I *have* faith in you," he growled, his frustration bleed-ing through the guttural words. "But that doesn't mean I'm not terrified of losing you."

"You've trusted me with your lust, even though you

were worried it would be too much for me. Can't you trust me to be strong and smart enough for my job?"

"I wish to hell that I could, Rey. But it terrifies me. I *hate* it," he scraped out, "and I don't know how to make that change."

"I don't know, either," she said in a throaty voice that was thick with tears. "I just know that this isn't healthy. We can't do this, no matter how we feel about each other."

He looked at her so hard and intensely that she felt like he was trying to change her mind with the sheer force of his will, his eyes dark and angry and troubled, his throat working as he swallowed. But she could tell he had no idea what to say to her.

Pushing his hand away from her face, she let go of his wrist and stepped back from him. "Later, Eli. We can sort things out later. But *now* is not the time."

He worked his jaw again, looking like a man who'd been pushed far beyond his limits, then turned and walked away, slamming the door behind him.

The instant she was alone, Carla covered her face with her hands, breathing hard, and all she could smell was *him*. His scent covered her, inside and out, and she wondered if she would ever be free of it.

The day went by in a blur of tension and frantic activity, and twelve hours later, as she pulled in a deep breath of the nighttime air, she realized that her head was finally clear of Eli's scent.

But that was only because the night smelled like death. And Shadow Peak looked like a warzone.

Keeping to the shadows, Carla surveyed the scene before her with a pounding heart. The night winds howled through the quiet town, eerie and hollow, like the lamenting cry of a banshee. As a trickle of sweat slipped its way down her spine beneath her tight, long-sleeved black top, the thick, meaty scent of blood filled her nose from the drenched street that currently resembled a crimson river. Voices from the street carried easily in the silence as the wind took a brief respite, and she heard someone say, "It's just as the call said. All that talk of the Silvercrest pack coming together was just a trick to try and put us off, and now the idiots have slaughtered themselves."

She moved closer to the corner of the building she was hiding in the shadow of, eyeing the two males standing among the bodies. They were human, and she recognized them both from the descriptions Kyle had given her of Jack Bartley and his second-in-command, Joe Mackey.

"It's disappointing," Bartley muttered, nudging a body with the toe of his boot. "I was looking forward to seeing their fall."

"Me, too. But now Claymore has gotten what he wanted without shedding a single drop of Whiteclaw blood. That's going to do wonders for our reputation."

"There is that," Bartley drawled, before giving a low laugh. "But he'll die if he thinks this means he no longer owes me our final payment."

Mackey grunted his agreement, then asked, "So what do we do now?"

Voice thick with disgust, Bartley said, "We bring in the soldiers and let them get to work. It will take forever to deal with this mess. Bloody mongrels."

Flexing her hands at her sides, Carla had to physically restrain herself from lunging into the street and ripping the merc's throat out, knowing she had to bide her time. One false move and everything would be ruined.

A few minutes passed, and then the Whiteclaw soldiers poured into the town square that lay at the end of the street, cursing and muttering to each other. Peeking around the edge of the building, she watched as Roy

Claymore climbed the steps leading up to the Town Hall, and felt bile rise in the back of her throat as he looked out over the crowd and shouted, "Shadow Peak is ours!"

The crowd cheered, and then Roy yelled out, "Rid the streets of the filth and pile the bodies on the south field, where we'll burn them at tomorrow's celebration!"

Another raucous cheer went up, and her pulse slowed to a hard, thudding beat, the way it always did just before she engaged the enemy.

When Kyle had first brought the mercs' plan to the Runners' attention, he'd told them, "The control of information is key." And he'd been right. By controlling what was going out of Shadow Peak via the rumor mill, they'd set the stage, spreading tales of a growing dissention within the town. An escalating tension between those who supported the Runners and those who didn't, that tension supposedly exacerbated by the arrival of Eli and his fellow mercenaries.

Taking deep, controlled breaths, she watched the Whiteclaw soldiers make their way through the piles of bodies that covered the streets, and waited for the signal that Eric would give from the top of the Town Hall. She counted down the seconds in her head, and then the first signal came—a low, warbling whistle—and she undid the safety on the automatic machine gun strapped over her shoulder. Then she heard the second signal, and she lifted the weapon as she stepped out of the alleyway where she'd been hiding, spraying the Whiteclaw with bullets. At the same time, the blood-covered Lycans lying on the ground who had pretended to be dead rolled onto their backs, weapons at the ready, and fired from below.

Many of those Lycans were women who had wanted to defend their town, but didn't have enough training to effectively fight with their fangs byrd claws. But as Mason had told the group during another meeting they'd had that afternoon, even if the women weren't properly trained in hand-to-hand combat, they could still do a hell of a lot of damage with the right kind of gun, in the right kind of situation, and he'd had a good point. Eli hadn't been happy with the decision, but he hadn't gone against the Runner. Instead, he'd used his expertise to create the safest situation that he could for the women under the circumstances, and she was hopeful that they would have limited casualties.

Hating the violence, but understanding that it was necessary when one group had to protect itself from another, Carla kept firing as wave after wave of Whiteclaw soldiers, many of who had clearly taken the "super soldier" drugs, swarmed into the streets. She could sense Eli somewhere near her left side, and she knew he was purposefully staying close to her. But as long as he didn't interfere with her job tonight, she wasn't going to complain. An argument right now would only get someone killed.

When her machine gun fired the last of its bullets, she tossed it to the ground. A quick glance at her watch told her that the women in the street would soon be making a run for the security of the buildings, where they would hide while those who had been trained in physical combat dealt with the second phase of the battle. They'd already taken down a good portion of the enemy, but the fight was far from over, and the soldiers who had been wounded by the bullets now needed to be killed.

Stepping back into the alleyway, Carla quickly did a weapons check on the blades she'd secured to her body, turning away from the group of mercs who were with her as they stripped down. Though she'd decided to fight in her human form, since she would be able to use a variety of weapons as well as her claws and fangs, the men would be fighting as werewolves, and she glanced over her shoulder just as Eli and the others allowed the shift to wash over their expanding forms. Bones cracked as fur rippled over their skin in a mesmerizing display of power, muscles increasing to nearly twice their original size. When the transformations were complete, they would stand at nearly seven feet in height, with wolf-shaped heads, lethal, claw-tipped hands, and long, deadly fangs that gleamed in the silvery moonlight.

Of course, that was what she'd *assumed* would happen, given her knowledge of Lycan transformations. But when Lev, Kyle, Sam and James completed their shifts, she realized they were even taller than Eli and the other Silvercrest males who were coming to join them, and she could only gape in shock.

"Um, Eli," she croaked, blinking her eyes in astonishment. "What *the hell* are they?"

Eli reached out and gently pushed her chin up with a claw-tipped hand, a crooked grin on his wolf's muzzle-shaped mouth as he said, "Not the time, Rey."

"Uh, right," she murmured, shaking her head.

"Stay close," he told her, not giving her time to argue as he turned and headed back out to the street. The others followed behind them, and it didn't take long before they were embroiled in battle, the Lycans they were going up against a mix of ones who'd been enhanced by the "super soldier" drugs, and ones who thankfully hadn't. Most of Bartley's men, it seemed, had been taken out in the initial wave of the attack, and Eli was grateful as hell to his guys for coming up with such a brilliant plan.

"Sam," he said in the deep, guttural voice of his beast, "watch your right. They're coming in hard and heavy from the next street over."

"Got it covered, boss man," Sam replied, sounding like he was actually enjoying the fight, and Eli figured once a mercenary, always a mercenary. Or maybe his friend just liked kicking bad guy ass and helping those who needed it, the same as he did. Either way, Eli was glad to have Sam and the guys there, and if they survived this, he was going to make sure he told them how much their loyalty meant to him.

Carla was fighting beside him, and like the night they'd been ambushed on their way up to the Alley, they were working together in perfect synchronicity. It should have made him feel better, but he was still raw inside with fear over the danger she'd put herself in by coming here. He knew she was still seriously pissed off at him, but damn it, he'd only done what he'd felt was right. What he'd felt he *had* to do, because he loved her and couldn't imagine ever losing her.

A little farther down the street, he noticed Cian working his way closer and closer to Sayre, who was fighting with a skill that was remarkable in an eighteen-year-old. But then, Sayre was more than your average girl, her powers apparently some of the strongest that either her mother or sister had ever seen in a witch. But Cian clearly wasn't any more comfortable with her fighting than Eli was by Carla's determination to be there.

When three burly Whiteclaw soldiers charged Sayre all at once, the Irishman roared for her to run for cover as he tore through the Lycans in a deadly flurry of claws and snapping jaws that was truly impressive. Well, to anyone but the witch. She shouted at the Runner to leave her alone, going so far as trying to use her power to hold him back when Cian snarled that he was getting her out of there. But to her obvious shock, the Irishman stormed right through the crackling wall of light she'd raised between them, hooking his arm around her waist and leaping onto the top of an RV that'd been left parked against a tall building on the far side of the street.

Eli could have sworn he saw Constance Murphy give the Runner a nod of thanks, or maybe even approval. But then her attention was drawn away by a fallen Silvercrest Lycan who needed her help, leaving Cian to deal with a furious Sayre all on his own. She growled something at him that Eli couldn't hear, but the Runner stiffened and growled something right back, before jumping off the top of the RV and ripping any of the Whiteclaw who tried to get near it to pieces, while a still enraged Sayre looked as though she wouldn't mind blasting him with another shot of light from her hands.

Yeah, the Runner definitely had his hands full with that one, and he almost felt sorry for the guy, until Eli realized that he was in the exact same boat. Because *his* woman was also a serious little badass. And as he finally took a moment to stop letting his fear control him, and really *watched* her in action, he saw that Carla Reyes was truly breathtaking when she fought…and he was a major, shit-for-brains jackass.

Christ, I'm an idiot.

He might have been slow on the uptake, but he was starting to see that he'd been wrong to worry so much. It didn't mean that he *wouldn't* worry, because he loved her and would always put her safety above his and anyone else's. But he knew a natural warrior when he saw one. In truth, the realization had been creeping up on him for days, though he hadn't wanted to acknowledge it. And his men had been hammering it home, none of them shy about telling him that it'd been a dumb move he'd pulled on her during the meeting at Mason's that morning. But it wasn't until right then, until that very moment, that it truly sank in. That he saw what they had all been telling him.

She was a friggin' goddess on the battlefield, gorgeous and deadly and seriously skilled, and he needed to get a grip, because that wasn't ever going to change.

When another heavy wave of the enemy suddenly poured into the street, Mason and Elliot quickly joined them, and the fighting became brutal. "Reyes, fall back!" Mason shouted, tearing his claws through one soldier's throat, before breaking another's knee. "This is getting too intense!"

She shot the Runner a blistering glare as she took down one opponent and then immediately engaged another. "What the hell, Mase?"

"I mean it, honey," Mason grunted, cutting her a worried look. "These assholes know they've lost, which means they're desperate."

Knowing he needed to speak up, Eli said, "Mason, it's okay, man. I know you mean well, but she's where she's meant to be."

Both Runners turned their heads toward him the instant the soldiers they were fighting fell, their shocked expressions almost identical. Mason recovered first, growling for her to be careful, then got back into the fight. It took Carla a little longer to recover, but she finally shook herself out of her daze, took a deep breath, and then gave Eli a tender look of thanks that he swore he could feel reach all the way down to his soul.

"You ready?" he asked, a wry grin tugging at the corner of his mouth.

Carla blinked, thinking that crooked grin of his was about the most beautiful thing she'd ever seen on a sexy-as-sin Lycan.

"What?" he asked, when he caught the way she was looking at him.

"I can't believe you just did that."

He had the audacity to shrug one of those massive, muscular shoulders, as if he didn't know what the big deal was. "Why wouldn't I? In case you hadn't noticed, you're a serious little ass kicker."

I will not smile...I will not smile...I will not smile. She repeated the words over and over in her head, still too hurt by what he'd done to forgive him that easily.

As if he sensed the confusing rush of emotions she was feeling, he winced and said, "I'm sorry, Rey. In case you hadn't noticed, I've been a blind, stupid son of a bitch."

Not knowing what to make of the change in him, she shook her head a little to clear it and got ready to get back in the fight. But a few moments later, when she saw the group of Whiteclaw soldiers who had just come around the corner up ahead, she knew what she needed to do. "Hey, Eli?" she called out, drawing his attention.

He hurried to her side, as if he'd just been waiting for her to call him closer. "You okay?" he asked, his bright eyes narrowed with concern.

"I'm good," she told him, gesturing toward the Lycans. "I just thought you might want to help me take out those assholes over there. They're the ones who knocked me around when I was in Hawkley."

"With pleasure," he growled, flexing his deadly claws at his sides. Together, they fought the soldiers, easily taking them down, working with that same startling precision and intuition that they'd used before. By the time the bastards who'd beaten her had fallen, more Silvercrest fighters, along with many of the Runners, were making their way into the street, since it had been set as their primary meeting point before the battle that had waged across the entire town had started. From what she could hear everyone saying, it sounded as if those Whiteclaw soldiers who were still standing were abandoning the attack and making a run for it.

Looking over the group, Eli spotted Jeremy, who had returned to his human form and was dressed in a torn pair of jeans, and asked, "Where are my brother and sister?"

Using his forearm to wipe the specks of blood from his face, Jeremy said, "They're helping Wyatt and Brody search for Roy. The last thing we want is for that asshole to slink away."

"I'm not going anywhere!" a belligerent voice called out from the far end of the street.

Turning around, Carla stared at the Lycan who'd spoken, thinking he was the most unattractive male she'd ever seen in wolf form, his fur a dingy gray and his head too small for his shoulders. "It's Roy. He's here," she said, and the mercs around her growled with aggression, while Eli simply watched Claymore with a cold, deadly gaze.

Walking across the fallen bodies of his soldiers as if they were nothing more than dirt, the monster responsible for all this bloodshed looked over the gathering of Silvercrest wolves and snarled, "I want the bitch Runner who brought the goddamn mercs here to help you. Give her to me, and we'll leave."

"You're leaving anyway, just not on your feet," Jeremy growled from Eli's side. "Because you have a hell of a lot to answer for, you twisted bastard."

"That's the problem with you Silvercrest," the Lycan sneered. "You let emotion get in the way of everything."

Instead of charging forward and taking Claymore's head off, the way she'd fully expected him to do, Eli turned his head and looked at her, holding her sharp gaze with his. Speaking in the wolf's garbled, gravelly voice, he asked, "You gonna let me take this one?"

"If you want him, go for it."

The instant the words left her mouth, she felt the change coming over him, and knew precisely what it meant.

Eli's *dark wolf*—that most deadly, primitive part of him that could only be created by a bloodline as powerful as the one he and his siblings shared—was awakening.

She'd heard it said that a dark wolf could only fully awaken, embracing its total power, once it had found its true life mate. Like so many things in nature, the rule was meant to keep balance, since it was a dark wolf's need for its mate that was meant to temper its savage, visceral aggression.

However, the rule no longer applied when that aggression was being channeled toward someone who had threatened the wolf's woman. In that event, all bets were off, and the threat was destroyed by any means necessary.

And that was just what Eli was getting ready to do.

Yes, in this case, Carla was perfectly capable of defending herself. But she freaking loved that Eli felt so protective of her that he was taking the shape of his dark wolf *now*.

Eyes burning with emotion, he looked down at her and said, "This doesn't mean that I don't believe in you. It only means that I love the hell out of you."

With those incredible words buzzing through her head, she jerked her chin toward Claymore, silently telling Eli to get on with it, and he gave a low, wicked laugh that struck her as impossibly sexy, even in these dangerous, deadly circumstances. Though the danger and death at this point were all for Roy.

There was an aura around Eli as he prowled forward,

a power pulsing like a physical force that you could feel in the air, and it made her shiver as it swept over her skin. Everyone around them was watching in awe, including his fellow mercenaries, who she would have guessed had never seen a dark wolf in action before, though they would have surely heard of them. He stood even taller than he had just moments ago, his body more muscular, while his eyes burned a deep, mesmerizing shade of amber. And when he started to fight, leaping through the air and catching Roy around the neck, slamming him into the side of a building, it was clear that Claymore didn't stand a chance. The older Lycan might have experience on his side, but he was no match for Eli's ferocity, speed and strength. His body was like a blur as he punched and clawed and kicked, and within mere moments the encounter was over.

When Roy finally fell, his head no longer connected to his shoulders, Eli turned and locked his hooded, burning gaze with hers. Then he gave her a slow, sexy smile, and the crowd erupted in cheers.

The battle had reached its end, and the Silvercrest were victorious.

Chapter 15

Six days later, Carla stood on her front porch, watching Eli and his men hard at work at the far end of the glade. They'd cleared the area of trees, and looked to be putting in some kind of series of foundations, but she couldn't be sure without going down there and checking it out firsthand.

And that was something she wasn't prepared to do, her panic now at an all-time high.

The days after the battle had been difficult, and she knew it would take time for normal life to resume. The pack mourned the loss of those who'd fallen, while holding those who'd survived a little closer to their hearts. And though there was a lot of work still to be done in those parts of the town that had been hit the hardest, they had made their stand and shown the Lycan nation that they weren't to be trifled with. Not unless you were looking to have your ass kicked. She knew they had Eli and his men to thank for so much of their success, and she'd personally spoken to each one of the mercenaries and expressed her gratitude.

Well, except for Eli.

Despite how he'd stood up for her during the battle, she'd been avoiding him. She hadn't even gone after him about the bond breaking, since Jillian and her mother and sister had exhausted themselves after the fighting, using their powers to heal the wounded. Jilly needed to recoup her energy now, especially in light of the small life she was carrying, so Carla hadn't even broached the subject.

And, yeah, she knew she was running scared by not talking to Eli, but damn it, she was just so...so terrified of what would happen when he finally grew tired of this place and left her again. Despite everything that he'd said, all the beautiful things that he'd told her, she couldn't get past her fear that that's exactly how this would all play out.

And strangely enough, Eli wasn't pushing the issue. There'd been no stolen kisses...no tries for sex...no pleas for her understanding. She saw him often, but they were always in a group of people. And things had simply been crazy busy since the war, so he probably hadn't had the time to seek her out on his own, especially with all the work he and the mercs had been doing.

Either that, or this was some kind of new battle plan he was waging against her. One that had her twisted in knots...and thinking about him constantly. Was he just wearing her down, waiting for the moment when she would snap and go running after him?

A few women had come down from town to see him—including the one who'd tried to visit him before—but he'd sent each one of them away, and apparently asked them not to return. She knew because his friends loved talking about it in front of her, as if the idea of Eli having to constantly tell his former lovers to get lost was the funniest thing they'd ever seen. On the surface, she was afraid to read too much into it. But deep down in her heart, Carla couldn't help but fall for him a little harder each time she heard that he'd sent another woman from his past back home, hoping that it meant he was saving himself for her. That he knew what he wanted, but just hadn't managed to secure the deal.

Not that it would make any difference in the end, considering she fully expected him to bail. But it was still something that she cherished, fool that she was.

Another loud noise came from the far end of the glade, drawing her attention back to the area, and she glared. What the hell were they doing down there, anyway?

Damn it, she was *done* wondering. She was going to go down there and find out for herself once and for all!

Starting down the porch steps, she saw Jeremy carrying what looked like the box for a crib into his and Jillian's cabin, which made her think of the dinner she'd had with all her girlfriends a few nights ago. Every single one of them, with the exception of Jilly, had been chatting about how they were trying to conceive. Even Elise, who had only been bonded with Wyatt for a short time, was giving it a go.

As Carla had watched their faces and listened to their excitement, she couldn't help but be happy for them and wish them all the best. And knowing their mates, she had a feeling they'd all be knocked up before the end of the summer. Which meant that it wouldn't be long before little rugrats were taking over the Alley, and she was looking forward to being the awesome aunt that all the kids adored. She would put her freaking heart and soul into spoiling those munchkins rotten.

But as thrilled as she was for her friends, it hurt that she didn't have any chance of bringing her own baby dreams to life. Not that she was ready now, mind you. But she'd always wanted to have a big family someday. When she'd been younger, those dreams had always revolved around Eli. And now...*no*, she thought, shaking her head. She wasn't following that dangerous train of thought, knowing damn well that she wouldn't be able to handle where it led.

Fired with an even greater sense of frustration, Carla cursed under her breath as she walked through the crisp blades of grass in her bare feet, the guttural sound catching Max's attention as he walked by. Sliding her an easy smile, he said, "Hey, Reyes. Those foundations for the cabins the mercs are building look pretty awesome, don't they? I think it's so cool that they're staying."

In that moment, she was pretty sure that her heart had just stopped. "What did you say?"

Max lifted his brows, looking a bit concerned as he took in her stunned expression. "That they're staying?"

"So then...they're building...you mean the cabins are for..." She broke off, unable to go on, shaking so hard her teeth had started to chatter.

Jesus Christ, she couldn't believe it. They were building cabins. For *all* of them. Freaking cabins for them to use on a permanent basis.

Oh, hell, no.

He wasn't going to pull this on her. Give her foolish hope and then leave nothing but a pile of rubble behind him in the place where her heart had once been.

Dodging anyone who got in her way, she stomped across the clearing, not even bothering to say goodbye to Max, who was no doubt watching her like she was a crazy woman. But, damn it, that's what she felt like. She knew something weird had been going on with Eli and the others, but she'd never expected *this*. Never! And she couldn't believe that none of her friends had told her. What was this? A freaking conspiracy?

Before she could reach the place where Eli and the others were working, he came around the side of the cabin he was still staying in with Kyle, a sudden grin on his lips when he caught sight of her. "Hey, Reyes. What's up?" he asked, his tone so deliberately casual it made her want to bite him.

When she didn't respond, just stood there seething and glowering at him, he nodded his head toward the cabin. "You want to come in and take a look at the plans for the place I'm building?"

Her nostrils flared as she pulled in a rattling breath, but she managed a thick, "Yeah," and followed him up the porch steps, through the door, and back to his room. The detailed blueprints had been laid out over his bed, and after looking them over, she turned her head to stare at him. He stood only a few feet away, at the foot of the bed, his hooded gaze locked in hard and tight on her flushed face. "Is this…is this some kind of joke?" she pretty much wheezed, since she couldn't get enough air into her lungs.

"A joke?" He rubbed a hand over his stubble-darkened jaw as he shook his head, and said, "No."

"Then why?" Breathing in rough, choppy bursts, her pulse roaring in her ears, she said, "Please, just tell me why you're doing this, Eli."

With a wry arch of an eyebrow, he asked, "You sure you want to know?"

She nodded, her throat so tight she could barely swallow.

He closed his eyes for a moment, took a deep breath,

and when he opened them, they were burning with so much brilliant emotion it made her light-headed. Then she heard that deep, bone-melting voice of his say, "Because you might not want to be mine right now, but it doesn't mean I'm not yours, Rey."

"No," she whispered, her eyes stinging. "You were *never* mine."

His voice was soft, and so damn delicious. "Hell, yes, I was. I always have been. From the first time I ever set eyes on you." Shaking his head again, he said, "I was just too afraid to admit it."

She blinked, wondering why his face was swimming out of focus. "I know you, Eli. You're not afraid of anything."

"You know that's not true, Rey, because I've been terrified of a lot of things." He came around the foot of the bed until he stood right in front of her, then reached out, swiping something hot and salty from the corner of her mouth. "But I'm also man enough to admit when I'm wrong. And I was so wrong, sweetheart. About…about so many things. But never about how I feel about you."

"It doesn't matter," she said unsteadily. "It's…it's too late."

Taking her face in his big, warm hands, he kept his glittering gaze focused hard on hers. "Carla, listen to me. It's never too late, baby. You're just feeling scared, and trust me, I know how hard that is. But I'm not giving up on you. *Ever.*"

Sniffing, she whispered, "This won't work, Eli."

"It *will*. When we're husband and wife, completely bonded, it will be the most incredible thing that's ever happened to me, and I will do whatever it takes to make you happy."

"Oh, God." She knew the look of shock on her face had to be priceless. "You want us to get *married*?"

"That's what this has all been about," he murmured, his voice getting huskier. "I want you. Not for a moment, Rey. I want what's *mine*. I want it forever." He threaded his fingers through her hair, pulling her head back as he lowered his face over hers, so impossibly gorgeous she couldn't think straight. "And you know what else? I know you love me. You aren't ready to tell me, but I *know* it's there inside you, and one day, you're going to give me the words." His dark eyes gleamed with emotion. "I have enough faith in that happening for both of us, Rey. Whatever it takes, I'm going to wear you down."

"You're mad," she gasped, unable to stop the tears spilling over her lashes.

A beautiful grin tugged at the corner of his mouth. "Maybe. God knows you won't make it easy on me. But I'll see this through. I have to. I can't accept any other outcome."

"You don't get to make that decision."

"Yeah, well, you don't get to decide everything, either," he drawled with a quiet, rugged laugh. "We need to do it together."

Stepping back from him, she swiped at the tears on her face. "You won't stay. Not for long. You'll be bored out of your mind before that cabin is ever even built."

His shoulders lifted in a casual shrug. "I'm sorry you believe that, but I guess you just don't know me as well as you think you do. Because as long as you're here, then I am, too."

She shoved her hair back with shaking hands, her voice thick with panic as she snapped, "Fine, whatever. I…I've got to go now."

"Then go, Rey. But I'd like to see you tomorrow."

Despite her words, she didn't leave. She didn't even move. She just stood there staring at him, while her heart pounded so forcefully in her chest it felt like it was trying to escape.

"See something you need?" he asked after a moment, hooking his thumbs in his pockets, acting as if he had all the time in the world to wait her out.

She licked her lips with a nervous flick of her tongue. "I...I feel tricked."

His lips twitched with another one of those sinful, crooked smiles. "I think the word you were actually going for was needed. Or loved. Worshiped. Adored." Raising his eyebrows, he asked, "Should I go on?"

"Oh, God, you *are* crazy."

"Crazy about *you*," he muttered softly, suddenly grabbing her and pulling her against him. His arms wrapped around her like steel bands, holding her close, while his mouth caught her startled gasp, his tongue thrusting past her lips as if he had every right to put it there, and she forgot all about resisting him. His hot, addictive taste pulled a helpless moan from her as she wrapped her hands around the back of his neck, holding him to her, the soft strands of his hair tickling her skin.

Muttering a thick, guttural curse, he lifted her and carried her across the floor until he could push her against the wall, trapping her there, grinding against her as she wrapped her legs around his waist. "I want to be *here*," he growled against her lips, and she wished she wasn't wearing her stupid jeans. "Live here. I want to be inside you again so badly I can taste it."

Shoving her fingers into his thick hair, she arched against him and cried, "Just do it, damn it!"

He groaned like a man who was desperate for his woman, but he didn't start ripping her clothes off. Instead, he pressed a tender kiss to the corner of her trembling mouth, and rasped, "I want to, baby, but I can't."

"What?"

Staring deep into her wide eyes, he slowly shook his head. "It's not gonna happen, Rey. Not until you're willing to give me everything."

She blinked, unable to believe what she was hearing. "Are you freaking serious?"

He set her back on her feet and took a step back, the gray cotton of his shirt stretching tight across his broad shoulders as he pushed his hands in his pockets. "I know how this works," he murmured. "If I keep giving it up, you're going to lose all respect for me, right?"

"You manipulative son of a bitch," she growled, fisting her hands at her sides. The bastard had gotten her all worked up, and completely played her!

He arched his brows, looking as if he was trying hard not to smile. "Sexual frustration makes you cranky, Rey."

"Not for long it doesn't," she snapped, the words rushing from her mouth in a surge of anger before she could hold them back.

His arm shot out, stopping her forward progress as she tried to storm around him, heading for the door. He waited until she turned her head to pin him with a sharp glare, and then he said, "Before you go causing trouble, there's something you should know."

"What?" she snapped.

"I'll kill any man who touches you."

She snorted. "Including your own men?"

He held her hostile gaze as he lowered his hand. "Anyone, Rey. So keep that in mind."

She sighed, knowing damn well that she was only bluffing. She didn't want anyone but him, and the cocky jackass knew it. Crossing her arms over her chest, she turned to face him. "So your men, they're staying, as well?"

"Does it matter?" he asked, his neutral tone giving nothing away.

"I'm not complaining. They're good men. But what the hell are they going to do here?"

"What they've always done. Just not all over the world. They're going to focus on the Eastern seaboard, which makes this a prime location for a permanent base. Something they've never had. But it means they'll have a chance for stability. Hell, they might even start families."

A quiet laugh fell from her lips. "Wow, then you've all lost your minds," she murmured, knowing she sounded like a bitch. But that's what fear could do to a person. Make you too afraid to even be honest with yourself, much less the man you loved with every single miserable part of your soul.

"Keep telling yourself that if it makes it easier," he said, the tender look in his dark eyes nearly breaking her down. "I'm prepared to wait you out, however long it takes. Just remember that I'm here, Rey. Waiting for you. And thinking about you every single moment of every day."

She started to pace from one side of the room to the other, knowing she should leave, but unable to just make herself do it. She couldn't get past the gut-wrenching feeling that if she walked out that door right now, it would be the biggest mistake of her life.

Finally, she stopped and whirled toward him, her chest heaving with her sharp breaths as she asked, "And just why is your cabin so big?"

He gave another one of those relaxed, easygoing shrugs. "I'm a big man."

She glared, biting her tongue, while her mind churned the question over and over in her head.

With a knowing grin on his perfect lips, he waited for her to say something more. To point out the obvious. And it didn't take long for her to crack.

Pointing at the blueprints still laid out over his bed, she said, "So you have like…what? *Five* bedrooms planned? What's that about? Are you planning on having a harem, Eli?"

"More like a family," he murmured, keeping his beautiful eyes locked tight on hers. "*Our* family, Rey."

"What?" she mouthed, frozen in place with shock, while her heart tried to climb its way into her throat.

He gave her a greedy, smoldering look, as if to say that he knew just how deeply his words had touched her, reaching those secret tender places where her dreams lived, because he felt the same way. Dreams she'd been terrified for so long would never come true.

Softly, he said, "You heard me, baby."

Oh…oh, God. In that blinding, breathtaking moment, she could finally see it—*feel it*—what it would be like to build that wonderful, incredible life with him, and it was the most magnificent feeling in the world.

Her throat tight with emotion, she whispered, "You're such a liar, Drake."

"It's not a lie," he said roughly, giving her a fierce look of determination. "I've never meant anything more."

"Not about this." She lowered her gaze so that he couldn't spot the happiness that was surging through her before she was ready for him to. "I'm talking about the bond. You never had any intention of breaking it, did you?"

She heard him exhale a ragged breath. "Not without one hell of a fight."

The sensation in her chest was so warm and sweet she was surprised she hadn't melted, and in an aching voice, she said, "You really do love me, don't you, Eli?"

He made a hard, thick sound, as if he'd finally realized he *had* her, and when she looked back up at him, she could actually see the tears in his eyes. God, was there anything more seductive than a badass alpha willing to cry?

Reaching out and yanking her close again, he buried his face in her hair, his body shaking with a visceral wave of emotion. "I love you more than you could ever possibly understand, Rey. And I'll never regret anything more than letting my old man take you from me for all those years, when we could have been together. Not just the ones while I was gone, but the ones before that, when you belonged with me and I was just too damn scared to do anything about it. I was such a stupid jackass."

He lifted his head, connecting that bright gaze with hers, and he held her head in his hands as he growled, "I've missed you so damn much. It was killing me inside a little each day, not having you in my life. In my arms. Not being able to tell you how much I love you. How deeply I will *always* love you."

"Damn it, you are *such* an ass for making me cry again," she sniffled through her tears, leaning up on her toes to press her trembling lips to his. He groaned as he quickly deepened the kiss, his arms locking around her, lifting her off her feet as he crushed her against his body.

"God, I need you," he said in a guttural burst of words, turning and laying her down on the bed, the blueprints crinkling beneath them as he came down over her, putting his face close to hers. "I need you to be *mine,* to be my *wife,* Rey, because there isn't any part of you that I don't love. I love your strength and your mind and your wicked sense of humor. I even love that you're a little badass, because it means I can do whatever the hell I want to your beautiful body and you'll be able to take it."

She arched against him, rubbing her breasts against his chest as she gripped the hem of his shirt and tried to rip it off him. They struggled for a moment, panting and giving breathless moans of excitement as they tore at each other's clothes, until they were both blessedly naked, her legs spreading wide for him as he rubbed his heavy erection against her sensitive folds. "Tell me, Eli. What are the things you want to do?"

His eyes scorched as he braced himself on straight arms and looked her over. "Everything," he said in a dark, velvety rasp that made her shiver. "I want to do every single thing there is to do to you, Rey."

"I want that, too," she gasped, lowering her gaze as she reached between them and curled her hand around his impressive length, the plump tip so swollen and succulent it made her mouth water. Did other women think this part of their male was so beautiful? She didn't know. She only knew that she loved looking at him, tasting him, holding him inside her. Loved the weight and the veined ridges and the sleek skin. Loved how powerful it was and what he could do with it. The intimacy and the trust she felt from him when she held him like this, stroking him with her hand.

Leaning down and pressing his forehead against hers, he groaned, "Christ, you really are trying to kill me."

"No," she whispered, lifting up and running her lips across the stubbled edge of his jaw. "But I love making you crazy."

"You do...I am...and I can't wait," he growled, reaching down and positioning himself at her entrance. "I need inside you, Rey."

"Then get inside me," she said, smiling up at him as he lifted his head and stared down at her with those smoldering, thick-lashed eyes. "It's where you belong."

His expression tightened with lust as he slowly started to thrust, working himself in deeper...and deeper, while his lips parted for his jagged breaths. He seemed even bigger than he'd been before, and it wasn't easy for him to get inside her, even though she was drenched with need. Then he was *there,* hitting the end of her, both of them breathing hard and fast, their mouths coming together in a kiss that was raw and wet and deliciously wild. His body started to move in a hard, shattering, devastating rhythm, and as wonderful as it'd been with him before, this was...different. Richer, and more intimate, as if something that had already been the best had somehow become even better, and in that blinding, poignant moment, Carla realized that she no longer wanted to forget their past, because it had taught her the valuable lesson to never take love for granted. To be brave and say what needed to be said.

"Eli?" she whispered against his mouth.

He lifted his head and locked her in his dark gaze, while his body kept thrusting deeply into hers, so thick and hot and hard that she was already completely addicted to the feel of him. "Yeah, baby?"

Clutching his broad, muscular shoulders, she said, "I just wanted to tell you that I love you."

He froze, lips parted and eyes gleaming, and she felt his cock get even harder...thicker, throbbing inside her. She'd stunned him, but it was clear from the look on his face and the reaction of his body that he'd *liked* what she'd said. The words had completely wrecked him, and she couldn't help but smile.

"I do. I've loved you forever," she told him, cupping his gorgeous face in her trembling hands. "I always will. And I should have told you that years ago. But I'll always say it for as many years as we have to come. I'll say it until you're sick of hearing it."

"That," he breathed out shakily, "will *never* happen."

Tilting her head to the side, she wrapped a hand around the back of his strong neck, and pulled him down to her as she said, "I'm *ready,* Eli. Show me how much you want me."

He made a rough sound that was so much more animal than man, and it drove her wild, knowing that she affected him so deeply. Even the most primal, possessive parts of him. He fisted his hand in her hair, holding her head tight, and she shivered when she felt the soft warmth of his breath against her sensitive flesh. He flicked his tongue against the smooth column of her throat, moaning with pleasure at her taste, and then she felt the hot slide of his fangs. He dragged them across her tender skin, teasing her, making her writhe, until she reached down and grabbed his magnificent ass, pulling him even deeper inside her. He shuddered as he gave a raw, guttural growl that was smothered against her throat, then drove his fangs deep, and it was so freaking good that she screamed.

Holding him to her, she opened her heart and soul to the beauty of the emotions that were flooding into her—to the love and tenderness, so protective and everlasting, combined with a greedy hunger that was so fierce and ravenous she could only shiver in rapture—and she wrapped her arms and her legs around him as tightly as she could. She was undone by the beauty of the bond as it built between them, twining their hearts and souls together until they couldn't ever be torn apart. She could feel his throat working as he swallowed the rich spill of her blood, his body driving into hers with all the raw, primal ferocity of their connection, until they were both gasping and shuddering. And then they were both crashing into a dark, savage pleasure that completely consumed them, and everything in her world went warm and soft and black.

She didn't know how much time had passed when she finally came back to her senses, but Eli was still inside her, and her lips curved as she blinked her eyes open, finding his gorgeous face right above her.

"There's that beautiful smile," he said huskily, nuzzling his nose against hers, and she could feel her smile growing, spreading through every part of her. Pulling his head back, he stared down at her with a breathtaking gaze that was molten with love. "I've waited a lifetime to see you look at me this way, Rey."

"You know, as badly as it hurt, I'd do it all again," she told him, her own eyes burning with tears.

"Do what?"

Sniffing, she said, "Relive every moment of pain, of anguish, that I've gone through. I'd do it all again if it meant we got to this point. Because it was so worth it, Eli. *You're* worth it."

"God, I love you so much," he groaned. "I love you more each day, woman, and it scares the hell out of me, because I don't know how to hold it all inside."

"Don't. You can trust me with it. I'll keep it safe, because I'm never letting you go," she whispered, pulling him down for another tender, soul-searing kiss, the moment so perfect and right she wanted to freeze it in her mind for the rest of eternity.

They'd completed their bond, her man was buried deep in her body, and she was wrapped up tight in his arms.

After all this time, they were both exactly where they were meant to be.

Epilogue

Standing on Carla's front porch, Eli looked out over the twilight-colored Alley, watching the preparations being made for Elise and Wyatt's wedding, which would take place in two days. His life was more blessed than he could have ever imagined it would be—and he knew, without any doubt, that it was only going to get better. He had his woman, his family, and a new sense of purpose to fill his days...while his nights were for Carla alone. And, God, were they incredible.

Someone called out a greeting to him, and he waved with his free hand, a cold beer in the other, looking forward to the event that had the entire Alley buzzing with excitement. Though the glade had seen its fair share of weddings lately, this one would be different, because it would no longer be just their small group of friends and family. For the first time in history, after the ceremony took place in the Alley, there would be a reception held up in Shadow Peak, since the townspeople had insisted on taking part in the celebration. The social divide between the Alley and Shadow Peak had been all but laid to waste after the war, and those who hadn't been willing to accept the change and move forward with an open mind had been invited to leave and make their homes elsewhere.

But while they'd lost some members, they'd gained others. After the battle, the Bloodrunners had offered sanctuary to the women and children from the White-claw pack who had wanted a new beginning, and the town, for the most part, had accepted them. Were there still some assholes who would never change or learn? Of course there were. Nothing was ever going to be perfect, because this wasn't a bloody fairy tale. But things were finally on the right track for the Silvercrest, and he knew the coming years would only see greater changes that brought *everyone* on the mountain closer together.

Instead of creating hatred, his father's legacy had accomplished the complete opposite of what he'd wanted, and none of them were happier to see that happen than Eli was.

Once the Whiteclaw had been defeated, Eli had taken Eric and Elise aside one night and confessed about the help he'd given their mother. They'd been angry, just not over what he'd expected. Instead of blaming Eli for what he'd done, they'd been pissed at him for not trusting them with the truth…and for not having the faith in them to understand. It'd been an emotional moment for the three of them, but it'd brought them closer together than they'd been since they were kids, and he'd slept lighter that night for having the burden off his chest.

Then he and Carla had finally gotten the new begin-

ning they deserved, and sleep had been the last thing on
Eli's mind. They'd been holed up in her cabin the entire
week, and the bed was pretty much shredded, seeing as
how his wolf had definitely wanted to come out and play
now that they'd finally claimed their mate.

No matter how wild Eli got with her, she never feared
him. If anything, the little hellcat reveled in his absolute need for her, pushing him harder, demanding everything he had to give her, including the parts of himself
he hadn't thought anyone would ever want or accept.

The way Eli saw it, a person could easily go through
life living with fear, letting it strangle them. Fear of someone they loved getting hurt. Fear that they weren't good
enough. Of loss. Heartbreak. They could let that fear
hobble them—or realize that all it really meant was that
they had something worth keeping...worth *loving*. Someone worth giving the very best parts of themselves and
finally letting the fear go. So that's what he'd done during the battle. And though it'd taken her a bit longer to
realize, he could have sworn he'd felt Carla do the same
on the day she'd come to him and they'd bonded.

That had been the best damn moment of his life, and
he'd be grateful for it, for *her,* until the day he died.

As if she could sense that he was thinking about her,
Carla came out onto the porch with him, snuggling up
against his side as they watched the flurry of activity
together. They'd offered to pitch in, but everyone had
shooed them away, telling them to take some time to
simply enjoy their bonding. They'd definitely done as
they were told, and Eli was wearing the claw marks on
his back to prove it.

And he was sure as hell wearing them with pride.

Of course, in another month, he'd be wearing something else that his mate had given him: a ring on his fin-

ger, on the day they had their own wedding there in the Alley. A wedding that his men had insisted on planning the reception for, which made him grin just thinking about it. With that lot, there was no telling what they might cook up. Eli only knew it was sure to be the party of the decade, and he couldn't wait to experience it with Carla right by his side, where she always belonged.

He was about to ask her if she wanted him to grill some steaks, when Jeremy came over and invited them to dinner with him and Jillian. They accepted the invitation, enjoying the evening they spent with the couple, and then Carla took him home and had her wicked way with him. He'd fallen asleep in her arms, and found himself waking up hours later with a damn grin on his face. At first, he didn't know what had roused him, and then he realized someone was tapping on the bedroom window.

What the hell?

Rolling out of bed while being careful not to wake her, he raised the blinds and found Lev standing outside in the moonlight. "What's going on?" Eli asked, after lifting the window.

Lev jerked his chin toward Cian's cabin. "I thought you might like to know that the Irishman's running."

With a scowl, he muttered, "Why should I care if he's going for a run?"

Shaking his head, the merc said, "He's packing, Eli. As in *leaving*."

"What? You mean...?"

Crossing his arms over his chest, Lev nodded. "That's exactly what I mean."

It took Eli only seconds to throw on a pair of jeans and head outside. Lev was nowhere to be seen, leaving him to deal with the situation on his own, and he choked back a curse, thinking he'd have to thank the jackass for that later.

He hadn't seen how things had worked out on the night of the battle between Cian and Sayre, but it'd become clear to everyone in the Alley that the Runner and the witch were doing everything they could to avoid each other in the days since. Eli had thought that meant the Irishman had finally come to terms with his feelings for the young woman. But he'd apparently been wrong.

Making his way down the porch steps, he walked through the damp blades of grass, toward the Land Rover parked beside Cian's cabin. The Runner was leaning into the backseat through an open door, and it was clear that the interior of the car had been filled to the brim with the guy's belongings.

"What the hell are you doing, Hennessey?"

With a cigarette hanging from the corner of his mouth, the Irishman turned toward him and frowned. "You're a clever bloke," he drawled. "Give it a guess."

Working his jaw, he said, "All right. Then let me ask you this. *Why?*"

"I just need a break from things for a bit," the Runner offered in a bored tone that Eli knew damn well was forced.

"Bullshit," he grunted, jerking his chin toward the loaded Land Rover. "You're not packing a bag. That's damn near everything you own in there."

Cian leaned back against the open door, and took a sharp pull on his cigarette as he held it between his thumb and forefinger. "All right. I *can't* stay here," he bit out, exhaling the smoke on an angry, frustrated breath.

"Because of Sayre?" When the Irishman's head jerked back, his silver eyes gleaming, Eli said, "Don't look so surprised. We're not blind. We've all figured it out."

"You haven't figured out shit," the Runner snarled, curling his upper lip.

"She's your life mate?"

Cian didn't respond at first. He took another deep drag on the cigarette, the tip gleaming like a demon's eye in the moonlit darkness. The silence stretched out, punctuated only by their breaths and the wind whipping through the leaf-draped branches, until he quietly growled, "She's nothing but a little girl."

"I call bullshit again."

Throwing the cigarette butt on the ground, the Runner pushed away from the door. "Damn it, the *best* thing I can do for her is to get the hell out of her life."

Eli gave an irritated shake of his head. "You might think that, but I'd be willing to bet that you're *wrong*. And you have no idea what you're setting yourself up for. You're gonna hurt out there," he predicted, pointing his finger toward the road that led out of the Alley, "because there's a big ass difference between screwing around and being with the one woman who matters."

Cian's mouth curled in a slow, chilling smile. "Trust me, I know."

"Then don't be a jackass! You can't run from fate, man. Take that from someone who *knows*. Even when you try to convince yourself that leaving is the right thing to do, it's nothing but a goddamn lie. And it all comes back to bite you hard in the ass when it finally catches up to you."

Shifting his turbulent gaze to the interior of the Land Rover, Cian said, "That's a chance I've got to take."

"You could try taking a chance on her instead," he argued.

"No. She's not the problem."

"And you are?" he grunted, watching the Runner shut

the door to the backseat, then open the driver's door and climb behind the wheel.

Cutting him a sharp look from the corner of his eye, Cian said, "I'm something you've never even known."

And with those soft, ominous words ringing in the air, the Irishman slammed his door, cranked the engine, and drove away, disappearing into the night.

* * * * *

BLOOD WOLF DAWNING

To my amazing editor, Ann Leslie Tuttle.

Mountains and oceans of appreciation for all that you've done for this series.

It wouldn't have been the same without you!

Prologue

If this was what falling for someone did to a person—what *craving* them felt like—then Sayre Murphy wanted no part of it. *Ever.* She might be young, as well as inexperienced, but she was a woman, damn it, and she knew when she was done.

When she had finally had *enough*!

With her back straight and her hands fisted at her sides, she stood in a moonlit Maryland forest, high on the mountain that the Silvercrest Lycans, her brethren, had owned for centuries. And she wasn't alone. Standing a few yards in front of her was the most magnificent, infuriating, arrogant male she had ever known. One who treated her as if she were nothing more than a child and interfered in her life time and again, making it painfully clear that he never had any intention of seeing her as an adult female capable of making her own choices. It was an antiquated attitude—completely fitting with his dominant, alpha personality—and one she was entirely sick of.

Honestly, who cared that she was only eighteen? Did that make her a child? Hell no. A handful of weeks ago, she had fought beside her loved ones in a bloodthirsty war to protect their homeland. Had used the unique powers she possessed as a rare Lycan witch and sent grown male werewolves to their deaths. If that didn't make her an adult in his eyes, then she wondered with frustration if anything ever would.

"I've had enough of this insanity," she told him, determined to keep her voice from shaking. "It ends. Now."

The tall Bloodrunner approached her, his dark-as-sin hair gleaming in the moonlight, narrowed silver eyes burning with fury. "You do not dictate to me," he snarled, his lilting Irish brogue thicker than she'd ever heard it before. "Not now, not tomorrow and not the day after that. You will *never* control this. You understand me, lass?"

"I'm not interested in controlling you," she shot back, fisting her hands even tighter, while deep within she felt the fiery heat of her power swirling with energy, desperate to break free. A rising power that she only managed to hang on to by a thread. "I'm simply making my position clear. You're the one who's been acting like a jealous ass. Not me!"

"I'm protecting you!" he roared in a voice that held dark, dangerous things that were so much more than human. As a male who was half werewolf, he was as deadly as he was beautiful. But she knew he would never cause her physical harm, even when he was glaring at her with such raw, seething fury.

The safety of her heart, however, was a different matter.

"I don't need your protection. I never have." Words

rushed up into her mouth that were revealing and intimate—words she knew would make her vulnerable the moment they were spoken—and yet, she couldn't stop them. Couldn't hold them back. "I...I just need *you*," she whispered, loving the way the muscles in his strong, corded throat moved beneath his skin as he gave a hard swallow, his blistering gaze fixed on her tongue as she nervously wet her lips. He watched her mouth with the hungry avidity of a predator who wanted to play and claim and mate, his body expanding with need, his rigid biceps straining the sleeves of his T-shirt. But the human half of him was too stubborn to give in.

"No," he bit out, the denial emerging like a bitter piece of gravel stuck in his throat as he shook his head. And then again. *"No."*

"Finally take what's yours, or I'm finished," she warned him, tired of the maddening double standard that existed between them. Of the way he could sleep with endless numbers of women, and yet, she wasn't allowed to have a simple conversation with another male without him interfering. "I have friends," she snapped. "Good ones. *Male* ones. Lycans who won't reject me. Who won't be so opposed to the idea of enjoying my body if I offer it to them."

His head jerked back as if she'd suddenly struck him with her fist. Then his gaze sharpened and a muscle began to pulse rhythmically in the hard line of his jaw, while his breaths became rougher, eerily stark in the heavy stillness of the forest. The woods were unusually quiet, as if every living creature were tuned in to their argument, waiting with bated breath to see how it would end. This was a storm that had been brewing between them for months, its fury finally unleashed in a torrent of anger and hurt and maddening frustration.

"Are you seriously threatening to take a lover, Sayre?" he demanded, his deep voice causing chills to race across the surface of her skin. "To let another man touch you?"

Lifting her chin, she kept her own narrowed gaze locked in tight on his burning one. "I'm not threatening. I'm stating a *fact*. You either stop this archaic bullshit you've been pulling for months now, protecting my virginity like it's something you expect me to keep for freaking ever, or I'll end it for you."

He drew in a deep breath, then slowly exhaled, his shoulders seeming even broader as he came another step closer, his nearness causing her own breath to quicken. "You really think I'll allow that to happen?" he rasped in a low, almost silent slide of words.

Sadness stabbed her right through the chest as she stared up at him, seeing his resolve in that piercing metallic gray, the phrase *He'll never want you...need you... accept you* looping over and over within the darkness of her mind. She had asked him to meet her tonight so that she could make a final bid for her sanity. Had offered him her body, with no strings attached, desperate for a measure of relief from the incessant hunger rushing through her veins, her need for him growing stronger each day, until she was ill with it. But he'd turned her down, refusing to give her what he so casually gave to so many others, and all because fate had decided to screw with them for a laugh. The connection between them was nothing more than a sick, costly joke, and she and the Irishman were the ones who would pay.

But *she* was the one paying the most. Because while he eased his hunger with countless others, he refused to allow her to do the same. And though she didn't want another male—how could she when she so desperately wanted *him*?—she was tired of playing the pathetic pawn in his twisted game. Tired of being alone. Of sleeping in an empty bed when his was always full.

"Just try to stop me," she finally whispered, unable to shout when everything inside her was aching and raw. Incapable of enduring another moment in his presence, she turned and walked away from him. Though she was dying a little more with each step that she took, she kept her chin high, refusing to look back, even when he growled her name with that rough, delicious accent. She could feel the burning, savage intensity of his stare pressing against her skin until she was finally shielded from his view by the lush flora of the forest, the leaves and branches feeling as if they were reaching out to embrace her. She normally took comfort in the verdant plant life, loving the way its rich scent filled her head and soothed her nerves. But tonight she was too cold. Too shattered.

She would give him the rest of the night to brood and rage…and hopefully think over what she'd said. But that was all.

Pressing a trembling hand to her stomach, her next breath stuttered out on a broken sob, and yet, she refused to give in. She'd already cried enough over the stubborn male. All she could do now was pray that he would make the right choice and alter his path, embracing what they had, even if it were just for one night, instead of doing everything in his power to spurn it. But she was terrified that this was it. That it was over. Whatever *it* was.

Oh, God. Had she honestly thought that she could hold the tears inside? The hot, salty wetness on her cheeks was proof that she'd been wrong. But as awful, empty and alone as Sayre felt at that moment, it was nothing compared to what was coming. To the pain that waited for her, lurking like a killer in the darkness, ready to cut and rend…and completely destroy her.

Because when the sun rose over Maryland the following morning, the Irishman was already gone.

Chapter 1

Five years later

Morning sunlight glinted through the treetops as Cian Hennessey pulled onto the paved mountain road that led into Bloodrunner Alley. He tried to stay focused on what he was about to face, but his last night in the picturesque glade he'd called home for so many years kept playing through his mind. After his disastrous meeting with Sayre in the woods, he'd known he was done there—that he couldn't stay. He'd waited until everyone had gone to bed, and then he'd packed his Land Rover with as many of his belongings as he could. His plan had been to take off before anyone noticed, but Eli Drake, a badass Lycan mercenary who had recently returned to the Silvercrest werewolf pack after years of banishment, had found him before he could get away.

"You can't run from fate, man," Eli had lectured him.

"Take that from someone who knows. Even when you try to convince yourself that leaving is the right thing to do, it's nothing but a goddamn lie. And it all comes back to bite you hard in the ass when it finally catches up to you."

That had been five years ago. If he'd known just how true Eli's words would prove to be, he might have paid more attention to them. But he'd been so sure he knew what needed to be done. That the path he'd been set on taking was not only the right choice, but also his *only* choice.

In the end, Cian had finally realized that he hadn't known a damn thing. All he'd managed to do was postpone the inevitable. But he'd been around long enough to understand that there wasn't any point in wishing for a do-over. What was done was done, and nothing he could do would ever change that. He just had to chalk it up as another entry on the long list of regrets that he lived with, and focus on how to make the best of the situation at present.

So here he was, returning to the only place he'd ever truly thought of as home. At least since he'd left his childhood behind. The scenery might not be as dramatic as the craggy seaside cliffs near Killian's Mount in Ireland, where he'd been raised as a boy, but the mountains held an undeniable beauty. And the half-human/half-Lycan hunters who lived there were not only his friends, but also his family in the truest sense of the word.

Hell, the Runners were more like family to him than anyone who still walked this earth and shared his blood. And yet, he'd turned his back on them because of *her*. Because of a little slip of a witch named Sayre Murphy. Until today, he hadn't seen or spoken to them since he'd left that fateful night. Not even an email or a text. So there was no telling what kind of reception he was about to receive from the men and women who protected the Silvercrest pack from its enemies.

He only knew it wasn't likely to be a warm one.

Parking the black Audi he'd arranged to have waiting for him at Dulles in the grass at the side of the road, he turned off the engine and climbed out, his narrowed eyes taking in his surroundings while he shut the car door and slipped the key fob in his front pocket. As he drew in a deep breath of the crisp mountain air, the scent of the surrounding forest was so achingly familiar that, for a moment, he felt as if his chest might crush inward from the force of regret pressing in on him.

But despite the familiarity of that woodsy scent, the Alley hadn't remained unchanged in his absence, the passage of time marked by differences that were both big and small. He hadn't been there to see the picnic tables repainted, or to help with the completion of the impressive cabins that now stood at the far end of the glade. Had missed the paving of the road and the additions that had been built onto many of the original cabins, where his friends and their mates lived. He could have undoubtedly spotted more changes, but the sight of the tall, auburn-haired Bloodrunner headed straight for him diverted his attention.

The welcoming party, it appeared, was on its way. Though there definitely didn't seem to be anything remotely welcoming about it. No, if he were reading the situation correctly, his former Bloodrunning partner, Brody Carter, looked more likely to throw a bone-crushing punch than he did to go in for a bro hug, and something sharp twisted in Cian's chest.

What did you expect? the wolf part of his nature grumbled inside his head. *He might have been our best friend,*

*but you destroyed that when you turned your back on
him. Asshole.*

Knowing damn well how true the beast's snide words
were, he hardened his jaw, determined to take whatever
Brody felt like dishing out without retaliating. He pushed
his hands in his pockets and waited as Brody closed in
on him, surprised to see that the guy looked even bigger
than he'd been before. Brody had always been muscular,
but now he was cut in a way that was truly impressive,
his tall body rippling with power as he stalked toward
him. The Runner's auburn hair was long again, but pulled
back from his scarred face. And there were little laugh
lines that crinkled at the edges of his green eyes, attest-
ing to the fact that he was a happily married man who
loved his life—even if those green eyes were currently
narrowed in fury. Not that he could blame him. If Brody
had bailed on the Alley the way Cian had, he would have
been so angry it'd be hard to hold back.

Behind Brody's broad shoulder, he spotted the guy's
human wife, Michaela, as she came down the porch steps
of her and Brody's cabin. The Cajun's dark hair was still
long and curly, and even from that distance Cian could
tell that she remained incredibly beautiful. Marriage obviously suited the two of them, and he found himself
remembering back to the obstacles they'd faced when
they'd first gotten together.

During the last months that Cian had lived in the
Alley, there were times when he'd felt like one hell of a
matchmaker. On several occasions, he'd even gone so far
as to claim that he wouldn't make the same mistakes he'd
watched his friends make when his own woman finally
came along—but in the end, it'd been nothing but talk.
Talk he couldn't back up, because happily-ever-after had
never been an option for him.

Instead, finding *his* woman meant he should run as far and as fast as he could in the opposite direction, and never look back. The kindest that fate could have been was to connect him with a female who wasn't a part of the Silvercrest. One he could ignore and keep his distance from, without leaving his friends. But that hadn't happened.

No, he'd been linked with beautiful little Sayre. That right there just proved that the universe had an exceptionally sick sense of humor.

Though he tried not to fixate on her, he kept scanning the Alley beyond Brody, searching for that familiar heart-shaped face and strawberry-blond hair. But she wasn't there. Besides Brody and Mic, the place was unusually empty. He'd texted Brody's old number when he'd landed, warning him that he was coming, and had naturally assumed that Sayre would be waiting for him. She no doubt had a hell of a lot to say to him, after the way he'd left. Not to mention the fact that he hadn't once tried to contact her in the last five years. But there wasn't any sign of her. He told himself not to panic, that she most likely didn't live in the Alley and was probably up in Shadow Peak, the mountaintop town that the Silvercrest Lycans called home, which was only a few miles away. Hell, she could be on her way down to see him at that very moment.

But when he pulled in another deep, searching breath, his heart started to hammer even harder as he realized that Sayre's mouthwatering scent was *nowhere* to be found. Not even the slightest trace. It made a cold sliver of fear begin to coil through his insides, keeping company with his tension. From the moment her older sister, Jillian, had moved down to the Alley to live with a Bloodrunner named Jeremy Burns, Sayre had been a constant feature at the couple's cabin. So what was keeping her away now?

Looking at Brody, who had just come to a stop no more than five feet in front of him, he cut off whatever the Runner was going to say with a rough, impatient burst of words. "I know you want to tell me to get lost, and after the way I left, you have every right. But I came back for a reason. I need to talk to Sayre. Where is she?"

Brody's green eyes burned with an even brighter surge of anger. "You think she's with the pack?"

Cian scowled. "Where else would she be?"

God, if she'd found someone and moved away with him he was going to completely lose it.

Michaela reached her husband's side, a concerned look on her beautiful face as she said, "Cian, Sayre doesn't live with the Silvercrest anymore."

Thinking this must be some kind of ploy to either screw with him or protect the young witch, he held Michaela's troubled gaze. "I'm not here to make things hard for her, Mic. I just…I came back because I need to talk to her."

Though human, Michaela possessed the unique ability to psychically "read" others' emotions, and Cian could only imagine what she was picking up from him at that moment: frustration, fear, guilt, anger, regret and, beneath it all, a seething, never-ending need for something he could never have. She slid Brody a quick glance, then delicately cleared her throat as she looked at Cian and said, "We're not lying. As much as I hate to say it, she honestly isn't here."

So many raw, visceral curses suddenly crowded into his throat, he thought he might choke on them. He swallowed a few times, then finally managed to scrape out a single word. *"Why?"*

His insides twisted when he noticed the way they glanced at each other again, as if neither of them knew how much to tell him. Or *what* to tell him.

"After you left," Michaela finally murmured, taking a careful breath, "there were...well, some things changed."

"What kind of things? What the hell are you talking about?"

He'd kept up on the pack enough through third parties to know that the Silvercrest had flourished in the past five years, thanks to the hard work of the Runners. They might have still been recovering from their war against the neighboring Whiteclaw pack when he'd left, but it'd been clear even then that they'd become a force too powerful for anyone to mess with. Nothing had happened in these mountains that should have necessitated Sayre leaving. Not unless it was something personal, and the secrets he could see burning in his friends' eyes were seriously pissing him off.

"Stop worrying about how I'm going to react," he said, "and just spit it out."

Michaela sighed. "Cian, Sayre isn't the same." At his darkening look, she hurried to explain. "Not long after you took off, Sayre went into a decline and suffered a... breakdown. Not only was she wrecked because of the way you abandoned everyone, but she'd also been dealing with some pretty powerful issues in private. Her powers had been increasing at an abnormal rate, but she didn't want to worry anyone and tried to hide it as much as she could. But after the war, it eventually got to be too much for her, and she had to get away and be on her own. She hasn't lived here in over four and a half years."

Four and a half years? Reeling, he tried to suck in a sharp breath, but his lungs had locked down. He was sealed in a goddamn vise of disbelief, the roaring in his head making him flinch. *No. No, damn it. This can't be happening.* He didn't want to believe, but he could tell by the looks on their faces that they were telling him the truth.

Somehow, he managed to choke out, "Where. Is. She?"

"It's too much of a strain on her system when she's around other people, so she lives by herself just over the border, in a cabin in West Virginia."

His throat was so tight with fear he could barely speak. "And there's no one there to help her? She's completely alone?"

Brody jerked his chin up and scowled. "She doesn't like to be around anyone. Even Jillian and Jeremy. It physically pains her to pick up on others' physical and emotional energy."

Cian paced away from them and lowered his head, staring at the tips of his heavy black leather boots. He shoved his hands into his hair, pushing it away from his face as he squeezed his skull, working everything he'd just learned through his head. *Christ*, all this time he'd thought she was safe, surrounded by her family and friends, when he couldn't have been more wrong. She was alone, damn it. On her own in the middle of fucking nowhere!

Rage seared its way through his veins in a thick, eviscerating spill, and he lowered his arms and fisted his hands at his sides as he turned back around and took an aggressive step toward Brody. Five years ago, he'd left a single message for his partner that read: *Take care of her.* But that obviously hadn't happened.

Locking his furious gaze with Brody's green one, he snarled, "I trusted you."

"Yeah, I trusted you, too," the Runner shot back, curling his upper lip. "But that didn't stop you from running like a coward, did it?"

Cian struggled to control his temper and calm his harsh breaths, but the darkness inside him was rising, and he knew it wouldn't be long before he lost the fight against it. Which meant he needed to get the hell out of there. "I need directions to where she is," he growled. *"Now."*

Brody snorted and shook his head, looking at him with disgust. "It's been *five* years, Cian. Why the sudden hurry?"

Before he could respond, Michaela reached into the pocket of her long skirt and pulled out a small piece of paper. "You both just need to calm down. This isn't going to help anyone." Offering him the paper, she said, "I already wrote the information down for you after you sent Brody that text."

Her husband shot her a disgruntled look. "What the hell, Mic?"

She slid Brody an apologetic smile. "I'm sorry, honey, but she deserves the chance to deal with this on her own."

Cian didn't speak as he grabbed the tiny slip of paper from Michaela's hand. A quick glance showed that she'd written down a brief set of directions along with several names and phone numbers.

"The others will be sorry they missed you," she told him. "They've taken all the kids down to the beach for two weeks in South Carolina. But we chose to stay home because Jack's still too young for that kind of thing."

He opened his mouth, a hundred different questions on his tongue. Jack? Kids? Exactly how many did his friends have now? What were their names, ages and genders? His curiosity was strong—but his fear for Sayre's safety was stronger.

Snapping his mouth shut, Cian turned and headed back to the sleek sports car he'd left parked in the grass. Just as he opened the driver's-side door, Brody grabbed his shoulder and jerked him around, getting right in his face. "What the hell are you up to, Hennessey?"

"I'm bringing her back where she belongs."

The three thin scars that slashed across Brody's tanned face turned white as he grimaced. "She won't come back with you. We *begged* her, but she was adamant. You really think you'll be able to change her mind after leaving like you did?"

"The difference is that I don't plan on asking, or begging. I'm not giving her a choice," he ground out, digging the key fob from his pocket. "I'll tie her up and throw her over my shoulder if I have to, but one way or another, she *is* coming back to where it's safe."

The Runner's green eyes widened with comprehension. "What aren't you telling us?" he demanded, tightening the brutal grip he had on his shoulder.

Looking his former partner right in the eye, Cian said, "I don't have the time to get into this, Brody. But I *will* explain when I get back."

"Are we in danger?" he asked in a low voice, showing no signs of backing down.

Cian shook his head, hoping like hell that it wasn't a lie. But he had no reason to believe that the Runners were targets. If that were the case, something would have happened a long time ago, when Cian had been one of them.

A knowing light started to burn in Brody's eyes. "Is Sayre in danger? Is that what this is about?"

"If she is, what is it to you?" he growled, hating the way that Brody was looking at him—with years' worth of fury and hurt and disappointment that made him feel completely worthless.

Deep voice vibrating with rage, the Runner said, "It's important to me because I was your partner and your best friend, asshole. So that was on *me*. You don't think I felt responsible when you just up and ran? I had to watch that girl deal with your betrayal while everything was falling apart for her, and felt guilty as hell for not figuring out what you were up to. Because you can bet that if I had, I would have saved her from having to deal with whatever bullshit you've brought down on her head *now*."

Struggling to hold on to his control, he forced his response through his gritted teeth. "I don't have time for this, man. You want to beat me down when I get back with her, then fine. Go for it. I'm sure it's exactly what I deserve. But right now, I've got to go."

"You want to leave," Brody seethed, his towering height allowing him to go nose-to-nose with Cian, "then you tell me what's going on. *Is* Sayre in danger?"

Through the thrashing of his pulse in his ears, he heard himself say, "She's been in danger from the moment I first realized she was *mine*."

"From who? *You?*"

"No," he grunted, choking back the bile that rose in his throat. "From an old enemy of mine."

"What *old* enemy? What the hell does that mean? Don't we all have the *same* enemies?"

Jerking free of the Runner's hold, Cian climbed into the car and slammed the door. Brody banged on the window with his fist, but he ignored him as he cranked the engine, then twisted in his seat to look over his shoulder and floored the accelerator as he reversed down the road.

He felt exactly like the asshole Brody had called him for leaving like this, knowing they were going to worry. But, damn it, he didn't have time to waste on explanations. He needed to get to West Virginia, to the girl he'd left behind, before it was too late and he lost his chance.

Your chance to do what? Save her life? his wolf muttered. *Because that's the* only *thing you have a chance in hell of saving when it comes to you and her. You've screwed up too badly for any "second chances" with the girl. And don't think I'm ever going to let you forget it.*

He ground his back teeth together, not wanting to hear it—*any* of it. Then he felt something slick and cold stir to life inside him, meandering its way through his veins, and suddenly the beast's nagging seemed the far lesser of two evils. Yeah, the wolf part of his nature might be a pain in the ass at times, but at least it was noble. Hard and vicious and animalistic, yes; but it lived its life according to a code.

Unfortunately, the wolf wasn't the only thing living beneath his skin, and Cian wanted to claw at his heart until he could rip the blackened organ from his chest. Because that was where the "other" part of him lived. And it wasn't noble or honest or loyal. It was nothing but hunger and rage and greed. An evil so twisted he'd always hated its existence. Had hidden it away, even from those who were closest to him. Who'd fought at his side, and put not only their lives in his hands, but also the lives of those who meant the most to them.

But now there was no more running. No more avoiding the inevitable…or his past…or those parts of his life that he wished he could simply erase from existence, like a hard rain could wash away grime and filth.

He could search the world over, but he wasn't ever going to find a rain that came down hard enough to wash *him* clean.

Glancing over at the passenger's seat, he spotted the crumpled bit of paper he'd tossed there earlier, the handful of words penned onto its surface carved into his memory like a blade scoring flesh.

> Cian,
> I imagine you'd hoped I wouldn't learn your secret, but I have. I'll give you a head start—though you better hurry. It's time for the little witch and me to play.
> *A*

It was a message that had chilled him to the bone the instant he'd woken in his Dublin apartment and found it waiting on his bedside table. His worst nightmare had come to life, because it meant that his oldest enemy had finally learned the truth about Sayre. That she was *his*. His *life mate*. The one female in the world who had been created for him and him *alone*.

And now his bastard of a brother intended to kill her.

Chapter 2

Sayre Murphy stiffened at the sound of a car smoothly rumbling its way through the quiet forest that surrounded her home; a noise she didn't often hear these days. She pulled off her gardening gloves and moved to her feet, turning away from the flourishing herb garden she'd been tending to cast a worried look toward the narrow dirt road that led right to her cabin. It wasn't even noon yet, but the heat was already oppressive, which was why she was dressed in a pair of cutoff shorts and a tank top and nothing more. She no longer had any need to dress for company, and she sure as hell hadn't been expecting any. Jillian and the others knew better than to show up unannounced, which meant that whoever was coming up her drive wasn't going to be anyone in her family.

And that meant they could be looking for trouble.

She dropped her gloves beside a leafy, aromatic patch of basil and flexed her hands at her sides, confident that she could deal with any threat that might be approaching. As a Lycan witch, she didn't possess the ability to shapeshift like the others in her pack—but with the strength of her powers these days, it didn't matter. She could zap any person or creature that tried to get near her with a jolt of pure energy that had brought grown Lycans to their knees.

"Ohmyfreakinggod." The hoarse words slipped past her lips as a sleek black sports car came around the last bend in the road and she caught sight of the driver. Stunned, she lurched back as if she'd suddenly been kicked in the stomach. Cian Hennessey was the *last* person she'd ever expected to see, and she shuddered, every blasphemy she could think of screaming through her head. Gripping the front of her tank top, directly over the thundering beat of her heart, she pushed down as if she needed the physical pressure to keep the racing organ inside her chest.

His pale gray eyes were locked hard on hers as he killed the engine, opened the door and unfolded his long, powerful body from behind the steering wheel. The sight of him had her stumbling back again, and she nearly fell on her bottom when the right heel of her hiking boot connected with the wooden edge of a flower bed.

The morning sun was behind him now, shining directly into her eyes. It was difficult to make out his features as he headed directly for her, his long-legged stride making short work of the yards that separated them. But she *felt* him with every part of her. The pull between them was so strong she could have counted his thudding heartbeats down to the minute, or his quickening intakes of air. The closer he came, the more heightened her sensory perception grew, and she really hoped that it didn't work in the reverse. She didn't want this man reading her. Didn't want him to feel the rushing of her pulse or the heat gathering beneath her skin, warm and thick and wild.

And she sure as hell didn't want him to know that there was a part of her breaking into sharp, jagged little pieces deep inside just because she was looking at him, breathing him in, completely and embarrassingly glomming on to every exquisite detail, after believing for so long that she'd never see him again. She knew there wasn't a man alive who could make jeans, a black T-shirt and boots look so unbelievably good—his body appearing even harder than it'd been before, as if he'd spent the past five years engaged in brutal combat.

"What are you doing here?" she demanded as firmly as possible, when he came to a stop no more than ten feet in front of her and she finally managed to find her voice. The way his long-lashed silver gaze swept hotly over her figure, taking her in from head to toe as if he had every right to what he saw had her vibrating with pure, volcanic rage. The freaking nerve of the guy! "No, scratch that. I don't care why you're here. Just get back in your car and go away, Hennessey. I don't want you here."

He didn't respond to her outburst in any way other than to take a step closer, and she was surprised when she found herself pulling in even deeper breaths of air through her nose, just so she could soak in that sexy-as-sin scent of his. A heady combination of the outdoors, musk and salt, it sat on her tongue like something she wanted to savor and suck on, and keep it there forever. She'd always enjoyed the way Cian had smelled, even when he carried the faint scent of cigarette smoke on his skin, but...*whoa*, her reaction had never been this intense before, as if she wanted to rub up against him like a kitten and get that mouthwatering scent all over her. More than a little rattled, she snapped, "Well? Are you going to stand there staring at me all day or are you at least going to say something?"

"Sorry," he rasped, the lilting sound of the brogue she knew he'd developed while growing up in Ireland even stronger than she remembered it, making her wonder where he'd been living. His tongue touched the corner of his mouth, and his thick lashes lowered over eyes she could have sworn had started to glow like melting metal, despite the tiredness she could see in them. "I just...you surprised me," he added gruffly. "I didn't expect you to be even more beautiful than you were before."

Wearing cutoff denim shorts with a threadbare tank top and scuffed boots on her feet, her long hair in a crazy swarm of curls around her shoulders and dirt probably smeared on her cheek? Um, yeah, like she was really rocking an attractive look at the moment. Shaking her head, she snorted at his lame-ass attempt at flattery. "We've never lied to each other before, Cian. It would be pointless to start now."

"I'm not lying, lass. You're..." He trailed off as his breath left his lungs on a sharp exhalation, and he cursed as he slowly rubbed one of his hands over his wide mouth. "You were always pretty, but the only word I can think of that does you any justice now is *stunning*."

The scowl on her face became a little fiercer, and she wanted to tell him to take his bullshit and shove it up his backside. She knew she looked different than the scrawny eighteen-year-old he'd left behind—she was curvier now, her hair was longer and wilder, and God only knew she had more freckles on her nose and shoulders thanks to all the hours she spent outdoors—but she didn't look *that* different.

And he was...damn him, he was still just as gorgeous

as ever. Other than the shorter cut of his hair, he didn't look as if he'd changed at all, even though he had to be pushing close to forty by now. His features were still chiseled, but ruggedly male, the shadow of stubble on his lean cheeks and square chin giving his already danger-ous good looks an even sharper, more aggressive edge. All broad shoulders and masculine lines, ripped and lean and deliciously cut. The kind of guy that women acted like idiots over, losing their self-esteem somewhere down around their ankles, right along with their underwear.

Then there was his bravery and intelligence and his wicked sense of humor. His undeniable loyalty to his friends and family.

Well, that last bit could no doubt be scratched from the list now, seeing as how he'd turned his back on them as completely as he had on her. But before that…God, before that, Cian Hennessey *could* have been exactly what she'd wanted.

If he'd only wanted her in return.

"Cian, please," she said as carefully as she could man-age, praying her voice wouldn't tremble. "Say whatever you came to say and then leave. I honestly don't want you here. It isn't…it isn't good for me."

She watched his throat work as he swallowed, his voice low and rough in a way that had never failed to make her shiver from the inside out. "There's a lot I need to explain. I know that, Sayre. But we don't have the time. We need to leave this place."

"Not a chance," she said, wondering if he'd been hit over his gorgeous head with a crazy stick. "*We* don't need to do anything. I live here; you don't. Whatever you want from me is nothing but a waste of your time. I don't give second chances."

Frustration shot through his narrowed eyes, making

them as dark as smoke. "You never even really gave me a first chance, much less a second one."

Amazed by those quiet, almost bitter words, she slowly shook her head, then pulled her shoulders back and glared. "That's total crap and you know it. And don't make it sound like you even wanted one."

"Then don't act like you know what I wanted," he argued roughly, "because you never had a goddamn clue."

Her control shredded like a cheap pair of tights, and she heard herself snarl, "You made my life hell!"

He came another step closer. "Right back at you, Sayre."

"Then why are you even here?" she shouted, watching his eyes widen as he slowly looked her over again. Oh... *hell*. Her power had just slipped free of her hold with the galvanic rise of her temper, skittering around her body in a fine spray of tiny, golden sparks.

Damn it, it was just her luck that she looked like a freaking sparkler every time she lost control of her emotions these days. With her hands fisted at her sides, she waited for him to comment on the bizarre display, knowing it was shocking even in their nothing-is-normal world.

But he didn't.

Instead, he rubbed his hand over his mouth again, almost as if he were wiping away whatever words were waiting there. Then he cleared his throat, muttered a low curse and looked her right in the eye as he said, "There isn't time to explain, but you *can't* stay here, Sayre. I'm taking you back to the Alley, where you belong."

She blinked back at him, unable to believe his arrogance. He acted as though he had every right to just stroll back into her life and take control. "Cian, even if I *wanted* to go back to the Alley, I couldn't." Her voice almost shook with a telling tremor as she added, "I can't stand to be around other people."

It occurred to her, as soon as the words left her lips, that she wasn't experiencing any pain—at least physically—while standing there with *him*. If he didn't mention it, then she sure as heck wasn't going to. But he was staring at her so intently with those incredible metallic eyes, she felt as if he were trying to take an intimate stroll through her mind, to dig out all her secret thoughts and emotions and truths, and in a sudden change of heart, she almost wished that he could. It would serve him right, because while he wouldn't have any trouble finding her desire for him, he'd also witness firsthand just how deeply her anger and disappointment ran. And it was deep. As deep as her freaking soul.

Finally, he pulled in a somewhat ragged breath, slowly exhaled and broke the tension-filled standoff. "I went to the Alley this morning," he confessed in a low voice. "Brody and Mic told me why you had to leave." His tongue flicked against the corner of his mouth again, and he shook his head a little. "I didn't know, Sayre. All this time, I thought you were still *with* them. That you were protected."

"Don't," she muttered, realizing that Michaela hadn't even called to warn her that Cian was coming. She couldn't believe her sister's friend would do that to her. The traitor! "I don't need your pity, Cian."

His mouth twisted, and she couldn't help but stare, thinking about what it would be like to feel those sensual lips against hers. She might not know many things about pleasure, but she knew how to kiss. She'd kissed her share of cute boys in her teens, and had enjoyed the hell out of it, though she'd never been willing to go further than that. Turns out it'd been a stupid choice. Back then, she'd had her girlish head filled with the idea of an everlasting, romantic love when she found her life mate, like Jillian and Jeremy had. Not that their road to happiness had been all sunshine and roses, but she wanted what they'd worked so hard for and had found in the end. Wanted it so badly that she'd been willing to fight for it, too. To earn it. Cherish it. Him. *Her man.*

Then fate had played the cruelest joke possible, and given her the Irishman. Yes, he was the most insanely sexy and gorgeous and powerful male she'd ever encountered. But he was the worst womanizer in existence. Sayre had heard all the rumors about the pack females he'd bedded until they could barely walk straight. Of his extreme intensity. His talent, skill and stamina, and the way a woman was never quite the same after she'd experienced his bed...or any of the other hundreds of places Sayre had heard he'd taken them.

She'd wanted a man who would love her and build a life with her. And, instead, she'd been given the one who'd always looked at her as if he couldn't quite stand to be in her presence.

She still remembered the moment when she'd finally realized why there was so much tension between them—the moment she recognized *exactly* what he was to her. They'd been in a roomful of people, surrounded by their friends, and she knew he'd already picked up on what was between them, or at least suspected it, when he looked over at her and caught her stunned expression. She'd been torn between agony and a need that was so strong she'd had to reach out and brace herself against the wall. Her eighteenth birthday had already come and gone, but he'd looked at her as if she were nothing more than an annoying child.

In that moment, Sayre had been so frightened of how

badly he could hurt her. Of the pain he could inflict—
not to her body, but to her heart. But then, standing there
across from him in that crowded room, her conscience
had chided her for being judgmental and not even giving him a chance. For one brief, incredible moment, hope
had flooded her system, filling her with heat, and she'd
given him a tentative smile. One that no doubt said, *I
think you're beautiful and you're mine and I vow to do
everything I can to make you happy. Everything I can to
make you want me...make you love me.*

He'd answered her unspoken message by taking his
phone out and holding her stare as he called someone.
She was too far away to hear what he was saying, but
she could read enough of the words on his lips to know
he'd just called one of *them.* A woman he would take
to his bed and bury himself inside, giving her what belonged to Sayre.

Her girlish heart had died a little that night. And then
a little more with each night that went by and he lost
himself inside female after female, never attempting to
hide what he was up to.

Over the weeks and months, life on the mountain had
become intolerable because of him. It was obvious that
he had no intention of ever acknowledging the connection between them, and yet, he hadn't liked her spending time with other males. Not even with Max Doucet
and Elliot Connors, who were her closest friends, and
the youngest of the Bloodrunners.

The final straw had come a few weeks after the war
they'd won over the neighboring Whiteclaw pack. Finally deciding she was done with whatever stupid game
he'd been playing with her, the next time Sayre got him
alone, she'd given him an ultimatum: he could either stop
acting like a jackass and take her virginity, or she was

going to say to hell with it all and give it up to the first of her male friends who agreed. He'd been livid at her threat, but she'd refused to back down.

Instead, she'd left his ass standing there in the forest, and had walked away.

What had happened that night had been the most difficult thing she'd ever done, putting herself out there like that, but she'd been fueled by ridiculous hope that it would make a difference. A hope she'd refused to admit even to herself at the time. But now, looking back, Sayre knew she'd been gambling her pride on the idea that if she could just get Cian to touch her, he'd realize she was all he needed and that they were meant to be together.

God, she'd been such a pathetic little fool.

In the morning, she'd heard that he'd left the Alley and nobody knew where he'd gone, or if he would ever return. Her heart had been completely shattered, but within a few days it became clear that more than just her heart had been altered by his absence. And while the others had become aware of her increasing problems with her powers, none of them had ever figured out her secret—and she sure as hell never planned on telling them the truth.

Now, after everything that had happened and all the time that had passed, she could hardly believe he was standing in front of her. All the pain she'd tried so hard to bury these past years came rushing back in a surge of emotion, cutting its way through her insides like a scalpel, and she shuddered as she took another step back from him, shaking, no doubt turning as pale as a ghost. She watched his eyes darken with sympathy, and her palm tingled with the urge to slap his beautiful, faithless face.

"I didn't know," he said again, the rough words sounding scraped from his throat. "I would have come home sooner, Sayre. I wouldn't have stayed away. I was only trying to—"

"Stop!" she snapped, cutting him off. "Just stop. I don't want to hear it, because if you say you left to protect me from your big bad self, so help me, God, I just might have to kill you."

He pulled in a sharp breath, nostrils flaring as he shoved one of those big hands back through his thick, dark-as-midnight hair. She'd never seen it as short as it was now, the ends only just brushing the back of his collar. "You know, I *should* have left for that reason. But I wouldn't have. I wouldn't have had the strength. As bad as I am, Sayre, I left to protect you from something even worse."

"Oh, God, that's funny," she said with a choked laugh, wrapping her arms around her middle. But no matter how tightly she squeezed, she still felt like she teetered on the cusp of falling apart. "What could be worse than *you*?"

He flinched at that brutal assessment, but didn't back down. "It's a long story and we don't have the time to get into it now. I just…I need you to trust me."

"Cian, just stop," she said with a derisive snort. "I honestly didn't know you could be this freaking hilarious."

"This isn't a goddamn joke," he muttered, giving her a look that seemed to say he was thinking of putting her over his knee and swatting her backside. And, God, did that piss her off. He'd lost the right to even think about putting his hands on her.

"You're damned right it's not a joke," she seethed, crackling with so much energy she was in danger of singeing her beloved garden. "Now get the hell off my land!"

"Sayre." He said her name on a long, drawn-out sigh, sounding too much like an adult who'd lost his pa-

tience with an unruly teen, and she felt her fury tip from emotion…right into action. Bathed in a fiery shower of sparks, she reached behind her and whipped out the gun she always kept tucked against her lower back when she was outside on her own. Just because she didn't need the weapon didn't mean it didn't come in handy. Especially when dealing with rowdy human males who wandered onto her land, thinking they could cause trouble with the woman who lived there on her own. And right now, it felt unbelievably sweet to point the gleaming barrel directly at Cian Hennessey's no-good heart.

He shot her a dry look and slowly arched one of his raven-black brows. "It's a pretty toy," he drawled, the lazy way he crossed his muscular arms over his chest telling her he didn't believe for one second that she'd shoot him. "But you know that bullets won't kill me, Sayre."

"They might not kill you, but they'll hurt like a bitch."

"You really think I could believe that you'd pull the trigger? You're a healer, not a—"

"Seriously?" she laughed, cutting him off as she unlocked the safety with a practiced flick of her thumb. "You might have watched me grow up, Cian, but don't for an instant think that you know what I'm capable of as a woman. I've had to deal with more crap since you left than you could ever imagine. People change. *I've* changed. So when I pull a gun out, you can bet your ass that I plan to use it."

His sexy mouth pressed into a hard, irritated, challenging line. "Then do it."

She aimed for less than an inch from the toe of his right boot, and fired a perfect shot.

"Shit!" he cursed, jumping back a step. "What the hell, woman? Have you lost your bloody mind?"

"I told you I'd do it." She kept her tone hard and cold,

determined to make him see that she meant business, and slowly raised her aim. "So tell me, Cian. Do you really want to play this game?"

He worked his jaw for a few seconds, no doubt cursing her to hell and back. Then his scowl smoothed out, and his eyes narrowed to the point that it was impossible to read the look in them. Whatever he was thinking as he calmly turned on his heel and headed back to his car—the back view of his tall, powerful body damn near as mouthwatering as the front—was something he didn't want her to pick up on. And *that* made her nervous.

When she called his name out, just as he was opening his car door, he looked back at her over his broad shoulder, and she gave him a sharp, icy smile. "If you like your body without any extra holes in it, *don't* bother coming back."

Chapter 3

Knowing Sayre needed some time to calm down, Cian climbed back into the Audi. He drove nearly a quarter of a mile down the mountain, then pulled over into a flat grassy area on the side of the road and parked. Though he never would have believed it, the beautiful little witch *had* been ready to put a freaking bullet in him. He'd have been incredibly proud over the way she'd stood up for herself, if her target had been anything other than his own body…and the circumstances weren't so serious.

But they were, which was why there was no way in hell he was tucking his tail between his legs and running. This was nothing but a change in strategy, and a good hunter always knew when to step back and regroup. So while he might have let her think she'd won the first round, he was already focused on the second, determined to be the one who came out on top in the end.

On top of her, *you mean*, the wolf's gravelly voice

rumbled in his head, and he rolled his eyes at the beast's wishful thinking. Not that it wouldn't have been nice—and by nice he meant fucking exceptional—but he knew that sex was the last damn thing he could afford to think about in connection with Sayre. Too much of that already took place when he finally allowed himself to sleep.

Though he'd tried not to, Cian had been dreaming about Sayre Murphy from the moment he'd walked away. Hell, even before that, when he was still living in the Alley and fighting his need for her on a daily basis. But the dreams had been...*evolving* over the last few months, and while many of them were more nightmare than fantasy now, the erotic ones were becoming shockingly intense. Not that they'd ever been tame—but there was a feverish, visceral edge to them now that had him strung so tightly he was surprised he hadn't snapped. Over the past few weeks, he'd awakened so many times thrusting and clawing at his sheets that he'd started to feel like a perpetually randy teen again, and God only knew he'd spent too many years perfecting *that* testosterone-driven stage of his life.

But even his dreams hadn't done the reality of her justice.

Sayre at eighteen had been beautiful. But Sayre at twenty-three was enough to make him want to sell his goddamn soul for the chance to touch her. She was *that* incredible. So earthy and warm and sensual that it'd taken every ounce of his strength to claw on to his control when he'd approached her, instead of taking her down to the ground and claiming every inch of her lush little body for his own.

Only the certainty that she'd hate him in the end had enabled him to fight that fierce, possessive pull. That...

and the fact that he had no business touching her when he could never give her the things she deserved. Christ, he couldn't even give her next month, much less promises of love and a family and forever.

Careful to stay hidden, he made his way back up the mountain on foot and studied her cabin from the shelter of the woods. The place was small but pretty, surrounded by a large, colorful garden that was obviously well tended. But the location couldn't have been more remote if she'd moved to the wilds of Alaska, and it twisted his insides to think of her being stuck out here all alone. It was the last thing in the world he would have expected for the girl who'd always greeted everyone with a smile and a hug; she'd always been an effortless little social butterfly who people couldn't help but want to be around.

Though there were a lot of Lycans who went away to attend university among the human population, he knew that Sayre had planned on going to a local school for a degree in environmental studies. He hadn't understood why she was so determined to stay with the pack while she continued her education, but now he thought that maybe he did. If her powers had been increasing to the point that she was having trouble dealing with them, she might have worried over what would happen if she were too far away from her family. He hated that she'd carried that kind of burden back then; girls in their teens didn't need to be worrying about such serious issues. But Sayre had fought in the war right along with the rest of her family, and it'd been apparent even then that her powers were…different. She'd already been capable of firing powerful bursts of light from her hands, and had taken down the enemy with a skill that had completely shocked him—though young, she'd shown no mercy to those who would have harmed her loved ones.

And now this. Instead of finishing her studies and starting to find her way in the world, she was living like a recluse in the goddamn mountains, all alone. No family. No friends. He felt to blame, even though he hadn't been there. But wasn't it better for her to be alone than to be with someone like him?

Not wanting to think about the answer to that question, he glanced at the thick, military-grade watch on his wrist, surprised she hadn't come down to check that he'd followed her orders and left. Did she actually believe he would just turn and walk away when her life was in danger?

Only you never actually got around to telling her that part, did you? his beast muttered, making him scowl. He didn't need the animal telling him what he already knew. Yeah, he should have explained the seriousness of the situation to her right from the start, but he'd had his reasons for holding back.

At first, he'd simply been too dumbstruck by how she'd changed, and he couldn't blame himself for that. He'd all but been knocked back on his ass by the sight of her. But then he'd told her there wasn't time to explain, which was bullshit. He could have *made* the time, but the fact was that he simply hadn't been ready to spill the whole sordid story. Telling her meant giving her one more reason to hate him, and she already had enough of those.

But no matter how angry she was, or how much the situation sucked, he wasn't leaving this mountain without her. He might have turned his back on her before, but only because he'd thought it was the best way to keep her safe.

Only…the danger had found her anyway, hadn't it?

Which meant that for all his running, he was still stuck in the same destructive loop, and there didn't seem to be any way out of it. Not until Aedan no longer hung over his life like a malevolent shadow, ready to wreak pain, terror and death on anything that he wanted for himself.

The minutes moved by in a slow crawl, the air hot and sticky with humidity, though he barely noticed, his attention completely fixated on Sayre as the witch went about her daily routine. Every now and again, he would pick up the muted sounds of her voice as she talked to herself, the low words edged with anger and frustration. He'd definitely pissed her off by coming there, which meant that she was still angry about the way he'd left and hadn't gotten over it. That she hadn't forgotten him. And as wrong as it was, he liked that she'd been thinking about him all these years. That he'd made a big enough impact on her life to be remembered.

You're her life mate, dimwit, his wolf grunted. *Not like she can just forget that little tidbit.*

"Piss off," he muttered, knowing damn well that the beast was right.

Are we going to just stand out here all day? the animal persisted. *Because we belong over there with her. We belong* inside *her.*

He choked back a curse, the need searing through his veins making him sweat even more than the heat. He'd never so much as kissed Sayre, and yet, he strongly suspected that sex with her would be unlike anything he'd ever known. Just the fantasy of it overshadowed every woman he'd ever been with, and there'd been so many. *Too many.* Faces and bodies and names that he wouldn't have been able to recall to save his life—which only made him that much more of a bastard.

The wind finally picked up, but he was far enough
away that he didn't need to worry she would scent him on
the air. Though Lycan blood pumped through her veins,
she was unable to take the shape of a wolf, which meant
she didn't have the same heightened abilities as the rest of
them. Instead, the women in her bloodline were known as
witches, or healers. They were each powerful in their own
right, but he'd never felt the charge of energy surrounding a Lycan-born witch like he had with Sayre. She was
truly in a class of her own, and he couldn't help but wonder how those powers would mature as she grew older.

He seriously doubted that she needed the gun. Though
he'd once been able to force his way through her power,
when they'd been in the heat of battle and he'd been hell-
bent on protecting her, she was stronger now. If she'd
wanted, he was sure she could have blasted him with
enough energy to put him out of commission for the rest
of the day—and Christ, that was sexy. Everything about
the woman was…intoxicating. He'd always thought she
was beautiful in an ethereal, fey kind of way, and had
been intensely attracted to her. But now…*Jesus.* There
honestly weren't words to describe the way she affected
him. Her curly hair had to be a good seven inches longer, reaching the middle of her back, the color a deeper
red that was shot through with streaks of gold, no doubt
from all the time she spent outdoors. Her once thin, colt-
ish body was now deliciously curved, her breasts and ass
a little fuller, giving her slender figure a more lush, wom-
anly look. He couldn't help but imagine what this new
shape of hers would feel like spread out beneath him, all
that sweet, creamy flesh his for the taking.

But his attraction to Sayre Murphy had always been

about more than her looks, and that hadn't changed. If anything, the force of her will held an even deeper draw for him now, her fiery spirit when combined with her tender nature creating an alluring package that would entice any man, but especially the one chosen by fate as her perfect match. Everything about her was designed to please him, and a gruff, troubled burst of laughter softly fell from his lips as he scrubbed a hand over his face, knowing he was in some seriously deep shit. Even if she weren't the sexiest thing he'd ever set eyes on, he'd have wanted her. The fact that her innate sensuality was even more prevalent now, her mouth and scent and the husky sound of her voice calling to him on every primitive level, well...that was just overkill. A play of the universe to make the coming days as excruciatingly painful as possible. Hell, at this rate, he was pretty sure he'd feel like he'd gone ten rounds in a medieval torture chamber by the time this nightmare was over. And he'd no doubt bear the scars to prove it, on his skin as well as his blackened heart.

Keep her alive and keep my hands to myself. That needed to be his new mantra—but the second part wouldn't be easy. When she stood up after tending another colorful flower bed and lifted her arms over her head to stretch her back, the little tank top she wore rising up to reveal her sexy tummy and a tiny, dark tattoo that was scrolled around her navel, he realized it would be damn near impossible.

Sweet little Sayre had a tattoo?

Holy...shit. He was fairly certain that his jaw had just dropped down to somewhere around his ankles, his cock so hard he probably wasn't going to be able to walk straight. He didn't know what the intricate symbols of the tattoo meant, but he'd have sold his damn soul in that moment for the chance to drop down on his knees in front of her and press his open mouth to that provocative little piece of artwork. And he sure as hell wouldn't stop there. Trailing his tongue down the center of her body, he would keep going until he was breathing in the sweet, humid scent of her where it would be the richest. Like hot, wild honey on his tongue, melting down his throat, making him hunger in a way he didn't think any human male could ever completely experience. A hunger that went deeper than his flesh—that bled down into his veins and his bones and pumped through the very heart of him.

A drop of sweat slid down the searing heat of his temple, stinging the corner of his eye, and he shook himself out of his thoughts, painfully aware that they weren't leading to any place he'd be able to go. And damned if it weren't enough to make him want to bawl like a friggin' baby. Or howl at the rising moon.

When she reached for something in the back pocket of those short-as-hell shorts and started to walk around the back of the cabin, Cian pushed off from the tree he'd been leaning against, ready to change his position so that she wasn't out of his sight. But he froze when his cell phone suddenly vibrated in the front pocket of his jeans, his brows lifting with surprise. He was unused to anyone trying to contact him, since the number was one he'd gotten after he'd left five years ago, and there were only a few informants he'd employed over that time who he'd given it to. They rarely contacted him, and how was he even getting reception out here?

This is so ridiculous. I know you're out there. Leave. Now. Before I go all West Virginia on your ass.

The text was from Sayre?

How the hell did you get my number?

I asked Mic for it.

Ah, that's right. He'd texted Brody that morning, so his number was in the Runner's phone. All Mic had to do was—

Enough stalling, his beast snapped, cutting him off. *Text her back!*

How did you know I'm out here?

That's not the issue, Cian. Leave. Like I told you before, I don't want you here.

He rubbed the back of his neck, wondering just how strong her powers had gotten over the last five years. Christ, she couldn't read his mind, could she? No, if she could, then she'd know about the danger from Aedan, which meant she'd understand how serious he was about taking her back to the Alley, where the others could help him protect her.

Knowing he just needed to get it over and done with, like ripping off a bloody bandage, his fingers flew across the keypad as he typed in his response.

I can't leave, Sayre. I'm here because you're in danger. You need to give me the chance to explain.

She didn't text back right away, and he hoped she was finally taking him seriously. Then his phone vibrated again.

No explanations needed. If that's true, then I can take care of myself. Just go.

He cursed, hesitating, then forced himself to write: I can't. It's because of me.

Huh. So what did YOU do? Do I have some psychotic jilted lover coming after me now? Did you accidentally let it slip that you have a mate? Should've told the poor woman you want nothing to do with me. She's wasting her time.

Oh, Jesus. He barked out a dry laugh, even though there was nothing remotely funny about the situation. Not want her? There were parts of her he wanted so badly he was surprised the need hadn't permanently damaged him.

Would serve you right, his beast muttered with disgust, as disappointed in him as everyone else who had ever meant anything to him.

You're damned right I am. And you sound pathetic.

Irritated that the animal had just called him out for taking part in an embarrassing private pity party, he started to make his way toward the cabin, ready to face the wrath of Sayre *and* her gun, when he and his beast both instantly realized something was wrong. While the wolf chuffed in his head, Cian lifted his nose and sniffed the mountain air, searching for what had snagged his attention, and promptly finding it. Two...no, three human males were closing in on Sayre's cabin from the north, and Cian stealthily headed in their direction, until he could pick up their muted conversation.

"Oh, man, he didn't tell us she was such a hot little piece. I'm thinking we need to try this one out before we deliver her," one of them said, obviously eyeing Sayre through the trees.

"I get her first," argued a second male.

"Like hell you do," a new voice cackled. "You always break them and then they aren't any fun for the rest of us."

"But I've got a thing for redheads," the second one whined.

"We don't give a shit. You can wait your fuckin' turn."

Cian moved silently through the trees, drawing nearer, every part of him completely focused on his prey. Did these idiots actually think he was going to let them get close to her? Did they have any idea what they were walking into? Either way, it didn't matter. Their fates had been sealed the instant they voiced their intentions.

"Let's spread out, blocking her exits. That asshole who hired us said it might be a few days before he showed up to collect her, and I'd rather spend the time we've got with her having fun than running her down."

One of his friends snickered. "That's just because your bum knees don't hold up anymore. But I kinda like the thought of chasing her down like a bitch."

In that moment, Cian almost regretted the necessity of killing them quickly. It no doubt made him a brutal bastard, but he would have enjoyed making these assholes suffer long and hard before he finally finished them off.

He quickly texted Sayre, ordering her to lock herself inside the cabin. Then he shoved the phone in his pocket, and released his long, lethal fangs and claws, the sharp tips piercing through gum and skin with a brief but familiar bite of pain. Without the light of the moon, this was as much as his body could shift form, but it was more than enough. Whatever weapons the humans possessed, they weren't going to be any match for his speed and skill.

In normal circumstances, he would have never revealed the deadly, animalistic side of his nature in front of humans, since the Lycan race's existence was a carefully protected secret from the vast majority of the population. But these weren't normal circumstances, and these assholes weren't ever going to leave this mountain.

Relaxing his tether on his beast, Cian allowed the wolf to prowl closer to his surface, the animal's possessive, visceral need to protect its mate punching deeper into his system, ramping his adrenaline at the same time he shifted into a state of total focus. His objective was extremely simple: destroy the threat by any means necessary. With a deep breath and a flex of his claws, he launched his attack.

It took only seconds to find the first male in the line of trees behind her cabin, the vile stench of body odor impossible to miss for someone with Cian's acute sense of smell. He slashed his claws across the human's throat and swiftly retreated to avoid as much of the thick, crimson spray as he could. Its rich scent had his pulse ramping up, the blackened part of his soul that he hated with such ferocity awakening with the rush for *more*. For that wet, slick spill to slide down his throat and feed the darkness. Forcing himself to abandon the kill and move on, he quickly closed in on the second human from behind, the bastard never even knowing he was there until he felt the sharp press of Cian's blood-covered claws tearing across his throat as his body crumpled to the forest floor.

Two down, one to go.

The third male had made his way around the eastern

edge of her property, intending to cut off Sayre from the south. Following the scent of cheap beer and stale sweat, Cian easily found the human standing between two towering trees as the last vestiges of sunlight held on, not yet ready to release its claim to the day. There was a nauseating leer on the bastard's face as he stared at her cabin, his tongue slicking across his lips while he tapped the blade of a hunting knife against his thigh. Cian was giving private thanks that Sayre had actually listened to him and gone inside, when she suddenly stepped out from behind the small shed not ten yards away from where the man stood, holding a rifle in her arms. He heard the click of the gun a fraction of a second before she fired a bullet into the male's thigh. The force of Sayre's shot sent the human crashing to the ground, and Cian quickly finished him off with a fatal swipe of his claws before turning toward the headstrong woman who apparently didn't know how to follow orders to save her life.

It took him six strides to reach her, and while she lowered the gun, she didn't even try to run. Retracting his blood-drenched claws, he ripped the gun out of her hold and tossed it aside. Then he quickly gripped her upper arms, yanked her up onto her toes and roared, "What the hell, Sayre? I told you to stay inside the cabin!"

"Like I give a rat's ass what you told me to do!" she shouted back at him.

"You got a death wish, little girl?" He got right in her face, his voice dropping to a sibilant hiss. "Because that was the dumbest move I've ever seen anyone make."

Shaking with fury, she began using her power to try and make him release her, but he refused to budge. If he'd been human, the palms of his hands would have no doubt been blistered within a few seconds, unable to endure the searing burst of heat she was generating without letting go. He growled at her, but she didn't so much as bat an eyelash, and he realized this female—*his female*—was a woman who would never cower before a man. Raging, intense pride and lust fired through his system, his blood thickening low in his body, while his heart thundered like something trying to break its way free.

With another rough, guttural growl, Cian forced himself to slowly set her back on her feet as he loosened his grip on her arms. He knew that if he didn't put some distance between them right then, there was a strong chance he was going to take her to the moss-covered ground beneath their feet and drive himself so deep inside her he wouldn't ever find his way back out.

"Who were those men?" she demanded, ripping out of his hold.

"My brother," he grunted, only to realize that his words didn't make any sense. "I mean, none of those men were Aedan. But I'm guessing they were working for him."

She blinked up at him with dark, gold-tipped lashes. "What are you talking about? You don't have a brother."

"It's a long story, but I'll explain on the road." Well, he'd explain some of it. No way in hell was he telling her everything.

"Cian."

"Listen. Next time, he won't send a bunch of human thugs. Those guys were just a game to him, Sayre. A message meant to let us know that he's found you and has you in his sights. But he won't play the game for long. Eventually, it will be *him*, in the flesh, and I know you don't trust me, but you can believe me when I tell you that going head-to-head with Aedan isn't something we could walk away from without paying for it first. Not here. Not alone."

She cut her gaze to the side and frowned. "I—"

"Damn it, Sayre, look at me!" He worked his jaw as her narrowed gaze locked with his, then grated out, "I can't let that happen. I *won't*. I will throw you in my damn car and tie you up if I have to, though I'd rather you come on your own. I don't want to hurt you, but there's no way I'm letting you stay here. He's *not* getting you."

She opened her mouth, then snapped it shut. He could see the indecision shadowing her gaze, her intuition battling against her desire to be rid of him. He could understand her anger, but he couldn't let it get in the way of keeping her alive.

"If not for yourself, then think about Jillian. About Jeremy and their kids," he told her. Jillian had been pregnant when he'd left, so he knew the couple had at least one child. "You don't think he'd go after them if he thought it would hurt you?"

Color leached from her face, making the spray of freckles across her nose stand out in stark relief. "What the hell do me and my family have to do with any of this?"

"He wants to hurt me, and he thinks you're the way to do that."

A bitter laugh burst from her pink lips, and she shook her head in disbelief. "Then he's a fool. I didn't even mean enough to you to fuck. I was just a troublesome little girl you wanted out of your way."

Christ, she couldn't have been more wrong, but he couldn't tell her that. And he sure as hell couldn't let himself think about that four-letter word that had just fallen from her lips—a word he'd never heard her say before. "Sayre, we don't have time to argue. We need to be on the road ten minutes ago."

She stared up at him as the seconds stretched out,

each one seeming to last longer than a lifetime while his hands itched with the need to reach out and grab her so that he could get her to safety. "Fine," she finally agreed, looking as if someone had just thrown her firstborn off a cliff. "I hate it, but I'm not going to cut off my nose to spite my face."

"Smart girl," he murmured with relief.

"*Woman*, Cian. Smart *woman*. I'm no longer a child."

"Uh, yeah. Got it." Then he tacked on a "sorry" for good measure.

Jabbing him in the center of his chest with her finger, she said, "You're damned right you had better be sorry. Because this is *all. Your. Fault!*"

Guilt settled heavily in his gut, and he knew he needed to tread carefully. "I know, and I'm sorry. But can we please just get on the road?"

Shaking her head, she said, "No."

"No?" He sucked in a sharp breath, struggling not to shout at her again. "I thought we just went over this."

"I believe that you've landed me in the middle of a freaking problem, but that doesn't mean I'm running back to the Alley. However—" her voice sounded like she'd swallowed a handful of razor blades as she held one hand up to him in a hold-it-right-there gesture "—I'm willing to let you come inside and talk to me."

"I'm not letting you stay here alone, Sayre."

"Then you had better not piss me off," she huffed as she walked over to where he'd tossed her gun and picked it up, "because I was planning on letting you take the sofa until we have this figured out."

Shit, he thought, shoving a hand back through his hair. Staying here wasn't what he wanted. He needed her in the Alley, where he knew it would be easier to protect her. "It's safer there, Sayre."

With the gun propped on her shoulder, she turned back to him, her expression impossible to read. "That may be. But I'm not going to let you rush me into any decisions right now. I will give myself some time to process this, and then I'll let you know what I've decided to do."

He closed his eyes for a moment, dropping his head back on his shoulders, and counted back from ten.

"While you're struggling with whatever's going through that thick head of yours," she told him, sounding as if she were gloating a bit, "I'll just run inside and grab my keys, then take you down the road so that you can grab your car and bring it back here."

Opening his eyes, Cian lowered his head and watched her walk away, wondering how she made the money to pay for the truck and the cabin, knowing she wasn't the type to live off her parents. Then again, the truck that was parked beside the shed was fairly ancient, so he knew she hadn't unloaded a ton of cash on it.

"You were wrong," he said in a low voice, when she came back outside, keys in hand.

"About what?" she murmured, keeping her gaze focused straight ahead as she made her way over to the faded blue Ford.

"When I first saw you today," he muttered, following after her, "you said we'd never lied to each other. But we did. *I* did. I lied to you all the time."

She didn't ask what he'd lied about as she opened the driver's-side door and climbed behind the wheel, and he wondered if she knew.

He'd told her time and again that he didn't want her.

And each time, it'd been a lie.

In his entire life, he'd never wanted anything like he wanted Sayre Murphy. In his bed. Under him. Completely full of him, his body packed so deeply into hers she could feel him in every part of her. Every cell and breath and thought.

He just didn't want the rest of her.

The last thing in the world that Cian needed was a woman's heart, because he knew exactly what he'd do to it. And while he might not love Sayre Murphy, he liked her too much to want to see her crushed, which is what would happen. It wasn't arrogance or his ego talking; it was a simple fact. She was too young to clearly separate sexual need from higher emotion, and he knew that if he touched her, she'd likely end up thinking she was in love with him. Wasn't there a saying about how hate and love were simply two sides of the same coin? So while she might hate him now, that feeling could be twisted into the other. After everything he'd done, he owed it to her to keep that from happening.

Does that mean you plan to keep your hands to yourself? his wolf demanded, prowling beneath his skin. *'Cause I gotta tell you, that doesn't work for me. If given the chance, I plan on getting between those perfect thighs of hers and staying there, where we belong.*

He made a gruff sound in the back of his throat, wishing the animal would just shut up and leave him alone.

And by the way, I still think you're an idiot. Jackass.

Irritated, tired and at the end of his rope, his grip tightened on the passenger's-side door handle until he'd nearly ripped it off, the beast's guttural laughter echoing through his head as he climbed up into the truck. It knew it'd gotten under his skin, and he wondered if his friends all had this much trouble with the possessive predators who lived inside them, or if it were only him. Seemed just his luck that his wolf would not only be a pain of the first order, but a sarcastic son of a bitch, as well.

"Cian?" Sayre said as she cranked the engine and slid

him a curious look. "Are you going to sit there growling at your door all day or are you going to shut it?"

He didn't bother to respond. He didn't dare. He didn't trust anything that might have come out of his mouth at that moment, and his pulse was thrashing in his ears too loudly to carry on a conversation anyway.

Instead, he slammed the door shut, rolled the window down and focused his attention on the surrounding woods, knowing that Aedan could very well be out there, watching and waiting, slowly biding his time. The human thugs had been his brother's first play, but they wouldn't be his last.

And now the clock was ticking.

Chapter 4

As soon as he parked the Audi behind Sayre's truck and climbed out, a terrible sense of doom settled over Cian, hanging around his shoulders like a leaden weight. It sounded embarrassingly dramatic, but there was no denying the emotion. It was like a thundering death knell echoing in his head, warning him that nothing about this situation was going to end in the way that he wanted it to. He *knew*, damn it…and yet, he couldn't turn back.

Instead, he simply followed her into the small cabin, doing his best to keep his attention focused on their surroundings and not on how tight her little ass looked in those too-short-for-his-sanity shorts.

Seriously? You sound like an old man who doesn't even know how to get it up anymore.

"Fuck off," he muttered under his breath, mentally giving his wolf the finger. It wasn't a question of not being able to get it up. It was knowing how quickly she'd have his friggin' balls kicked in if he let the sight of her in those shorts take hold of him.

While she closed the door behind them, he did a quick survey of the room. The cabin was built with an open floor plan, the walls lined with row upon row of packed bookshelves, the bindings on the books creased from use. A hallway on the right led to what he assumed would be her bedroom and the bathroom, the kitchen located off to their left. There was a high-tech sound system on a small table in the corner of the main room, but no television. If she watched movies, it was likely on her computer or iPad, and he recalled Jillian once talking about her sister's penchant for comedies.

A scowl twisted his brow as he tried to recall the last comedy he'd watched. It'd no doubt been something he'd caught down at one of the cinemas in the human town of Covington with Brody before he'd left, but he couldn't remember the title. Just that he hadn't felt like he got even half of the jokes, and he'd hated how old that'd made him feel.

He hated it even more now, when there was a so-beautiful-she-hurt-his-eyes twenty-three-year-old walking away from him as she headed toward the kitchen. She would probably laugh her ass off if she knew he'd "technically" be pushing fifty in a few years.

His body might be young—he halted the aging process when consuming blood as one of his main food sources—but his spirit felt freaking ancient, as if he'd lived three times that long.

As she washed her hands at the kitchen sink, she looked at him from over her shoulder, eyeing his blood-spattered jeans and T-shirt, and jerked her head in the direction of the small hallway. "You're messier than I am. Why don't you go ahead and grab your shower? It's the first door on your left. Towels are under the sink."

Taking a few steps toward the kitchen, he said, "Actually, I should go and bury the bodies first."

She turned around as she dried her hands on a towel, blinking back at him with those big, storm-colored eyes. "Um...of course. I wasn't...I don't know why I didn't think of that."

Because she wasn't a natural born killer, like he was. And because she was also probably a bit in shock, after everything that had happened. She might have grown up in the hard, often brutal world of the Silvercrest, but Sayre Murphy had always been a dreamer at heart. And dreamers weren't the kind of girls who were accustomed to burying three dead bodies out in the woods behind their homes.

"Is there a shovel in your shed?"

She pulled her lower lip through her teeth and nodded.

The sight of her white teeth on that plush lip had him sweating, and he cleared his throat a little as he swiped his arm over his forehead. "Then you go ahead and grab your shower," he told her, the roughness of his voice telling him he needed to get back outside and cool the hell off. "This won't take me long."

Her eyebrows lifted slightly. "Don't you need help?"

Shaking his head, he said, "I'm not letting you anywhere near them, Sayre. But I won't go too far. I'll be close enough that I can hear you if you need me."

He turned and walked back outside before she could say anything more, and pulled in a deep breath of the humid air as he headed for the shed. A half hour later, he was shoveling the last scoops of dirt over the place where he'd buried the bodies, the grave situated between two thick blackberry bushes that would quickly grow over it. He'd checked all three males' clothing before putting them in the ground, looking for anything that might give him a clue about Aedan's plans, but wasn't surprised when the search turned up nothing. His half brother might be seriously twisted, but he was too smart to make a dumb-ass mistake by trusting anyone like these jackasses with vital information. That was why Cian hadn't bothered to keep one of them alive for questioning.

That...and the fact that he'd been too bloody furious to let them live.

After putting the shovel away in the shed, Cian made his way back inside the cabin, locking the door behind him. He couldn't hear the water running, so he knew Sayre was out of the shower. The sound of a hair dryer clicking on told him she'd be busy for a while longer, so he washed his hands in the kitchen, then went through the French doors that opened onto a small deck and took out his phone. After scrolling through his contacts, he called Brody's cell phone number.

Within two rings, the Runner answered the call. "Where the hell are you? I thought you were bringing her back."

"That's still the plan," he said in a low voice, unsure how much of this shit storm he should explain over the phone. "But it looks like we're staying here tonight."

Brody exhaled a rough breath. "I told you she wouldn't do it."

"Yeah, well, she doesn't have a choice. We ran into some trouble, which I've handled, but this place isn't safe enough for her in the long term. I need her *in* the Alley, with all of your full security measures in place."

"I've sent Michaela up to Shadow Peak with our kids, since you wouldn't tell me what's going on. And I've told Jillian to stay up there, as well, right now. The others are going to stay down in South Carolina until we know it's safe for them to return with their families."

"That's good," he murmured, wondering what had kept Jillian behind. Had the witch had a premonition that her sister would need her?

Brody's next words pulled his attention back to the conversation. "Max and Elliot have been out on a Blood-run, but they'll be back in the morning. And the mercs have been working a job over in Tennessee, but they're expected back in the next day or two. So we'll have security covered, and I'll have the scouts from up in Shadow Peak double their patrols. But we need to know what we're dealing with."

At the mention of the mercs, Cian's already tensed muscles coiled even tighter, and he pinched the bridge of his nose between his thumb and forefinger. The mercenaries were four badass warriors who had worked with Eli Drake for years, and had decided to stick around once Eli had returned to the Alley and married Carla Reyes, the only female Runner in the group.

"This silence is getting kind of tiring, man. You there?" Brody asked.

"Yeah, I'm here," he muttered, keeping a careful eye on the surrounding forest.

"You ready to tell me what's going on?"

He swallowed so hard he could feel the movement all the way down his throat. "This…it's not something I want to get into over the phone, Brody." Hell, it was something he'd rather avoid altogether. But that wasn't going to be an option. "And before you try to argue, don't. You're just going to have to trust me on this."

Brody's deep voice was gruff with frustration. "Yeah, well, it was easier to trust you before you disappeared for five years."

He bit back a guttural curse, knowing there wasn't anything he could say to that particular piece of truth. Part of him was eager to prove to his friends that he was still the same man he'd been before, while another part kept wondering what the point would be, when he would only leave again when it was all said and done.

"Cian, man, I'm serious. You better talk to me or you won't be welcome back in the Alley. I hate to say that, but I don't know where your head is anymore."

He scrubbed his free hand down his face, his insides knotting. So many emotions roiled through him, clashing like warring, blood-drenched sides on a battlefield, that it was impossible to keep them straight. "I swear I'll tell you everything when we get back. I just…" He worked his jaw as his words dried up, hating that he couldn't simply avoid this problem forever. With a tired sigh, he said, "In all honesty, Brody, I need some time to figure out how to say it all."

Silence met his admission, followed by a rough, quiet burst of words. "It's that bad?"

"Yeah. But I won't leave you in the dark. I give you my word on that."

"Then we'll talk when you get back," Brody muttered. "But I need to know if Sayre is okay. Jillian gave Mic and me an earful for not warning the girl that you were coming for her. Jilly's been trying to get her on her cell phone, but Sayre won't take the calls. Just texted back that she was fine and would be in touch later."

"She's good. Pissed, but she's all right."

"Okay then. You need any backup on the road when you head back?"

Unable to resist having her all to himself for just a little longer, he said, "Thanks for the offer, but I think we've got a few days before we need to worry."

"Then keep me updated."

"I will. And stay sharp. There's no reason for you to see any trouble when she's not there, but it's better to be safe."

"On it," the Runner murmured, then disconnected the call. Shoving the phone in his pocket, Cian walked back inside just as the bathroom door clicked open, releasing a wave of warm, Sayre-scented air into the cabin. He couldn't see into the hallway from where he stood, but what was probably her bedroom door snapped shut a moment later. He debated going back outside for a smoke, but decided to simply wait her out, loving the way that intoxicating scent was filling his lungs, working its way through his system.

He spent the next moments looking over the titles on her bookshelves, surprised she was into gritty suspense novels, many of the books ones he'd already read. He lost track of time as he walked around the room, soaking up all the telling details like a sponge with water, hoarding them in his mind. They were like tiny clues that he needed to unlock the mystery of her life, his brain cataloguing everything from the scent of her candles to the type of pen she'd left sitting on top of a notebook. The sofa was off-white and deep, his mind easily picturing her cuddled up among the matching throw pillows with a book, while the evening sunlight touched on the feminine curves of her body. The sensual slope of a shoulder. The lithe shape of her thighs. He stood in the middle of the room, each breath drawing more of her provocative scent into his lungs, while his hands flexed and released at his sides. His tension just kept winding tighter…and tighter, until he nearly stumbled from the jolt of hunger that slammed into him when she came back into the room a few minutes later.

Christ, he thought as he got a good look at her. *Is she trying to kill me?*

The cutoffs had been exchanged for a pair of jeans that hugged her curves like a second skin, her tight black T-shirt molding to a pair of breasts so perfect they made his mouth water. Her skin was still dewy and pink from the shower and the sun, and he had to physically hold himself back from her. Had to fight the animalistic urge to yank her against him and run his tongue up the slender column of her throat, taking all that salty warmth into his mouth. Summer heat had never looked so good on a woman, and he knew he needed to get out of there before he did something stupid.

"Shower's all yours," she told him, her gaze focused on the base of his throat instead of his eyes.

"Thanks." His voice was gruff, but he couldn't help it. She'd taken a step toward him, bringing her into the last wash of sunlight that spilled through one of the front windows, the shimmering beams highlighting the strips of gold buried in all those waves of strawberry-blond. He wanted to search out every strand…wind the long skeins around his fist…and hold her tight. Pull her to him. Into his arms. Until she was trapped there.

And that's my cue to get the hell out of here.

Grabbing the leather bag he'd left by the front door, Cian headed toward the bathroom without so much as another glance in her direction. But it was hardly any better once he was alone in the tiny white-tiled room. Her scent lingered in the steamy air, and he pressed his shoulders against the door as he dropped the bag on the floor, his head pressed back against the wood as he squeezed his eyes shut and clawed on to every ounce of self-control he could find. He needed it like an alcoholic standing before an open bar, the shiny bottles tempting him with *drink me...drink me...drink me.* Though in his case, the words were coming from Sayre's soft lips, her husky voice curling around him like sensual tendrils of heat.

It actually hurt a part of him deep inside to be near her like this. And, yeah, it'd been pure hell to be so far away from her for so long. But this...*Jesus.* This was torture on a level he'd never experienced before, and he still hadn't managed to get a handle on the right way to deal with it.

He ended up taking the coldest shower of his life, knowing if he lingered he was liable to take matters into his own hands. And he instinctively knew it wouldn't be enough.

Fifteen minutes later, when Cian headed back out into the living room, it felt like he was walking into some kind of surreal new reality that didn't fit in his world. The delicious scent of sizzling vegetables and Asian spices drifted to his nose, and he looked toward the kitchen, surprised to see Sayre standing with her back to him as she stirred something in a pan on the stove.

What the...? Was she making him *dinner*?

A slight flush warmed her cheeks as she glanced at him over her shoulder, sweeping those big eyes over the clean clothes that covered his body. "It's getting kinda late, so I figured I should throw something together for us to eat."

"Thanks."

"It's not much," she murmured, her gaze seeming to linger a bit on his chest before she quickly looked away. "Just some veggie stir-fry and salad."

"That sounds great, Sayre. Anything I can do to help?" he asked, biting back the words he really wanted to say. *Lose your clothes and let me touch and lick and nibble on every mouthwatering inch of you* wasn't the kind of thing he needed to be thinking when it came to this woman, much less saying out loud.

He joined her in the kitchen, the two of them working in silence as she finished the noodles and he pulled down plates and glasses from the glass-fronted cupboards. Though they weren't speaking, he could see her clever mind working overtime as he watched her from the corner of his eye, the hammering pulse at the base of her throat telling him she was anything but unaffected by his presence.

"Do you want to sit outside?" she asked him, once the stir-fry and salad had been dished onto their plates. "It's probably cooler out there."

"It'll be safer inside," he replied, carrying his plate and glass of iced tea into the living room.

"Suit yourself," she said, taking a seat in one of the chairs while he sat on the sofa. "But I don't have a TV for you to veg out in front of."

"Not a problem." He never watched TV much anyway, which seemed to be something they had in common. He preferred to be outdoors, his time indoors usually spent in a bed. Though since he'd left the Alley, he'd gotten damn good at losing himself in a book, during those brief periods of time when he hadn't been searching for Aedan.

He was nearly halfway through the delicious meal, enjoying simply being in her presence without arguing, when she finally looked over at him and said, "Your accent seems stronger now. Have you been living back in Ireland?"

"I've traveled a lot, but I have an apartment in Dublin."

She swallowed a bite of salad, then sighed. "I bet it's beautiful."

"Dublin?"

Sounding more than a little wistful, she said, "Ireland.

All of it. I've always wanted to go, but...well, traveling isn't something that really works for me now."

He took a drink of his tea, then slid his gaze back to hers. "That sucks," he offered in a low voice, wondering why he was stating the friggin' obvious. Of course it *sucked*. She'd basically been living like a recluse up on this goddamn mountain, and on that note, he muttered, "I can't believe Brody and the others didn't put anyone on you for protection out here."

"They tried," she said flatly, turning her attention back to her plate. "But no matter how sneaky they were about it, I could still pick up on them. When they realized they were only hurting me more, they finally just let me be."

Since hearing that made him want to destroy something with his bare hands, he forced himself to change the subject and think of something positive to say. It wasn't easy, considering all he felt like at that moment was kicking his own ass for all the mistakes that he'd made, but he finally came up with a worthy compliment. "You've turned this into a beautiful place, Sayre. The, uh, garden is incredible."

Her mouth twisted with something caught between a wry smile and a grimace. "Thanks. It keeps me busy."

"Well, you're obviously amazing at it."

Shrugging one feminine shoulder, she kept her attention focused on the noodles she was twirling around her fork. "They like my touch, so it's easy."

His chin shot up like he'd just been clipped on it. "Your touch?"

"Yep," she replied, lifting her gaze. "I've always had a green thumb when it comes to growing things."

"Yeah," he murmured, shaking his head a little. He was *not* going to get jealous over a bunch of leafy green shit, damn it.

Keep telling yourself that, his wolf laughed. *I, for one, would give anything to be a mother-lovin' daisy if it meant I got to feel her hands on me.*

He grunted under his breath, and they finished eating, then carried their plates into the kitchen. He dried while she washed, trying like hell to take shallow breaths, since her scent was seriously screwing with his head. Unable to take it anymore, he set the towel down after drying the last pan and muttered, "It's getting late, Sayre. You should get some rest."

Propping her hip against the counter, she gave him a look that said she didn't like being told what to do. "I'll go to bed when I'm ready. Right now, Cian, we need to talk. Not chat about mundane crap. We need to actually discuss something important."

Figuring he knew exactly what she wanted to discuss, he tried to find the words to come clean, but couldn't. He swallowed, struggling for the right way to explain, but nothing was there. It was like the fucking well had just dried up, his tongue thick in his mouth. Shaking his head with frustration, he somehow managed to rasp, "I know we need to talk, but…I'm not ready to tell you everything. Not yet. I need a little more time."

A quiet, bitter laugh fell from her lips. "That's such a jackass attitude, seeing as how I seem to have been thrown into the middle of some bizarre family feud you have going on with some *brother* none of us ever even knew existed. But that's not what I was getting at."

Relief swept through his system as he leaned back against the opposite counter. "What then?"

"It's the Alley. I'm not exaggerating when I say that it's hell for me there these days."

"I'll be there with you, Sayre."

"You'll be there with me, huh?" She laughed again,

shooting him a baffled look of amazement. "Is that meant to make me feel better?"

He flushed, grinding his molars together so hard he was surprised they hadn't cracked. "I just meant that I'll do whatever I can to help make it easier for you there. But we don't have any other choice at this point, because we *need* the protection."

"And when you're gone?" she asked softly, her slender brows slightly raised in challenge.

"Let's just get through the present. We can worry about the rest later."

"Seriously? That's all you're going to say? You don't even think I deserve the courtesy of a full explanation?"

"Jesus, Sayre. I don't want to talk about this right now," he growled, his heart hammering so hard he wondered if he were on the verge of a friggin' panic attack. And the more she stood up to him, the harder it was for him to remember why he had to keep his goddamn hands to himself.

Brow knitted with a fresh wave of anger, she said, "Yeah, I picked up on the fact you don't want to talk. But guess what? I don't give a damn!"

"You *should*," he argued, his voice rising. "Because there's a good reason for why I want you to just shut the hell up. Every time you open your mouth, I want—" He broke off, cursing at his crumbling self-control as he shoved both hands back through his hair so hard he nearly ripped it out. "Christ, woman. If you knew what I want to do to you, you'd run screaming all the way back to Maryland. So just let it go for tonight!"

Given the situation, Sayre knew that "letting it go" was probably a damn good idea, but she couldn't do it. Not when Cian Hennessey was suddenly looking at her as if she were the embodiment of every primal sexual fantasy that he'd ever had. "Wait. Are you...are you saying that you *want* me?"

"I *always* want you."

The gritty words were so sharp with emotion she almost felt cut by them, and she slowly shook her head in wonder. "But you *always* said I was too young for you."

His hands tightened into fists until his knuckles turned white. "You're no longer a child, Sayre."

"And I wasn't a child at eighteen," she snapped, sick of this archaic attitude he had about her age. "If I was old enough to go to war for my pack, then I was old enough for sex, Cian. But you left me anyway."

"That was only part of the reason I left," he said roughly, his chest expanding with each of his hard, ragged breaths.

Narrowing her eyes at him, she kept her tone deliberately calm. "I left, too. But not right away. I lived in the Alley for nearly six months without you there, and it was nice to learn that there were *some* men on that mountain who didn't think I was too young for what they wanted."

An immediate scowl twisted his brow, his silver gaze going dark and diamond-hard. She could feel the powerful force of his anger surrounding her, blasting against her, but unlike with the others, Cian's emotions didn't cause her physical pain or discomfort. They simply fed her own, making her feel...charged, like a draining battery that had finally been given a potent boost. The jolt was as stunning as it was delicious, raising the fine hairs on her skin, and the fact that it felt so freaking good only made her angrier. So furious, she didn't even flinch when he straightened to his full height and snarled, "What exactly are you saying, Sayre?"

Crossing her arms over her chest, she threw him a

taunting look that she knew would rile him, her voice a soft, sultry drawl. "That really isn't any of your business, is it?"

He advanced on her so quickly he was there before she'd even noticed he was moving, getting right up in her space until he was looming over her and she had to crane her head back just to see his face, his expression one of pure, seething fury. "Everything about you is *my* business, little girl. And if any male has put his hands on you, I will fucking *kill* him. Am I clear?"

Sayre blinked up at him in a mild state of shock, unable to believe he was actually reacting this way—as if he truly gave a crap about what she did or who she did it with. Sure, he'd acted like a jealous ass before he'd abandoned the Alley, but the guy had dropped off the grid for *five* years. That was half a damn decade! For all he knew, she could have run off, married some amazing man and started a family by now. He'd had no way of knowing what she was doing or who she was doing it with. His actions couldn't have made his feelings toward their connection any clearer than if he'd looked her right in the eye and told her she meant *nothing* to him. Not a single goddamn thing.

Though the women he'd taken back to his cabin in front of her had certainly gotten the message across before he'd left. Nothing like watching your life mate hook up with an endless stream of females to make it clear he didn't want you.

Pulling in a deep breath, Sayre took a few steps back to put some much-needed space between them. "What I'm clear on is that you'll never know what I've done or who I've done it with. So this is a pointless argument, *Gramps*."

His eyes widened at the name she'd used for him, and

she had to bite back a satisfied smirk. Now that she'd found a chink in that titanium-plated armor of his, she was sure as hell going to exploit it. Heck, she might even look up old-man jokes online just so she could have them in reserve, ready to use when needed.

He opened his mouth, then closed it, his nostrils flaring as he pulled in a sharp breath of air. The seconds stretched out, each one heavy and weighted with possibility and tension, until he finally cursed something thick and guttural under his breath and stalked around her, making his way toward the front door with long, angry strides. Then, without so much as a backward glance, he slammed out of the cabin. She waited, wondering if she'd hear the roar of the Audi's engine, but his shadow moved across the curtained window a few moments later, and she realized he was outside pacing. A brief spot of flame sparked as he paused to light a cigarette—the first one she'd seen him smoke all day—and then the pacing resumed.

It wasn't anything to necessarily be proud of, but she'd have been totally fibbing if she'd said it didn't feel good to know that she'd gotten to him. *Hah! Score one for the witch! In your face, wolf boy!*

But as she turned and headed back to her bedroom, she had to face the harsh reality that he'd gotten to her, as well. Her body ached a little deeper with each step that took her away from him, her heart thudding to a jarring, painful beat that sounded suspiciously like *go back...go back...*

And the sex-hungry wild woman living inside her was practically screeching her head off, furious that Sayre wasn't giving her what she wanted. Unfortunately, Sayre pretty much felt the same way.

She might be a twenty-three-year-old virgin, but damn

it, that wasn't by choice. And while she might still be innocent, she embraced her sexuality. Had learned to touch
herself and make it feel good. Liked reading about sex
and imagining what it would feel like when she could
finally give her body the freedom to enjoy it one day.
After Cian had left, if there'd been a man she'd wanted,
she would have gone to bed with him. But there hadn't.
So she'd taken care of herself, and hoped that one day
that would change.

The last few weeks, however, had been…different,
her need becoming sharper, more focused, until she'd
wondered if it weren't time she invest in some "things"
to help her out. She wasn't thrilled about walking into a
sex shop, because while she might be a modern woman, it
was still probably going to make her blush. Even the idea
of ordering something online and having it delivered to
her PO box in town made her cheeks warm. But now…
now she wondered if maybe her body had started quickening in preparation for *this*. For his return. For the man
she'd always wanted showing up out of the blue and acting all protective, as if he actually gave a crap about her.

Was she really willing to let him walk away without taking everything that she could from him before
he went?

She didn't know, but she needed to figure it out, and
fast. There was no telling how long he would stick around
this time. She couldn't count on forever. And after the
way he'd treated her, she no longer wanted a lifetime
with him anyway.

But she needed to decide if she could go all in for
nothing more than a good time. If she could use him for
that mouthwatering, kick-ass body of his for as long as
she dared, and then turn around and walk away before
he got around to it.

Would the pleasure be worth the inevitable pain that would follow?

As she crawled onto her bed and turned out the light, Sayre could have sworn she heard a voice in her head murmur, *How will you know if you never give yourself a taste?*

Chapter 5

For Sayre, the following morning put the phrase *leap of faith* in a whole new light. One that was up close and personal…and as exciting as it was terrifying.

Cian had prowled outside the cabin until just after two in the morning, then finally dragged himself inside. Sayre had dozed off at that point, too, awakening later than usual after a restless night's sleep. Dressed in soft cotton shorts and a tank top, she padded out to the living room and stopped at the end of the hallway when she saw that he was still asleep on the sofa. His long legs hung over the end, one powerful arm thrown across his face to block out the morning sunlight flooding in through the French doors.

As she stood there with her shoulder propped against the wall, staring at his sunlit body sprawled across the off-white cushions, she knew she'd made her decision. Knew what she wanted. And while things usually went to hell in a handbasket when people started making decisions based on what they felt they deserved, rather than on what was smart, she didn't care. She figured this was her one shot at joining the masses and being a "normal" girl. Even if it were just for a brief moment in time.

But there was more on the line here than her need for sexual discovery and satisfaction. More than her need to finally get herself a "little somethin'" before she ended up a crazy old recluse who had nothing but chipmunks and squirrels for company. She needed to think about what the right answer was for their current safety situation. Not so much for herself, because she knew that while Cian might be an ass when it came to women and relationships, he would do whatever it took to protect her. His coming back to the States was a clear indication of his determination to keep her safe from this unknown brother of his. But she was most likely putting him in a dangerous situation by making him face it alone, with only her to help him. If they went back to the Alley, he would have others to watch his back and ensure his own safety.

And as long as he was there with her, she had a feeling she would be able to deal with the issues her powers created. When she'd mentioned how difficult it was for her there during their argument the night before, she'd been thinking more of the emotional strain it would put her under—not the physical one. Being there with Cian, when everyone knew how he'd just upped and left her, was going to be anything but peachy. She didn't plan on actually spelling any of this out for him, though. It would simply be a lie by omission, and she could live with that.

Plus, she knew most of the others were on vacation at the beach with their kids, enjoying a summer getaway, so the group would be small. Brody and Mic were there, and Jillian had had to stay behind, because she was needed in

town to help deal with several premature babies who had
been born within the last few weeks. Sayre was aware
of the details, because her sister had been blowing her
phone up with texts since yesterday. Instead of calling
Jillian back, like the texts had begged, she'd replied that
she was fine and would be in touch, and left it at that.
Yeah, it was bitchy, but she didn't have the energy for the
guilt she knew she'd feel when she heard the worry in her
sister's voice that was always there whenever they spoke.

And God only knew Jillian would have a lot to say
about Cian showing back up in her life. Cian's leaving
had drastically altered her sister's perception of the Irishman. Words like *bastard*, *selfish* and *coward* were the
ones Jillian used to describe him these days, whenever
he happened to come up in conversation. And Sayre had
always agreed with her.

But now…now she didn't quite know what to believe.
Sure, there were parts of her that still felt he was all of
those things and more. But she was starting to see that
the "more" part had a lot more to it than she'd ever realized. That there were things about Cian's life, like this
so-called brother he'd mentioned, that she and the others had never been told about. A brother who for some
reason wanted to harm her simply because of her connection to Cian. Who was crazy enough to have hired
those human assholes to come up here on her mountain
and mess with her. It made her wonder what other secrets
Cian had been keeping from them—and why he'd felt he
needed to keep them in the first place.

Unable to resist this stolen moment, where she could
stare at him at her leisure and simply soak him in, she
pushed all of that to the background and padded quietly into the room, until she stood only a few feet away
from where he lay. His ebony eyelashes were long and

thick and ridiculously beautiful—the kind of lashes most women would have killed to have. His brows slashed arrogantly across a face that pretty much left her breathless. And then there was the long, powerful body, his tight skin wrapped around chiseled muscles that would make any hot-blooded female a little weak in the knees. It wasn't fair for him to be this mesmerizing, as if everything about him had been designed to draw in a woman and make her *want* him. *Crave* him. *Need* him in a way she'd never needed anything in her entire life.

And the fact that fate had chosen him as her perfect match meant that Sayre felt those things in the extreme, as if they were two magnetic fields being drawn together with incredible force—even when he so obviously wanted to fight it. That particular little fun fact made her long to slap him as desperately as she wanted to lean over that fallen-angel face of his and kiss him until he forgot his own blasted name. Until he was as lost in her as she'd always ached for him to be, his need matching hers in a way that was guaranteed to burn the cabin down around them, it was so freaking hot.

As if he sensed her presence, he made a low sound that rumbled deep in his chest and lifted his arms over his head as he stretched out his big, muscular body. He'd thrown his shirt over the back of the sofa and taken off his boots and socks, leaving him dressed in nothing but those low-slung jeans he'd changed into after his shower. Every mouthwatering inch of his wide chest and ripped abdominal muscles were on dazzling display, and she actually had to lift her hand and wipe the corner of her mouth, the rush of her pulse pounding in her ears like the warning blare of a siren. *Get back! Be careful! Don't touch!* The guy was just too beautiful for his own good.

Damn it, even his bare feet were sexy!

She tried to be strong and walk away. She really
did—because using him for pleasure was different from
mooning over him like a lovesick idiot. But the way he
suddenly turned his head, those sleep-heavy eyes warm-
ing with pleasure when he blinked them open and saw
her, his wide mouth curling in a slow, sin-tipped smile,
was just too much. Too perfect. Too freaking emotional.
And the way that for just that single instant he looked
genuinely happy to see her…damn it, it broke her stupid
heart all over again. Put foolish, dangerous thoughts in
her head. Made her dream, when that was the last thing
in the world she should be doing where he was concerned.

"You okay?" he asked in a low, sleep-rough rumble,
his accent even thicker than when he was fully alert.

She wet her lips, took a shallow breath and searched
for her voice. "I…I'm fine. I still need to get dressed, but
first…I just wanted to let you know that I'll go back with
you. We don't need to have another argument in order
for you to convince me."

He pushed up on an elbow, looking like something
on a goddamn hunk calendar. Only Cian was more gorgeous and rugged and sexy than any model she'd ever
seen photographed. Sounding a bit more awake than he
had before, he said, "I'm glad to hear it, lass. But what
changed your mind?"

"I don't want your death on my hands," she murmured,
wrapping her arms over her middle, her confession making her feel even more exposed than her skimpy sleep-
wear. "You'll be safer there."

He sat up and swung his legs around until his feet were
flat on the floor, confusion joining in with the surprise
and relief she could read on his handsome face. "It's *you*
I'm worried about, Sayre."

She slowly arched one of her brows. "Are we really

going to argue about this, or are you going to just be happy that I've decided to make your life a whole lot easier? Would you prefer it if I threw a tantrum and refused to leave?"

"Hell no."

Her lips twitched as she took a step back. "Then get up and get dressed so that you can help me."

Pushing his hair back from his face, he shot her a wary look. "What are we doing?"

"I might be able to suck it up and endure a visit, but I'm no more moving back there permanently than you are. So I need to make sure things are in good working order around here before I go."

His jaw got tight, as did the skin around his eyes. He didn't like hearing that she would be coming back to the cabin. Though why it would matter to him, she couldn't understand.

"This place is that important to you?" he asked, as he leaned forward and rested his elbows on his parted knees.

"The garden here isn't just a hobby, Cian. It's my job, because I run a blog called *The Green Witch*," she explained, wondering why her body felt the ridiculous need to blush as she revealed this information. "My income feeds in from my YouTube subscribers, as well as the companies that advertise on my site. I use my garden to make instructional videos on how to do everything from planting and general maintenance to horticultural design."

He blinked a few times, then scratched the shadow of stubble on his jaw. "Hell, Sayre. That's pretty damn impressive."

"I'll never be a millionaire, but I don't need to be. I just need a roof over my head and money for the bare essentials."

His look of admiration slipped into a grimace, and she shook her head, wondering what his problem was. Before she could ask him, he switched gears and said, "*The Green Witch*, huh? Cute name."

She smirked. "What the humans don't know about the truth in the name won't hurt them."

A deliciously low laugh rumbled up from his chest, the corner of his mouth kicking up a bit. "I guess not."

That laugh, as well the freaking lopsided smile that went along with it, was about to put her in meltdown mode, so she quickly retreated, mumbling something about needing to change clothes and would he please put on some coffee.

When she came back out not even ten minutes later, dressed in denim shorts and a white T-shirt, he'd thankfully thrown his shirt back on, and they quickly ate some toast and cereal before heading outside. It took her the better portion of the day to get the automatic watering system set up, as well as the wire netting that would protect her precious plants and flowers from hungry animals.

By the time they finally had the place secured enough that Sayre felt comfortable leaving it, Cian gave off a vibe like he was coming out of his skin, his attention constantly focused on the surrounding woods. She knew the delay in leaving had pissed him off, but he'd been smart enough not to voice his complaints out loud, understanding she was stubborn enough to change her mind. Not that she was going to. Cian's tension had rubbed off on her to the point that even *she* was anxious to get the heck out of there. She didn't know much about this mysterious brother of his—okay, she knew next to nothing—but the fact that he worried the Irishman was enough for Sayre to know he was going to be a crapload of trouble.

After they'd wolfed down a late lunch of sandwiches

and chips, she locked up the shed, grabbed her things and they climbed into the Audi.

"Nice car," she murmured, stroking her hand over the sumptuous leather. The seats in her truck were so cracked that she'd covered them with a quilt her grandmother had made. Her parents, as well as Jillian and Jeremy, had tried to buy her something newer, but she'd refused, unwilling to take their charity. They'd already done too much, helping her remodel the cabin up there in the middle of nowhere, when she'd needed to get away before she suffered a total breakdown.

Her brows pulled together as the memory of how helpless she'd felt during those dark days pressed in on her, and she mentally shoved it to the back of her mind, along with all the other things she didn't want to think about at the moment. Things like the fact that even if there had been someone she'd wanted to sleep with before she'd left the Silvercrest, like she'd warned him she would do, the problems with her powers would have likely made it impossible. That despite hoping her powers might one day mellow out enough that she could return home, there was a strong chance that she would *always* be this way. That Cian Hennessey's absence from her life meant she would forever be alone. That fooling around with him might very well be the *only* chance for intimacy that she ever had, and boy did that thought suck, seeing as how he'd admitted to wanting her…but clearly hated that he felt that way.

Knowing Cian, he was probably terrified she'd mistake passion for love and start following him around like an adoring puppy dog, constantly begging for his attention.

God, I'd rather die a virgin!

Since she desperately needed to get out of her negative head space, she pressed forward with more chatter about the car. "When do you have to have it back to the rental company?"

"It's not a rental," he murmured, handling the powerful engine with ridiculous ease as he took the winding mountain roads. And looking entirely too freaking sexy while he did it.

She whistled under her breath at his response, shocked that he'd spent so much money on a car. The Runners were all financially comfortable, but they didn't have the kind of wealth that made them able to throw around the amount of cash it took to buy a set of wheels like the Audi. "So what's the story with that, then? You win the lottery while you were gone?"

He shifted his long body in his seat, his energy moving from relief that they'd finally left to restless again. "Didn't need to," he muttered under his breath.

Sayre sensed he'd be happy if she dropped the topic, but given the situation between them, she wasn't particularly interested in giving him what he wanted. "Then how did you afford it?"

He worked his stubble-covered jaw a few times, then exhaled a sharp breath through his nose before he admitted, "I used money from my trust fund, which I finally started to spend after I quit Bloodrunning. And since I didn't know how long this thing with Aedan was going to take, I didn't see the point in renting anything when I could just buy it."

Her mouth actually hung open for a moment. "Trust fund? Are you serious?"

He grunted in response, and she had to laugh. No wonder the guy had always seemed a little out of place in their small mountain community. He was probably used to living in a freaking mansion, rather than the rugged beauty of Bloodrunner Alley.

She didn't know much about Cian's family, other than that his mother had been a member of the pack who'd fallen in love while on vacation in Ireland and had never returned. But Cian never talked about her much, and she couldn't recall him *ever* talking about his father. "Do the others know?"

He slid her a shuttered look that was impossible to read, then shook his head and returned his attention to the winding road. He'd explained when they set off that it would likely take them hours to reach the Alley, since they'd be avoiding the main roads, taking smaller ones that were less traveled…and less likely to be monitored by his homicidal brother. She let the conversation about money go, thinking instead about the possible reasons for the Hennessey brothers' apparent feud. Was it over a woman? The family money? Or something even darker than that? Wouldn't it have to be, if Aedan wanted to hurt his brother badly enough to kill over it? And that was definitely the point of all this. Cian's behavior made at least that much apparent.

"So," he murmured, his deep voice startling her when neither of them had said a word for the past half hour. "I was wondering what your powers are like now."

Her shoulders lifted in a brief shrug. "Oh, you know. Just typical witch stuff."

He shot her a look before turning his attention back to the road. "Can you go into a little more detail than that?"

A quiet laugh slipped past her lips. "I can't read your mind, if that's what's worrying you."

"It wasn't," he remarked in a dry tone, "but thanks for clarifying."

"I can sometimes do that with animals, though, and

communicate with them. But it's pretty rare, and usually only when they need my help."

"Like with the snakes?" he asked, shifting the Audi into a lower gear as he took a particularly tight turn in the road.

"What?"

"When Elise first came to stay with Wyatt, he and I came back from being out on security patrol one evening and found all the women freaking out because some rattlesnakes had wandered into the Alley. But you were as calm as could be when you came outside and spotted them. Instead of screeching, you just lifted your hands in the air, your eyes all glowing and bright, and those fucking snakes listened to whatever you told them, slithering back into the forest."

"I remember that," she said with a small smile. "Chelsea was so pissed at Eric because he couldn't stop laughing at how ridiculous her and the others looked, jumping up and down on top of Brody's truck and screaming their heads off."

He gave a low laugh. "It was one of the craziest, funniest damn things I've ever seen."

"You calling me crazy?" she asked, playfully smacking him on the arm.

A sensual smirk curved the firm line of his beautiful mouth. "Only in a good way."

Sayre rolled her eyes. "Gee, thanks."

"So what else can you do?"

Picking at the frayed edge on her shorts, she said, "Well, there's the healing ability, and the energy, light-shooting-out-of-my-hands part. Other than that, I've occasionally had some moments of what I suppose you could call 'sight'—but it's been a long time since anything like that happened." Looking over at him again, she said, "As the energy thing's become more powerful, it's like it's eclipsed everything else."

He glanced her way, then focused once more on the road. "So then what's the story with the gun that you pulled on me yesterday? I've seen your powers in action, and that was before they hit full throttle. So why not use them?"

"They're not something I use in front of humans if I can avoid it, so I carry the gun."

"That's understandable. But you could have used them on me."

"I could have," she admitted, momentarily caught up in watching the way he was holding the steering wheel with his left hand, his thumb stroking over the smooth leather in a way that struck her as incredibly erotic. Clearing her throat a little, she added, "But the gun was more… impersonal."

He grunted again, which seemed to be his standard response when she said something he didn't care for. They drifted back into another heavy silence for a few minutes, until her impatience finally got the better of her. Before she could stop herself or talk herself around in circles over whether it was the right move or the wrong one, Sayre tucked her left leg up under her, turned to face him and said, "So, I've been doing some thinking, and I need to talk to you about something."

The way his body seemed to brace itself, his muscles tightening beneath his skin, told her that he'd picked up on her nervousness. "Go on," he said in a low voice, sliding her another shuttered glance before looking back at the road.

"I'm, um, still coming to terms with how to handle this, but I don't…I don't want the time we're together to be spent fighting. I want to call a truce. One where we don't keep arguing about what happened before. All I ask is that you're honest with me, even if it's painful."

"Sayre," he rasped, so softly she almost couldn't hear him. His chest lifted with a deep breath, and she could literally *feel* the heat pouring off his big, powerful body, his jaw hard as he probably tried to work out where she was going with this.

"I don't know what you want from me, Cian. I don't even know what I'm willing to give you. But I know that I feel better when I'm with you than I've felt in a long time. Maybe, if we work together, then just *maybe* we can somehow find a way to be...friends."

He swiped his tongue over his lower lip, his face and throat flushed with a heat that she wanted to feel under her mouth and against her tongue. "There's just one problem with that, lass." His voice was rougher than she'd ever heard it before, husky and deliciously thick. "I want to do things to you that I wouldn't want to do to any of my friends, if I had any these days. Things I've wanted to do for *years*, Sayre."

Trying not to let herself get carried away with excitement over hearing him say he wanted her again, she pointed out the obvious. "You never seemed all that attracted to me before. Just possessive."

"Because I fought it with everything I had," he growled, the tendons in his neck straining in a way that made her want to nip them with her teeth.

Knowing this was make-or-break time, she clutched on to every ounce of courage she could find and went for it. "I don't want to argue about the past anymore. What's done is done, and there's nothing you could ever do to make it right. But I...I want things from you, too."

His head turned sharply to the side. "What are you talking about?"

Her confession came in a soft, breathless rush of words. "I want to know what all the fuss is about when it comes to pleasure and the man who was meant to be mine. I want to enjoy my time with you, the time that we're together, however short it is."

Slowing the car, he veered onto the grassy shoulder, then slammed the brakes so hard she had to brace her hands against the dashboard. "Say that again, Sayre."

"I think you heard me just fine," she whispered.

The way he was looking at her made it difficult to breathe—her body all ramped up on hunger for the things she'd been missing out on. For a split second, she froze, wondering if she were doing this because it was the logical, mature decision, or if she were simply being steered by her hormones. Then she exhaled a shaky puff of air, watched his eyes darken as she licked her lips again… and realized that she just didn't care about the reasons and justifications. She was doing it, to hell with what was stupid or dangerous or unwise for her future. The future was never going to be what she'd once hoped for, so she needed to take her happiness when and where she could find it. And that was here. *Now.* Right that very second… and as many seconds as she could have afterward.

"Let me get this straight," he said in a low rumble. "Are you saying I can touch you now?"

"I'm not saying you *can't.* I'm still figuring things out, and it's not easy when you're still not answering my questions."

"Christ, Sayre." He sounded equal parts frustrated and turned on, which made her want to grin…maybe even laugh, which wasn't something she'd done much of in a long time. She knew there weren't many people who surprised him, and it felt good to be one of them. "Are you…are you *blackmailing* me with your body?"

Instead of outright denying it, she gave him a look of open curiosity. "Could I do that?"

The look he gave her in return was so freaking hot she could have melted right there in the sumptuous leather seat. Quietly, he said, "You're playing games, lass, that you're not prepared to lose."

"Not really," she murmured, determined not to let him rattle her. "Because I think you're making a bigger deal out of this than it actually is. All I'm interested in is scratching an itch that should have been dealt with a long time ago. So long as you don't bite me and make a bond, why not indulge while we can?"

Because of the life-mate connection they shared, Cian held the ability to create a permanent blood bond between them if he ever sank his teeth into her throat—and that was something she intended to avoid at all costs. She couldn't think of anything worse than being stuck forever with a man who didn't want the same things as her. Not that she even wanted a bond with him anymore. She would have to trust him...and love him first, and those were two things that this particular male would *never* have from her.

He turned his head away from her, staring out the front windshield, his profile so stark he looked like he'd been carved from stone. "It's not that simple," he eventually said, sounding as if he'd had to force the gritty words from his throat.

Sayre sighed. "Fine. If you don't want me, then just say so."

"Not want you?" he muttered with a harsh, humorless laugh, shaking his head again. "I want the touch and taste of your body so badly it's all I can do not to just *take* it."

"Then look at me, Cian."

He did as she said, the heat and hunger in those smoldering gray eyes making her feel stripped down to her bare flesh, despite the clothes chafing against her warm skin. In that moment, she could have been wearing freaking Eskimo furs and she still would have felt completely exposed. It was a heady feeling, being the center of such intense focus, and the answering part of her soul gloried in it. Soaked it up like a freaking leaf with sunshine, even though her heart was screaming to be careful...cautious.

"I'm not playing a game," she told him, working hard to keep her voice even. "Yes, I want answers to my questions, and I'm hoping you'll eventually give them to me. But I want more than that, and I don't want to wait for it."

His eyes narrowed, the gray glinting like piercing chips of silver. "Then spell it out for me. In *exact* terms, Sayre."

She took a deep breath, refusing to let herself break eye contact as she put it all out there. "I don't want either of our emotions involved. And I don't even know if I want the full sex act. But I...I want everything that leads up to it."

"No emotions, huh?" It was clear from his tone that he didn't like hearing that any more than he'd liked some of the other things she'd said to him since he'd suddenly burst back into her life. "Can you honestly tell me that you feel nothing where I'm concerned?"

She couldn't hold back the sharp burst of laughter that rushed up from her chest, her lips twisting with chagrin. "Oh, I *feel* plenty, Cian. Anger being first and foremost the majority of the time, along with a lot of other nasty things like pain and humiliation. But there's also hunger, and I'm tired of aching for something I can't find anywhere else. My powers have been keeping me prisoner for years, but here I am, sitting beside you, and I'm okay. Maybe...maybe if I work you out of my system, things will be different when you leave again. Maybe *I'll* be different."

She could tell he hated that idea, as well, but didn't have an argument for it. And, really, what could he possibly say? That he planned on sticking around this time? That he wanted her in a forever kind of way, just like her girlish heart had once hoped he would? Even if he tried to sell her on the idea, they both knew it would be a lie.

Without a single word, he tore that heated stare from her face and looked over his shoulder, checking for other cars before he pulled back out onto the road and floored the gas. Disappointment settled heavily in her gut, but she refused to beg. "Is this your answer then?"

"No," he growled, squeezing the steering wheel so hard she was surprised it didn't crack. "You want my hands on you, then they're going to be on you. But that wasn't the time or place."

Sayre was half convinced he was simply trying to buy himself some time to think of a way to let her down gently—until she noticed something that made her ridiculously happy.

The hand he'd just shoved back through his hair was actually shaking, and she couldn't help the small smile that crept its way into the corner of her mouth.

Yeah, this was bound to end badly. And yep, she was most definitely playing with fire. Hell, she had the matches lit and was dancing in the middle of a sea of gasoline, splashing through it like a kid in a puddle. But maybe that was okay.

Maybe—just *maybe*—it was about time she stopped playing it safe, and actually got a little burned.

Chapter 6

By the time they'd crossed into Maryland, Cian was in a world of pain unlike anything he'd ever known. He took shallow breaths and tried not to draw too much of Sayre's mouthwatering scent into his lungs, but it was a wasted effort. Now that she'd admitted she still wanted him, there wasn't any point in trying to keep his hands off her. He was locked on to every single detail of her, his hunger increasing with each second that ticked by, coiling tightly through his insides. Like a physical thing, it prowled beneath his hot skin, keeping perfect company with his beast.

To make matters worse, the more time he spent with her, the more it became increasingly clear that he genuinely *liked* her. Yeah, he lusted after the little witch to the point that it was going to damn near kill him to walk away from her. To leave without claiming her in *all* the ways that he craved. But he liked the woman beneath that beautiful surface to an equally dangerous degree. She was funny and spirited and fascinating. Different from the girl he'd known, and yet, the same.

Sweet, smart, beautiful Sayre. If he'd been a different man, with a different past…and a different future, he would have claimed her in a heartbeat. Even with that smart-ass mouth and attitude that could so easily rile him.

Finally reaching his breaking point, he sent up a silent word of thanks to whomever might be out there listening when he saw the sign for a small rest area a mile up the road. They were in a remote part of the mountains and hadn't passed another car for the last twenty minutes, so when they reached the turnoff, he took it and followed the dirt path into the trees, parking at the back of a small clearing that sat at the edge of a cliff. Restrooms and a few empty picnic tables were the only amenities, but the view out over the mountains was incredible.

"Is there any particular reason that you've parked here?" she asked, staring out at the view as she undid her seat belt.

He cut the engine, the air leaving his lungs in a rough exhalation. "You know damn well why I brought us here."

With a feminine little snort that he found entirely too adorable, she turned her head and gave him a cocky grin. "You're too old to drive for long periods of time without getting out to stretch your legs?"

Arching his right eyebrow, he said, "You've developed quite a gift for sarcasm, haven't you?"

Her next breath released on a sigh. "Sometimes life will do that to a girl. Does it turn you off?"

"There isn't a damn thing you could do to turn me off, Sayre."

She blinked at him with wide eyes. "Wow, you're not holding back, are you?"

"Why the hell should I hold back about wanting you? I wanted you when you were too young for me to even think about. Wanted you so badly it nearly drove me out of my goddamn mind. I want you even more now."

"Good," she breathed. "Because I want you, too."

"Then come on," he rumbled, reaching for his door handle. "I'm not kissing you for the first time in this small-ass car."

With a low, kind of nervous laugh, she opened her door and started to climb out. "This is a beautiful car, you know. You're just too big for it."

Did she just call us big? his wolf growled, sounding smug as hell. *She's got that right.*

Shaking his head at the arrogant idiot, Cian climbed out and slammed his door shut. His stupid hands were still trembling like a boy's, and he couldn't help but shake his head at himself, as well. So much for his legendary reputation and control. All it took was a single heated look from this girl, like the one she was giving him as he came around the front of the Audi, and he was undone. Damn near knocked back on his ass like someone who'd had their legs swept out from under them.

"I don't understand," he said when he was standing right in front of her and staring into those big, beautiful eyes, a shimmering ring of gold beginning to gleam around the smoky blue. It was like she'd been shocked wide open, her desire laid bare for him to witness, and it humbled him just as much as it scared the ever-loving hell out of him. "How can you do this, Sayre? How can you look at me like that? Don't you blame me for what's happening? For the fact that your life's in danger?"

She pulled in a deep breath as she stared up at him, and then slowly let it out. Voice thick with emotion, she said, "I actually blame you for a lot of things, Cian. If that bothers you, then don't touch me. It's your choice. I'm simply being as honest as I can be with you about what I want."

"You were never this bold before."

"True," she agreed, keeping her gaze locked tight with his as she leaned back against the passenger's-side door. "But a person can change a lot in five years."

"And some things don't change at all."

"Are you talking about yourself?" she asked, some of the light in her eyes fading, and he knew she was thinking about the women. About the ones he'd gone through faster than packs of cigarettes.

"I was. But it's not what you think, Sayre. I was thinking about the way you affect me."

The frown between her slender brows smoothed out. "Oh."

A slow, crooked smile tugged at his lips. "Yeah, *oh*."

"Tell me," she said, the words soft and husky with need. "I mean, I know it's really just the connection, but I'm curious if it's as strong for you as it is for me."

"You want me to speak plainly?" he asked, his throat so tight with lust he could barely voice the question.

She nodded. "Please."

Cian stepped closer and allowed himself to touch his fingertips to the pink flush on her cheek, her skin so smooth and soft it was unreal. She'd left her hair down, and the wind was playing havoc with the wavy strands, silky tendrils brushing against his forearm and across the back of his wrist. "I'll tell you what I want, Sayre. I want you open and bare beneath me, your beautiful little body *mine* to do with as I please," he confessed, the lilting burr of his accent thickening with each word. "I want you wet and desperate and begging for me, lass. I want to make you feel so bloody good you can't do anything but scream when you come for me, your nails digging into my back and your body writhing. I want to get inside you, any way I can, and bring you off so many times you won't even be able to remember what it was like without my hands and mouth on your skin, laying claim to every part of you."

She shivered, and he loved the way he could feel the warmth of her blush surge beneath his fingertips, her temperature spiking with the fiery energy of her power, tiny sparks of light beginning to glitter in the air around them. Her eyes were glassy with desire, storm-dark and eager, those slim rings of gold at the outer edge of her irises starting to burn even brighter.

"I'm, um, good with all that," she whispered, her little tongue swiping across that succulent lower lip that he wanted to catch between his teeth and suck on, *hard*. It was juicy and pink, the sweet rush of her blood lying just beneath the tender surface, and Cian quickly shoved that dangerous thought behind thick iron gates in his mind, determined not to let it take hold of him and ruin this unexpected moment.

Given their past, he'd never once believed that she would let him get close to her like this. And there was always the chance that she would change her mind. Which meant he needed to get the hell on with it, enjoying it while it lasted, and pray to whatever higher power might be listening that he didn't blow it by losing control.

Lowering his head, he gently swept his lips across hers, using every ounce of strength he possessed to hold himself back, still terrified he'd scare her off. The wolf inside him shuddered with pleasure to finally have the taste of her, and their breaths blended together, the tips of her breasts pressing against his chest as he made a low, thick sound of hunger in the back of his throat. When he pulled his head back to check her reaction, making sure she was still with him, she frowned up at him. "What's wrong?" he rasped, curving his hand around her nape.

"Is there some kind of problem? Because despite what you keep saying, you seem pretty reluctant."

You fucking idiot, his wolf snarled, seething beneath his skin. *We've finally got her and you're blowing it!*

"Not reluctant, Sayre. Just trying to figure out if I'm dreaming."

Another soft burst of laughter seemed to catch her by surprise as it fell past her lips, and she smirked up at him. "Oh, man. That was a smooth line."

"I wish it was a line," he groaned, caging her in with his arms as he pressed his palms flat against the sun-warmed side of the car, her breaths coming in little pants of excitement that he couldn't get enough of. Then he leaned down and brushed his mouth over hers again, unable to believe how impossibly sweet her lips were. "This would be so much easier if it was," he growled against that tender mouth, flicking the center of her bottom lip with his tongue.

When she moaned and rubbed her tongue against his, he lost it and thrust past her lips, the kiss turning deep and deliciously wet. It was terrifying as hell, how damn perfect she tasted, the tender recesses of her mouth and that kittenish tongue that kept tempting him to take more on the cusp of landing her in some serious trouble. His gums burned with the weight of his fangs, every dark, dangerous part of him shocked into awareness by the feel and scent and taste of her.

Unable to keep his hands off her, Cian reached down and grasped her hips in a hard, possessive hold, preparing to pull her into his lower body, against the part of him that was getting harder by the second, when she gasped against his mouth in a way that almost sounded like fear. Breaking away from the kiss, he pressed his forehead against hers, his body shaking with the effort it took to stop and wait for her to tell him that she was okay.

"Sorry," she whispered unsteadily. "I didn't want you to stop. I'm just…I'm not used to people touching me."

He knew she meant in a casual way, seeing as how she'd been living on her own for so long. But he also sensed that she was talking about physical intimacy. Whatever the little witch had done with other men after he'd left, there was still a part of her that was somewhat shy when it came to sex, and he both loved and hated it with equal ferocity. Yeah, he was relieved that she hadn't gone out and banged every guy she could find just to get back at him for being a jackass. But on the other hand, he didn't quite know what to do with someone who didn't share his level of sexual experience. That was something he hadn't messed around with for decades, and, for a moment, he was worried he'd do this all wrong. Go in for too much, too soon, and end up pushing her to call a halt to the whole thing.

He couldn't let that happen. Not when the taste of her had just hit his system like a shot of pure whiskey. She was even more addictive than he'd feared, and now he was hooked. Walking away from her at this point, before he'd gotten his fill, might damn well finish him off. And while he might not care all that much about dying, he wasn't going anywhere until he'd dealt with Aedan. No way in hell was he leaving this world until his brother had been taken care of, once and for all, and Sayre was safe.

The touch of her hands curling over his shoulders jerked him from his troubled thoughts, and he couldn't stop himself from lifting his head to ask, "Why are you really doing this, Sayre? With me of all people?"

Holding his gaze, she said, "I don't have to tell you my reasons, Cian. You're either game or you're not. No pressure. But if we do this, I want it to be worth it."

"And what, in your mind, makes it worth it?"

"In all honesty? Lots of things. But the pleasure is a part of it. Until this problem with your brother is over, I want you to make me feel good. I want you to rock my freaking world." Her beautiful eyes gleamed with challenge. "So are you up for it?"

Despite her mention of Aedan, which should have turned his blood cold, his shoulders shook with a silent laugh. "Poor choice of words, lass. I'm always *up* for it with you."

"Wow," she murmured with a smirk. "Look at the old man playing the comedian."

"I'm not that old," he grunted as he dipped his head and nipped the delicate edge of her jaw with his teeth.

"Sure you aren't, baby."

He rubbed his nose against hers, a smile on his lips that he couldn't have gotten rid of to save his life. "You're riling me on purpose, aren't you, you little witch?"

"Either way," she quipped, "you'll never know."

"Ah, lass. I told you that you shouldn't play with me," he growled, holding her head still with his hands as he brought his mouth down over hers again, claiming that damp, succulent part of her like he owned it. The kiss was nothing but pure, unadulterated craving, raw and aggressive and dirty as hell. His tongue pushed into her mouth, stroking against her own in a way that was suggestive of how he wanted to lick at that sweet flesh between her thighs, and he knew that she got it. That she understood what he was trying to tell her with the greedy, explicit demands of his lips and tongue and teeth. His hands burrowed deeper into the silken mass of her hair, turning her head at the angle he needed so that he could get to even more of that hot little mouth, the breathless sounds that she made and the way she clutched at his shoulders as she kissed him back driving him out of his goddamn mind.

Needing to learn more of her, he lowered his arms and pushed his hands under the hem of her shirt, touching her soft, smooth skin. His heart was hammering so hard he was surprised it hadn't torn free of his chest, his pulse roaring in his ears, the thumping beat keeping perfect time with the guttural howls of his beast. Loving the way she felt, he trailed two fingertips across her soft skin, his path leading to the shallow indentation of her navel. But just as he started to trace his fingertips over the sexy tattoo he knew was inked there, something dark and savage burst inside his head like an explosion, slamming into him with the force of a racehorse at full tilt. He cursed against her mouth, burning with the predatory need to take her down to the ground and bury every inch of his brutal erection deep inside her, at the same time he drove his fangs into the tender column of her throat and bit the holy living hell out of her.

What. The. Fuck?

Was it the force of her own desires suddenly pushing him to take the hot, rich spill of her blood into his mouth and drink her down, marking her as his? The draw of her power? Their connection? Or did the violent craving for complete possession have something to do with *him*? With what he was? With that part of him that he struggled so hard to keep contained?

Cian wished that he knew the answer, but he was at a loss. All he really knew was that touching her like this, being with her like this, was more incredible than anything he'd ever had before. Even better than he'd imagined it would be, and he'd played out this scenario in his head so many excruciating times it was permanently etched into his memory. Had hungered for it until he'd felt hollowed out inside, bled dry with need.

But if he didn't stop now, he understood what would happen.

There would be a damn good chance he wouldn't stop at all.

Sayre wanted to scream with frustration when Cian suddenly pulled away from her. One second she was lost in the dark, velvety heat of his mouth, his tongue rubbing against hers so wickedly it made her ache for more, and in the next she was staring up at his cold-as-stone expression as he took a step back from her, wondering what on earth had happened.

"Cian?"

He gave one sharp, curt shake of his head, then jerked his chin toward the car. "Get in," he said in a voice so low it sounded more predator than man. "We need to go."

She blinked, feeling like he'd just tossed a glass of ice water in her face. "You're kidding, right?"

His response punched from his lips with so much force it made her flinch. "You want to get down and dirty in a goddamn rest area, Sayre?"

"No," she returned, though her voice wasn't nearly as strong as she wanted it to be, her system still reeling from the way he'd kissed her. "I made it clear that I don't plan on having sex with you. But I thought we could... that we could at least do *other* things."

"We could," he muttered, shoving one of his big hands back through the windblown strands of his hair, "but I need to think."

"Does this mean you've changed your mind?" she demanded, wanting to know *now*, so that she didn't make even more of a fool of herself later on.

The look he gave her said he thought she was crazy for even asking such a ridiculous question. For a moment, a warm, sensual buzz of pleasure swept through her, until her next thought quickly sobered her up. Of course he wanted her, at least in a sexual way. The laws of nature wouldn't have connected them if they weren't primed for intense attraction to one another. But even though he was finally admitting his need, it didn't mean that he had to like it. Or accept it. Or embrace it.

From the dark expression on his face, he didn't plan on doing *any* of those things. Not a single damn one of them.

As if he could read her mind, he growled, "You don't need to doubt my desire for you, Sayre. I'm harder than I've ever been right now, and it's because of you."

She couldn't help but look down, the sight of his thick erection trapped behind that denim fly making her heart leap into her throat. She gave a hard swallow, embarrassingly aware of the heat burning in her face. Damn it, she wanted to be sophisticated about this, but that just so wasn't her. All she could do was stand there and gape, wanting to know what the weight of him would feel like in her palm. If he would be smooth or ridged with veins, and how hot his flesh would be to the touch. If she could make him shout with pleasure, and how he would taste and feel on her tongue.

But as she watched him make his way back around the front of the Audi, his tension like a physical force blasting against her in the late-afternoon sunshine, she knew her curiosity wasn't going to be appeased today. Heck, maybe not ever, if he didn't manage to let go a little and relax.

She opened her door and climbed inside, her thoughts snagging on something that she couldn't quite put her finger on. She could understand Cian being worried about taking things too far, seeing as how the life-mate connection they shared naturally drew them together, even though there was only so far they were willing to go, neither of them wanting to be permanently stuck with the other. And if they had sex, that connection would no doubt compel him to bite her and mark her in a way that would be damn difficult to resist.

But she couldn't help thinking that there was more to it than that. That something darker than the magnetic, fate-driven "pull" between them was behind his reticence. And her gut told her it had something to do with the man who was trying to hurt her to get to him. She had so many questions about Aedan Hennessey that she didn't even know where to start. And she didn't even bother, knowing Cian wouldn't answer them.

After pulling her door shut, she latched her seat belt and then turned to look at him, surprised to find him just sitting there, watching her, his troubled gaze dark and endlessly deep, filled with so much confusion...as well as frustration. "Does it bother you at all to be around me?" he asked her.

"You mean with my power or just in general?"

His nostrils flared as he pulled in a deep breath, and he muttered, "Your power."

"So far? No," she said, giving him an honest answer.

He nodded, then looked away from her and started the engine. As they pulled back out onto the winding mountain road, he seemed to get lost in his thoughts, but the silence didn't bother her. Her emotions were too raw at the moment to make casual conversation.

Pulling the backpack she'd left on the floorboard into her lap, Sayre took out the iPod Jillian had given her for Christmas and her headphones, then scrolled through her playlists until she found the one titled *Free*. She'd paid for every track on the list, the meaning of the name going deeper than her measly bank account. It was an eclectic mix of songs that embodied what she wanted most out of life: freedom from her past and the things that held her back.

But as she listened to the first song, she realized that it wasn't quite fitting for her current set of circumstances, and she wondered if maybe she should put a new list together and call it *Strength*.

After everything that she'd been through, the last thing that Sayre considered herself was weak. But she was also realistic enough to know that there were times when even the strongest of people needed a little more.

And if she were going to make it through this thing with Cian without any permanent damage to her heart, she had a feeling she was one of them.

Chapter 7

As he steered the powerful sports car into the Alley, Cian couldn't help but recall the night Eli Drake had returned to the mountains he'd grown up in after an absence of three years. Was this how the mercenary had felt that night? Like he was walking into a dream? One that was both calming and familiar, and yet, oddly terrifying?

Had he felt as out of place as Cian did in that moment, like a stranger in his own home?

Shaking off the uncomfortable thoughts, he put the car into Park, turned off the engine and twisted toward Sayre. She was worrying her lush lower lip with her teeth, her gaze shadowed with something that seemed remarkably close to fear. It made his insides tighten, as if he physically rejected the idea of her feeling that sour emotion when it was his job to protect her.

He might fail disastrously when it came to upholding most of his duties as her mate, but ensuring she felt safe was one that he had every intention of carrying out.

For the moment, his wolf muttered. *Some hero you are.*

Ignoring the sarcastic jibe—leave it to him to have an inner wolf that constantly sported an attitude—he studied her as she slipped off the headphones she'd been wearing for the past hour and dropped them back into her pack. "You feeling okay?"

She pulled in a slow breath. "So far, so good."

"If it gets to be too much, let me know. We can have as much privacy as you want."

"Privacy didn't help before."

Knowing exactly what he was doing, he shot her a heated look, and let a slow smile lift the corner of his mouth. "If you need me to, I think I can find a way to get your mind focused on something besides your powers."

She narrowed her eyes at him. "*Now* you decide to flirt with me? God, you have some seriously craptastic timing."

He didn't know how she managed to make him laugh in the middle of some of the tensest situations in his life, but she did. "Craptastic? Is that even a real word?"

Shrugging a slender shoulder, she sighed. "I don't know. I just…" Confusion clouded her gaze. "You mess with my head, Cian."

Since that didn't necessarily sound like a good thing, he let it go as he opened his door and climbed out into the warm, slightly humid evening. Pulling in a deep breath of the forest-scented air, he almost felt light-headed from the way it hit his system. Not as potent as Sayre, but still meaningful, like he was pulling in a deep breath of home. There was no other place in the world that smelled like

this to him, and it made his heart hurt to think that he
was going to lose it again when all was said and done.

Only because you're too stubborn and pigheaded, his
beast grumbled.

Mentally flipping off the wolf, he closed his door,
shooting Sayre a look over the top of the car as she did
the same. Worry for her punched him low in the gut, and
even though he knew this was the safest place she could
be once Aedan made his appearance, he also knew that
he wouldn't force her to stay if it became too much for
her. With a nod of encouragement, he turned and faced
the small group that was making their way toward them.
Jeremy must have decided to come back to be there for
Jillian, because he was walking right beside her, while
Mic and Brody followed just behind them.

The mercs who worked with Eli Drake were there,
as well, and he found a frown tugging at his mouth. He
could have done without them, seeing as how Sayre had
been pretty close to a few of them before he'd left, but
he knew they were permanent residents in the Alley
now. Single ones, from the looks of it, since the four of
them—Lev Slivkoff, Kyle Maddox, Sam Harmon and
James Bennett—were still without wedding rings. But
that was hardly surprising. They were even bigger wom-
anizers than he'd once been, though that seemed like a
lifetime ago.

Keeping a wary eye on the group, Cian moved to stand
at the back of the car, his muscles tightening with awareness as Sayre came to stand beside him. The wind was
tossing her wild mane of curls against his arm, the silky
caresses striking him as oddly sensual, considering it
was simply the touch of her hair. But it seemed that his
mind equated everything to do with the little witch with
sex, from that devastatingly sensual scent that he wanted

to draw into his mouth and bite down on, to the way she chewed on her bottom lip when she was deep in thought. If he didn't know how much she resented being linked to him, he would have thought she'd put some kind of spell on him. One that made him crave the scent and touch and taste of her.

I'll never *forget that hot little mouth of hers*, his wolf snarled, baring its fangs at him. *Could gladly kill you for pushing her away today.*

Yeah, he had to agree with the jackass on that one. But he hadn't had any other choice. If he hadn't pulled away from her, he'd have ended up screwing her beautiful little brains out in the middle of a rest area while he marked the shit out of her throat, and then everything would have gone to hell so fast it left his head spinning. And the results would be just as bad for her, seeing as how she would have been stuck with him. No matter how badly he wanted her in his bed, he wasn't so much of a bastard that he would ruin her life that way just for the sake of his dick.

Not that the idea wasn't tempting, because, *hell*, it was Sayre, and he wanted her in ways he still didn't even fully understand. Ways he refused to look at too closely, convinced he wouldn't like what he found.

Jillian was the first to reach them as she hurried away from Jeremy's side and grabbed her little sister up in a crushing embrace. "Ohmygod, I've missed you so much," she said in a broken rush, while Sayre hugged her back.

"Me, too," she whispered, and he could hear the tears she was holding back in those quiet words. Sayre raised up on her tiptoes and hugged her sister even tighter, and while it no doubt made him a perv, he couldn't help but notice the way her shorts had hiked up with the action, revealing even more of her smooth, sleek thighs.

And he wasn't the only one who'd noticed.

Turning his head back toward the group, he caught the way the mercs, as well as Max and Elliot, were checking her out, and had to choke back the sudden urge to snap at them with his jaws. But while he hated it, he couldn't fault them for their primitive interest, given that they were hot-blooded males and she was the embodiment of lush, guileless femininity. A sensual feast to each and every single one of a man's senses, and he couldn't help but wonder which of them had knowledge of that first-hand. Given his reputation, it made him a complete and total bastard, but he wanted to know which ones had stroked and tasted her and made her come. Which ones had touched what was *his*, and enjoyed her in the ways he'd never been able to allow himself to do before.

Damn it, he'd barely managed to get through kissing her today without seriously screwing it up, and he knew he needed to get a white-knuckled grip on himself before the next time. And there would *definitely* be a next time. No way in hell could he keep his hands off her now.

"It's good to have you back, scamp," Jeremy drawled, pulling Sayre into a hug when Jillian had finally released her, the healer's eyes damp with tears as she smiled at them.

While Sayre spoke with Jeremy, Cian stepped back to give them some space, and the others obviously took that as their cue to move in closer.

"That's an awfully nice ride you've got there," Lev murmured, grinning like a jackass. "One might think you were trying to impress someone with it."

Kyle laughed. "I doubt a guy with Hennessey's reputation needs a fancy car to impress a girl."

"Yeah, that's right," the blond merc drawled, with a

certain edge to his voice that spelled trouble. "He was the tomcat of the wolves, wasn't he?"

Max muttered for them both to shut up, shooting Cian a cautious glance. The kid was worried he'd lose his cool with the mercs, but he wasn't going to get into an argument over his reputation in front of Sayre. He didn't need to have that tossed in her face, and he knew exactly why the cocky mercenary had started in on him. Slivkoff had been close to Sayre before Cian had left, and from the way he kept stealing looks at her, he was interested in getting even closer. And that didn't sit well with him. Especially given how the guy's golden good looks and unusual blue-green eyes, not to mention his shit ton of muscles, never failed to make him popular with the ladies. Hell, he could have given Cian's rep a run for its money, and he was just about to pull the merc aside and explain why it would be in Lev's best interest to stay away from Sayre, when Jeremy slapped him on the shoulder, a little harder than a friendly clap, and told him they were all heading over to Brody and Mic's place for some dinner.

Given that it would mean spending an hour or two with a group of guys who were clearly lusting after his woman, along with two of his former friends who were pissed at him for the way he'd walked out on them, dinner was the last thing that Cian wanted to suffer through. But Sayre was already walking away with her sister, and there wasn't a chance he was letting her go without him. So he sucked it up, gave Jeremy a tight smile and followed after her, figuring this was going to be about as much fun as having a tooth pulled.

But it actually didn't turn out that bad. The steak and baked potatoes were better than anything he'd had in a long while, aside from Sayre's stir-fry, and even though things were strained with Brody and Jeremy, they didn't spend the entire time telling him to go screw himself. He ended up taking a seat off in a corner of the room, and let himself simply enjoy watching Sayre interact with her family and friends in a way he knew she hadn't been able to do in years. He watched her carefully, looking for any signs of pain or distress, but she seemed to be doing fine so far. She maybe looked a little overwhelmed by all the noise and conversation, seeing as how she'd been on her own for so long. But he was relieved she was holding up all right, even if it did make him a little uneasy.

It wasn't that he wanted her to suffer. That was the last damn thing that he wanted. But he couldn't get rid of the unsettling feeling that something wasn't quite right. That there had to be an explanation for why she was handling things so well, and the knot in his gut hinted that it might not be one that he liked.

As the others finished off the meal with coffee and cake, she stood by the empty fireplace, talking with Max, Lev and Sam. He still needed to warn the males to watch themselves where she was concerned, but figured it would have to wait. They'd had a hell of a day, and he'd noticed Sayre trying to hide a few yawns, which meant it was time to call it a night and get his woman out of there.

He shook his head at himself for still thinking of her as *his*, seeing as how he'd never done anything but push her away. But the wolf in him couldn't think of her as anything but something that belonged to him.

And the man in him just wanted… *Hell*, he didn't know what he thought or felt or wanted anymore, other than to keep her safe, no matter the cost.

He crossed the room, caught her eye and motioned for her to join him. She said something to the guys, then came over to him, her expression difficult to read, which didn't make him feel any better. Was she angry? Tired?

Irritated that he'd taken her away from her friends? He didn't know, and that just made him feel even edgier, as if he were already losing control of the situation.

"What's up?" she asked.

"I think it's time to call it a night. You've had a long day and should get some rest."

"You're probably right," she agreed with a soft, easy smile that should have warned him she was up to something. "I'll go with Jilly and see you in the morning."

She'd already started to turn away from him, but he stopped her by taking hold of her arm. "What the hell, Sayre? I thought you understood that you're staying with me."

She blinked up at him, that pink, sin-inspiring mouth suddenly pressed flat with irritation. "Not if you're staying in your cabin, I'm not."

His brows knitted with frustration. "What do you have against my cabin?"

Michaela's dry voice cut into their quiet argument, making it clear that she'd been eavesdropping from her nearby spot on the sofa, while Brody sprawled at her side with his arm draped over her shoulders. "Use your head, Cian. I doubt Sayre wants to bunk down in the place where you did most of your *entertaining*. That's asking a bit much, isn't it?"

He stiffened, the urge to argue and defend himself instantly building. But what could he say? The beautiful Cajun had spoken nothing more than the truth, and he made a silent vow to thank her for making him look like a prick. He knew Mic cared about him as a friend, and was grateful for the way she'd helped him find Sayre. But she also loved her husband beyond anything, and was no doubt angry as hell with him for cutting off Brody like he had.

Giving Mic his back, he focused completely on Sayre. "If not my cabin, then where are we meant to stay?"

Jeremy came over and clapped him on the shoulder again, not quite as hard as the last time, but still enough to jar his teeth. "Mic's just razzing you. I mean, yeah, we all agree with what she said. But your cabin isn't exactly how you left it."

Cian scowled, not liking where this was headed. "What the hell does *that* mean?"

Though Jeremy tried to play it cool, Cian could tell something was up. The sparkle in the guy's hazel eyes was making him worry, and he gritted his teeth as Jeremy told him, "When we didn't hear from you for an entire year, we tossed your things into storage up in town and redid the place. We've used it as a guesthouse for the past four years."

Irritation shot through him like the searing slice of a blade. "You turned my cabin into a damn bed-and-breakfast?"

Ignoring him, Jeremy looked at Sayre. "I swear the place has been stripped and repainted. Even the furniture is new."

"Son of a bitch," Cian snarled, but no one was paying him any attention.

They were too busy heading out the front door, and taking his woman with them.

Cian was still cursing under his breath about meddlesome assholes as they walked across the grass-covered Alley, and Sayre had to bite her lip to keep from laughing. Without saying a word, she climbed up the front porch steps of his cabin, caught between embarrassment that everyone knew what had been bothering her about staying there with him, and relief that they weren't going to have to bunk down with her sister and brother-in-law. She loved Jilly and Jeremy like crazy, but she wasn't sure how much interaction with others she could take before needing some space. She was doing fine for the moment, but was still cautious and didn't want to push her luck.

The others left her and Cian to make their way inside on their own, and she could have sworn she heard Jeremy snickering under his breath as he and Jillian headed back to their place after hugging her good-night. She wondered just how bad it could be as Cian used his old key to unlock the door and walked in. Moving to his side, she heard his swift intake of breath as he flicked on a light, and she swept the room with a glance, then looked over at him. The expression of horror on his face was so hilarious she had to spin away, using the excuse of shutting the front door as she tried not to burst into choked gales of laughter.

Gone were the rustic furnishings, cream walls and gleaming hardwood floors. Everything had been redone in a brilliant shade of shamrock green, from the upholstery on the furniture to the carpet and the paint on the walls. It looked like some kind of psychotic nightmare— one where a demented leprechaun had thrown up all over the room—and she had to silently commend the creative nature of their revenge.

As if he'd been listening in on her thoughts, he shoved both hands back through his hair and said, "I can't believe they were so angry at me that they actually spent money on all this shit. Jesus."

"It's, um, interesting, I'll give them that. But maybe they thought you'd like it."

He sent her a *get-real* look. "They knew damn well that I'd hate it, Sayre. You know that as well as I do."

"If you don't like Ireland," she murmured, pushing her hands in her pockets, "then why do you live there?"

"This isn't Ireland," he growled, running his tongue over the edge of his teeth as he looked from one eyesore to another. "This is the seventh circle of Hell."

"So then you do like Ireland? Is that where your family lives? Is that why you moved to Dublin?"

He grunted in response, then rolled one of those muscular shoulders. Apparently, that was the only answer he was going to give her, and she held back a frustrated laugh. He took stubborn to a whole new level when it came to being closemouthed about his past, but she was willing to cut him some slack, since there were things she didn't want to tell him, either.

When a soft knock came on the front door, he muttered something under his breath as he stalked down the hallway, leaving her to see who it was. She smiled when she found Jillian standing on the front porch, and stepped outside to join her, leaving the door open so that she could see when Cian came back down the hall. Judging by his reaction to the living room, he was probably searching the rest of the cabin to see what else they'd done to it. It was either that, or he'd scented Jillian on the other side of the door and decided to give them some privacy.

"First off," Jillian said with concern, keeping her voice low enough that they couldn't be overheard, "how are you feeling?"

Sayre crossed her arms over her chest to ward off the slight chill in the air. "So far, so good. There's…I don't know how to describe it. I'm tuned in to everyone's energy, but it's not overwhelming me. At least not yet."

As a wave of relief spread across her beautiful face, Jillian nodded. "That's good. Maybe you're learning to control it."

A slight shrug lifted her shoulders. "Or it could be that there simply aren't that many people here at the moment."

"Maybe," Jillian murmured, tucking a long strand of blond hair behind her ear. "But promise you'll let me know the moment you start to feel that it's too much. Please don't keep it to yourself."

"Stop worrying, Jilly. I'm a big girl."

"I know that. But...God, Sayre. What are you doing?"

Not really wanting to have this conversation, she deliberately misinterpreted the question. "Um, I'm pretty beat, so I was planning on getting ready for bed."

Her sister didn't look amused. "You know I meant with Cian."

Softly, knowing her sister was only looking out for her because she cared, she asked, "Is that really any of your business? You know I love you. But there are some things that should be private, don't you think?"

"If he was committed to you, then yes. But that's not the feeling that I'm getting from the two of you."

With a lopsided grin on her lips, she said, "Can't a girl just be in it for a good time?"

Jillian didn't so much as crack a smile. "Some girls, yes. But...that's never been you. And with the male who's your life mate? This is a recipe for disaster, Sayre. You *know* that."

"Maybe. Probably." She tilted her head a bit to the side, willing her sister to understand. "But what's my other choice, Jillian? Go through life never knowing how incredible it is to experience what the rest of you enjoy on a daily basis?"

Shaking her head, Jillian argued, "Sex without love is different than being with the person who holds your heart, Sayre."

"And you know this how?" she asked with an arched

brow, fully aware that her sister had never been with anyone but Jeremy.

But Jillian wasn't going to concede her point so easily. "I know from watching others."

"Well, even if you're right, you don't need to worry about me." Trying to look strong, she lifted her chin and straightened her spine. "I know what I'm doing."

"I just don't want to see you get hurt. Either physically *or* emotionally. You've been hurt enough by all this." Jillian blinked, and Sayre hoped like hell she wasn't about to cry, because then she'd cry right along with her. "I can't help but feel like I've lost you."

"Maybe this will help me," she said gently. "Maybe I can actually get to the point where I can function normally. Then I could come home, and maybe even start a life with someone else." But they would have to be human. She wouldn't risk depriving another Lycan of their life mate.

Though she'd tried to be convincing, she could tell by her sister's expression that Jillian wasn't buying it. "I'm worried for you."

"I know," she whispered. "But you don't need to be. Really, Jillian. Just trust me, okay?"

"I'm afraid that's easier said than done. And not because I don't think you're equipped to handle whatever life throws at you. I just… I don't trust Cian not to break your heart."

She shot a quick look through the open front door to make sure they were still alone, then gave her sister a solemn smile. "He doesn't have my heart. At one time, that might have been a possibility, if he'd…if he'd wanted the same thing. But he didn't, and what's done is done."

"And what of the danger he's brought down on you? Something we still don't know anything about!"

"I don't think that was on purpose, Jillian. I *know* it wasn't. So as much as I'd like to, I can't blame him for it." Not that he'd bothered to share any of the details with her, either. She could only hope that now that they were in the Alley, he'd open up and tell them exactly what was going on.

Jillian's next breath released on a heavy sigh. "I know that Cian wouldn't put you in danger on purpose. It's just...I'm worried and I'm angry, and right now blaming him sounds like a really stellar idea. And it doesn't help that I've missed you so much. You hardly ever even email me, Sayre, much less call."

"I know," she said, feeling incredibly guilty, "and I'm sorry. It's just...staying in touch makes it harder. But I think about you guys all the time."

"Just please promise me that you won't shut me out again."

"I promise," she murmured, giving her sister another hug.

Before she left, Jillian warned her that their mother was going to flip when she found out she was back, but assured her that she would try to buy her a little time before Constance Murphy descended on the Alley like a force of nature. As Jillian headed back to her cabin, Sayre walked inside and locked the front door, hoping they were done with visitors for the night. She went in search of Cian, and instead found her things sitting on the foot of the bed in the master bedroom, which had been decorated as hideously as the living room. He must have gone out the back door and brought everything back from the Audi while she'd been talking to Jillian, and she hoped like hell that he hadn't overheard any of their conversation.

Stepping back into the hallway, she saw that the cabin's back door had been left slightly ajar, and she could smell cigarette smoke, which meant he was probably out on the back porch polluting his lungs. Deciding to get ready for bed while he enjoyed his vice, she changed into a small tank-and-short set, then went into the horrendously green bathroom to brush her teeth. When she came back into the bedroom, a magnificently bare-chested and barefoot Cian was sitting on the bed with his back resting against the gaudy headboard, his long legs stretched out in front of him and crossed at the ankles.

"You look exhausted," he said the moment she walked into the room.

She snuffled a soft snort under her breath. "Thanks. Lines like that must get you laid *all* the time."

Instead of laughing, he gave her a hard, steady stare that brought a rush of heat to the sensitive surface of her skin. "You could look dead on your feet and you'd still be the most beautiful woman in the world, Sayre. I was just trying to say that I'm worried about you."

"Oh. Um, thanks."

"Come on," he said, jerking his chin toward the empty side of the bed.

"Are we both sleeping in here?" she asked, unable to hide the surprise in her voice. After the way he'd pulled away from her today, she hadn't thought he'd want to get near her again so soon.

She watched his strong throat work as he swallowed. "Yeah, we are. I...I don't want to take any chances being away from you. Especially at night. And the bed is big."

She didn't say anything more as she put her toothbrush back in her bag, then made her way over to the bed. Trying like crazy not to drool at the mouthwatering sight of him sprawled on top of the far side of the mattress, his lean, muscular body the most mesmerizing thing she'd ever seen, she pulled back the blankets and climbed in.

There was a hole in the left leg of the faded jeans he'd thrown on, and she could see a glimpse of the dark hair that was sprinkled over his strong, powerful thigh. Given how hot that little glimpse of his leg was making her, she knew better than to let her gaze drift higher, taking in his ripped abs, rugged chest and those broad, sink-your-nails-into-them shoulders. And then there were his big, round biceps, corded forearms and thick wrists that led to large, beautiful hands.

God. Her body temperature was rising, her heart pounding like a freaking jackhammer, and she knew her power was on the verge of breaking free in an embarrassing display of sparks any second now. Doing the only thing she could, she squeezed her eyes shut, praying he would turn off the bedside light as she started to roll over, giving him her back. But he stopped her with the touch of his big, warm hand on her arm.

"Don't," he groaned, pulling on her arm until she'd rolled onto her back and found herself staring up into his breathtaking face, his lips slightly parted for his uneven breaths. He lifted his hand and gently tucked a strand of her hair behind her ear, a slight smile tugging at the corner of his mouth. The look in his molten, heavy-lidded gaze made her shiver, and she licked her lips, so nervous and excited she thought she might come out of her skin.

Then he completely blew her mind as he said, "You forgot to let me kiss you good-night, lass."

Cian didn't know where those words had come from, but he couldn't take them back. Didn't *want* to take them back. He didn't want anything but the feel of her mouth under his again, slick and hot and opened wide for the ravenous demands of his lips and tongue, and so that's what he took. With his weight braced on his elbow, he leaned over her and ran his tongue over her juicy lower lip, then sank it deep inside that sweet-as-hell hollow of flesh. And, Christ, it was perfect. Soft and wet and impossibly addictive, making him crave even more of her—*all of her*—in a way that was even deeper than the visceral hunger for this woman he'd been carrying with him for years.

"I want *more*," she moaned, curving her feminine hands around the back of his neck, his skin hot and damp beneath the softness of her palms.

With his right hand cupping the side of her face, he tilted her head back at a deeper angle with his thumb under the delicate edge of her jaw. "More of what, baby?"

"Of this. Of you."

"Sayre," he groaned, rubbing her name into those cushiony, kiss-swollen lips, fighting the instinctive urge to reach down and cup one of her perfect breasts in his hand, her nipples tight and thick as they pressed against the thin cotton of her top in a way that was guaranteed to drive him insane. "Damn it, you little witch," he panted, his blood pounding in his ears. "You're going to be the death of me."

She broke away from the kiss and pulled on the back of his hair to get him to lift his head until she could see his face. "Don't say that," she whispered, stroking her fingertips across the stubble that covered the lower half of his face, reminding him that he still needed to shave. There were too many tender, intimate places on her body that he *needed* to put his mouth on, and he didn't want to be worrying about scratching her when he explored every single one of them. "With everything that's happening," she added, "I don't want to hear you talk that way."

He ran his tongue over his lower lip, loving how he could taste her there. "And I can't hear you say you want me without wanting to do things to you that should have me drawn and quartered."

Her lips twisted with a rueful grin, some of the fiery heat in her gaze dimming. "I'm sure it's nothing you haven't heard a thousand times before."

"It doesn't matter, Sayre." They were gruff, husky words that were thick with his need for her. "None of it matters, because you're different."

"Good," she murmured, looking relieved, if not entirely convinced. "I should be different for you, considering what's between us."

"No," he argued with a snarl, unable to soften the frustration scalding him from the inside out. "It's not good. I'm not talking about the life-mate connection. I wanted you *too much* before I even realized it was between us."

Surprise filtered through her smoldering look of need. "You did?"

"You're damned right I did," he growled, clawing on to his crumbling self-control with everything that he had. "As wrong as it was, I wanted you even when you were practically jailbait. I wanted to get you naked and under me, Sayre. I wanted to keep you trapped there, at my mercy, taking every inch of me until I was buried so far inside you there wasn't any chance I was ever coming back out."

"Cian," she moaned, just as her power started to break free in a shower of tiny, golden sparks that glittered around them like fireflies. Pulling away from her, he forced himself to sit up, needing to give himself a moment to think, to get his head on straight, since he was about two seconds away from completely losing it. But she followed after him, bringing that breathtaking body of hers up right beside him. He opened his mouth, ready to tell her that he wasn't leaving, that they just needed to

be careful and take things slow—not because he wanted to, but because it was the only way he could keep his shit together—when she reached down, grabbed the hem of her tank top and ripped it over her crazy little head.

Holy mother of God, someone whispered inside his head, but he wasn't sure if the choked words belonged to him or to his wolf. His head jerked back so quickly it was like she'd smacked him, his lips parting as his eyes narrowed to piercing, focused slits. Her nipples were very small, and very pink, the way they topped her firm breasts making his mouth water and his blood burn.

Somehow, she was even more perfect than he'd imagined, and now he was seriously in trouble, his hunger like a living thing inside his body, foaming at the mouth, champing at the bit to get closer to her. "What the fuck, Sayre?"

"I want this," she said in a voice that was soft but steady, her long hair streaming over her freckled shoulders, framing her mouthwatering breasts so perfectly she looked like a centerfold. Only he'd never seen a centerfold who even came close to looking as devastatingly gorgeous as Sayre Murphy. She was…damn it, there weren't even words, and he couldn't have torn his gaze away from her to save his bloody life.

Blushing so hard she looked sunburned, that adorable mix of shy and bold the sexiest damn thing he'd ever encountered, she added, "They're not as big as you usually went for, but—"

"Shut up," he growled, quickly finding his voice so he could cut her off. He'd walk over jagged shards of glass before he sat there and listened to her say shit like that. "Your breasts are beautiful, Sayre. *You're* beautiful. Every addictive little inch of you is perfect."

And then he was done talking, because he couldn't

wait another goddamn minute to get his mouth on her. Gripping her upper arms, he pushed her back into the god-awful green pillows that had tiny pink shamrocks all over them, and came down over her. Everything else faded away, and he lost himself in the girl he wished like hell he could be the right man for. Holding her blistering gaze, he touched just the very tip of his tongue to one of those swollen nipples, the taste and texture so damn good he groaned. She was exquisite, and he shuddered with a hard jolt of lust as he lapped at her and rubbed the flat of his tongue over the pebbled, succulent pink flesh. She was exceptionally sensitive, her skin flushing with color, those tiny sparks of light still pinging around them. It was like being caught in the center of a star, surrounded by the surreal bursts of color and heat, while waves of sensation crashed into him again and again.

Keeping his heavy-lidded gaze locked tight with hers, he loved watching the emotions flash through those hazy blue-gray eyes. Excitement. Hunger. *Want*. Unable to stop himself, he scraped his teeth over the tender flesh of her nipple, a choked curse rumbling through his mind when she arched into the sharp caress. She might be the softest thing he'd ever gotten his hands on, but she liked a bit of bite with her pleasure, and his head went dizzy with the possibilities. It was like she'd been friggin' made for him.

She was. Jackass.

"God, Cian." She clutched handfuls of his hair as she held him to her, a husky cry slipping from her lips as he took the tip of her breast in his hot mouth and started to hungrily suck on her. "No wonder all the women made fools of themselves over you."

He flinched as if she'd suddenly poked him with something sharp, letting her nipple pop free of his mouth as he pulled his head back. "Don't," he ordered, forcing the word through his gritted teeth.

"Don't what?" she asked, as he put his face directly over hers, a scowl wedged deep between his brows.

"Don't talk about other women. They don't have any place in bed with us."

She stared up at him, rosy and damp with desire, those tiny sparks of light still glittering around her. But she was being careful to keep her expression neutral, even as she pulled that succulent lower lip through her teeth. "If you don't want me obsessing about your past and not being enough for you, then tell me what you want me to do. Tell me what you like, and I'll do it."

God...damn...it. Though he wanted her so badly it hurt, he knew he needed to stop. He was too close to losing control, and too irritated by the way she was coming at this thing between them to keep it together. He knew why she kept bringing up other women, using the reminder to help her keep things from getting too emotional, and it was bugging the hell out of him.

That was...bad, because he was too aware of how easily that frustration could get the upper hand on him, his need for possession overshadowing his common sense as what he wanted battled against what he could take without being a total asshole.

Closing his eyes, he rolled away from her and threw his legs over the far side of the bed as he sat up. "It's been a long day, Sayre. You should go on and get some sleep."

"Wait, what?" He could easily hear the disbelief in those breathless words. "Where are you going?"

"I need another smoke." He sounded like he'd swallowed a mouthful of gravel, and got the hell out of there before she could say anything more. Once he was out on the back porch, he propped his shoulders against the cabin's rough cedar planks and tilted his head back, pulling in deep breaths of the crisp mountain air, trying to make sense of what was happening to him.

Every time he touched her, he could feel his need for the little witch ramming against the defenses he'd built inside himself, stone by stone. Shields that made it possible for him to get through each day without her…and without doing something stupid.

There were things behind those walls in his head that he did his best to avoid. Pain lay there. As well as despair and disappointment. Failure and regret and guilt. So much that it made his insides feel like a festering wasteland. They'd driven him away from her before, and he honestly didn't know what would happen this time around, now that Aedan had already learned the truth about her. Yeah, he knew what he *wanted*. But how badly did he want it? What was he willing to do for it? How much was he willing to reveal? To lay out on the line?

Before, he hadn't been willing to dig any deeper for the answers, because he'd known he wasn't right for her. And he still wasn't. But that didn't mean he had any of this shit figured out.

The only thing Cian knew with absolute, unchanging certainty was that he would never be what she needed.

Or even close to what she deserved.

Chapter 8

It was time to come clean.

Cian wasn't looking forward to it, but he knew he couldn't put it off any longer. After a shitty night's sleep on the green velvet love seat that sat beneath the window in his bedroom—since he hadn't trusted himself to sleep beside Sayre in the bed—he'd awakened at dawn. Standing on his back porch with a steaming cup of coffee in his hand, he'd watched the sun rise above the line of trees, struggling to find the right words for the explanations he would soon be making. He'd told Brody the night before that he wanted to talk to everyone today, and the Runner had told him to be at his cabin at nine.

Since he didn't want Sayre around when he was admitting all his ugly secrets, they'd decided that Max and Elliot could keep her busy, and then the two youngest Runners could be brought up to speed later. It wasn't an ideal solution, seeing as how she'd be spending time with the young men without him there, but he would deal with it because he had to. Anything was better than her sitting in Brody's living room and listening to his confessions.

While the sun continued its steady rise into an azure blue sky, he was careful to be quiet so that he didn't wake Sayre, who was damn near cocooned in the ugly shamrock sheets, only her glorious hair and the cute little tip of her nose visible. He grabbed a shower, then dressed in jeans, his black boots and one of his favorite old gray T-shirts that he'd filched off Brody years ago. It was sappy and sentimental, but it made him feel better to wear it, knowing damn well that the meeting could go one of two ways, and he wasn't entirely certain of the outcome.

As he put his empty cup in the sink, he glanced out the kitchen window and spotted Jeremy working on a children's swing set at the edge of the glade. In that moment, it really hit him, how drastically his friends' lives had changed since he'd left, and he lifted his hand to rub at the center of his chest, where there was a sharp pang. He could see it so clearly it was like he was replaying a memory, all those big, badass warriors out there playing with their kids, making them laugh and squeal as they tossed them up into the air and blew raspberries on their little bellies, while the women looked on with heartwarming smiles.

You could have had that with Sayre, his wolf pointed out quietly, its tone more solemn than he'd ever heard it. *We could have had it, if you hadn't left.*

That was true, but at what price? Five years ago, Cian could have convinced himself that the danger wasn't as real as he'd feared—that Aedan would let go of their feud and never mark her as a target—just so he could have her. But it wouldn't have been fair to her. Would

have just been one more sin to add to his many, and she
hadn't deserved that.

*So you left. And look where we are. Right here, deal-
ing with the same things you were trying to avoid.*

He grimaced, hating that the beast was right. And,
yeah, if he'd known this would happen—that his past
would find her anyway—he probably would have never
found the strength to leave in the first place. He would
have claimed her, despite knowing he wasn't good
enough for her...that he could never love her the way
she deserved, and they would probably have at least three
kids by now.

Did you honestly just say that? his wolf roared, seething with sharp-edged, visceral fury. The beast had been
against leaving her from the moment the idea had first
come to him, never wavering in its conviction. In its primal world, a male didn't walk away from what belonged
to him. He conquered and claimed and worshipped, de-
voting his entire life to ensuring the happiness and protection of his female, while doing everything in his power
to plant his seed in her womb and create life.

"I didn't say I wanted kids," he muttered quietly to
the animal. "I was simply stating a fact. If I'd stayed, I
have no doubt the two of us would have kept her knocked
up. We'd have done everything we could to make that
happen."

And that was the truth. All of it. But it would have
been wrong.

*You call her living out in that cabin on her own, with
no family and friends, a better outcome?*

He cursed under his breath, unwilling to concede that
the animal had a point. But then, his wolf had never
bought in to his feelings about his bloodline...or the guilt
he carried over his past. In its world, when mistakes were

made, you moved on and didn't let them hold you back. It was a simple, primitive view, and one he was jealous as hell of. Because he would have given anything to be that way, too. To say to hell with his concerns over what Sayre deserved, and simply take her because it was his goddamn right to do so.

Unfortunately, his humanity was too much a part of him, his guilt woven into the very fabric of his character.

And now he had to go and unload his darkest, ugliest secrets to the people he cared about most in this entire world, aside from Sayre, and it sucked.

He took a moment to compose himself, shoved his hair back from his face, then turned and headed over to Brody's. They were all there before him, including the mercs, the curiosity in the air thick enough to cut with a knife. While coffee was being handed out in the kitchen, he kept himself occupied studying the framed photographs that covered the mantel. Most of them were of holidays they'd had there in the Alley, when everyone had been together. A few at Christmas, and then Easter, and what looked like the Fourth of July.

There were more kids in the photos than he'd expected, though he shouldn't have been surprised, given how his friends hadn't been able to keep their hands off their mates before he'd left. But what he really couldn't get over was how happy the Runners looked in the photographs, as if everything they could have ever wanted or needed was right there with them.

If it were possible for people to be blessed or rewarded for their hard work and sacrifice, then Cian knew that's what he was looking at. These families were a blessing, plain and simple, and he finally had to turn away before he started getting all maudlin about it. As everyone came back into the room and took their seats, he pulled in a shaky breath, ready to confess every shameful, appalling part of his story.

"So, yeah. There's something important that I never told you—any of you," he forced past his tight throat as he leaned back against the mantel, his hands shoved deep in the front pockets of his jeans so that no one could see them shaking. Forcing himself to look around the room, instead of staring at the floor like a coward, he went on. "It's something I hoped like hell you would never learn. That I'm not proud of. Not for the reasons you're going to assume, but because...because of the choices I made."

"Cian, just tell us," Brody urged, his elbows braced on his parted knees as he sat beside Mic on one of the leather sofas. "If you'd just trust us, we'd be here for you. You know that."

"I'm... I have... Shit, this isn't easy."

Brody gave him a supportive nod. "Just go for it, man."

"Right. Okay." He sucked in a deep breath, then quickly blurted, "My, uh, father is a vampire."

Silence immediately followed those six little words. Dead, heart-thudding silence. The kind where you couldn't even hear anyone breathing. And then a pale-faced Jeremy kind of coughed to clear his throat, and managed to croak, "What?"

Before Cian could respond, everyone started talking at once as they grappled to understand his shocking revelation.

He understood their confusion. In the Lycan world, vampires were a reclusive, seldom-encountered species. They were coldly calculating, elitist and basically assholes. Immoral, amoral and arrogant as hell.

Huh. When he put it like that, Cian thought it was kind of hard to believe they'd never figured it out for themselves.

When Brody finally got tired of the noise, he yelled for everyone to calm down, then turned his attention back to Cian. "We can't scent it on you," the Runner said in a low voice that surprisingly held more curiosity than it did anger. Aside from Sayre, it was Brody's reaction he'd been the most worried about, and he couldn't help but be relieved by how things had gone so far.

Exhaling a slow breath of air, Cian said, "You can't detect it because my father is also part human, which means my blood is too diluted for scent recognition."

"So then you're a combination of three different species," Sam murmured. "Human, Lycan and vampire?"

Cian nodded, then reached over for the mug of coffee Mic had set on the mantel for him earlier, wishing it had a hefty dose of Irish whiskey in it. He took a large swallow, then set down the mug and tried to explain to them how it worked. How his vampire instincts weren't a voice in his head, like the wolf part of his nature, but more of a…a *hunger.* A greedy, chilling, twisted craving for blood and gratification, like a powerful internal drive that was continually focused on consuming more…and more. And one he was only able to control thanks to the dominance of his beast.

When he was done, he had to wipe the sheen of sweat off his face with his sleeve, his insides knotting as he waited to see how they would react. After a few moments, it was Jeremy who spoke first again. "So if vamps can halt the aging process by feeding on blood as their main food source, then…Jesus, man. How old *are* you?"

A rusty laugh rumbled up from his chest. "Of all the things you need to ask me, *that's* your first question?"

"I've just always assumed you were around my age," Jeremy went on, looking him up and down with a critical eye.

"Close," Cian murmured.

"How close?" Jeremy persisted, obviously unwilling to let this one go.

A heavy sigh slipped past his lips. "I'm roughly ten years older than you are, because I spent a decade at the age of sixteen. Then I came here to visit my mother's family—I met you and the others—and I decided to change the way I'd been living. I stopped feeding from the vein, and allowed myself to begin aging again. All because I wanted to be one of you. To make my home here."

Everyone took a moment to digest what he'd just told them, and then Lev spoke up for the first time, scratching his jaw as he said, "You know, that actually makes a lot of sense."

Cian raised his brows, wondering where the guy was going with that statement. "It does?"

Lev smirked. "Hell, yeah. You spent damn near close to twenty years being a know-it-all, smart-ass teenager. No wonder you turned out to be such an asshole."

It was Brody who tilted his head back and laughed the hardest, while the others either snorted or smiled. And even though Cian started off scowling, he soon found himself shaking his head and joining in. "Nice one, jack-ass."

Mic was the one who commented next, her blue eyes bright with emotion as she stared up at him from her place beside Brody. "I have so many questions, I don't even know where to start. I mean, I could sometimes sense that you carried a tremendous burden inside you. But I honestly never realized that it was this, Cian. I wish you had told us. You have to know that we would have never judged you for it."

Sliding her a grim smile, he said, "I know that, Mic."

But he also knew that he hadn't even gotten to the bad part yet.

Stalling for a bit more time before he dropped that final bit of "craptastic" news on them, as Sayre would say, he looked at Jillian. She'd been sitting beside Jeremy the entire time, her blank expression completely at odds with the flurry of emotions he could see rushing through her wide-eyed gaze. "Didn't you ever pick up on it, Jilly?" he asked her gently, searching for the truth in those velvety brown eyes. "Every time you had to heal one of my injuries, I thought for sure that you would see—"

She cut him off, saying, "Never. I…I tried not to pry. I *always* try not to pry."

"You honestly never suspected?" he asked, surprised that she'd never seen the truth when helping him, since a witch's power enabled her to often see into the mind of the person she was healing.

"I didn't," she told him, shaking her head. "I thought… I mean, I *sensed* that there was something different about you. I guess I just figured that you were part of some powerful, unique bloodline, or…I don't know. That you'd inherited *something* on your father's side. But I sure as hell never suspected vampire."

"What about you?" he asked, looking at Brody.

"I don't know what I thought, man. Maybe that you'd… Hell, I don't know. I figured you'd been scratched by something, or fed on something you shouldn't have, and it'd affected you in some way. But I never suspected it was something that was as much a part of you as your wolf."

"Huh." He looked around the room. "With all those comments you all used to make about the damnation of my immortal soul, I sometimes wondered if you didn't already know."

"Naw," Jeremy drawled with a wry, lopsided grin. "That was just because you're an ass."

Everyone laughed, releasing some of the lingering tension in the air. As if they suddenly felt more comfortable, the questions started coming more quickly, one after another, and Cian did his best to answer each one as honestly as possible, even though he hated talking about that part of his life.

But he did it. For them. Because they deserved to know everything, seeing as how he'd brought this nightmare with Aedan directly onto their doorsteps.

Breaking out in a cold sweat, he eventually explained how the "black" or "dark" blood that created a vampire came in different strains: old lines and new lines. Somewhat sane ones…and ones so evil the creatures shouldn't even be allowed to exist. As if he sensed where Cian was going with the information, Jeremy suddenly gave him a sharp look of concern and asked, "What does this all have to do with Sayre being in danger?"

He pretty much flung out the answer, needing to get the words off his chest. "I have a brother. A half brother named Aedan who is a year younger than me. We share the same father, but his mother was also a vampire, which means that the vamp part of him is dominant, overshadowing the human part. He's the reason I came back to protect Sayre, and he—"

"Wait a minute. You have a goddamn *brother,*" Brody cut in, looking ready to bolt to his feet. Cian figured the only thing holding his former partner back was the touch of his wife's hand on his arm.

"Brody, calm down," she murmured.

"No, that's not gonna happen. Because it's one thing not to tell us about the vamp blood," the Runner growled, his scarred face ruddy with anger as he glared up at him. "I don't like it, but I get it. But why the hell did you need to keep your family a secret? What the fuck is that about, Cian? I didn't think we kept shit like that from each other."

"We didn't," he said, hating the hurt he could see that was fueling Brody's anger. "But Aedan is a twisted son of a bitch and there wasn't any way to tell you about him without telling you about the other."

"How about 'Hey Brody, I have a brother. He's a jackass, so I don't like to talk about him. But I just thought you should know'?"

"Christ, Brody. He's not a jackass." He couldn't stop his voice from rising, each word torn out of him like a bleeding chunk of flesh. "Aedan's an evil piece of shit, and I spent ten years of my life acting just like him! *That's* why I didn't want you to know!"

The Runner's face paled so quickly it was like he'd been gutted.

Dropping his head forward in defeat, Cian screwed his eyes shut, hating that look of shock that had just spread across his friend's face. Voice weary and thick with disgust, he forced himself to explain as much as he could stomach to reveal. "He's a hundred times more powerful than a rogue wolf. Their drive and their frenzy—that's Aedan on a mellow day. I heard he once took out an entire Lycan family of eight on his own, within a mere matter of minutes. He's *that* strong. That screwed up in the head, and I spent an entire decade with him when he was a boy. At the age of sixteen, I traveled the world at Aedan's side, doing more shit than I could ever possibly name that I'm not proud of. But Aedan always took things even further. I tried to get him to…hell, I don't know. To tone it down, I guess, and I made excuses for him for a long time, like he was someone I needed to

look out for and stand by because he was my brother."
Lifting his head, he forced himself to look Brody right
in the eye before he went on. "Then, one day, I ran dry.
He'd done something that I couldn't make any more excuses for, and I got out. But not before I'd made a life-
long enemy of him."

Jeremy's deep voice cut into the heavy moment of silence that followed. "And now he wants to hurt Sayre because of you? Because she's yours, and he holds a grudge
against you for something that happened all those years
ago?"

Before he could respond, Brody shot to his feet and
paced away to the far side of the room, then turned
around to face him with a dark, vicious scowl. "That's
why you left," the Runner snarled, his thick chest rising
and falling with the harsh force of his breaths. "Goddamn it, Cian! When you realized what she was to you,
you took off to protect her. You didn't even ask for our
help. You just left!"

Hardening his jaw, he managed a curt nod, feeling
sick to his stomach. In that moment, standing there in the
face of his best friend's pain, he hated himself...and he
hated his old man more than ever for not ending Aedan
when he'd had the chance.

Though their father's vampire strain was one of cun-
ning and strength, the "dark" blood from Aedan's mother
was as evil as it came. Their father had always claimed
that she'd used that ancient power to enthrall him, leading him to her bed against his will. But Cian knew better.
Colin Hennessey was nothing more than a self-serving
son of a bitch who thought of nothing but himself, and
he always would be.

When his father should have destroyed Aedan, once
they'd realized just how far he was slipping away from

them, he'd refused. Because of power. The fool had seen Aedan as a weapon that could be used to defend his position in Ireland, not understanding until too late that *no one* controlled Aedan, including the man himself. Aedan had been lost to the darkness inside him from the moment his vampire instincts had gained the upper hand, and there was nothing anyone could do that would ever bring him back.

"Jesus," Kyle rumbled, locking his fingers behind his head as he leaned back in his chair, while Brody completely turned his back on the room, his hands braced on his hips. "I knew you had some serious shit going on under the surface that none of us knew about, Hennessey. But I never guessed it would be this messed up."

He didn't know what to say to that, so he didn't say anything at all.

"I wish you'd talked to us," Jeremy said with a tired sigh, his blond hair falling into his eyes as he shot a worried look over at Brody. "That you... Shit, man, I just wish that you had trusted us."

He swallowed so hard that it hurt, knowing there wasn't anything he could say at this point that would make things better. This wasn't one of those times when *sorry* was going to cut it. Not unless he wanted to sound like an even bigger dick than he already did.

It was Jillian who finally cut to the heart of the matter. "How does this affect Sayre? Does she even know?"

He braced himself, knowing exactly where this was headed. "She doesn't know specifics about the threat, but she knows that Aedan is my brother."

"And the vampire part?"

Locking his jaw, he shook his head.

Perched on the edge of her seat, she gave him a look that would have brought a lesser man to his knees, the love she held for her sister making her fierce. "You have to tell her, Cian."

"I know." He swallowed, then wet his lips, each thudding beat of his heart making him feel like he was sinking deeper into a pit of quicksand. "I just…I don't want her to be afraid of me." *Or disgusted by who I was…*

Damn it, he didn't want to lose what little part of her he had!

"I can understand that," Jillian offered with a husky note of sympathy. "But it doesn't mean you get a pass, Cian. The only choice you have is to *trust* her."

Scrubbing his hands down his face, he muttered, "It's not that simple, Jilly."

"It's *exactly* that simple. You're going to have to man up and tell her everything. All of it." Her dark eyes burned with conviction. "Even those parts that are the… hardest."

In other words, the secrets he was holding closest to his chest. The ones that would cause him to lose her, and not for a handful of months, or years.

But forever.

Chapter 9

Cian spent another hour with the group, questioning them about how things had been since he'd left. Not long after his strained exchange with Jillian, Brody had cursed something guttural under his breath and stormed out of the room, his office door slamming shut behind him a moment later. Mic excused herself and followed after Brody with a worried expression on her face, but the others were willing to let Cian turn the tables and ask some questions of his own.

Even Slivkoff managed to offer some helpful information without sounding like a jackass, and Jillian spoke up a time or two, though it was apparent her thoughts were a million miles away, undoubtedly with her sister. But, together, the group filled him in on the problems they'd had to deal with during his absence, as well as the challenges they'd taken on. It was clear that the Silvercrest were now thriving, and that the pack had the Bloodrunners to thank for their success. Relations between the Alley and the pack's mountaintop town of Shadow Peak had never been better, and he was glad that his friends were enjoying the recognition they deserved.

The only part that sucked was that he hadn't been there with them. That he'd missed each of the milestones that had marked the passage of time in their lives. Hell, the simple fact that all the Runners, with the exception of Max and Elliot, had kids now would be something that took time for him to wrap his head around. Before Mason had found Torrance nearly six years ago, Cian had never imagined the group would all be settled down and doing their best to add to the pack's growing population.

Before they ended the meeting, they talked over the Alley's security issues, and Jeremy assured him that extra patrols were already in progress. If Aedan wanted to get to Sayre, it wouldn't be easy for the vampire, and that was what Cian needed. A way to slow down the bastard so that he could deal with him one-on-one, while the others got Sayre the hell away from him.

When Kyle asked if he wanted a tour of the security procedures they had in place, Cian took him up on it, and he said a somewhat awkward goodbye to the others before heading out. There wasn't any sign of Sayre as he walked across the sunlit glade, and it worried him, how desperately he wanted even the tiniest glimpse of her— so he told himself it was good that he was getting away for a bit and putting some space between them. He and Kyle left the Alley in the merc's Jeep, and headed for Shadow Peak, to the security headquarters that the Runners ran there. They grabbed lunch while up in town, his presence at the diner drawing more than a few curious stares, and he knew that news of his return would have spread like wildfire before the end of the day. Not that he cared. The few remaining relatives he'd had in the town had moved away years ago, and there was no one else he would have wanted to catch up with, aside from some of the Runners' parents. But he figured he could pay them visits after this shit with Aedan was over, before he took off again.

After lunch, he and Kyle headed back down the mountain, leaving the Jeep at one of the new security outposts that had been built out in the forest. From there, they spent hours walking most of the security routes on foot, then grabbed the Jeep and made their way back.

By the time he and Kyle, who had been surprisingly easy to get along with, were parting ways, the evening sun was already setting behind the trees, and Cian was bordering on desperate to see Sayre again. He wasn't so naive that he thought she wouldn't have heard about the meeting that had taken place that morning, and didn't doubt that she'd demand to know what he and the others had talked about. And when he refused to tell her, she would definitely be pissed at him. But it didn't matter. He still wanted—and maybe even *needed*—to be close to her. To see her. Breathe her in. Soak her into his memory so that he'd have a full reservoir to pull from when this nightmare was over and he was no longer a part of her life.

Jesus. He had to stop on the way up his front porch steps and brace his right hand against the railing, as that last thought slammed into him like a high-powered kick to his sternum. Whatever his frame of mind had been when he'd come after her, he was man enough to admit that things were...*changing* on him. His need for her was taking on a new face and shape, until it was something he no longer even recognized. Something that seemed to be shifting on him with each second that ticked by, becoming stronger…sharper, like a reflection in the fogged surface of a mirror as it slowly cleared.

Which meant he'd just have to claw on to every bit of control he could find. And when he reached the bottom of the well, dig even deeper.

When he didn't find her in the cabin, his teeth snapping together so hard at the sight of all that damn green that it made his jaw ache, he went back outside and ran into James. From the looks of it, the sweaty, bare-chested merc had spent the better part of the day cutting the plush green grass that covered the entire expanse of the glade, the crisp scent of the freshly cut blades thick in the air.

"You didn't happen to see Sayre out here, did you?" he asked, while James chugged back a bottle of water.

The tall, dark-haired merc wiped the back of his wrist over his mouth, then said, "She's playing poker with her boys."

He froze, hoping like hell that he'd heard him wrong. "Her *what?*"

James's brown eyes crinkled at the corners, the smirk on his face making it clear he thought Cian's jealous reaction was funny. "Her guys. You know, Max and Elliot and Lev. They always used to play together over at Lev's place, before she moved. Me, Sam and Kyle would sometimes join them, but it was always the four of them together."

Something hot and uncomfortable crept its way up his spine, then curled around the backs of his ears and settled sourly on his tongue. He'd never experienced the vile touch of jealousy before Sayre, but he'd felt it nearly every day since. Even in the years they were apart, it was a constant emotion weighing heavily in his gut, forever reminding him that she was somewhere out there in the world, enjoying her life…with someone who wasn't him.

Only, she hadn't been. Instead, she'd been living in her own personal prison, isolated and alone, and that was on him. Not because he'd made it happen, but because he hadn't been there for her, in whatever way that she'd needed him.

Feeling like an even bigger jackass than he did before, he headed over to Lev's cabin.

Without even bothering to knock, he gripped the heavy metal handle that was still warm from the sun and opened the front door, the music and laughter he could hear coming from inside telling him that everyone was still there. After letting himself in, he saw that they were all gathered around a card table in the middle of the merc's living room, and he knew, before she even opened her mouth, that Sayre had been drinking. The alcohol had slipped into her scent, giving it a ticklish edge that would have been intriguing, if she weren't sitting there getting wasted with a table full of guys who looked as if they'd like nothing more than to put her in their laps and let her wriggle that sweet little ass of hers all over them.

The instant she looked up and saw him standing just inside the archway from the hall, a wide smile spread across her pink face and she flung her arms up in the air, throwing cards everywhere as she shouted, "I knew you'd find me!" Then she reached over and grabbed Max's beer, lifting it high and damn near spilling it all over the place.

Christ, she wasn't just a little tipsy. She was *hammered.*

"'N case you were wondering what I'm doing with this bottle, I'm toasting fate for being such a bitch," she said with a tiny hiccup, while Max tried to rescue his beer and Lev and Elliot just looked on with stupid grins on their faces.

Making his way around the table, Cian crouched down

beside her, drawing her face toward him with the touch of his fingers on her chin. Sensing that there was something bothering her—and hoping like hell that she hadn't found out what was discussed at the meeting—he asked, "What's going on, Sayre? You were fine when I left this morning."

A bitter laugh slipped past those pink, velvety lips. "That's because you ran out while I was *asleep*. And then…then your *harem* started showing up!"

His harem? What was she talking about?

In a moment of clarity, she must have read the confusion on his face, because she leaned in closer so that she could explain, her breath smelling like peach schnapps. "There's been a steady stream of 'em all day. Blondes, brunettes, redheads. Slim, curvy, short, tall. Pale, dark, and everything in between. And every single one of them was beautiful." Her voice got soft, and she made the saddest little damn sound that he'd ever heard, whispering, "So freaking beautiful. And they've missed you."

He bit back a guttural curse, understanding now how Eli had felt when his past bed partners had tried to visit him in the Alley, after he'd returned. Carla hadn't reacted well, and neither was Sayre. Not that he blamed her, seeing as how that green-eyed monster was one he was only too familiar with these days.

"I didn't ask them to come here," he told her. "And I've no desire to see them, Sayre."

She rolled her eyes, or at least tried to, ending up a little cross-eyed instead. "Sure you don't. That's *exshmactly*…I mean *expactly*…damn it, I mean *ezfactly* what I expected you to say!"

"God, you're cute when you're wasted," he rumbled, easily catching her in his arms as she lost her balance on the chair and slumped to the side, crashing right into him. Moving to his feet, he held her soft weight cuddled against his chest as he turned toward the table and the three guys who were watching them, their expressions almost tender as they glanced at Sayre, who had gone as limp as an overcooked noodle in his arms. It was clear that they'd been looking out for her, even while enjoying her drunken revelry.

"I'm taking her back to my place," he told them, hoping they were smart enough not to give him any grief about it.

Max and Elliot smirked, while Slivkoff gave a low laugh. "'Bout time, don't you think, Irish?"

Cian narrowed his eyes at the jackass. "You got something you'd like to say to me, *Russian*?"

"Oh, I have lots of things that I'll say eventually. When it's just the two of us." The merc cracked his knuckles. "That way I can make sure that you're listening. Real careful-like."

Cian flipped him off with the hand near Sayre's knees, then turned and headed back outside, unable to get enough of the way she felt in his arms, even when she was too drunk to lift her head. He could feel her lips moving against his chest, and was trying to make out the words as he carried her across the grassy glade. Then her voice got a little louder, and he thought he caught something about letting a wolf out of a closet.

"Hey, are you singing that Shakira song?" he asked, nuzzling the top of her head with his nose, her hair so silky that the animal in him wanted to feel it stroking over every inch of his body, the wolf more tactile than a human could ever be.

"What's wrong with that?" Her voice was a little sleepy, but not quite as slurred as before, the fresh air no doubt helping to clear her head a bit. "Shakira is *hawt*!"

she added, and he could sense her smile. "If I were a dude, I would so tap that."

He gave a loud snort. "If you were a dude, seeing you drunk off your ass in those little shorts you're wearing wouldn't be nearly so much fun."

She pulled her head back, her pretty mouth hanging open in a way that was putting some seriously dirty thoughts in his head. Not that he didn't always have those around her. "Ohmygod," she gasped, blinking up at him. "Did you just crack a joke? I didn't think you even knew how to do that anymore."

His lips twitched, but he managed to choke back the laugh burning in his throat, not wanting to encourage her.

She snuggled back against his chest and shimmied in his arms until she could bury her nose in the crook of his shoulder, almost as if she were trying to breathe in more of his scent, and a sizzling spike of lust shot straight to his dick. "This is so weird," she said around a yawn, making him wonder if she'd sensed that he was getting hard.

"What's weird, lass?"

She danced her fingertips across his chest, her voice so soft it was nearly lost in the evening breeze. "Being here, in the Alley. In your arms. I mean, a girl spends years thinking she'll *never*—as in the freaking moon will turn into cheese and pigs will fly before it happens—never, ever, *ever* be in a certain place, and then *boom*, there she is."

"Huh. That was quite an emphatic never about ever being in my arms."

"Well, I might not be human, but I get a clue as quickly as the next girl. You leaving like you did didn't beed… um, bade…I mean *bode* well for ever seeing that gorgeous face of yours again."

He couldn't stop himself from pressing his nose back

into her hair, the sweetness of having her close somehow making him feel better than he had in…hell, in
years. With a cocky smile in his need-roughened voice,
he asked, "You calling me gorgeous, baby?"

This time, she was the one who snorted. "Like you
don't already know. You've seen a mirror, Hennessey."

His response was heartfelt and low. "Yeah, well, I
don't have anything on you."

"Oh, get real. I'd rather you just be quiet than lie to
me. I'm so, so, sooo sick of all the lies."

She was finding her words better now, but her voice
still had that singsong quality to it that was a sure sign
of someone who'd tossed back a bit too much. And from
what he knew about Sayre when she was younger, she
wasn't a drinker. Which meant it probably hadn't taken
much to get her to this point.

Cian got her into the cabin and onto the bed with rela-
tive ease, surprised to find she was still awake when he
came back from the kitchen with a cold bottle of water
for her.

"So, I've been meaning to ask you about your tattoo,"
he murmured, after she'd finished taking a couple of sips
and was snuggling down into the pillows while he sat beside her on the edge of the bed. He'd slipped her sandals
off her cute feet, but left her in her shorts and tank top,
knowing better than to tempt himself with the exposure
of too much flesh.

"Hmm." Her eyes were closed, and he thought she
might have passed out, when she suddenly asked, "Which
one?"

His own eyes went a little wide—though she missed
it because she wasn't looking at him. "You have more
than one?"

"Yep. I've got three of them little puppies."

He laughed, which had her opening her eyes just enough to glare at him. Catching a pale strand of hair that was stuck to her flushed cheek and tucking it behind the delicate shell of her ear, he said, "Please don't tell me you have a puppy tattooed on your sweet little ass."

"What?" she gasped, smacking him in the shoulder. "No, you goober. No puppies."

Bracing his left arm over her body, he watched her try to keep her eyes open, thinking she was probably going to have his head for questioning her like this once she'd sobered up. But he wanted answers enough that he was willing to risk it. Apparently, he was that much of a *goober*. "So if you're not sporting a slew of killer puppy tats, then what are they?"

"Well, the one on my belly is Sanskrit. It's meant to help me find peace and to keep me centered. And then there's one between my shoulder blades. You haven't seen that one yet. It's a…mmm, you smell *really* good."

Christ, she was killing him with that hungry look on her face. Coughing to clear the lump of lust that had just lodged itself down near his voice box, he said, "I'm glad you think so, lass. But you were telling me about the ink on your back."

She blinked as if coming out of a daze, making him wonder where her thoughts had drifted. "Oh. Right. It's a pretty little owl in flight that's meant to help me be wise."

"And where's the third one?"

"The third what?" she mumbled, just as her eyes fluttered shut again, her pink lips parted just enough for her gentle breaths.

Knowing he had it bad when just watching the witch breathing made him so fucking hard that he hurt, he groaned, "Tattoo, remember?"

"Oh, that one's high on my inner thigh." She cracked

one sleepy eye open. "And no, I'm not showing it to you. It's a secret," she told him, looking so incredibly young lying there on the shamrock-covered sheets, the spray of freckles over her cheeks and nose too damn adorable for words. He honestly didn't know what fate had been thinking to link her with someone like him, but it sure as hell wasn't what she deserved. In another world, where fairness ruled, she'd have been connected to a male who could be everything that she needed. Not only a protector and lover, but also a partner. A male who made seeing that she was happy his single most important mission in life.

Without even realizing he was going to do it, he heard himself ask, "What do you want, Sayre?"

Since he'd thought she'd finally dozed off, she caught him by surprise when she said, "You. I want to trust you, Cian, but I'm scared."

Though his heart had just lodged itself in his throat, he somehow managed to rasp, "Why? What are you afraid of?"

She turned onto her side so that she faced away from him and wrapped her arms around her pillow, her voice so soft it was barely a whisper. "It's not your brother, because I know you'll deal with whatever's going on between the two of you. But I'm frightened by how badly I want you. Of not being enough for you. Of you walking away again, like you did last time. If I decide to trust you, and then you cheat or get bored or just move on, it's going to hurt so much. Worse than when you left me before, and I don't know how I would..." She pulled in a shaky breath, and with a catch in her voice, she finished the thought, saying, "I don't know what I would do, except hate you. And I don't want that to happen."

His gut cramped with a powerful shot of self-loath-

ing, because he knew he would no doubt end up hurting her in the end. Not with another woman. Never like
that. The last five years had clearly shown him that if he
couldn't have Sayre, he apparently couldn't be satisfied
with anyone else. But he couldn't stay with her. She was
honestly the best person he'd ever known, and he cared
for her more than he was comfortable admitting, even
to himself. The most honorable thing he could do for her
was to walk away once she was safe, if he managed to
make it through this in one piece. To give her a chance
to live her life without his shadow hanging over it, dragging her down with him.

So it's better for her to live alone than with us? his
wolf snarled. *We're her mate. Hers. There is no other
male out there who can make her as complete as we
can. No one!*

"I don't expect you to understand," he quietly told the
beast as he leaned down and pressed a kiss to Sayre's
freckled shoulder. She didn't even twitch, her even
breathing telling him that she'd drifted off. Being careful
not to wake her, he headed out onto the back porch and
lit a cigarette, needing the quiet so that he could think.
But the animal wasn't ready to let him be.

*Of course you don't expect me to understand. You just
expect me to live with your choices and suck it up without complaint because of mistakes you made a bloody
lifetime ago. Haven't we suffered enough?*

"I won't do that to her," he growled, exhaling a sharp
stream of smoke. "I can't."

*What you can't do is live without her. And if you think
it's only because of the mating connection, then you're an
even bigger fool than I feared. I guess that vamp blood
inside you really has screwed with your head.*

"Piss off," he grunted, wishing he could get his hands

on the beast and wring its bloody neck, not wanting to hear it. Any of it. "And learn how to shut up every once in a while!"

"What the hell, man?" someone drawled off to his right. "I didn't even say anything."

Twisting to the side, he found Jeremy standing at the bottom of his back porch steps, the guy's hip propped against the railing and his hands shoved in the front pockets of his board shorts. "I wasn't talking to you," he muttered, feeling like an idiot for getting caught arguing with his wolf.

Jeremy's hazel eyes glittered with humor. "Good to know. I mean, I get that I can be a pain in the ass. But that was a little harsh."

Fighting the urge to roll his eyes, he sighed. "What do you want, Burns?"

"Can't I just hang out with an old friend?"

His right eyebrow shot up as he took a deep drag on the cigarette, then slowly exhaled. "Are we still friends?"

"You really asking me that?" Jeremy demanded, sounding pissed.

"I haven't exactly been welcomed back with open arms," Cian pointed out, his tone dry.

Some of Jeremy's irritation softened. "Brody'll come around. Just give him some time. When you left, we all took it hard. But Brody—man, it really wrecked him. Thank God for Mic or I think he might've gotten so lost in his anger he couldn't find his way back from it."

He took another deep drag, needing the burn in his lungs so that he didn't have to think about what a bastard he was. "So that's just one more thing I get to feel shitty about, huh?"

Leaning his head back to stare up at the blanket of stars that were beginning to light the darkening night sky,

Blood Wolf Dawning

Jeremy said, "You know, I fought my feelings for Jillian for a decade. An entire goddamn decade." A harsh laugh tripped over his lips and he lowered his head, locking that sharp gaze back on Cian. "It nearly killed me, and it was all because I was too stubborn for my own good."

"But you got her in the end because you deserve her."

"And you don't deserve Sayre?"

He couldn't hold back a grim bark of laughter. "I don't even deserve to breathe the same air as she does."

Jeremy whistled low under his breath. "That bad?"

"Yeah," he muttered, finishing off the cigarette, then stubbing it out in the ashtray he'd left sitting on the porch railing.

"I don't recall you ever feeling unworthy before when it came to women. You've always been one of the cockiest bastards I've ever known."

"That was screwing," he said flatly, avoiding the Runner's gaze, "and it had its purpose. I didn't make promises, and I wasn't expected to."

"And Sayre expects promises?"

"She doesn't *expect* anything from me." He locked his hard gaze back on Jeremy's steady one. "But she deserves more than what I can offer."

"That seems like something she can decide for herself, without you doing it for her."

Narrowing his eyes, he made a sharp, bitter sound of frustration deep in his throat. "Isn't there some kind of unspoken Lycan law that says 'thou shalt not screw over the woman meant to be yours'? We're meant to cherish our mates, not use them."

"Well, maybe she's the one who wants to use you. And if that's the case, then what the hell is holding you back?"

"Christ, Jeremy." He scowled as he shook his head.

"You really suck at playing the concerned brother-in-law, you know that?"

A gritty laugh rumbled up from the Runner's chest, and he lifted his right arm, then rubbed at the back of his neck. "If you don't think this is awkward for me, think again, Cian. I love that girl like she was my own blood. But this thing between the two of you, it's screwed up. Normal rules don't apply."

And with those insightful, irritating words, Jeremy headed back over to his own cabin, leaving Cian to his heavy thoughts and dwindling pack of Marlboros.

Staring up at the same expanse of starry sky that had held Jeremy's attention moments before, the glittering pinpricks of light reminding him of the beautiful witch passed out in his bed, he wondered if it was possible to live with this much regret and not lose one's mind. To find a way to make things right and change what seemed an unchangeable course.

He honestly didn't know. But as Cian sat down on the top porch step and pulled out another cigarette, he realized that for the first time in what felt like forever, he was ready to try for a little hope.

Chapter 10

After another uncomfortable night spent sleeping on the love seat in the bedroom, while Sayre sprawled across the bed, completely passed out, Cian found himself sitting on the edge of the cushions with his elbows braced on his knees, his damn eyes glued to the sight of her. He'd known better than to snuggle up beside her when she'd been so soft and warm and open. Without a doubt, he would have ended up taking things too far, and then he would have regretted the hell out of it. So he'd been a good boy and slept on the love seat.

And. It. Had. Sucked.

I blame you, his beast grumbled, its frustration like another living thing in his body, burning beneath his skin.

"Yeah, I blame me, too," he muttered quietly, shoving his hands back through his hair as he moved to his feet. He needed to make himself get a move on, or he'd still be sitting there staring at her like a skeevy perv when she finally woke up, and that was the last thing that he needed. The girl already thought he was a faithless ass-hat. No sense in dragging her opinion of him down any lower.

Then do something nice for her for a change.

With a low laugh, he headed out of the room and toward the kitchen, surprised that the wolf had actually offered a helpful suggestion.

I'm not the jackass in this partnership. Jackass.

Smirking, he opened the refrigerator door, scoping out his options. Twenty minutes later, he was carrying a tray back into the bedroom, complete with toast, bacon, eggs and a glass of orange juice.

"Holy cow, Cian. Is that for me?" She'd opened her eyes when he'd sat down on the side of the bed with the tray, her eyelids puffy from sleep. "I didn't even know you could cook."

Trying not to blush like an idiot, he set the tray over her lap as she sat up, her back propped up against the gaudy headboard. "Breakfast is about all I can manage. Thought you might need a little pick-me-up this morning."

"Thanks." She picked up a crispy piece of bacon and took a bite, her gaze sliding toward him as she chewed. "I'm almost afraid to ask what happened last night," she murmured, not quite looking him in the eye. "I know you carried me back from Lev's, but the details of our conversation are kind of sketchy. Did I make an idiot of myself?"

"Naw," he drawled, his lips twitching as he recalled her singing Shakira to him. "You're actually pretty cute when you're wasted."

"Hmm." She took another bite of bacon, then grinned. "I'm even cuter when I'm chocolate wasted."

"Chocolate wasted?"

She laughed as she reached for the toast. "Never mind. It's from a comedy. You wouldn't get it."

His immediate reaction was to stiffen a little, but he tried to play it off like she hadn't just insulted him. Did she think he was too old to appreciate a funny movie? Jesus, did he seem like that much of an uptight asshole around her? Not that she was wrong, but that didn't mean he *wanted* her to see him that way.

"Hey," she said softly, leaning over to the side until she could catch his gaze. "I didn't mean anything by that, Cian. You just don't seem like a slapstick kind of guy. Your sense of humor is more...smart-ass."

"Thanks," he said drily, letting the conversation go so that she could finish eating.

He carried the tray back to the kitchen when she was done, planning on making a few calls into the security posts to check in on things while she took her shower. After seeing how tightly the security was being run around the Alley, he knew his brother was too sharp a hunter to simply charge right in without first evaluating the situation, searching for a weakness in the system. He figured they still had a day or two before Aedan made his next move, in the flesh this time, and he wanted to make sure that the scouts the Runners had posted were ready for him, knowing a single mistake could cost lives.

To Aedan, killing men and women was as inconsequential as crushing a bug under his boot. Hell, his brother didn't even discriminate when it came to age, killing children these days as willingly as he did adults. He seemed determined to live up to the monstrous expectations that their world had of the vampire species, and Cian had heard from more than one source that there were numerous bounties out on Aedan's head.

He put on a fresh pot of coffee as he made the first call,

the Lycan in charge giving him an update on the routes they were currently running. Just as he was getting ready to call the security headquarters up in Shadow Peak, someone knocked on the front door. He found Brody standing out on the porch, massive arms crossed over his chest, his scarred face settled into an expression that fell somewhere between irritated and resigned. The guy definitely didn't look happy, but Cian figured this was better than the fury that had been blasting his way most of the time since he'd returned.

"Let Sayre know you're gonna be gone for a while," the Runner muttered. "Jillian will keep an eye on her so that she's not alone."

Mimicking his former partner's pose, he tried to keep his expression as stoic as Brody's, but it wasn't easy. He was relieved the guy was actually talking to him, and more than a little nervous about what Brody had in mind for their outing, hoping he wasn't about to get taken out to the woods and hunted. "Where are we going?"

"Just get your damn boots on so we can get moving."

Sayre was taking the longest shower in history, so he knocked on the bathroom door and shouted that he was heading out, his imagination working overtime at the thought of her tight little body turning rosy and slick beneath the hot spray of water. He'd have given his bloody right arm to open the door and climb in there with her, letting his tongue get up close and personal with every silky inch of flesh, licking away each meandering drop of water…working his way closer to that most private, intimate part of her that he wanted to lick and suck and fuck so hard it was killing him. Wanted to take her until she couldn't do anything but beg and claw and chant his name.

"What the hell, Hennessey? Do I need to drag your

ass out of there?" Brody shouted impatiently from the
porch, and he cursed under his breath, yelling through
the door again to remind Sayre to be careful and stay
near the cabins.

He met Brody outside, and they walked in weighted
silence over to where a shiny new Chevy truck had
been parked around the side of the Runner's cabin. As
he climbed up into Brody's new ride, the two car seats in
the back making him smile, Cian found himself thinking about the first time he'd met Mason's wife, Torrance.
They'd all been gathered in Mase's kitchen, and he'd
been ribbing Brody about being broody, like he always
did, while flirting outrageously with Torry just to get a
rise out of Mason. Even with all the chaos surrounding
them at that time, with the hunt for a serial killer going
on and all the crap that Eric, Eli and Elise's father had
been involved in, life had been so much simpler then. It
might have sounded corny, but it was true.

God, in so many ways, those days seemed like a million lifetimes ago. And now look at him. Sitting beside
his former partner while they headed up the road that led
to Shadow Peak, without a damn clue what to say. Back
then, he'd have started singing Julio Iglesias or some
shit like that just to mess with the guy, but now he was
afraid to even speak.

Ah, to hell with it, he thought. He was just going to
say something and if Brody didn't like it, he could kick
him out or turn around and take him back to the Alley.

Clearing his throat, he looked over at the guy and
said, "So what's going on? Is this the part where you
take me out to the woods and break my neck for being
such a jackass?"

"Tempting, but no. We're going up to my grandmother's place." Brody slid him a narrow look, then turned his

attention back to the road before muttering, "Mic wants Cianna to meet you."

Oh…Christ. This was *big*. He knew, from talking to Kyle yesterday, that Cianna was Brody and Mic's three-year-old daughter.

Propping his elbow on the door, he rubbed his fingers along his unshaven jaw, and was unable to keep the grin off his face. "So Cianna, huh? Cute name."

Brody snorted loudly. "Mic's the one who insisted on it."

He swallowed against the lump in his throat, then shook his head, wondering when he'd become such an emotional pussy. "I know you don't care, but it…it means a lot to me, man."

Brody didn't bother to respond until they'd pulled into his grandmother's driveway and he'd cut the engine. Turning his head, he pinned Cian with a hard, don't-screw-with-me look of warning. "You make her love you and then leave again without a single damn goodbye, then I'm gonna kill you. Understood?"

"Yeah, got it," he rasped, wiping his damp palms on his jeans. He'd never spent much time around kids—hell, he'd never really spent *any* time around them—so he wasn't sure what to expect, and that made him…nervous. What if she took one look at him and ran screaming? What the hell did he do then?

They climbed out of the truck and were heading up the front walkway, when the front door burst open and a little ball of pink came flying out, crashing right into his legs. Cian reached down, careful to keep his hold gentle as he gripped the little girl's shoulders to stop her from falling over.

"Up!" she shouted, her little voice imperious as she craned her head back and lifted her arms.

Unsure what he should do, he glanced at Brody, who jerked his chin at him in a get-on-with-it gesture.

It's just a kid, his wolf snickered. *Hold her by the scruff of her neck and feed her when she bellows. How friggin' hard can it be?*

Choking back a laugh, he said, "Right then," and reached down and lifted her tiny body into his arms— holding her under her arms, instead of by the neck. She seemed to know exactly what to do, as she perched her little bottom on his right forearm and braced her hands against his chest. She was a beautiful child, with long black curls like her mother's and Brody's bottle-green eyes, the scent of fresh-baked sugar cookies and cinnamon clinging to her in a way that reminded him of Christmas. She blinked a few times, and stared at him so intently he felt like she was trying to read his mind. Then she leaned in a little closer, grabbed his cheeks with her chubby little hands and quickly kissed him right in the middle of his forehead. "That's how Mommy does it!" she said with a giggle, then pulled back and gave him an adorably dimpled smile.

"Thank you." He had to give a little cough to clear his throat before he could go on. "That was the sweetest kiss I've had in forever."

She giggled again and started rubbing her hands over the stubble on his cheeks. "Your face is all scratchy like Daddy's."

"It sure is."

"You's ticklish?" she asked, that dimpled grin of hers infectious.

"Nope," he said, smiling back at her. "But I bet *you* are."

She wiggled to get down, and he and Brody spent the next thirty minutes playing chase with her in the front garden, while Abigail, Brody's grandmother, looked on with a smile from the porch. When Brody looked at his watch and told the little munchkin they were going to have to go so he could get back to work, she threw herself around Cian's right leg, squeezing him with surprising strength while looking up at him and shouting, "Kisses! I wants more kisses!"

"Come on, you little flirt," Brody rumbled, a smirk on his face as he came over, pulled her off and lifted her up into his arms. With his face close to his daughter's pouty one, Brody said, "What did Daddy tell you about mauling people for kisses?"

"But I likes him!" she wailed, blinking like she was on the verge of tears. "I wants to *keep* him!"

Muffling a laugh under his breath, Brody gentled his voice. "Cianna, baby, he's not a toy for you to keep. Now stop it with the crocodile tears and give your old man some goodbye squishes."

"Yes, Daddy," she whispered, as she threw her arms around Brody's neck and hugged him tight.

"You gonna be a good girl and help take care of Nana?" he asked, nuzzling her curls.

She nodded as she lifted her head, but her lower lip started to tremble. "Whens you come back?"

"I'll come see you tomorrow, baby girl. And Mommy's going to be here to stay with you when she gets back from taking Jack over to visit with her friend Rachel. Okay?"

She nodded, and Brody lowered her back to the ground. As soon as her little feet touched the grass, she ran over to Cian and hugged his leg again. He figured he knew exactly what the Grinch felt like at the end of that holiday movie, because his damn chest was feeling all mushy and big.

As soon as he and Brody were back in the truck and

reversing out of the drive, he waved to Cianna one more time, and said, "She's adorable, man." His chest shook with a low laugh as he turned his head and looked at Brody. "You know you're gonna have your hands full when she's older, right? Boys'll be lining up from Shadow Peak all the way down to the Alley, wanting to ask her out."

"They can try," he muttered, flicking his signal on as they neared the next corner. "But if they're smart, they'll stay the hell away from her."

They had the windows down, letting in the fresh air, and Cian braced his arm along the top of the door. "How old is Jack?"

"Two months." Brody slid him a rueful grin, then looked back at the road. "Between the two of 'em, I'm already going gray. But Mic wants to have a few more, so I figure the more the merrier."

He shook his head and grinned. "It's crazy to think of you having a family, but I'm happy for you, man. I always knew you'd be great at it."

Brody grunted in response, and they sat in silence for a mile or so, until the Runner made a rough, frustrated sound in the back of his throat and smacked the top of the steering wheel with his hand. "I want to be able to forgive you, Cian. But you pissed me off." Keeping his narrowed eyes on the road, Brody went on. "I've spent years feeling guilty as hell for not realizing you were going to bail on Sayre and everyone else. But you blindsided me like you did the rest. Made me wonder if I ever knew you at all."

"You didn't," he said, the quiet words filled with regret. "I made that clear yesterday."

"I'm not talking about some damn strain of vampire blood. You think any of us give a shit about that?"

"You should. And you sure as hell would if you knew the way I'd lived all those years I traveled with Aedan."

"Bullshit," the Runner scoffed, while a muscle started to pulse at the rigid edge of his jaw. "You were a kid, Cian. What the hell did you know? Do we blame Elliot for the mistakes he made before we brought him into our group? Hell, no. We just found a way to help him move on. That's what friends and family are about."

Dropping his head back on the seat, he closed his eyes and let those words soak into his system, wishing he could believe them. Because if he could, it meant that at least one of the obstacles keeping him from what he wanted most would no longer be an issue. And what he wanted was a certain little strawberry-blonde witch. Even now, she was in his head, never far from his thoughts, his need just to be near her so intense he had no frame of reference for it. No idea what the hell he was doing, or how he was going to find the strength to walk away when all this was over.

"I know I screwed up," he heard himself say, "and I'm sorry, Brody. I was just so terrified of what he would do if he found out about her." He scrubbed his hands over his face, exhaled a ragged breath as he lifted his head and stared sightlessly out the windshield. "Leaving was the hardest damn thing I've ever had to do, after struggling to keep away from Sayre during those months before the war. But I believed it was the right choice, so I *forced* myself to do it. And it had to be the way it was. I knew if I tried to talk to you, I'd cave. If you'd said the things you just said to me right now, I never would have gone. And he would have found her even sooner than he did."

"I hate it," Brody grumbled with a rough sigh, "but I get why you did it. I'm not saying it was the right thing, but at least it makes some sense to me now."

"I feel like there is no right fucking answer anymore. As if this is all inevitable somehow, and no matter what I do, bad things are gonna happen." A hard laugh jerked from his throat, and he shook his head again. "Probably some twisted-as-shit karma coming back to kick my ass. I just wish Sayre didn't have to pay for my mistakes."

Turning onto the road that led to the Alley, the Runner said, "She's not going to pay for anything. You came back to protect her. That says a lot about how you feel about her right there, Cian."

He swallowed, wondering if the color was draining from his face as quickly as the blood. "It's not like that, Brody. I don't want her getting hurt, but I don't...I don't have those kinds of feelings for Sayre. She's an amazing woman, but what's between us is purely physical."

The jackass didn't argue. He just threw back his head and laughed, the deep sound gruff and full of humor. And he was pretty sure he could hear his wolf joining in right along with him.

Cian scowled. "Shut up, you ass." *Both of you!*

"Sorry." Brody's shoulders shook as he pretended to wipe away tears from his eyes. "You're just pretty damn funny."

"You know, I'm starting to wonder why I even wanted you talking to me again," he muttered, sounding like an irritable jerk.

"Don't try to hide it, man. We both know you missed the hell out of me."

He grunted, but couldn't stop the corner of his mouth from twitching when the goofball winked at him.

Jesus. Broody Brody had just winked at him. And grinned!

Just like that, the five years that Cian had been gone suddenly felt like fifty. He'd known having a family would change the guy, but he'd never imagined Brody could be so...so friggin' happy. He was pleased as hell for him, but a part of him was also burning up with jealousy.

"And while we're having this gooey heart-to-heart," the Runner murmured, parking the truck beside his cabin, "I'll go ahead and apologize for losing my shit when you told us about Aedan." His auburn hair brushed his shoulders as he shrugged. "I don't know why that hit me so hard. I guess I just always thought of you as the closest thing to a brother I would ever have. It threw me to learn you already had one."

"Brody, man, you were more of a brother to me than Aedan ever was."

"Yeah, I kinda got that after I cooled down and thought about it," the guy rumbled, cutting the engine. He looked over at Cian as he opened his door. "Just don't forget that we're here to help. There's no need for you to handle this shit on your own."

He managed a jerky nod, but his damn throat was too tight to get any kind of verbal response out.

They climbed out, meeting around the back of the truck, both of them standing there with their hands shoved in their back pockets, no doubt looking awkward as hell. "If you and Sayre don't have plans later," Brody said, "why don't you come over to our place again? I know Mic would like to spend some time with the two of you."

Cian smiled. "That'd be great. I'll talk to Sayre and let you know."

Brody nodded, and Cian asked him to make sure the scouts posted at the bottom of the drive into the Alley didn't allow access to any more female visitors from town, seeing as how that was something he didn't want Sayre having to deal with. And he didn't want to deal

with it, either—none of those women interesting him in
the least. With a speculative glint in his green eyes, Brody
said that he would, then turned and headed toward his
cabin, while Cian made his way back over to his.

He took the porch steps with an eagerness that should
have given him pause, but he was tired of trying to control every single damn emotion and desire that he felt
where Sayre was concerned. He'd just started to reach
for his keys so he could unlock the front door, when he
heard a voice coming from inside the cabin that made
ice sweep through his veins, the blood no doubt draining
from his face for the second time in the past ten minutes.

"You're making the biggest mistake of your life!" Jillian and Sayre's mother, Constance Murphy, snapped,
her sharp voice rising with each hard, slashing word.

In contrast, Sayre's tone was calm and controlled,
though she definitely sounded tired. "Considering how
you almost destroyed things for Jillian and Jeremy, you'll
forgive me for not listening to any of your relationship
advice, Mom."

"That's not fair, Sayre."

"Not fair?" Leaning a little closer to the door, Cian
caught the sound of Sayre's soft, bitter laughter. "What
wasn't fair was you lying to her all those years ago to
keep them apart."

Though everyone in the Alley was aware of how Constance had tried to sabotage Jillian and Jeremy's relationship, he was surprised to hear Sayre calling her out on it.
That took a lot of guts, considering her mother was one
hell of an intimidating woman.

"I didn't want to see her hurt!" Constance argued, her
tone making it clear that she still believed she'd been in
the right.

Sayre obviously didn't agree. "But what you did hurt

her more than anything. I won't let you do the same to me and Cian."

He sucked in a sharp breath, his heart hammering as Constance shouted, "Don't be so naive, Sayre. There is no you and Cian!"

"That might be," she conceded, her voice still coming through clear and strong. "But it doesn't give you the right to talk trash about him. I won't listen to it."

Cian slumped against the door, a little dizzy with shock, unable to believe what he was hearing. After the way he'd treated her, Sayre was the *last* person in the world he would have ever thought he'd hear defending him.

"You're making a mistake." Constance's clipped, harsh words vibrated with her anger. "He'll lie to get what he wants from you, promise you whatever you want to hear, and then where will you be?"

"He hasn't broken any promises, Mother. He's been honest with me about what he's willing to give, and I've been honest about what I'm willing to take."

"You *slept* with him?" the older witch croaked, sounding *more* than horrified. She actually sounded afraid. "You know what that means. He'll know—"

Sayre cut her off, her tone firm but gentle as she said, "I love you, Mom. I really do. But what I do with Cian Hennessey isn't any of your business. It's between him and me and no one else."

"He's your life mate, Sayre," Constance said unsteadily. "You… God, you have no idea how dangerous this game is that you're playing."

"It's not a game."

"He doesn't deserve you! He's nothing more than an arrogant, no-good—"

"Stop!" Unlike the calm tone she'd used up to that

point, this time Sayre's words cracked like a whip. "Just stop. I don't ever want to hear you talk that way about him. If he wanted me, I'd be damned lucky to have him."

"You just like his looks!" Constance cried. "It's lust, Sayre, and you're too innocent to realize it!"

"That's not true," she countered, her low voice thrumming with emotion. "Do I think he's quite likely the most badass, rugged, gorgeous male to ever walk the planet? Of course I do. Every woman with eyes in her head knows he's beautiful. But he's *more* than that, Mom, and you would know it if you had ever taken the time to talk to him. He's intelligent, witty and he can be incredibly kind. He's one of the most honorable men I've ever known. And believe it or not, I think he's trying to do the right thing by me."

"By leaving you broken and alone when he takes off again?" her mother scoffed, sounding surprisingly bitter.

Sayre's response was soft. "I didn't break the first time."

"Didn't you?" Constance questioned with a catch, as if she were on the verge of tears. "How is losing your home and the people who love you not breaking?"

With a swift intake of air, Sayre said, "I know you mean well, but you need to leave now."

"Sayre."

"I mean it, Mother. This is Cian's home and I won't have you coming in here and acting this way. He doesn't deserve it."

Angry footsteps neared the door, and Cian had only seconds to move back a few steps before Constance ripped it open, her dark eyes narrowing with fury the second she caught sight of him. Mouth pinched even tighter than before, she pulled the door closed behind her, then stepped toward him. "You're a bastard," she hissed, the loathing in her voice impossible to miss.

"Actually," he murmured, hoping like hell she wasn't about to turn him into a friggin' newt, "my parents were married. Much to my mother's misfortune."

She cursed under her breath and stalked past him, no doubt plotting some awful revenge against him for daring to come back into her daughter's life. Constance had never liked him before, and she obviously didn't like him any better now.

He smoked a cigarette while he waited for the woman to make her way over to her car and drive off, his thoughts churning with everything he'd overheard.

He didn't know what to make of her. Not Constance, but Sayre. He'd never known anyone so brave and strong and giving. *Forgiving.* He didn't deserve her concern or loyalty or any of what she was giving him.

But, Christ, he wished that he did. He'd have given anything in the world to go back and change those years he'd spent at Aedan's side. To undo his past and all the countless scores of women. To be a different person, with a different bloodline. To have a different emotional makeup.

This was, in all honesty, the worst sort of punishment he could be forced to endure. Being so close to what he would claim in a heartbeat if he could, but unable to have it. Thank God he was too damaged to love her, because he'd be relentless then, doing everything he could to make her love him back. And she'd be crazy to give her heart to him. Damn it, just having her loyalty was more than he'd ever expected.

Needing to see her, to be close to her, he quickly turned and opened the front door. The sight of her leaning back in the ugly green velvet chair that sat across from the equally ugly sofa, her eyes closed and her mouth soft and pink, made something in his chest flip over.

She smiled when she opened her eyes and saw him coming toward her, after he'd shut the door behind him. "Hey you. Where'd you end up going with Brody?"

With a grin tucked into the corner of his mouth so she wouldn't take him seriously, he said, "He took me up to town to meet a young lady."

She laughed, shaking her head, her expression making it clear she knew exactly who they'd gone to see.

"You're not even jealous?" he asked, lifting his brows with mock surprise. "I got a kiss and everything."

"I'll bet you did," she drawled. "I'm going to have to warn the little flirt that you're a heartbreaker."

"She's a cute kid." He took a few steps closer to where she sat, loving the way the sun shining through the side window was setting her hair alight, the red strands looking like fire. Clearing the knot of lust forming in his throat, he said, "Brody, man, he's a great dad. It's obvious he adores her."

Her head tilted a bit to the side. "Why do you sound surprised?"

Pushing his hands in the front pockets of his jeans, he shrugged. "I'm not. I just…it's kinda strange, seeing the way things have changed."

She nodded, her gentle expression telling him that she understood.

Reaching up to rub at the knots of tension at the back of his neck, he said, "I, uh, heard you talking to your mom."

Her eyes went wide, and she turned an interesting shade of pink as she shot to her feet, then quickly took a few steps away, as if she needed to put more space between them. "Wow…that's, uh, really embarrassing."

"Sayre...the things you said. I just wanted to thank you. It's been a long time since anyone has said anything like that about me."

Avoiding his gaze, she snorted under her breath. "Then you should be keeping better company."

"To be honest," he rasped, "I haven't had much company since I left."

Her eyes immediately cut back to his, narrow and wary. "Now that I'll *never* believe."

"Before you get your claws out," he said, taking a step toward her, "and we get off track, I was just about to get to the good part."

"And what's the good part?"

His voice got lower. "Me showing you how much I appreciate it."

Both her eyebrows shot up with surprise. "And just how were you planning on doing that?"

Knowing he was about to shock the hell out of her, Cian moved with the speed his father's "dark" blood afforded him as he picked her up and carried her into the bedroom. Her back hit the mattress with his body braced above hers before she'd even managed to draw in a breath to scream, and he said, "I want to show you by making you feel good, Sayre. I want to make you cry out my name until everyone in the Alley can hear it."

"Why?" She studied him through her long, gold-tipped lashes, her provocative scent rising with the heat of her body and making him feel like the animal he was. "Because you're trying to prove a point?"

"No, baby." He lowered his head, burying his face against the slender curve of her throat, her skin tender and infinitely sweet beneath his open mouth. "Because I need to know what you look and feel and sound like when you come. And I don't want you holding back when it happens."

He knew the exact moment she chose to surrender—her hands fluttered against his shoulders as a shiver coursed through her strong, feminine little body. Then her head shot back as she arched up into him, her beautiful breasts pressing against his chest, while her scent became something so lush and thick it was like being drenched in her.

And that was it. He friggin' lost it.

Chapter 11

Chanting under his breath in a low, husky stream of words, Cian told her how incredible she was, how beautiful and sensual and how goddamn hard she made him, while he sat up, straddling her hips, and stripped off his shirt. Then he reached for hers. Seconds later, her bra had joined their shirts on the floor, he'd forced a knee between her legs and his hand was pushing into her unbuttoned shorts. His fingers slipped beneath the elastic waistband of her white panties, while his hot, heavy-lidded gaze devoured every inch of her, from her flushed cheeks to that sexy little tat circling her navel.

Breathing so hard and fast he was damn near panting, he lowered his head and took one of those plump, candy-pink nipples between his lips, sucking hard and then rubbing it with his tongue, his hand in heaven between her legs. She felt insanely perfect, her breasts firm and ripe, the folds between her legs deliciously wet and as soft as

satin. Swollen and slippery with slick, warm juices that
had his mouth watering with the visceral need to taste
her. To lap at her like a cat with cream...or a *wolf* with
something that it couldn't get enough of.

And then there was that darker, chilling part of him
that was painfully aware of each hard, pounding beat of
her heart...the enthralling rush of her pulse. But he fought
that bastard back with everything he had, refusing to let
his fangs drop from his burning gums.

"God, Sayre. I've waited forever for this," he growled
against her wet nipple, as he slipped a blunt fingertip
through that hot, slick cream, stroking between the silken
folds of her sex, every part of him focused with predatory
precision on how good she felt. How right. Keeping his
eyes locked hard on hers, he moved his mouth to her other
breast, tonguing that delectable nipple while he watched
the hunger and excitement spill through her as he circled
the tender, puffy entrance between her legs, then pushed
just his fingertip inside. She gasped, her beautiful eyes
darkening as he pushed in another inch, the plush sheath
so soft and tight he was only managing to hold himself
together by a bloody miracle.

"I like it," she breathed out, each throaty word slipping over his skin like a physical touch, as she pulsed
her hips, taking him deeper. They were both breathing
loud and harsh by the time he'd buried his finger in her
up to the knuckle, their skin damp with sweat and burning with a heat that the gentle breeze blowing in through
the window did little to cool.

Her eyes slid closed as he found the tight knot of her
clit with his thumb, rotating the callused pad with firm
pressure against the sensitive bundle of nerves, and he
let her plump nipple pop free from his mouth. Rising up

over her, he put his face above hers and said, "Eyes open, baby. Let me watch you."

Her lashes fluttered, then lifted, and... *Oh, Christ*, there she was. It was like looking directly into the heart of her, as if he could literally see every sensation pulsing through her, rushing through her system. Hot, violent, wild. She was coming undone right before his eyes, and he'd never seen anything so painfully perfect in his entire life. Never felt anything like thrusting his finger in and out of her plush, slick sex, the tight hold making him shudder.

"Don't stop," she gasped, her nails biting into his skin as she squeezed his shoulders. "Please."

"Stop? Jesus, Sayre. I couldn't stop even if the bloody roof was coming down on our heads," he groaned, covering that succulent mouth with his, his tongue sliding between her parted lips, mimicking the primal, penetrating rhythm of his finger. She was so tight, he had to work to get a second finger inside her, forced to break away from the kiss and suck in air, his blood roaring in his ears as the lush sheath gave a hard pulse, his hand soaked all the way to his wrist. She was close, pink-faced and damp, those glittering sparks that he loved so much breaking free, skittering in the air around them, making her shine.

"God, I love this!" she cried, breathless with need, her lashes fluttering as her gaze went hazy and dark. "Your fingers feel so big. I can...I can feel them stretching me."

In that moment, Cian wanted nothing more than to strip her goddamn shorts and panties down her beautiful legs, spread her firm thighs as wide as they'd go and devour every glistening inch of her with his hungry gaze...then devour her even harder with his mouth. But the tremors coursing through his tensed muscles and the savage clawing of his beast to be set free—so that it could mark and bite and claim—told him he wasn't there yet. That his control wouldn't last if he pushed it that far. So he shoved his own needs down deep enough that they couldn't screw this up for him, ignoring the fire in his gums and the raw, throbbing ache in his steel-hard cock, and focused on making her come.

Moving his mouth to her ear, he nipped the tender lobe with his teeth, his low voice rough with emotion as he said, "One day soon, when I have more control, I'm going to give you three fingers, Sayre. You won't be able to take them at first, baby, but I'll put my head between your legs and suck this tiny clit that's under my thumb into my mouth. I'll lick it with my tongue. Sip on it. Nibble it. Suck it so hard you're gonna claw at my shoulders until you draw blood. And you'll be so greedy for me that this sweet little sex will suck those three fingers right in. It'll be tight as hell, but will feel *so...fucking...good*, and you'll come so hard you scream my name, over and over, until that sexy-as-hell voice of yours just gives out."

"Oh, God," she moaned, gasping for each breath. "Cian!"

He ran his parted lips over her feverish, delicate skin, the muscles in his wrist flexing as he shoved his fingers deeper inside her, stroking the tips against the front wall of her sheath, until he found what he was looking for. He knew he had it when her nails dug into his rock-hard biceps and she gave a breathless, keening cry, her beautiful body writhing as he aggressively stroked that cushiony spot while his thumb worked hard on her clit. "You're getting so wet that you're soaking me, Sayre." His voice was dark and raw and deep, too guttural to belong to anything other than a Lycan male in the throes of lust.

As if his words and the sound of his voice were what she needed to push her over the edge, her head went back, she sank her nails into his bare shoulders and screamed like a little banshee. Crashing over that dark edge and into oblivion, she came so hard and hot and wild, her scent rising, getting richer...deeper...sinking into his system like a goddamn narcotic. And all the while, her tight sex was throbbing against his hand, convulsing around his fingers so perfectly it was like a dream, while these throaty whimpers kept spilling past her rosy lips.

"Sayre, Christ, no more," he choked out, shaking so hard it was making the bed rattle. "Shh, baby, shh. I can't take it."

"Wh-what?" she gasped, blinking her eyes open, the look in them so hazy and sweet, he had to lower his gaze. But it didn't help. The sight of her bare breasts and trembling belly, her shorts wrenched open, his big hand shoved down the front of her panties, was the most provocative thing he'd ever seen. So beautiful it was burned into his mind, carved into his flesh like a scar.

"I'm barely holding myself together here," he growled, feeling his wolf punch against his insides, desperate to get out, while that savage, aggressive pull that he'd felt the first time they'd kissed started blaring in his head again, roaring for him to take and mark and possess. "If you make one of those little sounds again, I won't be able to...to keep...to keep from *nailing* you to this goddamn mattress."

"Mmm. If it feels anything like *that* did," she moaned, grinning up at him, completely oblivious to the fact that she needed to be...careful, "I doubt I'll complain. Heck, I might even beg you."

Sayre quickly squeezed her eyes shut again. The way Cian had just stiffened, as if he couldn't believe what she'd said to him, made her wonder if she'd lost her mind.

Honestly, when was she going to learn?

"Sayre," he growled, his voice even grittier as he pressed closer against her, his cock a hard, thick ridge shoved against her hip. "*What* did you just say?"

She forced her eyes back open, and as if listening through a fog, she heard herself tell him, "I want you, Cian. I…I don't think that should come as a surprise."

His heavy gaze was savage and hot, full of molten, primitive need. "How? *How* do you want me?"

Her breath came in short, sharp pants, and she licked her lips. "All of you. Every part. But I can't do it with so many secrets between us. Are you…I mean, will you tell me about Aedan now?"

He froze, not even breathing…then cursed so viciously it made her blink. And before she even knew what was happening, he'd pulled his fingers from her body and was rolling away from her in one smooth, effortless move. One moment she'd been surrounded by his heat, and in the next, she was lying on the cold sheets, staring at the sleek, powerful length of his back, his shoulders tight with tension. His head hung forward, the dark fall of his hair shielding his profile, but she knew that firm jaw would be locked, that telling tic pulsing beneath his tanned skin.

Sounding as if the stark words were being ripped out of him, he said, "I'm going outside for a smoke."

She would have laughed, but wasn't sure it wouldn't come out as a sob. "Sure, whatever. Like I haven't seen you do *that* before."

"I don't want to." The confession seemed to punch its way free from his chest, his biceps so hard they looked like boulders. Shoving one of his big hands back through his hair, he said, "But I *have* to, Sayre. I can't…I don't have any other choice right now."

"It's fine, Cian. Go."

Without another word, he shot off the bed, grabbed his shirt and got the hell out of there. She knew it would be useless to wait for him and hope he'd come back to her, ready to open up and let her in, finally answering her questions. This, his leaving the room, *was* her answer. And while there was a part of her that felt like a fool for defending him earlier, she couldn't regret it. She just… she needed to be smart where her emotions were concerned, and not lose sight of what was happening between them. Needed to remember that with the life-mate connection, there was some powerful mojo working to draw them together. So while they wanted each other, it didn't necessarily mean that they wanted the same things…or in the same ways.

Yes, she knew that he cared enough about her to want to see her safe and protected. He was just *that* kind of guy. But he was also the "other" kind of guy, and while he wanted her now, she knew she couldn't let herself think in terms of him wanting her forever.

But when he made her feel the way he had just moments before, touching and kissing her as if she were something…*God*, as if she were something *vital* to him, it was difficult to keep those rational threads of reason woven into the framework of her thoughts. To remember, and not forget. Not dream. Because dreaming could be fatal to her heart, and that particular organ had already taken too many hits. Each time she'd seen him with another woman, it had been like a physical strike. Like a blade stabbed into the middle of her chest.

It was up to her to protect that part of her that could be too easily broken for good this time. In a way that never healed. And that could never be forgiven.

Feeling decades older than she was, she forced her-

self to get up and get a move on. She sorted her clothing, pulled her hair up into a ponytail, put on the hiking
boots that she gardened in and decided working outside
was a better use of her time than sitting in Cian's cabin
and brooding over him.

But, hey, at least he hadn't walked away and left her
hanging again. Her body was still buzzing with a warm,
sensual burn of pleasure from the mind-blowing orgasm
he'd given her, her muscles deliciously loose, and she no
doubt had some kick-ass color in her cheeks. And it was
a beautiful day, the sun shining in a cloudless sky, which
meant she needed to get her butt outside and enjoy it.
She figured she could hunt down some gardening tools
and do some maintenance work on the colorful flower
beds that had been planted between the cabins. Maybe
she'd even try to find Kyle, since she'd missed the way
he teased her and that soft-edged Southern accent of his,
and see if he wanted to help her.

And seeing as how he'd spent the better part of yesterday with Cian, she was hopeful the merc might have
some useful information for her. But as it turned out, she
never ran into Kyle. She spent the day out in the summer sunshine, working on various projects, and enjoyed
herself, for the most part. Although…she couldn't quite
shake the feeling that something was, well, *off.* Yeah,
she knew everyone was on edge because Cian's psycho
brother was apparently out there somewhere, preparing
to make a move against her. And since she wasn't a fool,
she was freaked out about it, too. But there was more
going on than she knew about. It didn't matter who she
was talking to, they all seemed to be looking at her in an
expectant way, as if there were something they wanted
to ask her, but weren't sure if they should.

As the day wore on, it became increasingly clear that

something was definitely going on. And that something was seriously pissing her off.

Not only had Cian not shown his face again and gone off to God only knew where, but it was like everyone had suddenly learned a secret she didn't know about, and now they didn't know how to act around her. She knew it must have something to do with the meeting Cian had held with the others the day before—the one she hadn't been invited to. And when she finally bit the bullet and just asked her sister for details, point-blank, Jillian wouldn't tell her a damn thing.

It was obvious she felt bad about that. But Jilly clearly thought she should be talking to Cian. Which was easier said than done, since the man was doing a damn good job of avoiding her. She'd even tried texting him, but he wasn't responding.

"Fine," she huffed to herself as she opened the front door of his cabin and headed back outside. She'd gone back to the cabin an hour earlier, after bombing out on getting some answers from her sister, and was tired of wearing down the floorboards with her pacing. "I'll find something else to do to keep busy," she muttered, heading down the porch steps again. She was trying to decide if she wanted to go back to gardening, or if she should just find a cool place in the shade and read a book on her smartphone, when someone called her name.

She turned and saw Max jogging over to her, a wide smile on his handsome face. "Hey, Max. What's up?"

"I was wondering if you wanted to hang out tonight," he said as he came to a stop right in front of her, the wind playing havoc with his dark curls. "I haven't got to spend much chill time with you since you came home."

Her lips twitched as she tilted her head back to stare up at him. "Drunken poker games don't count?"

He laughed as he pushed his hands in the front pockets of his jeans and lifted his brows. "Not that it wasn't fun watching you get obliterated, but I was hoping you might come over and have dinner. I think Elliot was planning on stopping by, so it'll be just like old times."

She almost winced, but somehow managed to hold it back. Old times for her hadn't necessarily been happy times, though she'd always been grateful for Max's friendship. He had a mellow, natural cool that made it impossible not to like him, and she'd always found him easy to be around. Despite what she'd insinuated to Cian the night he'd left the Runners, she never would have gone to Max or Elliot for sex. Their friendship had always been too close for that, and she never would have jeopardized it just to make a point.

Not that she ever planned on confessing any of that to Cian. The guy was already cocky enough when it came to his appeal. God knew he didn't need any encouragement.

She accepted Max's invitation, glad that Elliot could join them, and spent the rest of the evening trying to shake off her funk and simply enjoy spending time with two of her best friends. She'd missed these guys like crazy. Max was still the easygoing, nowhere-near-ready-to-settle-down guy that he'd always been. And Elliot was still kind of quiet, but funny as hell. He didn't talk about having a woman in his life, and it made her heart hurt that he was still so wary of trusting himself, after going through a horrific ordeal five years ago. One that had resulted in the deaths of two innocent young women, and had nearly turned Elliot into a rogue wolf. The Runners had saved him, but she knew he still carried the scars of that experience on the inside, and hoped he'd one day be able to leave it in the past.

When she finally headed back over to Cian's around

nine, she was surprised to find him sitting in the velvet chair in the living room all alone, as if he'd been waiting for her, the only light a soft glow filtering in from the kitchen.

"What's up with all the plants out on the porch?" was the first thing she said to him, having seen them as she'd come in. Small ones, big ones, some with colorful flowers and others with big, waxy green leaves that looked so beautiful it stole her breath, like something from the tropics. There was a fortune in plants sitting out on his front porch, and it made her a little giddy to think he might have gotten them just for her.

Leaning forward, he braced his elbows on his parted knees and answered her question. "I spent most of the day running patrols out in the woods, but I did a quick run up to town with James to check in with the security headquarters there, and we passed the new garden center just as they were getting a delivery. So I asked him to stop so I could grab you a few things. I figured you might want something to keep you busy while we're here, and I know it's something you enjoy."

She blinked, no idea what to say in response. This guy…he seemed to do nothing but put her off balance. Pull her close; push her away. An ebb and flow that went against everything inside her, every part of her, because fate wanted nothing more than to pull them so close they became one and remained that way. A unit. Unbreakable and unstoppable.

But fate wasn't life. It wasn't what would protect her heart. Keep her from shattering into so many pieces she couldn't ever be put back together again.

"Have a good time tonight with Max and Elliot?" he finally asked her, breaking the awkward silence.

A little surprised that he'd even bothered to find out

where she'd been, she said, "Yeah, it was great to catch up. I've missed them."

"I'm sure they've missed you, too." He moved to his feet and hooked his thumbs in his front pockets, his shuttered gaze impossible to read. "Brody and Mic invited us over for dinner, but I told them you were busy."

"Oh. You didn't mention it before."

Voice a little too tight for her not to pick up on his tension, he said, "I didn't realize you were going to stay out."

"Yeah, well, I didn't realize you were coming back," she replied just as tightly, a fresh wave of irritation spiking through her at the way he'd avoided her for almost the entire damn day.

He frowned as he rubbed a big hand over his mouth, and she realized this conversation was going nowhere fast. Getting it back on track, she exhaled a rough breath and added, "You know, you should probably give Max a big ol' thank-you."

His dark brows started to draw together. "And why's that?"

"Because I tried to get him to tell me the big secret," she explained, crossing her arms over her chest, "but he held firm and wouldn't budge."

Agitation spilled over the quick spark of surprise she'd spotted in his sharp gaze, veiling its light like clouds over the gleaming heat of the sun. "You questioned Max about me?"

She gave a soft snort. "Cian, I'm not stupid. I know something went down at the 'briefing' you held with the others yesterday. It's obvious that everyone knows something big that I don't. Not even Jillian would tell me, and that *hurt*. She just kept saying to ask you about it."

He lifted his powerful arms and gripped the back of his neck, then ran his hands up the back of his head, his body so tense and hard he seemed even larger, when his presence was already so overwhelming it blotted out everything else around him. He constantly burned like a pulsing star in the center of her existence, blindingly white-hot and elusive, always too far away to touch, even when he was right the hell in front of her.

She couldn't help but wonder if she would still feel that way if he were buried deep inside her. Would she stare up into that beautifully masculine, fallen-angel face and finally feel at home? Or would it be like staring into the eyes of a stranger, cold and lonely and empty?

Swallowing her grief like it was a bitter pill she'd been forced to take, she choked out, "Is it another woman?"

Slowly lowering his arms to his sides, he shot her a startled look. "What?"

"If it's about your brother, I can't understand why you wouldn't tell me. So is there someone else? Up in town? Or somewhere else? Did you learn you have a child with someone? Is that what everyone's hiding from me?"

His shoulders dropped as if the weight of the world had just landed on them. "Sayre, stop," he said, shaking his head. "There are no kids, and there's sure as hell no other woman. I don't want anyone but you." Scrubbing his hands over his gorgeous face, he muttered, "God, life would be a whole lot simpler right now if I did."

She flinched, hating that he noticed, those molten eyes darkening to stormy gray.

Giving her a piercing look, he took a step closer to where she stood. "Let me finish, lass."

"What more is there to say? You want me—I believe that. But it's the connection. You can't help it. And you don't *want* it, Cian. You don't want to feel that way. *That's* why you keep pulling away from me."

"You're wrong," he said, softly but with an unmis-

takable vein of anger. Or maybe it was…hopelessness.
Something lost and filled with pain. "Despite everything,
how wrong and completely shit this is for you, the truth
is that I *wouldn't* change it. I know that's unfair as hell
to say, but I wouldn't want this connection with anyone
but you."

She blinked, more than a little undone, and thought
God. Just *God*. They were pretty words from a pretty
mouth on a pretty face. Hard, rugged, masculine—but
undeniably beautiful. And yet, it was what was beneath
his skin that had her tied in knots. Ever since they'd returned to the Alley, the pieces had been coming back
to her. Fragments and memories and emotions. The
ones that had drawn her to him all those years ago. That
had made her fall for him so hard she was still crashing through space, waiting for the landing. Terrified it
would be unforgivably brutal and break her, but secretly
hoping, like a fool, that he would be there to catch her
in the end. That when she crashed, it would be *into* him,
into the private, most intimate part of him, and she'd be
safe. Rather than against the hard, jagged edges he kept
trying so hard to hide behind.

Drawing in a slow, steadying breath, she asked, "If
not another woman, then what?"

Frustration scored his words. "Why, Sayre? Why do
you keep pushing this?"

"Because everyone knows but *me*. And I deserve to
not be left out in the dark, because it's my life that this
brother of yours supposedly wants. *Mine*, not theirs. And
after everything that's happened, that's happening *now*,
you owe me this. The truth. What are you so afraid of?"

The skin around his eyes pulled tight, that muscle
pulsing like a heartbeat in his hard jaw. "If I tell you, it
will…change things."

"What things?"

"Sayre." He sounded like a man being forced over the edge from a terrible height, but she knew if she backed down now, he might never tell her. Not until it was too late and she was being faced with a cold, hard reality in the middle of Hell.

If Aedan were coming for her, she wanted to know what she and everyone else here was up against.

Thoughts spinning, she studied him, using everything she had to understand him…read him and pick the clues out in not just what he was saying, but what he wasn't. "Is it me, Cian? You think whatever you confess is going to change *me*?"

He scowled, turned away from her and stalked to the window, then braced his hands on either side of its dark, reflective surface. His posture was rigid, his powerful muscles bulging beneath the tight stretch of his skin, making him look exactly like the hard, dangerous creature she knew he could be. He squeezed the sides of the window frame so tightly she was surprised the wood hadn't cracked, sensing a deep-seated anger and pain seething inside him, and in a dizzying moment of clarity, she suddenly understood what had been holding him back.

"You think it will change this. *Us*. The way that I feel about you."

He smacked his open hands against the window frame so hard it made the glass shake. "I know I don't *have* you. I *know* that. But I don't want to lose you, either. I don't want to lose the small part of you that I *do* have."

"Then you're just going to have to trust me."

A low, humorless laugh jerked from his chest. But he remained silent, his shoulders heaving with the harshness of his breaths.

"It isn't that hard, is it? I've trusted you. With my life. With my body."

He groaned as he leaned forward, pressing his forehead against the glass. "Don't want to lose that."

"Then trust me when I say that you won't," she told him, taking a few cautious steps closer, wanting so badly to reach out and run a soothing touch over the rigid length of his spine, his broad shoulders stretching the cotton of his T-shirt until she was surprised it hadn't shredded. "So long as you're honest with me, you won't lose anything."

Quietly, he said. "No, Sayre. I'm going to lose everything. I don't see any other way."

"Just tell me. *Now*."

He turned then, the look in his beautiful eyes so dark and pained, it made her gasp. Voice little more than a choked thread of sound, he rasped, "I'm...a...vampire."

She blinked, thinking she must have heard him wrong. "Um, say that again, please."

"My father is part vampire, and he passed the bloodline onto me. It's not as dominant as my wolf or my human sides, but it's there. A part of me."

"Ohmygod," she breathed, her thoughts flying so fast she couldn't keep up with them. So many things were crashing together in her mind, mysteries that suddenly made sense, holes filled with an answer that she'd never, *ever* expected.

He drew an unsteady breath. "God didn't have anything to do with it, lass. It's pure evil."

She straightened, glaring daggers at him. "Bullshit."

Cian figured it was his turn to look surprised, because she'd just shocked the hell out of him.

"Don't look so stunned," she snapped. "You're a lot of things, Cian Hennessey, but evil isn't one of them."

He laughed low and rough, the bitter sound making him cringe. "I wish that were true. But you don't know the things I've done."

Her gaze glittered with challenge. "Then tell me. If this is part of the reason you left me, then I deserve to know."

"Sayre," he said with a tired, wrecked sigh.

"*Tell me*, Cian."

Almost as if he had no control over himself, he could hear the graveled words bursting from his throat. "At the age of fifteen, we're fully matured, at least physically. At that point, if we consume blood as one of our main food sources, we can halt the aging process."

Her eyes went wide. "Have you ever done that?"

He gave a jerky nod, and stared at the pulse rushing at the delicate base of her throat, unable to meet her eyes as he said, "I spent a decade by Aedan's side at the age of sixteen. I...I was angry, at my parents, because of... well, because of *him*."

He turned, braced his shoulder against the wall beside the window and explained it all. Everything. How he hadn't learned of Aedan's existence until he was fifteen. Aedan's mother had been killed, and the boy had come to live with them at his father's estate in Ireland. He'd been...God, he'd been so angry, when he'd realized what it all meant for his family. That his father had betrayed their mother, their vows, their so-called love, and taken another woman. He'd felt as if everything he'd ever believed had been turned upside down, torn apart and destroyed, his rage toward his father so consuming he'd burned with it. A raw, seething rage toward everyone and everything, except strangely enough, for the boy.

The connection between him and Aedan had been... impossible to resist. They'd bonded over their shared hatred of their father, and that bond had grown fast and furious, until they were nearly inseparable. Though his arrival had changed the way Cian looked at his family, destroying everything he'd believed about honor and loyalty and the kind of man his father had taught him to be, he'd never blamed Aedan. He'd seen Aedan as the innocent. The one without blame, and it'd been obvious that the boy's life with his mother had been nothing like the supposedly perfect childhood Cian had been given. One that, it turned out, had actually been built on nothing more than lies. Unable to let it go, with Aedan by his side, Cian had searched and investigated, uncovering more and more of his father's infidelities, each new discovery making his hatred for the man grow.

And his mother...*Christ.* That had been the straw that broke the camel's back as they say. The one that had driven him away, setting him on a path of destruction.

Voice graveled and raw, he told Sayre of how he left home, and began his life as an angry sixteen-year-old with Aedan at his side, as if it were the two of them against the world. "I seduced innocents," he growled, the guttural words stark with disgust. "Got them in my bed, or against a wall, or over a table, and used them. Fed on them, whether they were willing to give me their blood or not. Killed the dregs of society for sport. Because I *could.* I was angry at everyone and everything, other than Aedan, and I took it out on whoever was unlucky enough to catch my eye." A quiet, painful laugh fell past his lips, and he squeezed his eyes shut, as if that could somehow shield him from what was happening. "I thought I could take what I had finally started to see that my father glorified—a vampire's power and strength and ruthlessness—and shove it in his face. Show him what a bastard he was. But the joke was on me, because he didn't give a shit what kind of destruction I caused."

Softly, she asked, "And what about your mother?"

"I don't know," he whispered, the words halting and low. "The last thing I said to her was how pathetic I thought she was for continuing to stay with him, for not leaving him, after what he'd done to her. I told her she embarrassed me for being weak, and then..."

"Then what?" she persisted, when his voice had trailed off.

He opened his eyes and turned his head to look at her, his breaths coming hard and fast, his throat burning. "She died before I ever made it back to see her again."

"Oh, Cian," she whispered, her gentle voice cracking. "I'm so sorry."

He flinched, but buried the pain beneath the rage that had been his constant companion for so many years. Even when he'd been playing it up as the womanizing jackass, trying to act as if he didn't have a care in the world. "Don't be sorry," he snarled. "It was *her* choice. I begged her to leave him, to go back to her pack and start a new life. But she refused."

With an impossibly sad look in her eyes, she said, "You sound so angry with her."

"I am. I always will be. She didn't fight for herself."

She nodded, her dark eyes soft with understanding. "And she refused to let you fight *for* her, didn't she?"

He blinked, feeling just as lost as he had all those years ago, and stunned that Sayre had read him so perfectly. Swallowing, he managed to say, "She forbid it."

She took another step toward him, close enough now that he could feel the delicious heat of her body against his arm. "Did you ever think that maybe she was protecting you?"

His brows pulled into an even deeper scowl. "From what?"

Almost afraid of how easily she could seduce him—*intoxicate* him—he watched as she lifted one smooth, perfectly freckled shoulder. "I don't know. But if you're anything like she was, then I think it's a possibility that you need to look at."

"Christ," he groaned, closing his eyes as he dropped his head back on his shoulders. It was barely past nine, but he was exhausted. Tired down to his very bones, the revelations of his sins draining him in a way that physical exertion could never do. When she prompted him with the gentle touch of her hand against his bare forearm, he said, "I will, Sayre. I will. Just…not now."

"Will you tell me the rest?" she asked, her other hand softly stroking his spine, her position at his side cocooning him in warmth. He knew she was asking for the rest of the story with Aedan, but he simply didn't have it in him to unearth any more skeletons that night.

"I'll give you the long version tomorrow, if you want it. The short version is that I finally got my head on straight, and realized what I was doing. What I had become. I…I went against Aedan because of it, righting one of his wrongs, and he took it as the ultimate betrayal, swearing to take his revenge against me one day."

"And then?"

He lowered his head, and could no more stop himself from looking at her beautiful face than he could stop needing air. "Then I tried to go home, but I couldn't stand to be near my father. So I bit the bullet and decided to visit my mother's family. After she'd married my father and became pregnant with me, she'd never returned, knowing they would never accept us as vampires. She never even told them the truth about my father's bloodline. They had no idea when I'd been born, or how old I was meant to be. I came to her relatives as her teenaged son, and that's when I met the Runners."

A soft smile touched her lips. "You found a home with them, and wanted to stay."

Nodding, he said, "I did. I stopped drinking blood as a main source, allowing myself to begin to age again, and when I was old enough to be a Runner, I moved here permanently. I became one of them, and I left that old life behind as best as I could."

With a slight catch in her voice, she asked, "So then you can grow old with your friends?"

"I can. I can grow old and die, if that's what I choose." A wry grin tugged at the corner of his mouth. "And I will, Sayre. There isn't a single goddamn part of me that wants to live forever."

Chapter 12

Sensing his exhaustion, Sayre took Cian's hand and led him back through the quiet rooms of the cabin, until they'd reached his bedroom. Trying not to blush like the virgin she was, she pulled his shirt over his head and tossed it to the floor, the sight of his broad shoulders and all those hard-edged muscles on his abdomen making her mouth water. The guy was just too freaking gorgeous for words. Taking his hand again, she pulled him with her until they were lying down in the middle of the bed, the open window allowing the wind and moonlight to filter in, their heads resting on the pillows as they lay on their sides and gazed at one another.

Keeping her voice soft, she asked him questions as they popped into her head, both serious and silly, and he answered each one in a deep, husky rumble that made her shiver with awareness, her body heavy and aching with desire. He explained that garlic didn't have any affect on him, and he could see his reflection in a mirror, as well as walk into a house uninvited. When she asked about sunlight, since it was rumored among the Lycans that they shared the night with vampires, he explained that he was naturally more nocturnal than a human, even more so than his fellow Runners, but that the sunlight didn't physically harm him.

She had no idea how much time had passed when his breathing deepened and his eyes fluttered closed, sleep overtaking him as his voice trailed off. She could sense him relaxing in a way that was whole and complete, as if he were resting easier now that he was no longer carrying the burden of so many secrets, and she had to bite her lip to stop herself from saying his name. If he needed sleep, then she would simply lie there and watch over him, while everything that he'd told her carefully worked its way through her mind.

There was still so much that she didn't know, or understand. But there was also so much that now made sense, like pieces of a puzzle slowly working themselves into place. The way that his arrogance had most likely been a cloak he'd used to hide his self-loathing for the things that he'd done when he was young. She'd also wondered, over the years, if his relentless womanizing was because he'd had his heart broken at some point. And now she knew that he had. Just not by a woman. By his family.

But he had a new family now. One that he could claim, if he would only stop running long enough and let it happen.

She just…she just didn't know if she could be a part of it.

But, *oh, God,* how she wanted to. She wanted to hold him and take him into her body and keep him forever, but didn't know if she could be that brave. If she could say to hell with the fear and simply follow her heart, knowing there was such a strong chance that he would break it.

Trusting his touch had hardly been an easy decision, but this, tearing down that last barrier and letting him in, now that she was seeing things in a clearer light...*this* was so much *more*. Infinitely more intimate, because she would be showing him more than just her outer layer. She would be letting him directly into her heart, and there would be no more secrets, then. Not even from herself. Because of her bloodline—because she was *witch*—everything would be out in the open if they had sex, her true feelings laid out before him like a sacrifice, his to do with as he pleased.

That was what her mother had feared. And now Sayre feared it, too. Not because of his bloodline or his tortured past, but because she could feel the walls between them breaking down, crumbling to dust. Could feel herself being drawn dangerously close to the emotional truths she wasn't yet ready to face.

But she wasn't going to let it pull her away from him. Instead, she shifted closer, put her face close to his on the pillow he was using, and lifted her arm, curling it over him, her fingers pressed against his broad, powerful back. They were still lying like that nearly a half hour later, when his eyelids quivered, then slowly opened. Neither of them said a word as their gazes locked together, the only sound that of their rough, quickening breaths, the air around them building with a crackling tension that was thick and rich and provocative.

It was like they'd slipped into another world where the two of them were the only inhabitants. His eyes narrowed, focusing on her mouth as she caught her lower lip in her teeth. It was the hunger, the *need*, she could see tightening his beautifully masculine face and darkening the tops of his cheekbones that gave her the courage to reach down and undo the top button on his jeans. Then she undid his zipper, biting her lip even harder when it became abundantly clear that he wasn't wearing any underwear, and she eagerly reached for him.

He grabbed her arm so quickly it made her blink, his low voice little more than a choked whisper. "What are you doing, Sayre?"

"Learning you." She flicked her wide-eyed gaze up from where she'd been watching her trembling fingers try to curl around his long, shockingly thick erection, and she smirked when she caught his stunned expression. "What's wrong, Cian? Did you expect me to run and hide when I finally got a good look at your goods?"

"Uh..."

She laughed softly, loving the way he felt against her palms, so hard and feverishly hot, the thick veins that pressed beneath his skin throbbing with the pounding beat of his heart. "I might not have your *extensive* experience in these matters, but I'm not afraid of you or the way you make me feel." She stroked him tightly with both hands. "I'm not afraid of *this*."

"That's good," he groaned, shuddering so hard that it shook the bed. "'Cause you're his favorite thing in the entire fucking world."

She smiled so big it made her face hurt. "That's awesome," she drawled with a wealth of satisfaction, unable to get enough of the way he was looking at her. His hooded gaze pierced her with its intensity, his every reaction telling her how much he loved the feel of her hands on that utterly magnificent part of his body. Her confidence built with each tremor of muscle and serrated moan, her touch becoming bolder as she gave herself the freedom to explore him like she'd always wanted to do. With her hot gaze focused on her actions, she gently tested the weight of that heavy, rounded part of him with one hand, while she stroked the other to the top of his shaft, studying the broad, flushed head. He was getting hot and slick there, and she used her thumb to rub the slippery moisture into his hot skin, encouraged by the way he hissed through his teeth, his nostrils flaring as he sucked in a harsh, ragged breath.

"Damn it," he growled, the rigid shaft getting even harder—and *bigger*—in her hands.

If it weren't obvious by her scent and the drunk-on-lust look on her face that she was thoroughly enjoying herself, the skittering sparks of light suddenly shooting off of her were an unmistakable sign.

"You gotta stop before this goes too far," he rasped, his hooded gaze burning with molten heat, as if his beautiful eyes had been lit from within.

"Not gonna happen," she responded, shaking her head.

He made a guttural sound deep in his throat, and pushed her onto her back. "You're so playing with fire, little witch."

She shot him a feisty smirk as she continued to stroke him, her power crackling in the air like an electrical storm, illuminating the room with glittering points of light. "Look around you, Cian. Fire doesn't exactly scare me."

His incredible silver eyes smoldered with craving as he lowered his face over hers, then lower, until their lips were softly touching. She shivered, loving the way he breathed her in, as if he couldn't get enough of her scent, or her taste, his tongue stroking against her bottom lip once…then again. He nipped it with his teeth, his next breath a little harsher, tension coiled tight in the long length of his body as he pressed harder against her, his heavy erection throbbing in her grip. With a guttural curse on his lips, he shifted position, kneed her legs apart and moved between them. Then he pulled her hands off his cock and pinned them near her head as he pressed that massive shaft right against the seam of her shorts. She gasped, thinking it felt beyond wonderful, until he pulsed his hips, grinding against the moist cushion of her sex, and *that* felt so insanely amazing that her eyes nearly rolled back in her head.

God, in that moment, she would have given *anything* for there to be nothing between them. To feel him so deliciously hot and hard against her naked flesh.

"I want you so badly," he growled, the gritty words vibrating with need as he braced himself on his elbows, his forehead dropping against hers. "So badly, Sayre, I think it could break me." He reached down with one hand and shoved her shirt up under her breasts, his body pressed so close she could feel the mouthwatering flexing of his abs. Then he lowered his hand again, curled it behind her left knee and jerked it up against his hip, his next rolling thrust rubbing against her in a way that made her sob with pleasure, her nails digging into the sleek, powerful muscles in his back.

"Cian," she moaned, unable to say more than his name.

"I would sell my goddamn soul for the right to take you," he panted. "Take you for fucking ever."

Her nails dug in a little harder, and she could tell by the flare of heat in his eyes that he liked the bite of pain. "It *is* your right."

He grimaced at her husky burst of words and stilled at the end of a powerful stroke, his color fever-high as he started to pull his head back, his eyes wild. "God, I wish that were true."

Curving her hands behind his strong neck, she pulled his mouth to hers as she gasped, "It is." Then she kissed the hell out of him, hard and wet and aggressive, tangling her tongue with his...until he ripped the control right out of her hands, and took it for his own.

Claiming the sweet, sleek inner surfaces of her mouth with his tongue, Cian kissed Sayre so deep and explicitly, it was like he was trying to decode her. Lure out her unspoken emotions and secrets, craving the flavor of them. Needing anything of hers that was private and sacred, just so he could feel *close* to her. So he could hold a little part of her that no one else had ever held. Needing it to be his, and his alone.

He was thrusting against her with so much power now that the bed was slamming against the wall, and he wasn't even inside her. But that wasn't going to stop him from crashing over the edge so hard he damn near turned himself inside out. When it hit him a moment later, the force of his release was so intense it was like his heart had stopped, every muscle and tendon in his body straining and taut. He kept his mouth locked tight against hers, growling hoarse, broken curses into that sweet, honey-flavored space as his body shuddered and pulsed, his climax spilling him all over her soft stomach and that sexy-as-hell tattoo. He could only breathe out a huge groan of relief that she'd climaxed with him, her throaty cries echoing in his ears, while the rich, drugging scent of her pleasure hit his system so powerfully he gave another hard pulse, completely drained.

Collapsing onto his side, back in his original position, he couldn't stop himself from pulling her onto her side, as well. She lay facing him again, her flushed cheek pressed into the pillow, eyes closed, and he didn't even spare a second glance at the god-awful shamrocks. He was too lost in Sayre, his heavy-lidded gaze devouring the sight of her still flushed from her orgasm. Then she lifted those long, gold-tipped lashes and looked right at him, and the smile she gave him was so damn beautiful it made Cian feel as if he'd been knocked upside the head with a bat, his ability to think all but obliterated. So he simply let himself feel...and enjoy. They lay there for what felt like forever, faces close together, breathing the same air, completely lost in the moment. Unable to keep the words burning on his tongue inside, he eventually said, "I know it doesn't change anything, but I just...I want you to know that the women who came here to see me yesterday, they don't mean anything to me, Sayre. They never did."

She touched her fingertips to the stubble darkening his jaw, the tender caress making him tremble. "God, Cian. I don't know if that makes it better, or worse."

Understanding what she meant, he shifted forward until he could press his lips against the center of her forehead, trying to show her the tenderness she deserved as he cupped the side of her face in his hand and stroked her soft, warm cheek with his thumb. When her breathing became deep and slow, he gently pulled his head back, lost in the precious sight of her as she fell asleep against him, those beautiful lips curved in another soft, satisfied smile that made him feel like he'd conquered worlds. He wanted to stay there and watch her forever, but the gnawing feeling in his stomach reminded him that he hadn't eaten dinner. Forcing himself to get up, he changed his jeans for clean ones with hands that still weren't quite as steady as they should be, and headed into the kitchen to make himself a sandwich. A few minutes later, he went out onto the front porch for a cigarette, needing some more time to think in the quiet about everything that had happened…and how the little witch had surprised him, once again.

Instead of pushing him away after he'd unloaded about his bloodline and his past, she'd pulled him closer, and he didn't know what to make of it. How to wrap his head around it, when he'd been so sure she would run screaming and never want to set eyes on him again.

Not yet ready to go inside after he finished his smoke, and not wanting to spend any more time worrying about Aedan, he pulled out his phone, took a seat on the top porch step and spent a long time cruising her blog, watching videos of her with the sound low. It was probably kind of stalkerish, but damn it, he was drawn to every part of the woman, and he couldn't help feeling incredibly proud at what she'd achieved. Isolation would have broken most people, but Sayre had found a way to survive. And while he might be physically stronger, he didn't doubt for an instant that she was stronger than him where it counted.

He was still huddled over his phone minutes later, watching the way the sun turned her hair a fiery red-gold in another video, when Jillian's quiet voice came from just in front of him, at the bottom of the steps. "Did you tell her?"

Setting the phone down beside him on the porch, Cian lifted his head and nodded. "I told her tonight."

"And how did she take it?" she asked, just standing there with her hands pushed in her front pockets.

He gave a husky laugh. "Better than I would have, that's for damn sure. She's…she's friggin' amazing, Jilly."

She lowered her chin, her shoulders lifting as she pulled in a deep breath, and he suddenly picked up on her tension.

"What's going on?" he asked, moving to his feet, his

worried gaze locking tight with hers as she lifted her head and glared up at him.

"I've been so worried about her," she said in a voice so low it was barely audible. "About how she would get on being back here, with so many of us around. But she's doing great."

He nodded again, the tension between them slowly building, making his insides churn. He knew something bad was coming, but he didn't know what. Had Jillian seen Sayre with one of the other men? Had Sayre told her that she'd had enough of his bullshit? None of that fit with how she'd been with him earlier—but damn it, he didn't know what to think.

When she didn't add anything more, he asked, "Is there something else you want to say, Jillian?"

Her head tilted a bit to the side. "I was just wondering if you've figured it out yet? I didn't get it until today, when I was spending time with her. So have you?"

He could feel a muscle begin to pulse in his jaw, his nostrils flaring as he pulled in a slow, deep breath. "Figured what out?"

Stepping up onto the bottom step, she said, "Before you left, I actually felt bad for you. I knew you were afraid of what was between you and Sayre, but I had faith that you would find your backbone and do the right thing. But you didn't. You ran like a coward, and we... we *lost* her. Because of you!"

"What the hell are you talking about?"

She climbed onto the step just beneath him, fuming with rage. "She went into that meltdown with her powers because you left her! It wasn't the war or the battle or her powers growing too quickly—it was *you*!" she hissed, shocking the hell out of him when she reached up and slapped the side of his face so hard it jerked his head to the side. "I sensed it, when it started, when you started feeling that pull for her. But I didn't panic, because I was so sure you were going to figure it out and do right by her. I'd seen the way you stared at her, the way you watched her…like a man who'd finally found the answer to every wish he'd ever had. And then you ran!" she shouted, tears spilling from her glistening eyes and rolling down her cheeks. "Did you ever stop for one second and think about what that would do to her? Did you, you selfish son of a bitch?"

"Jilly, come on," Jeremy murmured, seeming to come out of nowhere as he wrapped an arm around his wife's waist and pulled her back against him. A sob broke from her throat as she glared up at Cian, waiting for his answer, and he felt like the lowest pile of shit that had ever existed.

"Christ, Jillian. I'm…sorry," he choked out.

"You should be. Because when you bail on her again, guess what? It's going to happen *again*, Cian. And she'll run. We're going to lose her, because you're too much of an asshole to grow up and do what's right!"

"Jilly, baby, that's enough," Jeremy rumbled, as he lifted her up and cradled her against his chest. She wound her trembling arms around his neck, pressed her tear-soaked face against his shoulder and let him carry her away, her muffled sobs echoing softly on the wind until the Runner had taken her into their cabin.

Feeling as if he were moving through quicksand, Cian turned and climbed back up the steps, the side of his face still stinging as he reached down and picked up his phone, thumbing it off. Then he went back inside, locking up behind him. When he walked into the bedroom, he was surprised to find that Sayre was still asleep, cuddled up in the middle of the bed. He figured it was a miracle that

Jillian's shouting hadn't woken her, but he was glad. He wanted nothing more than to crawl into bed and hold her in his arms, so after stripping off his jeans and slipping on a pair of boxers, that's what he did.

And then, with her body tucked up close to his, he finally let himself think about what had happened. About what Jillian had told him.

Yeah, he'd picked up on the fact that Sayre was handling being in the Alley better than any of them had hoped. And maybe he'd known, deep down, why that was. But he hadn't let himself admit it. Hadn't wanted it to be true. Hadn't wanted to be the cause of even more of her pain. More goddamn friggin' pain than he could ever atone for.

He knew he should walk away from her, but—

So she deserves to be alone? Forever? his wolf grumbled, cutting him off. *Because after what you learned tonight, you* know *that's what will happen!*

God, the beast was right. If he truly *were* the thing stabilizing her power, or buffering it, or whatever was going on between them, then what would happen when he left? It stood to reason that she would suffer the same problems as before, just like Jillian had said. That she would be forced back to her little cabin in West Virginia. Alone. Isolated. The most beautiful woman in the world, in his eyes, wasting away because of his screwups.

Not if we stay with her. Not if we claim *her.*

He gritted his teeth, hating how tempting that suggestion was. How deeply it called to him, the visceral need felt in every single cell of his body. One there was a damn good chance he would no longer be able to resist, whether it was best for her...or not.

But no matter what, he had to kill Aedan first. Had to destroy that threat. And if by some miracle he survived, well…there were things he would obviously have to figure out then. Sayre deserved more than a hollowed-out man who'd had the ability to love burned out of him, if he'd ever even had it to begin with. So he would have to figure out a way to…to somehow…

Shit! He didn't know. There was no goddamn magic answer in this twisted situation—but the one thing he vowed he wouldn't do was run. Not until he'd figured things out and knew, without any doubt, that she was all right. That she wouldn't have to go back to living in her own little world of seclusion.

But for tonight, he just wanted to hold the little witch in his arms…and find a moment of peace. As a man who'd never had many of them, he knew to hold on tight and grab them when he could. And none had ever been as perfect or as sweet as this one, which seemed fitting.

Because there was always the chance that it could be his last.

Chapter 13

Cian knew he was dreaming, but he couldn't stop. Couldn't make himself wake up. Like someone who'd been bound and gagged, he was forced to watch the horrific scene play out in his mind without any way to stop it. The nightmare was from the last night he'd spent with Aedan, in the fortress home they'd taken in Romania, after they'd killed the owners and acted like the dark lords of the castle. Well, acting on *his* part, because he'd already known at that point that he could no longer keep living at Aedan's side.

But his brother had believed. For Aedan, the monstrous reality of their lives had been no act.

On that particular night, Cian had come home earlier than planned, leaving Aedan in a nearby town, creating havoc at a local festival, drinking too much and fondling girls too young to be looked at with sexual intent, much less touched, plying them with liquor to make them forget

their fears. His brother's fondness for fresh-faced innocents was why Cian had started to draw away, as well as
Aedan's growing penchant for savagery and violence. The
anger that Cian carried toward his father, and even his
mother, was no longer driving him into the darkness, and
as slivers of light began filtering their way into his consciousness, the way they lived simply became too much.

He'd slipped away from the festival without Aedan
even noticing and wandered the halls in the ancient castle,
restless and uneasy, knowing he would leave soon…and
dreading the scene with Aedan when he did. Dreading
even more the decisions he still needed to make regard-
ing his brother's future.

Before he realized where his feet were taking him, he
was down in the lower part of the castle, walking stone
corridors that were cold and damp, his path illuminated
by the flashlight he carried with him. At first, he attrib-
uted the low whimpers to nothing more than the groans
of an old building. But the deeper he traveled, the clearer
they became, until he started following the odd noises.
His heart beat with dread the closer he got, the stench of
fear thickening in the cold, dark tunnels.

Then he found her, locked inside a rotting cell, the
padlocked wooden door easily breaking with his strength
as he smashed his way inside. The human girl was a
small, shivering lump on the floor, and she only shuddered harder when he asked if she was all right. Such a
stupid question, when the girl was clearly anything but
okay. Choking on the unspoken curses crowding into his
throat, Cian kneeled on the filthy stone floor beside her
and moved her to her back as carefully as possible. She
groaned, trying to push him away, and blood spattered
his face as she struggled. He blanched the instant he realized the sprays of blood were coming from her throat.

She'd been bitten there many times, the wounds left open and bleeding so freely he was amazed she was still alive. He clutched her tight to his chest and prayed he could get her out before Aedan returned, sick with disgust at what his brother had done. The girl was no more than twelve, and it was obvious she'd been horribly abused.

She was too out of it with pain, weakened by blood loss, to protest when he stood with her in his arms, her frail body like a doll's, her short blond hair matted with blood and things he didn't want to identify. He sniffed at her temple, relieved that while Aedan had fed freely on her blood, he hadn't given her enough of his own to harm her. Then he hurried to get her out of the fortress, hiding in the nearby woods for several minutes, until he was finally able to get her name and address out of her. She lived in one of the local villages, and within half an hour, he had her home and in the care of her terrified, yet grateful parents.

There were tears, so many tears he felt as if he were drowning in them, and all the while, he kept thinking of the other mothers who had cried over the broken bodies of their children. Young men that Cian had killed over the years, simply because his anger had allowed Aedan to convince him it was their way. Their *right*.

"If you want her to live," he told them, "get her to a healer and then take her away from here and don't ever come back."

When they asked how, he looked around their small cottage, and knew they were doomed without his help. He went back home and quickly retrieved enough money that they could travel halfway around the world and live comfortably for the next twenty years without ever lifting a finger, and brought it back to them. Then he loaded them on a bus that would take them into a bustling city, where they could make their way to a healer whom Cian knew could be trusted not to go to the authorities, before taking a taxi to the airport and flying out. That night, never to return.

Then he burned down their cottage, and destroyed the bus they'd taken, making sure there were no clues for Aedan to follow.

And after that, he went back to the cell. And he waited for Aedan. Waited for the battle he knew was coming. For the blood and the accusations and—

Enough! a deep, guttural voice roared inside his head, and he jerked awake with a gasp, sitting up in the bed, drenched in sweat, while his wolf's rough voice echoed through his mind. Cian scrubbed his hands over his face and shoved his damp hair back from his brow, then sent a silent thank-you to the beast, grateful for its intervention. He'd had enough of that goddamn dream to last a lifetime.

Glancing around the sunlit room, he realized he was alone and a frown pulled at the edges of his mouth. "Sayre?" he called out, his voice still rough from sleep. She didn't answer, and as he pulled in a deep breath, he knew she'd already left, since he couldn't scent her presence in the cabin. Just that sweet, lingering trace of her that now filled every room. It was infused into his sheets and the very air. Clean and pure, while his own repulsive nature damaged everything he touched.

He showered until he'd damn near taken off a layer of skin, but still couldn't shake the vileness of his memory. Recognizing that he was too raw and wound up to face her right then, he pulled on some clothes and his boots, needing to get out and get his head focused on something else. But his beast wasn't happy about it.

She's ours, you idiot, and you're blowing it, the wolf

snarled, losing its patience with him and the entire situation.

He ground his jaw, understanding the wolf's anger. But he knew they needed more than a life-mate connection to make things work. Nature could only add so much to the equation, and the cold hard fact of the matter was that he was most likely missing too many elements that were needed to complete it. And, God, did that piss him off.

Shoving the infuriating thought from his mind, he went outside and sniffed the air as he searched for any sign of Aedan, same as he'd been doing for days now. He didn't think for an instant that his brother had given up. No, Aedan was simply biding his time, no doubt loving the way they were all walking around on pins and needles, looking over their shoulders at every sound, just waiting for him to make his appearance. The security patrols were running like clockwork, but it didn't ease his tension. If Aedan wanted in to the Alley, he would find a way. Cian just had to be ready for him when it happened.

Heading down his porch steps, he looked toward Jeremy and Jillian's place, figuring Sayre was over there. Trusting her to be smart and stay inside the borders of the Alley, he decided to head over to Sam's. The merc had told him he could stop by anytime if he wanted to talk over possible strategies for dealing with Aedan, and this was as good a time as any. Sam had apparently had some experience dealing with vampires in the past, and he was a good sounding board. Cian ended up spending the next few hours there, while they came up with a couple of extra security ideas that he planned to talk to Brody about as soon as the Runner got back from checking on his wife and kids up in Shadow Peak.

Hoping that Sayre would be back at the cabin by then, Cian told Sam he'd catch him later and headed back over, calling out her name as he shut the front door behind him. She didn't respond, and he frowned, wondering if she were planning on avoiding him the entire day. Even though the idea irritated the hell out of him, he knew he'd been doing the same damn thing to her, and so he forced himself to give her the space that she needed. Using the time to check in with some of the informants he kept out in the field, hoping they might have heard of any sightings on Aedan, he didn't actually start to worry until lunchtime came and went, and she still hadn't made an appearance.

Standing at his front window, he stared out into the quiet glade, and wondered if Jillian had told her about the link between him and her loss of control over her powers. Was that why Sayre hadn't come back to the cabin...and to him?

Determined to talk to her about it, he'd just opened his front door and stepped back onto the porch when Jeremy came running up, his expression set in a fierce scowl that had Cian's heart pumping with dread. "What's going on?" he asked in a voice that was hoarse with fear, a thousand horrible scenarios running through his head. "Where's Sayre?"

Jeremy's scowl deepened. "She isn't with you?"

"Hell no, she isn't with me!" he snarled, his gums burning as his fangs prepared to drop, his beast roaring with fury.

"I don't know where Sayre is," Jeremy told him, talking fast. "She was with Jillian until a half hour ago, and we thought she'd come back here. But I just got word that one of our scouts has been found with his neck broken over on the east border."

"Shit!" he growled, spearing his fingers into his hair so hard that it stung, his mind racing. The only sure way to kill a Lycan was to either behead him, or sever his spinal column. And Aedan knew that.

Though he wanted to throw back his head and bellow with rage, Cian knew he didn't have the time. Lowering his arms, he told Jeremy to get everyone mobilized and searching for Sayre. "Make 'em spread out, but they need to go in pairs. Do not let anyone try to face him alone. And whatever the hell you do, don't underestimate him. He will cut you down without a second thought."

"What about you?" Jeremy grunted. "Who are *you* pairing up with?"

"I'm not," he muttered, moving too quickly for the Runner to stop him. Heading toward the east border, he caught Sayre's intoxicating scent not far from where the scout had been found, as well as the rancid odor that belonged to his brother. Moving with inhuman speed as he followed the scent trail, Cian was more terrified than he'd ever been in his life. He could recall moments as a child when he'd been frightened—the most memorable the night he'd learned about the vampire part of his nature, and realized he wasn't what he'd believed himself to be. But even that life-changing moment hadn't come close to this.

Though he followed a crazy trail through the woods that Aedan had clearly laid out to screw with him, the route like something a child would take while playing a game, Cian managed to find them within minutes of picking up her scent. The location was a small clearing the Runners had used for training purposes back before the war against the Whiteclaw, far enough from the Alley that no one would hear him if he howled. But he knew they would be able to follow the same trail that had brought him here—just not as quickly. Sayre sat straight-backed on a fallen tree trunk at the far edge of the clearing, while Aedan paced back and forth in front of her, his crimson eyes narrowing in hard and tight on Cian the instant he stepped out of the surrounding woods.

"See, Sayre," his brother drawled with a sickening smile. "I told you it wouldn't take him long to track us. It's that bestial nature of his. Like a dog with a bone, he could probably follow your mouthwatering scent straight into the depths of Hell."

Ignoring the asshole, Cian locked his worried gaze with hers. "Are you okay?"

She nodded stiffly in response, then immediately returned her attention to his brother, watching him the way someone never took their eyes off a snake that was preparing to strike. There was a nasty bruise forming beneath her right eye, and the corner of her lower lip had been busted, but he couldn't see any other marks on her. Not that the ones she had didn't matter. They made him want to rip the monster's heart out of his chest and then shove it down his throat, making him choke on it. But he was infinitely thankful that they weren't worse—that she was alive and breathing.

When he returned his full attention back to Aedan, his brother lifted his hands and showed him his raw, blistered palms. "I'm sure it will make you happy to know that the little witch gave me a hell of a jolt when I grabbed her."

"Too bad she didn't fry your psychotic ass to a crisp."

"Aw, I love you, too, big brother."

"Cut the bullshit, Aedan. What do you want?" he asked, studying his enemy as he came farther into the clearing. The boy who had been his brother, and was now a maniac, looked so familiar, and yet, different. It'd been years since Cian had seen him, and he knew he'd been right to warn the others not to confront him. They might be badass Lycans capable of ripping grown men in two if it were needed, but Aedan—Aedan was something else entirely.

His hair was still dark as pitch, so black it looked blue in the hazy afternoon sunlight, but instead of the longer cut he'd always worn it in, the thick mass was now shorn close to his scalp, making it easy to see the metal he wore in his eyebrows and ears. Though he was several inches shorter than Cian, only just reaching six-one, his whipcord-lean physique was more muscular than it'd been before. His once naturally pale skin was now ghostly white, most of it on display since he wore nothing but a low-slung pair of jeans that barely covered his lean hips. And those crimson eyes that burned with hatred would make it impossible for him to go out in public without dark glasses covering them. Not to mention the short, thick black talons that curved over the tips of his fingers, pointed and lethal.

But what was truly disturbing were the tattoos that covered every inch of skin on his arms and chest. They were horrific scenes of murder and sexual abuse, the victims' eyes shocked wide with fear and pain, their mouths hanging garishly open for their bloodcurdling screams.

"What do I want?" Aedan drawled, pulling Cian's attention back to those feral, blood-colored eyes. "I think that's obvious."

"If you wanted her dead," he grunted, "you would have already killed her."

"Oh, she'll die eventually. But…well, to be honest, this is more enjoyable than I expected it to be. Watching you worry and squirm. It would be a shame to end it too soon," he crooned as he stepped closer to Sayre and ran his hand down the gleaming fall of her hair. "So consider this visit a little gift to myself," he added, his thin lips spreading in a wide smile. "I got to spend some lovely *alone* time with your woman, and now you know how easily I can get to her whenever I want."

Hoping like hell that Sayre would keep her mouth shut and let him do the talking, he said, "She isn't my woman, Aedan."

Stepping away from Sayre, and closer to the place where Cian stood, his brother tsked. "Come now, Cian. Lying doesn't become you. It never did. Even when you were a sinner, you managed to be noble."

"There was nothing noble about the way we lived."

Aedan gave a snide rumble of laughter. "God, you're boring."

"And you're insane."

"At least I'll get the girl in the end, and not you. That's only fair, don't you think? Since you took my sweet little Elizabeth from my dungeon and stole her from me."

"Do you scent my mark on Sayre?" he growled. "No, you don't. Because I haven't claimed her, Aedan."

"Just because you haven't had the balls to make it official doesn't mean this beautiful little piece of ass isn't yours." Tilting his head back, he flicked his tongue out like a snake, then looked at Cian and laughed. "I can *taste* the possessiveness coming off you in the air. It's thick in your blood, brother."

"What does any of that matter if I have no intention of ever making her mine?" he countered. "You're wasting your time."

Aedan smirked. "I'm afraid I don't agree. I think you want her so badly it's *killing* you, Cian. Fucking ripping you to pieces."

His hands flexed at his sides, his claws beginning to prick his fingertips. "You're wrong, Aedan. I'll protect her because she's innocent in all this, the same way I've protected others from you in the past, like Elizabeth. But you're letting your madness cloud your judgment."

"You didn't protect Elizabeth from me. You stole her!" Aedan roared, his body rapidly changing, preparing for battle, as his temper got the better of him. The instant his fangs released, nearly two inches in length, his skin turned milk white, as if every ounce of blood had drained from his veins. Against that corpse-like background, the macabre tattoos looked even sharper, the violent scenes writhing as his muscles rippled. He was raw power, cut and lean and horrifically lethal, and Cian wondered how it'd taken him so long to see it when they'd been young. Had he been blinded by their joint hatred of their father? Or had it been the love he'd once held for Aedan that had made him such a fool?

He hated to admit it, but it was most likely the love. Despite what Aedan's birth had meant to his mother—a devastating sign of his father's betrayal—Cian hadn't been able to do anything but love the boy who had been nothing but scrawny limbs and shaggy hair. A familial love, which was the only type he'd ever been capable of feeling. And it's not like he could have blamed the boy for their father's infidelity. Aedan had had no one, and so Cian had taken over the role of protector.

Instead, he should have taken his head when he'd had the chance, but he'd been too weak, and he put the blame for that weakness where it belonged. On his love. If that right there wasn't a blinding endorsement for how that particular emotion was something he wanted no part of, he didn't know what was.

You know nothing, his beast muttered. *You never have.*

He wasn't surprised they disagreed on that particular point. Hell, most of the time they hardly agreed on anything. But the one thing they were both fully prepared to do was protect Sayre. At any cost.

Tired of letting this son of a bitch stand between him and his woman, Cian released his own lethal set of fangs, his long Lycan claws piercing through the tips of his fingers as he charged Aedan in a blur of speed. He managed to get in a solid strike across the bastard's ribs before Aedan backhanded him with so much power he was surprised his head hadn't snapped off, the hot rush of blood filling his mouth telling him that his lip had been smashed. Shaking it off, Cian rolled his head over his shoulders and narrowed his gaze, just as a deep, guttural growl surged up from his chest. Aedan might have the cold, calculating hatred of a vampire, but Cian had the scorching, primitive fury of his beast, and the ruthless animal was seriously pissed that their mate had been put in danger.

In the next second, Aedan flew at him in a flurry of strikes, his talons slicing across the front of Cian's shirt, shredding the cotton but only grazing his skin as he twisted to the side. He wasn't hurt badly—it was only a scratch—but Sayre reacted as if he'd been gutted. Surging to her feet, her face pale and her eyes wide with fear, she flung her arms forward, throwing up one of those crackling, blinding walls of energy between him and the vampire.

But Cian wasn't going to let it hold him back.

"Sayre, stay out of this!" he roared, gritting his teeth as he pushed into the light, his skin sizzling from the searing burn. But he didn't back down, determined to reach his brother and inflict as much damage as he could.

When he'd made it through the wall, stalking toward Aedan—who was watching the whole thing with another one of those chilling, maniacal smiles—Cian pulled off the tattered remnants of his shirt and tossed them on the ground. "Come on, you sick bastard. You want blood?" he snarled, knowing damn well that his eyes were turning the same haunting shade as his brother's, his rage fueling his bloodlust. "Then come and get it."

"Not today, I'm afraid," Aedan murmured, pushing his hands in his front pockets as if they weren't in the middle of a vicious fight to the death. "Like I said before, brother, this is proving so much more entertaining than I'd hoped. And I was already aiming high, after spying on your dreams these past few months."

He froze, unable to believe what he'd just heard. "What the hell are you talking about?"

Aedan laughed low in his throat, and took a step closer, though nearly ten yards still separated them. When Sayre had thrown up her light, his brother had scrambled away like a frightened cat. But now he was all cold, malevolent confidence. Lifting his brows, he said, "Think about it, Cian. How else do you think I learned about her after all this time?"

"You saw my dreams of her?" he growled, flexing his deadly claws at his sides.

Aedan smirked as he shook his head. "You're jealous I saw you thrusting like an animal between those silky thighs? That doesn't sound like you, brother. I can remember a time when you liked screwing your meals while others watched. It made you *hotter*."

He flinched and cut a quick look toward Sayre, who was still standing by the fallen trunk as she stared at his brother with complete focus, her expression impossible to read.

When Cian returned his attention to Aedan, he found the bastard staring right back at her. "You'd probably faint if I told you what my precious brother dreams about doing to you, little witch. Some of it was so depraved, I couldn't get enough of watching, just like a voyeur." His head cocked at an eerie angle, as if his neck wasn't attached correctly. "Though you've probably been having those dreams, too. It's because the two of you were quickening for one another. That happens when life mates spend too much time apart, at too great a distance."

"How the hell would you know?" Cian demanded, wanting to rip out the bastard's eyes so he couldn't look at her that way. As if he was seeing her like she'd been in so many of his dreams, passionate and wild and hungry for pleasure.

"I'm a hunter, brother, and hunters study their prey. I've been learning everything I could possibly need to know about your doglike nature for years." He finally tore his attention away from Sayre, and slid Cian a gloating look. "Although, it wasn't the sex dreams that truly caught my attention. They were just the cherry on the top of my *favorite* part. The thing that reached out across the world through our link and clasped on to me, digging its way into my mind."

He swallowed, knowing exactly what Aedan was talking about.

"You see, Sayre, Cian's been dreaming about more than just nailing you to every available surface he can find. He's been having bad, *bad* dreams. And it's funny, the things you can tell about a person's feelings, when they're afraid. You see what they care about most in those moments. What means the most to them. Like when a fire alarm goes off, who does the husband run to first, his wife or his kids?"

Cian bared his fangs. "Shut the fuck up," he snapped.

Ignoring him, Aedan went on. "And because Cian and I shared so many…meals together," he explained with an evil smile, "we formed a connection. One that bound us in a way others will never understand. I'm sure he would feel my fears, if I had any. But I can assure that I feel his. I feel them as if they were my own. And do you know what most people fear for the most? The things that they lo—"

"That's enough!" he roared, cutting the bastard off.

Aedan threw back his head and laughed. "Careful now," he chided. "You're giving yourself away, brother."

Catching the scent of the others in the air, he said, "My friends are almost here, Aedan. You're powerful, but you're also massively outnumbered."

"And you can't hide here with your animal pals forever. Our time is coming, Cian, whether you want it to or not."

"I'm an animal, too, Aedan."

The vampire's crimson eyes burned with madness. "Which is why I'll win. Vamp trumps your noble beast, brother. Always."

Voice thick with frustration, he asked, "Why can't you leave me be and get on with your own damn life?"

"Because I'm lonely? Because this is fun?" Aedan's eyes narrowed, a guttural tone to his own deep voice that sounded like tightly coiled rage. "Because you deserve it for betraying me? Do I really need a reason, *brother mine*?"

His jaw tightened. "You won't win this."

"You're suffering, Cian. You look as if you're living in the depths of Hell." A slow smile twisted his thin lips. "That means I'm already winning."

"It doesn't mean jack shit."

In a flash of movement, Aedan was suddenly at his side, his cold mouth pressed close to Cian's ear. "And just in case you were getting any ideas," he whispered, "killing yourself won't save her. It'll just mean I don't have to go through you to get to her. But she's still *mine*, even if you're rotting in the ground."

In the next moment, the Runners and the mercs, along with Jillian, caught up to them and burst into the clearing, and Aedan disappeared in a blur of speed that the others probably hadn't even caught.

"Where is he?" Brody demanded, his fangs gleaming beneath the curve of his upper lip. His massive body vibrated with rage, and Cian felt the sharp slice of guilt tear through him. He hated that he was putting his friends through this. Hated that he couldn't reach Aedan. Hated every part of it. Every miserable piece of this screwed-up situation.

And beneath it all, there was the sickening guilt that this was all *his* fault. For starting Aedan on this path. For not ending him when he'd first realized what his brother was capable of, after his father had refused to take action. For the niggling fear that he hadn't tried hard enough to find Aedan these past five years. The fear that there was a part of him that hadn't *wanted* to find Aedan badly enough, because he hadn't wanted to see his brother die. A part that had privately been relieved he couldn't go home to Sayre, knowing where that path would lead, too frightened of the things the little witch made him feel. Of how much stronger those feelings would be now that she was a young woman, and no longer untouchable.

Christ, had he ever wanted to touch anything as desperately as he wanted to touch Sayre Murphy? Ever needed anyone as badly, or simply craved their happiness?

The answer was as simple as it was obvious.

Not. Even. Close.

Chapter 14

Shoving away from Jillian, who had thrown her arms around her in relief, Sayre suddenly turned and took off, running as hard and as fast as she could back toward the Alley. Tears ran unchecked down her face, the enormity of the danger Cian had faced making it difficult to stand, much less move at this speed. But she made her way back to the cabin as quickly as possible. She was too raw to talk things over with anyone, including her sister, and she knew Jillian would try.

There'd been moments in her life when her "sight" had proven incredibly useful—but only for her loved ones. Never for herself. Never when she'd needed it, and God, could she have used it now. Being blindsided by an undeniable truth when she'd watched Cian fighting his brother had left her reeling. Left the ground shaking beneath her feet in a way that made it difficult to breathe... to think. All she could do was *feel*, seething in a maelstrom of emotion, the tears coming harder, faster, until she was sobbing with them, every part of her body trembling, breaking apart.

In that moment, when she'd thought he might actually die out there in that clearing, she'd realized that she didn't need to fear she was falling too hard and too fast for him, because it had already happened. Her heart was already his, irrevocably and completely, and *that* scared her in a way that Aedan Hennessey never could.

Had she known, when she'd agreed to come back to the Alley with Cian, that this was where her need would lead her? To loving him?

Whatever the answer, it no longer mattered. She was already at the point where it was too far to turn back, because he'd earned it. He'd *earned* her heart—every scared, agitated cell of it—when he'd faced off against that monster to protect her.

Now she just had to decide what she was going to do about it.

"You bastard!" she screamed only seconds later, when he shoved the bedroom door open, breaking the lock with ridiculous ease, apparently unwilling to let anything come between them—*except himself.* Fired with savage, visceral frustration, she picked up one of the heavy books from an ugly green bookshelf and hurled it at his head with surprising strength. "You son of a bitch!"

He'd ducked to avoid the book, but the breath whooshed out of him when she nailed him in the stomach with a wooden bookend. "I get that you're angry," he grunted, "but I need to know if you're all right. Are you okay?"

"You're damned right I'm angry," she snapped, her hair lifting slightly from her shoulders as the air between them began to crackle.

"You have every right to be. It's my fault he got near you."

She shuddered, recalling the sickening fear that had burst inside her the instant she'd set eyes on Aedan. But she wasn't going to let him distract her so easily. "I'm not angry about him coming after me. Yeah, it sucked. But that's not why I'm livid. I'm pissed *because of what you did*!"

His head jerked back as if her words had clipped him on the chin. "What?"

"Why would you do that? Why would you just...just try to throw your life away like that? You saw what he was like! How did you expect to fight him and come out alive? I could have watched you die out there!"

He sighed, his shoulders dropping as he took a step toward her. *"Sayre."*

The way he was suddenly looking at her, as if she were the most precious thing in the world, only made her cry harder. His bright, long-lashed eyes were still painfully beautiful, even when she'd seen them tinged with crimson. So unlike his brother's. Aedan's eyes had resonated with pure evil, especially when seen within a face that was so coldly devoid of emotion. She shuddered again as she relived the memory of Cian taunting that monster to fight him, and shouted, "No! Don't come any closer. I...I'm liable to punch you if you do."

He looked stricken to see her so upset, his breath leaving his lungs in an audible rush. "I wasn't trying to die out there, Sayre. I'll do whatever it takes to protect you, but I'm not going to throw myself on a fucking sword. If I thought it would help, then yeah, I'd be tempted. I'd be an asshole if I felt any differently, because *I'm* the one who got you into this mess. But it wouldn't stop him. It would just leave you alone to deal with him without me, and I can't let that happen."

Trembling, she said, "No matter how this ends, it will be bad for you, Cian."

"And that's what I *deserve*," he growled, his chest heaving as he fisted his hands at his sides, his claws and fangs already retracted.

But his chest and arms were still streaked with crimson smears of blood, and she knew, *she goddamn knew*, how close he could have come to dying out there.

"Why d-did you do this?" she sobbed, shaking so badly her teeth were chattering. "Why d-did you come back? I'm not yours. You haven't claimed m-me, and you never will. So why didn't you just k-keep screwing your way around the world and let him kill me?"

He took a harsh breath, his brow furrowing as he slid his gaze to the side. "I haven't."

"You haven't what?" she snapped, sniping at him like a child in a fit of temper.

He shoved a hand back through his hair and cursed under his breath. "I haven't…been…with anyone. Like that."

"What?"

He pulled in another deep breath, and slowly brought his hooded gaze back to hers. She jolted from the look burning in those molten eyes, feeling like she'd just been shoved hard in the chest, though no one had laid a hand on her. "I haven't been with another woman, Sayre. Not since I left you."

She swallowed so hard that it hurt. "Cian, that…that doesn't even make sense."

"You think I don't know that? I mean, I know I can't have you. Not like that. And I don't want to go through the rest of my life like *this*. But from the moment I walked away from you, I haven't even *seen* other women. Hell, before I even left, it'd been...weeks since I'd taken anyone to my bed."

"You still slept with them," she said unsteadily, "after...after we realized what we were. What we are..."

"I know." He exhaled a ragged breath and grimaced like a man in physical pain. "I tried like hell to ignore it, Sayre. To prove I didn't need you. That I could keep going the way I always have, doing the same things to cope."

"To cope?"

He shook his head as he looked away. "Never mind."

"No! No more freaking secrets. Or I walk."

"Fine. It was how I coped with the bloodlust," he growled, pacing away from her. His heavy boots were loud against the bedroom's hardwood floor, his hard-edged muscles rippling with power beneath his blood-stained skin. "The constant fucking—it was either *that* or keep feeding the monster inside me and stop aging. And I didn't want that. I wanted to live here, with the others. So I screwed my way through the pack and kept that twisted part of me at bay as best as I could."

"And after you left?" she whispered, her thoughts reeling so rapidly she had to reach out and brace her hand against the bookshelf.

"I've been feeding on supplies of human blood that I purchase on the black market. It's why I don't look as though I've aged, because I haven't. Not since I came back for you."

"And the blood worked?"

"When I've needed it," he muttered as he lifted one of his powerful arms and rubbed the back of his neck, the position causing his beautiful biceps to bulge. "For the most part, I've been...I don't know. Dead inside. I've felt nothing." He flicked her a shuttered look from beneath his lashes. "Nothing but the need for you."

She wanted to ask how he dealt with that need without going crazy, then blushed as she figured she already knew the answer, considering how she'd had to take matters into her own hands over the years. Not that her self-made orgasms were anything to brag about, compared to how Cian could make her feel. As if he'd read her mind, he arched one of those dark brows as he looked at her, and the corner of his grim mouth actually twitched.

Needing to put the conversation onto a different subject, before she embarrassed herself, she blurted, "I'm sorry for what Jillian did last night. She finally fessed up before I snuck away today. I honestly wasn't running. I just…I needed some time to myself to think, and then I…well, I ran into your brother."

He stopped pacing and took a step closer to her. "Promise me you won't do that again, Sayre."

"Yes, of course. I understand now. I…I don't think I really did before," she admitted in a nervous rush, wetting her lips. "Aside from those humans you killed at the cabin, I guess the threat didn't feel as real to me as it should have. But it does now."

His brows lowered over his sharp, steely gaze, and he took another step closer to where she stood. "And the thing with Jillian? You're not angry…about your powers?"

"Cian, that's *my* problem, not yours. And, anyway, I have enough things to be pissed at you about without throwing *that* on there."

He grimaced, until he caught the way she was smirking at him. "Smart-ass."

"In all honesty, I already suspected you were the reason."

He looked surprised. "You did?"

Nodding, she said, "I started feeling different the morning after you left. And from that point on, each day got a little worse. I'd hoped I was wrong, but I think that deep down, I always knew the truth."

"Christ, Sayre. I'm so damn sorry," he groaned, and the next thing she knew, he was right in front of her. His hands pushed their way into her hair, and then he claimed her lips with his, ravaging her mouth like he was trying to brand her with his need. The carnal, devastating kiss was heated and hungry, demanding everything she had to give, his slick tongue rubbing against hers in a way that was guaranteed to melt her down. But no matter how tempting it was, she couldn't let him distract her from what was important.

"Why did you do what you did?" she gasped against his mouth. Her trembling hands curled around his strong wrists as he held the sides of her head in his hands, the masculine sprinkling of dark hair tickling her skin.

With a serrated groan, he broke away from the kiss and pressed his forehead to hers. "Because I can't lose you. Not like that. I can't let him hurt you. I'd rather die."

"If you really feel like that—if you would be willing to *die* for me, Cian—then why are you fighting this? Why not just claim me?"

"Because I'm bad for you, little witch."

She moved her hands to his broad, muscular shoulders and pushed until he finally relented and pulled his head back to look at her. "Do you really believe that?" she asked him, staring into those smoldering, tormented eyes.

A gritty, bitter laugh burst past his lips. "Ask anyone who knows me and they'll tell you the same thing."

"I'm not interested in what anyone else has to say, Cian. I only care about what I feel and see. And I *see* the good in you. The more time I spend with you, the deeper I see it."

"You're seeing what you want," he muttered.

"No," she argued, willing him to believe her. "I want *you*. Not some fairy-tale prince. You're not perfect, and I don't care. I'm not perfect, either. But together, I think we might be. If you would just give it a chance," she finished softly, keenly aware that she'd just made herself incredibly vulnerable—but believing he was worth it. Worth fighting for.

"You deserve more than that," he grunted. "More than me."

She blinked up at him, giving him a shaky smile. "More than a life spent with the only man I'm meant to be with? More than the promise of a family with that man?"

His scowl deepened. "Use your head, Sayre. You know exactly what kind of family we would have."

She flinched, feeling as if he'd just slapped her, and pushed away from him. "If you think I wouldn't love and adore my children, no matter their breed, then it just goes to show that you really don't know me at all, Cian."

"Sayre," he sighed, "that's not what I meant."

"Isn't it?"

"No," he muttered, shoving his hand back through his hair again in a telling gesture of frustration. "I just...I don't want to screw things up for you."

"And what about you?"

"Lass, my life was screwed to hell and back a long time ago. And no one is to blame for that but *me*. You said so yourself, when I found you in West Virginia."

God, he frustrated her! "Cian, I was wrong. When I said it was your fault that I was in trouble, I was angry. And I was *wrong*. It's not. You're not responsible for what your brother does."

"Like hell I'm not." They were raw, graveled words. "I should have ended him a long time ago, when I had the chance. But I chose not to—I chose *wrong*—and now his actions are a result of that choice. Of that mistake."

"You know what, Cian? It's time for you to shut up."

"Sayre."

She glared up at him as she stepped back into his body, then reached up and curved her hands back over those broad, rugged shoulders. "I'm serious. Your words are just pissing me off, and I'd rather kiss you than listen to you put yourself down." Then she tugged him down as she rose up on her toes, and kissed him like she was going to die without his taste in her mouth.

He shuddered, then wrapped those strong arms around her, jerking her even closer as he thrust his way past her lips and raked the inside of her mouth with his wicked tongue. She opened her mouth wider, wanting to take in even more of him, desperate for all of him, body and soul. She didn't even care that her busted lip was stinging like a bitch, her desire for him burning through her like a wild, rushing flame, her power breaking free in a shimmering burst of those tiny, flickering points of light.

"God, your mouth is so damn sweet," he groaned against her lips, and she could feel the emotions burning in those husky words, the hunger and need and craving that went deeper than the physical, and it made her want to shake him until she could get to the truth. But she was too busy trying to open his jeans so she could get to even more of him, while he literally tore her clothes off her body, her underwear shredding beneath his hands as he pushed her back onto the bed. Everything was moving hard and fast and furious, their harsh breaths filling the air as he shoved her to the middle of the bed and came down over her, that hot, slick tongue curling around one of her sensitive nipples, the sensation so intense it made her toes curl. He gave the same attention to the other breast, sucking on her nipple like it was a juicy piece of fruit, then turned her to her stomach, moved the fall of her hair to the side and latched that talented mouth on to the owl she had tattooed there.

She hadn't thought that particular patch of skin between her shoulder blades would be an erogenous zone, but boy, had she been wrong.

She trembled, gasping, her hands clawing on to the bedding, her blood pounding as he made a hard, thick sound deep in his throat and turned her over again, his mouth going straight for her belly this time.

"I need you in my mouth," he growled against her navel. He flicked the ink there with his tongue, then licked at a patch of skin just beneath it. "Need to taste you so fucking badly, Sayre. Can I?"

Instead of giving him a verbal response, she simply pushed hard on those mouthwatering shoulders and spread her thighs as wide as she could, holding her breath with anticipation of his tongue touching that most private part of her. But it didn't. Instead, she felt his soft, warm lips brush against the tiny symbol she had tattooed high on her inner thigh.

"A beautiful little Celtic cross. For Ireland," he murmured, and she knew that what he really meant was *for me*. And he was right. It had been for him. A way for her to carry him with her, even when she'd so badly wanted to hate him, but couldn't. Her dark, tortured Irishman. So eager for connection, though he would never admit it.

"It's fitting," he said huskily, "seeing as how this part of you is like my own personal holy ground."

She was still laughing softly when he turned his head and pressed his open mouth right over the hot, drenched center of her sex, her laughter choking off into a breathless gasp. *Oh...oh, wow.* That was seriously mind-blowing. Bone-melting. He pushed his face into her, his tongue and lips everywhere, going at her with an aggressive, unapologetic hunger that felt so freaking good she could have cried, the guttural groans that he gave making it sound like he was feasting on something lush and sweet. Something he couldn't get enough of, as if he'd been starved for the taste of her.

Though Sayre had fantasized about this moment an embarrassing number of times, she'd had no idea it would be like *this*. That he would spend so much time with his dark head buried between her thighs, pulling pleasure from her writhing body as if it were *his* to control. His shoulders kept her spread wide and his thumbs held her tender folds open as he did things that would have shocked the hell out of her, if she hadn't discovered a love of steamy romance novels. She'd thought, given her extensive reading, that she had a good handle on what this would feel like. But the heroes in her books didn't have anything on Cian.

It wasn't just his skill, though the man was clearly incredible at it, every part of him made for sin. But even more than that, it was the way he didn't try to hide how badly he needed it, letting her feel every bit of his hunger. A craving that was as visceral and primitive as the animal that lived inside him. He moved his tongue inside her body like he might die if he didn't get *more* of her, his mouth nothing less than voracious as he licked and sucked at her slippery flesh, consuming her. Driving her out of her mind with pleasure. And then she was coming in a hot, mind-shattering rush, hoarse cries spilling from her lips as she trembled and pulsed, melting against his mouth in wave after wave of release, while he growled dirty things against her sensitive flesh, telling her how perfect she tasted. How he couldn't get enough of her. How he wanted her to keep coming for him...harder and deeper and wetter. And so she did. Over...and over...until she was as boneless as a rag doll, arms and legs flung wide, her head foggy, thoughts drifting somewhere out there in a glittering, throbbing darkness.

She didn't know how many minutes had passed by the time she finally came back to herself. He was still nuzzling her with his open mouth, lapping at her with his tongue, the sounds he made telling her how much he was enjoying himself. And while it was incredibly lovely, she was eager for her chance to return the favor, her mouth watering at the thought of getting that thick, beautiful part of him between her lips.

"What are you doing?" he growled, locking his gaze with hers when she sat up and pushed against his shoulders, shoving him to his back. She quickly moved to kneel between his thighs, wishing she'd gotten the jeans off him as she flicked her gaze up. Her breath caught when she found him watching her with a hot, heavy-lidded stare, his mouth and chin glistening with her juices.

"Don't even think about stopping me," she told him, tugging the waist of his jeans down enough that she could curl her hands around that thick, steely shaft, the head so ripe and succulent looking she couldn't wait to get her first taste. "This is *mine*."

Something hot and wicked flared in his eyes as she made that pronouncement, and she knew she had him.

"You want me in your mouth?" he asked in a graveled voice, licking his slick lower lip as he braced his upper body on his elbows, looking so freaking sexy it was unreal.

Desperate for him, she answered the question with actions instead of words, as she leaned down and covered the broad, wet tip of him with her mouth and swiped at his hot flesh with her tongue. Flicking her eyes up again, she caught him watching her from beneath the thick black fringe of his lashes, his color high, marking the sharp crests of his cheekbones, his sensual lips parted for his ragged breaths. In that instant, she realized that she could so easily get addicted to this. To the raw intimacy of the act, and how right it felt as she started to suck on him, taking him deeper while she stroked the bottom inches of his shaft with her hand, knowing she was making the most powerful male she'd ever known tremble with need. Her senses were in overdrive, her body vibrating with a fine tremor as she tried to soak in every part of him, from his warm, musky scent, to the salty, exquisite taste that sat on her tongue like that was where it belonged.

"Finish me," he growled, keeping his head lifted as he dropped down to his back, his eyes glowing like bright chips of molten silver.

"With my hands?" She whispered the words against the very tip of him, laving the moist flesh with her tongue. She knew exactly how much he liked it by the way he gasped, the muscles in his abdomen rippling as his fingers speared hard into her hair, clutching her to him. "Or with my mouth?"

"Christ," he hissed, his expression so intense it was almost a scowl. "Are you trying to make me crazed?"

"No. You just make me hungry."

He stilled, holding his breath. "For what?"

"Everything," she whispered, letting her lips rub against the hot, sensitive crown, the thick shaft throbbing in her hands. "All of it. I want to crawl inside your head and live in your thoughts. Taste your emotions. Feel your pleasure."

"You *are* my pleasure," he growled, the tendons in his strong, corded throat straining beneath his skin.

"Then *show* me," she told him, taking the succulent head between her lips again, ignoring the sting of pain from where Aedan had struck her when she'd tried to get away from him. Forcing that dark thought from her head, she focused on *her* male, making her mouth as hungry and as wet as she could for him, greedy for his release as her hands stroked the broad inches she couldn't reach. She loved his raw, gritty curses and the way he gripped her hair as he got close, but she was *crazy* for the way he shuddered and shouted when he came, his feet planted flat on the bed, hips pumping as she stayed with him, doing everything she could to make it good for him.

When she finally lifted her head, he grasped her by the arms and hauled her up over his chest, surprising her with the way he took her mouth, kissing her as if he would go mad without the touch of her tongue against his, their mouths moving together as they fought for a deeper angle, a deeper way to taste—until he suddenly made a sharp, guttural sound deep in his chest. Before she could react, he quickly rolled her onto her back, his big body caging hers in as he braced himself over her on all fours.

She started to ask him what the hell was wrong, only to break off with another gasp when she saw the fresh smear of blood on his mouth from her bleeding lip. It was clear from the way he'd reacted that the taste of her blood had been a shock to him, the way he was taking such deep, rough breaths and eyeing her mouth telling her he was still struggling to get himself under control.

Then he slid her a dark, glittering look from beneath his thick lashes, and there was a...a *precision* to the way he was watching her that told her he was up to something. That his clever mind had just come up with an idea...

or a plan of some sort. One he had no intention of sharing, judging by the hard cast to his masculine features.

"Cian," she whispered, her eyes going wide as he moved his hand to her face and pressed the pad of his thumb to the cut on her lip. Then he trailed the crimson-stained pad down the front of her throat, over the hammering beat of her pulse at the base, and lower, trailing it between her quivering breasts. Wetting the pad with her blood again, he coated both her nipples, then traced his thumb around her navel, lower, down into the strawberry-blond curls on her mound.

When he was done, he snagged her heavy-lidded gaze and murmured, *"Trust me,"* as he leaned down and pressed his open mouth to her throat, his warm tongue lapping against her bloodstained skin.

"Oh, God," she moaned, shivering with poignant arousal. Watching his beautiful mouth follow the same path that his thumb had taken was the most erotic experience of her life, her power so charged it was literally arcing from her body in shimmering bolts of light. He took his time licking her sensitive skin, the thick sounds he made in the back of his throat telling her how much he loved it. Especially when he'd followed the crimson path right into her curls, and lower, his mouth just as ravenous as he'd been before, making her come twice before he suddenly lifted his head and jerked away from her, crouching on all fours at the foot of the bed.

"Cian?" she whispered, moving to her knees so that she could reach out to him, his tortured expression tearing at her heart. "What's wrong?"

"I don't care if you want to or not," he groaned between his harsh breaths, his hands fisting the bedding as he lowered his head, hiding from her gaze. "I just need you to listen to me, Sayre, and I need you to do as I say.

Get dressed and get the hell out of this room. Then...run as fast as you can."

"What?"

"Go to Jillian and Jeremy's." He lifted his head, and she gasped when she saw that his eyes had turned completely crimson again. "Run, Sayre. Now!"

"No," she breathed out, unwilling to leave him.

"Goddamn it, woman! Get the fuck out of here!"

She shook her head, and he curled in on himself, shuddering so hard it looked painful, every hard, powerful muscle in his magnificent body coiled tight beneath his damp skin.

Careful not to make any sudden movements, Sayre shifted closer to him. "I'm not afraid of you, Cian. Please, let me help you."

He ground his forehead against the bed and groaned like a man in agony. "Christ, you're impossible."

"I don't mean to be," she said softly, carefully inching her way closer. "I simply care about you too much to run away from you when you need me."

He shivered like someone with a raging fever. "Even when the things I need aren't something I deserve?"

"I don't think you get to make that decision."

A raw, fractured sound tore from his throat, muffled against the bedding. "Damn it, lass, I'm trying to do right by you."

"Hmm. Have you ever thought that maybe you should just *do me* instead?"

"Don't!" he barked, breathing in rough, uneven bursts. "Christ, don't do that. Don't flirt with me right now. I can't take it."

"Then just let me comfort you," she murmured, reaching out and stroking his broad back with a gentle touch. They stayed like that for untold minutes, until his breathing had finally slowed and his body was no longer gripped in that terrible tension. He rolled to his side and let her put a pillow under his head, his expression still strained, though his eyes had returned to their natural silver.

When she laid down beside him and rested her cheek on her bent arm, he reached out and stroked his hand over her hair. Then he wrapped his arm around her and yanked her against him, tucking her head under his chin as he threw his long leg over hers. Burying his face against the top of her head, he spoke in a low, husky tone that was so solemn it made tears burn at the back of her throat. "No matter what happens, my biggest regret will always be that I wasn't able to claim you as *mine*."

Clutching on to him with desperate hands, Sayre had to fight back the urge to shout at him to open his damn eyes, look in a mirror and *see* the truth she could have sworn burned in that silver gaze every single time he looked at her. But what good would come of it? He wouldn't see the truth until he was ready. Until he finally allowed himself to move on from the past and was ready to fight for his future. To fight for *her*. Not in the way that he was fighting to protect her from Aedan, but for her heart. For the future she prayed they could have one day. That she so desperately wanted.

But there was no guarantee that he would ever reach that point—and she no longer knew if she could continue to play it safe. Doing so went against everything her instincts were telling her to do. She might have started out hiding behind her emotional armor, afraid of the damage he could leave behind—but she understood him better now. The damage was already done, which meant it was time to go all in or go home. And she didn't have a home without him.

She wanted Cian. The wolf, the vampire and whoever else he might have living inside of him. She didn't care, she simply wanted them all.

She wanted *her* man.

Chapter 15

Twenty-seven hours later...

Pure green, for as far as his eyes could see. That was what always caught Cian off guard when he came back to the land where he'd been born. The deep, vibrant green.

Would look incredible against Sayre's golden red hair, his beast murmured, its guttural voice as dejected as his own. He kept having to blink goddamn moisture out of his eyes, so what the hell was that about? He'd never cried in his life, and now *this*. He felt like he was in a sappy romance flick. And it didn't help that he'd spent the entire seven-hour flight across the Atlantic poring over all *The Green Witch* videos that he'd downloaded onto his phone before leaving, still marveling at what Sayre had achieved at such a young age, and completely on her own. He was so damn proud of her there weren't even words to express it.

And he missed her so much it was killing him, each moment that took him farther away from her cutting him like a blade.

Though it'd been the hardest thing he'd ever done, Cian had left her sleeping beneath the covers just after the sun had set, and gone to speak with Brody, pulling the Runner away from his dinner. Hating that he hadn't been able to tell her goodbye, he'd been in a grim, miserable state as he told Brody that he'd devised a plan for dealing with Aedan, and would need his promise to keep Sayre under heavy lockdown, whether she wanted it or not, as soon as he was gone.

Then he'd climbed in the Audi and left her. Again. Only this time had been a thousand times worse than before, because he damn well *knew* what he was leaving behind.

As he'd held the witch in his arms after she'd fallen asleep, Cian had finally started to understand what they'd been doing. How they'd both been navigating a minefield of emotion, both gut-wrenchingly terrified of getting hurt...and so determined to protect themselves, they were living in lies and half-truths.

At least he was. He had been for...God, for too many years to count.

And with that stunning realization came another one that would have taken his damn legs out from under him, if he hadn't already been lying down. One he still couldn't think about without feeling like the biggest idiot on the face of the planet. All these years since he'd discovered the truth about his old man, he'd always been convinced he *couldn't* love because he was too much like him. Because he carried his blood in his veins, and had done so many wrongs. But the truth was that he was too afraid of being vulnerable, just like his mother. Of giving his love to someone who didn't love him in return, and ending up completely destroyed.

He'd wanted to stay there in that bed with Sayre, and keep working these stunning revelations through his mind, feeling like a man who'd always been blind suddenly discovering the gift of sight. But as always, the timing hadn't been right. He'd been forced to leave her, and yeah, he knew how she must be feeling about that. No doubt cursing him to hell and back for walking away from her all over again.

That seemed to be another constant, the way that doing the right thing always made him a massive dick. Maybe that's what he should ask them to put on his tombstone. Then again, maybe not. He could just imagine the questionable array of "objects" that would be left on his grave as mementos.

Though that last thought made him snicker, the quiet burst of laughter quickly died as he steered his Range Rover onto the winding country road that would take him to Killian's Mount, the seaside estate where he'd grown up. Despite the fact that the sun was still shining, he was nothing but a cold, aching shell, every cell of his body suffering from withdrawal.

But nothing about the way he was feeling changed anything. In fact, it only made him more determined to follow his current course of action.

An alive and kicking Aedan Hennessey meant that Sayre would never be safe.

So Aedan had to die. As soon as possible. By *whatever* means necessary.

It was as simple as that.

Stopping at his first destination, an overgrown-with-ivy cottage that sat on the edge of his father's land, Cian went inside and set his plan in motion. Within minutes, he was back in the Range Rover and driving toward the main house, the salty scent of the sea crashing against the nearby craggy cliffs clinging to his hair and clothes.

More cottages had been added to the estate since he'd last visited, but it didn't surprise him. His old man had never managed the art of self-control when he'd been younger, and he obviously wasn't any closer now. God only knew how many half siblings Cian had within the borders of the estate. Aedan might have been the first of his father's illegitimate children, but he was hardly the last.

He was also the only one that Cian had claimed. A mistake he wished more than anything he could go back and change.

By the time he was climbing the stone steps leading up to the front door of his father's palatial home, he had his teeth clenched so hard he was surprised they hadn't cracked. He didn't bother to knock—simply let himself in, and hoped like hell that the bastard took offence at it. Pissing off his old man was one of his favorite pastimes— though it didn't come anywhere close to spending time with Sayre, or kissing Sayre, or making the beautiful little witch come so hard she screamed. Hell, *anything* that involved Sayre topped his list of favorites. Even when she was frustrating him to the point of tears, his life was better than it had ever been without her. And he knew, without any doubt, that particular little fact wasn't ever going to change.

For the first time ever, Cian was actually letting himself be happy about it. Was embracing the hell out of it, and holding on as tightly as he could, ready to fight for it with everything that he had.

As he made his way through the sunlit halls, it didn't take him long to track down the object of his visit. He found his father in the library, sitting in a heavy leather chair by the far wall of windows, a book on his lap. Colin Hennessey was a big, robust man who looked no more than fifty, and Cian had definitely inherited his father's height and his broad shoulders. Everything else, thank God, he'd taken from his mother. Her coloring. Her eyes. He was grateful for each and every trait that she'd passed on to him, wanting to see as little of this jackass as he had to when he looked in a mirror.

"Father," he murmured, crossing his arms over his chest as he propped his shoulder against the door frame. "I wish I could say it's good to see you, but we both know that would be a lie."

Colin sighed heavily as he set aside the book he'd been reading, and it was clear that he was unsurprised to see Cian standing there. But then, he knew one of his father's security detail had no doubt notified him the instant he'd driven onto the property. Steepling his fingers together as he rested his elbows on the padded arms of the chair, Colin said, "Still angry, I see."

Cian slowly lifted his brows. "Did you honestly expect a hug?"

Exhaling a tired breath, Colin replied with a question of his own. "How long are you going to make me pay for a sin that you know I'm sorry for?"

"I don't care if you're sorry," he said tightly. "I could have forgiven you for anything but breaking her. Betraying her. So your answer is forever. Any love or respect or care I held for you died the day I realized what a miserable excuse of a man you are."

"You hold me to your standards, but I'm not a Lycan, Cian. I'm part man, part darkness, and you don't know how impossible Alice was to resist."

"Don't. I know exactly how easily you fell into bed

with Aedan's mother. And she was simply the first of many."

Colin frowned. "I'm not like you," he repeated.

"If you'd loved your wife, you would have been true to her. You wouldn't have wasted your time on trash."

"Damn it, I *did* love her."

A gruff, bitter laugh jerked from his chest. "No, you didn't. You loved the way she made you feel. The way *her love* made you feel. Powerful. Strong. Worthy. But that was her mistake. She should have ran the instant she ever set eyes on you."

"Just because we never completed the blood bond doesn't mean she didn't belong with me. She was my wife, Cian! Her place was at my side!"

He shook his head, his tone thick with revulsion. "She always said you couldn't bond with her because of the darkness in your heart. The evil flowing through your veins. But I know differently. I know firsthand," he growled through his gritted teeth. "You. Lied."

Leaning forward in his chair, his father gave him a penetrating look. "You're not bonded. I would be able to tell."

"You're right, I'm not. But not because I *can't*." No, he knew damn well that if he'd lived his life differently, he would have already claimed the hell out of Sayre Murphy and forged a bond with her that was more powerful than anything their world had ever seen. "I haven't bonded with my woman yet, because unlike you, I'm willing to put her first."

Colin's thick brows rose. "And is that why you're here? Because you're putting her first?"

"I'm here because I'm ending this thing between Aedan and me once and for all. This is where it began, and this is where it will end."

Those thick brows pulled together in a frown. "You really intend to kill your own brother?"

Shaking his head again, he said, "The monster walking around with Aedan's face isn't my brother. The boy we both loved was lost a long time ago. There's nothing of Aedan left in him."

Colin's chest lifted with a deep breath, the look in his dark eyes almost painfully piercing. "I know you blame me for not helping you before."

"I blame you for a hell of a lot more than that. But I'm not here to ask for your help. The only purpose of this visit is to make my position clear. I *will* fight Aedan to the death when he comes, and I *will* kill anyone who tries to stand in my way. *Anyone.* So if you want your bloody family safe, tell them to stay the hell away from me."

He pushed off from the door frame and started to turn away, when Colin's next words stopped him. "I…I made a mistake." At Cian's look of disgust, Colin grimaced. "All right, *many* mistakes. We've already been over this, but your mother—what I did to her—is the greatest of my failures. I had something…something unique, and I tossed it away for what amounted to nothing."

Cian narrowed his eyes. "If you knew what you had to lose, then why did you do it?"

"Because I was…" He paused to clear his throat, and then went on, looking as if the gruff words were being torn out of him against his will. "I didn't handle the things she made feel at all well. After you were born, those feelings grew. And she was somehow even more beautiful. More precious to me. I didn't know how to embrace that, and it wasn't long before I started to resent the pull that she had on me."

"That's why she could never bond with you," he muttered, his insides churning. "What you felt for her, you never allowed it to take hold. You fought it every step of the way. But you were too selfish to let her walk away and be happy without you."

Colin gave a weary nod, and for the first time that he could remember, his father actually looked his age. He looked old. Hollow.

"And your loyalty to Aedan?" Cian asked. "How do you explain that?"

Sighing, Colin said, "Despite what he became, he's still my son."

"Not for long," he grunted, turning away again.

"By the way," Colin called out, "I have the bachelor's house ready for you, and your guests are in the lodge."

Stopping dead in his tracks, Cian slowly turned back around, his hooded gaze locking with his father's through the open doorway. "My *what*?" he asked in a low, ominous tone.

Studying him with a deep, measuring stare, Colin said, "Your guests."

"Aw, fuck!"

Without another word, Cian turned and slammed out of the house, stalking across the lush lawn as he headed toward the massive stone-and-timber lodge that sat near a thicket of trees. Fear sat in the back of his throat like something threatening to choke him and his pulse thrashed in his ears like the straining roar of an engine. He knew exactly who his goddamn *guests* were, and he was furious that he hadn't guessed they would do something this outrageous. God only knew how long they'd been here waiting for him. His trip had taken longer than usual because he'd flown directly into Dublin so that he could stop by his apartment and arrange to have his things packed and ready to ship out, once he provided the moving company with an address. He knew where he *hoped* he would be going after this nightmare was over, but he wasn't going to presume until things were settled. He just knew he wasn't going to keep hiding in Dublin, pretending his entire world wasn't back in Maryland.

You know damn well where we're going, his beast rumbled. *If we have to camp on her doorstep until she gives in, we're going back. Going after the girl!*

"Yeah, well, the bloody girl is already here," he bit out, catching Sayre's mouthwatering scent as he neared the lodge.

Oh, hell no. I'm putting her over our knee for this and swatting her little ass!

"Not if I do it first," he snarled, throwing the front door of the lodge open and letting out a thunderous roar. *"Sayre!"*

A group of people walked into the high-ceilinged entryway from various rooms, and his jaw clenched as he took them all in. The mercs must have been handling things back at the Alley, because nearly everyone else was standing in front of him. All the Runners and most of their mates. Even Max and Elliot were there.

But there wasn't any sign of Sayre.

Scraping the words from his tight throat, he demanded, "What the hell are you all doing here?"

Jillian came toward him, and for a split second, he thought she was going to slap him again. But she didn't. Instead, she shocked ten years off his life when she threw her arms around his middle and hugged him so damn tightly he could barely breathe.

"Uh…"

Tilting her head back, she looked up at him and said, "You left before I got the chance to talk to you."

His right eyebrow slowly lifted. "You came an awfully long way for the two of us to talk, lass. You could have just used my number."

She smirked, the spark in her brown eyes telling him that she'd figured something out. He just didn't know what it was.

"Jillian, what's going on?"

She gave him another hard squeeze, then let him go and moved back to Jeremy's side, before she said, "I knew I couldn't have been as wrong about you as it seemed."

As relieved as he was that Jillian no longer looked like she wanted to kill him, he needed to find Sayre. Cutting a sharp look toward Jeremy, he growled, "Where's Sayre? And for the second time, what the hell are you all doing here?"

"What do you think we're doing here?" Jillian asked, looking at him as if he were being ridiculous.

He tried to catch Brody's eye, but the Runner was purposefully avoiding his gaze. The bastard. Cian knew that Brody had told them all where he was headed, even though he'd asked the Runner not to say anything until he'd contacted him.

And if he hadn't heard from him by the end of the week, well...he'd given the Runner strict instructions on what he wanted to happen then.

Struggling for patience, he cast another frustrated look over the group. "Would someone *please* tell me what the hell is going on?"

Eli Drake, who was mated to the only female Runner, muttered something under his breath that sounded like *stubborn jackass*, but it was Cian's old friend Wyatt Pallaton who finally took mercy on him. "We're here to help you, man."

"I don't need anyone's bloody help," he argued. "I have a plan."

Brody finally looked him right in the eye and snorted. "You have an invitation to the psycho to come and face you, knowing damn well he's going to be foaming at the mouth. But you don't have the answer." His partner's green eyes narrowed with suspicion. "At least not one that you've shared with the rest of us."

"I know what I'm doing. That's all you need to know."

"What the hell, Cian? You never used to be this stupid," the Runner yelled, taking an aggressive step forward. "You really think that's how we're going to let this play out?"

"You aren't letting anything happen one way or another. This is *my* fight."

"That doesn't mean we can't be here to support you," Mason said, speaking up for the first time.

Cian rubbed his tongue over his front teeth and seethed with frustration, a goddamn red haze falling over his eyes as he snarled, "You're not doing jack shit but getting in my way."

"Even me?"

He flinched, that soft voice dragging his gaze up to the top of the stairs at the back of the entryway. And there she was. Sayre. Dressed in jeans, sandals and a summery white blouse, she kept those storm-dark eyes locked tight on his as she walked down the stairs, the group parting to make way for her as she came toward him. She was so beautiful to his starved senses, he didn't know how to take it all in. Luminous skin, fiery hair in a wave of curls that fell around her heart-shaped face. Those eyes…her pink, glossy mouth…and that pale, tender throat that he wanted to bite so badly it was a physical pain that ripped through his insides and twisted him into knots.

"We'll let you two have some time alone," Mason told him, "but you need to know that we're not going anywhere, Cian. Jeremy and Brody have been keeping us updated on what was happening, and we wanted to be there. The only reason we stayed away was because we didn't want to make things harder for Sayre. But we're here to stay for as long as you need us."

The group filed out then, going back to whatever they'd been doing before he barged in, and he found himself standing alone with Sayre.

"Baby," he breathed, shaking with fear and anger and too many other explosive emotions to put a name to. "I can't believe you're here."

Crossing her arms over her chest, she arched one of her golden brows and smirked. "Did you really think I was going to let you bring me back to this crazy bunch and then just let you leave me? That hardly seems fair, Cian."

"Who the hell cares about what's fair? You have no reason to give a fuck what I do. I left you. *Again*, Sayre. As far as you know, we're over."

Instead of bursting into tears, she looked like she was fighting back a grin, her big eyes shimmering with humor. "Yeah, that's not really going to work for me."

"S-aa-y-re," he growled, drawing her name out with a healthy dose of frustration.

Trapping him in that smoldering, breathtaking gaze, she said, "You've got some weird hang-up about your past and your jerk-face of a father, and that's fine. I get it. But I'm not willing to give up our future because of it."

"You're being unreason—"

"Why?" she asked, cutting him off. "Because I refuse to let you go? If I really thought that was what you wanted, then I would." Taking a step closer to him, she lowered her arms and straightened her spine, looking like a regal little goddess as she faced him down. "So go ahead, Cian. Look me in the eye, right now, and tell me you don't want me."

"It's not that simple," he snapped.

She lifted her chin, her sharp gaze burning with determination. "Tell. Me."

He opened his mouth, but couldn't force the words out.

She waited, her breath held, and then her gaze softened, the corner of her lush mouth tipping up in a heartbreaking smile of relief. "I knew it. I knew I couldn't be completely alone in this. Fate isn't *that* cruel."

"You might not feel that way when this is all said and done," he muttered, knowing there was no way in hell he could stay away from her now, and wondering if she were truly ready for him. For what he'd want from her. He'd missed her more with each second that went by since he'd walked away, and now…damn it, he was done. "God, Sayre. You have no idea how badly I want you."

"That's why you don't get to touch me until it's over," she told him, her voice dropping to a soft, provocative murmur.

"Wait. *What?*"

Her big eyes were beginning to sparkle with mischief. "You need incentive, Cian. Beat Aedan's ass down when he shows his ugly face, and then you can you do whatever you want to me. We're talking a completely open menu. I'm ready for your A game, big guy."

"Jesus," he hissed under his breath, squeezing his eyes shut as he covered them with his hand. If he'd ever been this painfully hard before, he'd blocked it from his memory. "Have you lost your friggin' mind?" he growled.

"Nope," she replied, popping the *p*. "But I've finally found my backbone. I thought that to be strong, I had to hold myself back from you. From what I wanted. But that isn't strength. That was nothing but fear. And fear doesn't have any place between two people like us."

Lowering his hand, he opened his eyes, needing to see her more than he needed to hide. "And what kind of people are those?" he rasped, forcing the words from his tight throat.

"Ones who *belong* to each other. Who *need* each other." Her lips trembled, then curved into a sexy, breathtaking smile. "Ones who are ready to spend the rest of their lives, every day and night, getting lost in each other."

"Christ," he groaned. "You're wrecking me, baby."

Unable to wait a moment longer to have her in his arms, he started toward her, but she held up her hands and said, "Stop right there, Cian."

He exhaled a sharp breath. "Damn it, Sayre. I *need* you."

She kept that beautiful, luminous gaze locked tight on his. "I need you, too. But I need *all* of you, not just the parts that you're willing to share with me."

"I'm using everything I have to protect you, lass. *Everything.*"

"But you're not *giving* me everything."

He couldn't believe she was being this stubborn. "I *can't.* Not yet."

Taking a step back from him, she said, "Then I guess we're at a stalemate. Because until you share your soul with me, Cian, I can't share my body. And no, before you look at me like that, it's not because I don't want you to see what's inside me. All you have to do is look at me to know that I love you. That I'm *in love* with you. So, so much."

He shuddered, unable to believe what he was hearing. Yeah, he'd known that she lusted for him—but he'd been too goddamn terrified to let himself believe that she might already be in love with him. And while it was what he wanted most, he couldn't accept it. Not now, when God only knew what would happen when he faced off against Aedan.

So he forced himself to bite out a foul-tasting response. "You shouldn't."

"Shouldn't what? Tell you? Love you?"

"Yes! Damn it, I don't deserve it," he snapped, feeling the weight of his old self-loathing climbing over his back like a clinging demon. He wanted to shake off that fucker, but he didn't know how.

"*I* deserve it, Cian. I deserve *you*."

"You have no idea how badly I wish that was true. But you deserve a hell of a lot better than me."

"Stop!" she shouted, and he knew she was pissed when those sparks started pinging around in the air. "I won't listen to you talk about yourself that way."

"Sayre."

"No, just stop it, Cian. I'm so sick of hearing crap like that. No more. You don't get to keep spouting that same old bullshit. It's *done*. Do you understand me?"

"I...*fuck*."

Bright eyes flashing with anger, she said, "You either believe that we belong together or you don't. And if you don't, then it's already over. All of it. You won't walk away from this thing with Aedan if you don't believe."

He froze, something in her tone telling him that she was keeping a secret. "What is it, Sayre? What aren't you telling me?"

She quickly tore her gaze from his, but not before he'd seen the confirmation in her eyes. Already turning away from him, she said, "Goodbye, Cian. I'll see you tomorrow."

He got it then, figuring that she must have had a vision—a moment of insight where she saw into the future. He didn't know if it'd ever happened that way for her before, but if any witch were strong enough for a premonition, it was this one. *His* witch. "Damn it, Sayre, what did you see?"

Still making her way toward the stairs, he could have sworn there was a smile in her voice as she said, "Sleep tight tonight. I wouldn't want you to tire yourself out with a bunch of dirty dreams about everything you're planning on doing to me. An old guy like you needs his rest."

Torn between wanting to kiss the hell out of her smart-ass little mouth and the sudden urge to put her over his goddamn knee, he growled, "Get back here!"

"Can't," she said over her shoulder. "And just so you know, the next time you touch me, this *is* finally happening. I don't care if I have to tie your sexy ass up, you are *mine*."

For a moment, all he could do was watch her walk away from him, wondering what she'd done to him. How she'd so completely turned his entire world around until he didn't even know which way was up anymore. And then he heard himself say, "Sayre."

She watched him over her shoulder as she slowly made her way up the stairs. "Yeah?"

"You…" His voice trailed off, and he ran a shaky hand down his face before continuing. "You mean everything to me. If it all goes to shit tomorrow, I just want you to know that."

She stopped about halfway up the staircase and turned around, one hand gripping the railing as she stared down at him. "You know, you've spent so much time worrying about what I deserve, but what about you?"

He gave a hard swallow. "What about me?"

Her precious face was flushed with color, and her bright eyes gleamed. "What do *you* deserve, Cian? What do you *want* to deserve?"

"Just you," he managed to choke out in a husky rasp. "I want to deserve *you*."

She turned around again, but not before he caught the beautiful smile that touched her lips. "And nothing's going to go to shit," she called out, looking back over her shoulder to give him a wink. "Just get your head out of your ass and try not to do anything stupid tomorrow."

Crazy, beautiful, kick-ass little witch. God, she was going to be the death of him.

I just hope you don't mean that literally, his wolf grumbled, and he had to bite back a sharp bark of laughter, in complete agreement.

Grinning like an idiot, Cian watched the sway of her hips as she climbed the stairs for a few more seconds, then forced himself to turn and walk away, knowing damn well that he couldn't stay in the same building as Sayre and not be all over her. It struck him, then, like a physical force that knocked the smile right off his face, that he was always turning and walking away from her, when all he really wanted was to have her in his arms, holding her as close as possible.

But fate was always working against him, blocking his shot, and he was tired as hell of it. He was ready to teach that bastard a lesson and make him bleed.

Then he wanted to grab up the girl, bare his fangs in a vicious snarl to anyone who tried to get in his way and carry her off into the night.

He wanted his own goddamn happily-ever-after. And he wanted it *now*.

He just had to get rid of the bastard standing in his way.

And that meant that it was time for Aedan Hennessey to finally meet his maker in Hell.

Chapter 16

Cian had spent the entire day doing his best to avoid Sayre, knowing he needed to be sharp for when Aedan arrived. And now that time was almost here. A violent storm loomed out over the churning sea, keeping company with the crimson sun as it made its final dip beneath the horizon, while a million stars looked down from above, the sparks of light like curious eyes, eager to see what would happen.

He'd known his brother wouldn't make him wait long. As soon as Aedan sensed that Cian had taken Sayre's blood, he would have been driven mad with frenzy. Aside from the fact that she tasted like friggin' nirvana, sumptuous and hot and rich, *that* was the reason why Cian had licked her blood from her body the night he'd left the Alley. Because he'd known it would turn Aedan into his puppet, ensuring his brother followed after him like a faithful bloodhound. And with Sayre safely under lockdown in Maryland, there'd been no reason for Aedan to think she wasn't traveling with him. Cian had even purchased an extra ticket in her name for the flight, just in case his brother had checked.

But she wasn't under lockdown in the Alley. The headstrong girl had followed him to Ireland, putting everything he'd planned in jeopardy.

In fact, she was there with him now, standing at the far side of the cliff-top clearing, the Runners flanking her sides. She looked so insanely beautiful it was difficult not to stare, the golden glow of one of the swinging oil lamps that had been placed around the perimeter making the red in her hair burn like a flame.

The only bright spot in his day had been when Brody came to see him at the bachelor's house where Cian was staying, and handed him a flask of Sayre's blood. According to the grim-faced Runner, she'd wanted him to have something to drink for *luck*. Of course, there'd been the added benefit of how her blood affected him, hitting his system like a shot of pure, high-voltage adrenaline. He was ready for this fight, and knew it wouldn't be long now. Moments ago, Colin had received word that Aedan was nearing his land.

"I know why you chose this place to face him," his father called out, standing on the opposite side of the clearing from Sayre and the Runners, surrounded by a sprawling group of people who Cian refused to look at too closely, not wanting to see his same features staring back at him. "And I spoke with Simone this morning. I know what you bought from her."

"What's he talking about?" his friend Eric asked him, but Cian shook his head, making it clear he didn't want to talk or make explanations. He knew the Runner was asking about Simone, because Cian had already explained to Brody why it was imperative that he fight Aedan in Ireland, on their father's land. It had to do with a unique spell Colin had paid to have cast over the grounds decades ago. A spell that ensured Colin remained the dominant male by weakening the power of any other male once they set foot on Killian's Mount. He didn't see it having much effect on males as strong as he and Aedan were, but given his brother's physical power these days, Cian was willing to take any advantage he could get, no matter how slight.

And as for Simone—well, if things went badly, the Runners would learn soon enough what he'd purchased from the elderly witch the previous day, when he'd first arrived at his father's estate.

They waited another breathless span of seconds, while lightning thundered and crashed out over the violent sea, the winds so strong they whipped at people's clothing and lifted their hair, shaking the trees like invisible monsters. And then the monster they'd all been waiting for finally made his appearance.

"Are we having a party that no one told me about?" his brother drawled, moving so quickly that he seemed to have come out of nowhere and assuming a place not five yards from where Cian stood. He could hear the Runners talking in quiet, worried voices, since this was the first time they'd set eyes on Aedan. But Sayre remained silent, her steady gaze giving him strength.

Come on, you bastard, he thought. *Let's do this.*

He didn't bother to respond to Aedan's inane question, determined to get this nightmare over and done with as quickly as possible. Unlike the last time he'd seen his brother, tonight he was facing Aedan beneath the full light of the moon, and as he pulled in a deep breath of the sea-scented air, Cian gave himself over completely to its power, letting it call not only to his beast, but also to that dark well of strength he always kept so firmly locked inside him. Within seconds, his clothes had shredded as his body expanded in height and muscle mass, bones cracking and reshaping themselves into the predatory shape of a killer, his fangs dropping as his claws burst through the tips of his fingers. Even his face reshaped itself into the intimidating muzzle of a wolf, complete with razor-sharp teeth that could tear through flesh and bone like a knife slipping into warm butter. And instead of the fur that normally covered his body when he shifted, his skin darkened to a sinister blue-black, while his eyes changed from gray to crimson.

This was the first time the Runners had seen him in his "true" vampire-wolf form, and he could hear their collective sounds of surprise, as well as Brody's guttural *"What the ever-loving fuck?"*

Before he could give his former partner a hard time about his reaction, Aedan let out a vicious snarl, allowing his own transformation to take place. Long, sinister fangs dripped with saliva from beneath his thin upper lip, his talons curling longer around his fingers as his body turned that cadaverous shade of white again, his bones popping and extending until he was nearly Cian's height.

They waited for a heaving, weighted second, then bared their fangs and charged. Their bodies met in mid-air, slamming together with a brutal sound of flesh hitting flesh as they spun, twisting, delivering blows that had the night quickly smelling of blood. They'd traveled nearly twenty yards by the time they hit the ground, rolling dangerously close to the edge of the craggy cliffs. As they sprang to their feet, a lightning-fast kick to Cian's back sent him careening precariously close to the edge again. Aedan's maniacal laughter rang out, and from the far side of the clearing, he could hear the Runners shouting. Someone had apparently tried to join the fight to help him, only to realize that Colin had put a shield in place to keep everyone out until either he or Aedan had fallen.

"It will be a fair fight or there will be no fight at all," his father called out across the clearing, while he and Aedan circled each other, searching for a weakness.

A muttered collection of curses filled the air in response to Colin's words, and Brody sounded angry enough to shift into the shape of his beast then and there. "The vampire's a goddamn psycho! How the hell is that fair?"

"My sons are *both* strong," Colin responded, which made Aedan laugh.

"Aw, isn't that sweet, Cian? Dear ol' Daddy actually thinks you have a chance. What a fucking moron. You and I both know I'll be the one pounding inside your little witch tonight."

He snarled, and then they were at it again, fighting with a ferocity that brought constant gasps and curses from those around them. But their father simply watched in silence, standing tall and proud, as if he thought he was a god among men. Arrogant bastard.

When Cian looked back on this day, if he survived, he had a feeling he wouldn't recall the gruesome individual details. Instead, he would remember the spray of crimson that constantly filled his vision, the blood both his and Aedan's, while pain seared his system, burning him from the inside out. Dark, engulfing, savage waves of pain that came like the raging of the off-shore storm, hitting him one after another, until he couldn't even catch his breath.

As if she sensed that he was reaching the end, Sayre's power was unleashing with a force unlike anything he'd ever witnessed. Hawks and gulls swarmed overhead, their stark, constant cries echoing over the crashing sound of the waves, almost as though she'd called them to bear witness to her rage. But it wasn't just the animals falling under her spell—the tall trees that surrounded the clearing leaned eerily toward its perimeter, as if they'd been bent by a violent wind. Snakelike, meandering vines slithered across the ground, thumping repeatedly against the metaphysical shield that Colin had put in place.

She was desperately trying to reach him, her husky voice screaming in his head for him to keep fighting—but he knew if he didn't make his final move now, it would be too late. And there wasn't a chance in hell he was letting Aedan walk away from this, knowing the bastard would make Sayre suffer long and hard before he killed her.

"Tell me, brother," he panted, when they'd broken apart to gain their bearings after another brutal bout of combat. "Was your little Elizabeth really worth all of this?" he asked, deliberately taunting the monster as he carefully made his way toward the spiky patch of broken limbs and rotting tree trunks that sat clumped together at the eastern edge of the clearing. "Was she really worth all the hate? Because all I recall is a broken little girl who detested even the sound of your name. She didn't love you. She despised everything about you!"

Rising to the bait, Aedan let out a bloodcurdling roar and slammed into Cian so hard that it sent them both crashing to the ground—but the bastard was already too late. After wrapping the "binding tie" that he'd hidden earlier that day in one of the rotting trunks around Aedan's wrist, Cian quickly looped it around his own, the simple-looking strip of black leather instantly searing its way into their flesh. Then he locked his burning gaze with Aedan's, and gave him a chilling smile. "Thanks to Simone's witchcraft, you're bound to me now. Which means it's time for you to die."

"You *can't* kill me," Aedan scoffed, looking at him as if he were the one who'd been lost to madness. "Not when we're bound, brother."

"Just watch me," he snarled, and it was almost enough to make him laugh, the look of shock that spilled over Aedan's face like a stain.

Shaking his head with disbelief, Aedan's pierced brows pulled together in a deep frown as he looked toward Sayre, who was watching them with wide, terrified eyes. And then he slowly brought his crimson gaze back to Cian. "Is this real?" he asked, and there was something in his tone that reminded Cian of the boy he'd known all those years ago, and it broke his fucking heart. "You're willing to do that for her?"

"I'm willing to do *anything* for her," he rasped, his goddamn eyes filling with tears. "Whatever it takes." And with those final words, Cian shot one last, smoldering look at Sayre, drinking in the breathtaking sight of her until it fueled him with the strength he needed for one final burst of energy—and then he launched both him and Aedan through the air. They crashed into the middle of the rotten, broken trees, both of them crying out from the shared pain of their landing. Blood gurgled on Aedan's lips from the gaping wound that had been made when a jagged, protruding branch pierced through his upper back and tore straight through his chest, the spearlike tip hovering just beneath Cian's throat. But as brutal as the wound appeared, it wasn't enough to kill him, and Cian knew what he had to do.

With Sayre's screams echoing in his head, he whispered, "Time to die," and shoved himself onto the branch, the wood puncturing his throat and driving straight through to his spinal column, severing it in two.

After that, there was nothing but a hazy, icy darkness, as if he were floating through the nighttime sky. He could hear arguing, but it was far away. Someone was shouting that he was dead, that Sayre was going to kill herself trying to save him, and he struggled to tell her *no*, not to risk herself, but she was screaming for everyone to stay away from her, threatening to zap them over the side of the cliffs if they tried to stop her. Then a strange, shimmering vein of warmth started to snake its way through his weightless body, growing steadily hotter and more brilliant, until it felt as if he were lying in the center of a burning flame.

Only…he wasn't burning. Yes, there was pain, but his skin wasn't charring, or turning to ash. Instead, it was his throat and spine that seared as though lava had been poured directly into his wounds, and he suddenly realized that it was Sayre's healing powers being injected into his broken body.

"Did you make sure that goddamn binding tie is off him?" someone grunted, followed by a voice that sounded like Jillian's still screaming, "Jesus, someone stop her. She's going to kill herself!"

"Don't you understand what's happening?" Sayre growled, sounding like an enraged goddess. "He was tied to that asshole when he died, so he goes where his brother goes. If I let go of the hold I have on his soul, he's going to follow right behind him, straight into Hell!"

"And if you're linked with him like this, then so will you!" Jillian sobbed.

"I don't care!" Sayre shouted, her voice cracking at the end. "He doesn't get to come back, make me fall in love with his cocky ass and then leave me. Screw that!

I won't let him! I know I can save him. Why the hell do you think I came here after he walked away from me all over again? I *saw* this, Jilly. I knew he would need me!"

"Whatever you saw, it's impossible to bring back a soul once it's gone. You know that, Sayre. You're not thinking straight."

"Maybe it's impossible for most," he heard Jeremy murmur. "But you Murphy girls are special, sweetheart."

Murphy girl? No! She needed his name, damn it. Needed to be a Hennessey.

And why in God's name was he just lying there, listening to them argue, when he needed to fight for her? When he needed to fight his way back to her, so that she didn't end up following him into the *after*? And while he was all for having this woman by his side for eternity—*though preferably not in Hell*—he wanted a lifetime with her first. He wanted the wedding and births. The holidays and family vacations. He wanted the whole goddamn package!

Scraping onto every ounce of strength he could find, Cian finally managed to force his heavy eyelids open. He found himself staring up at the tearstained face of the most beautiful girl in the world—but he didn't know what he'd done to deserve her. All he knew was that someone out there had given him a second chance, and he was taking it. Grabbing on with both hands and taking the hell out of it.

"Shh," she whispered against his ear, when he tried to speak. "Shh. Just lie here and heal for a moment. You're almost there."

Against his will, his heavy eyelids drifted shut again, and he existed in a strange dreamlike state, not asleep, and yet, not completely awake. Sayre's mouthwatering scent was all around him, soothing and warm, and he knew his friends were close by, their voices reaching out to him in soft murmurs and broken phrases.

"So she knew he was going to die for her?"

"Never thought it would happen to him."

"About damn time that it did."

No shit, his wolf grunted, its gruff laughter echoing in his head.

With a smile on his lips, he let himself go back under, no idea how much time had passed when he next opened his eyes. But he could tell that someone had put a pair of jeans on him, since he was once again in his human form, and Sayre was no longer holding him on her lap. Instead, he was lying on the blood-soaked ground in the middle of the clearing with something soft under his head, and Brody was crouching down beside him, a fierce scowl etched onto the Runner's scarred face.

"Hey, would you look at this," Cian croaked. "It's Broody Brody to the rescue."

Brody snorted, his green eyes glittering with relief. "Shut up, you lucky jackass."

Surprised by how good he felt, he managed a lop-sided grin. "I know that look. You want to hug me now, don't you?"

"I think I'll leave the hugging to your woman," the Runner muttered, shaking his head. "But I'm thinking I could probably welcome you back home now without constantly wanting to kick your ass."

"Thanks, man. You're all heart," he said drily.

Brody laughed, and Cian sniffed the air, searching for Sayre's scent. "Speaking of my woman, where is she?"

Jerking his chin toward his right, Brody said, "Right over there, giving your old man hell."

"That's my girl," he rumbled with pride, pushing himself up into a sitting position. He purposefully kept his head turned away from Aedan's body, not wanting to see it. Though he definitely didn't regret what he'd done, knowing it was the only way, it wouldn't be a sight he could stomach.

As if he'd read his mind, Brody lowered his voice so that no one else could hear him. "She saved you, man. Brought you back from a one-way trip to Hell. And you were ready to spend eternity there to protect her. I…I don't know what to say to that exactly, except that I'm happy for you. You went all in, Cian, and you came out breathing on the other side. Now you can leave the past in the past, where it belongs, and move forward by having a kick-ass life with your little witch."

"You know, when you put it like that, I'm pretty fucking happy for me, too."

"Yeah, I can see that you are." A low laugh rumbled up from the Runner's chest as he eyed Cian's smile. "Christ, that girl has you *so* wrapped around her little finger."

"That's only fair, since I plan on keeping her wrapped around certain parts of me pretty much twenty-four seven."

"Watch it, Cian." Jillian's laughing voice came from somewhere behind him. "That's my baby sister you're talking about."

"And she's *my* woman," he said with a wealth of satisfaction, watching her giving his old man absolute hell for not doing anything to help him during the fight. No matter what, the little witch was always fighting for him—fighting for *them*—and he knew there were going to be some serious changes taking place in his life, the first being that he was going to stop buying his own bullshit. Because he finally got it.

Anyone could walk away. *Anyone.* But it took a real man to face the truth and accept that one little slip of a girl held his entire world in her hands. The smartest, sexiest, most incredible girl there was.

"And she's ours," he growled under his breath.

About. Fucking. Time.

He gave a low laugh, agreeing with the beast completely.

Needing to hold her more than he needed his next breath, he managed to push himself up on his knees, and while he was a bit shaky, it was a goddamn miracle he was alive. Suddenly, kneeling in the middle of that godforsaken clearing, he realized something that was pretty damn important. For the first time, he saw, and actually *believed*, that everything really did happen for a reason. All the pain and heartbreak and fear and loss. He'd spent so many years wishing he could undo it all, but it was those things that had brought him here, to this point. Made him who he was. If he'd been different, fate might have never chosen him for Sayre at all, because it was the sum of all those parts of him that made him hers. That put the two pieces of them together, clicking them into one.

Each decision and step they'd made had led them to this point.

Every single goddamn one of them.

It was the kind of thing that could twist your brain into a pretzel if you thought about it for too long, and he didn't need to waste his time. He wasn't fighting this outcome. No, he was grabbing on to it as hard and as tight as he could, and holding on forever.

Holding on to her. His woman. His beautiful little bad-ass witch.

He didn't care what Colin Hennessey or anyone else thought of what he was about to do. The only person who mattered was Sayre, and Cian knew she would understand the symbolism behind the way he started crawling toward her on his hands and knees. Before his father and friends and God, he was humbling himself for her, making it clear to one and all that he would crawl after her over any distance, for any amount of time, until he finally had her in the end.

She ran toward him the instant she caught sight of him, tears streaming down her flushed face, and he moved to his knees again so that he could catch her against him, his head tilting back as he stared up at her, getting lost in those big, beautiful eyes. "You're *mine*," he told her, his big hands gripping her hips. "That means I'm never letting you go, Sayre."

He couldn't stop the slow, satisfied smile that lifted the corner of his mouth when she dropped to her knees before him. "It's about time you said that."

"And?" he murmured.

She blinked, looking adorably confused. "And what?"

"There's something else it's about damn time that I said to you." Looking her right in the eye so that she would know just how much he meant it, he cupped her precious, tear-drenched face in his palms, and told her, *"I love you, Sayre."*

"Oh, God," she whispered, crying even harder. "I can't believe you just said that."

He could hear his father bitching from somewhere behind her about how he was making a spectacle of himself and that real men didn't grovel, but Cian just tuned out the jackass, unwilling to let him intrude on this moment. Then he heard Jeremy mutter, "You know, I didn't think it was possible for someone to be an even bigger pain in the ass than Cian. But I was wrong. His old man *sucks.*" He snickered under his breath. "That's kinda fitting, I guess, seeing as how he's a vampire."

"Seriously?" Carla asked. "You're making jokes *now*?"

"You know what Jeremy's like," Mason murmured. "The End of Days could be here and he'd still be laughing it up."

"Speaking of jokes," Cian said, raising his voice so the group could hear him, "when we get home, I want my cabin stripped down to the baseboards, ready for Sayre and me to make it the way we want it."

Jeremy snickered again. "I think we can manage that. But what do you want us to do with all the green shit?"

Keeping his eyes locked tight on Sayre, unwilling to look away from the love he could see shining there in that smoky, smoldering blue, Cian grinned as he lowered his voice and said, "Let's ship it over here. I'm betting my old man would love it."

The others all laughed, but he was already sipping from Sayre's soft lips, her sweet taste fueling him with energy, making him feel like he could take on the entire bloody world. But the world would have to be taken on by someone else. All he cared about taking was *her*—as hard and as often as she'd let him—and he couldn't wait a goddamn second more.

"Let's get out of here," he growled against her hot little mouth as he quickly moved to his feet with her in his arms and carried her away from their cheering friends, up to the bachelor's house, his body growing stronger with each step that he took. He felt as though he'd existed in two parts: the man he'd been before he started to see clearly, who wanted to put his hands around fate's throat and squeeze the life out of him. And then this one, who was ready to embrace the shit out of that fucker and thank him for making this incredible woman a part of his life, because he wouldn't change it for anything.

Seriously. Not a single goddamn thing.

Though they managed to make it through the front door, they didn't get any farther than the entryway before their desire got the better of them and they went wild on each other.

"Shit," he muttered, dropping down on his knees, his hands digging into her sweet little ass as she wrapped herself around him like a vine. "I'm still covered in blood, baby."

"Don't care," she gasped, kissing her way up the side of his throat, her lips and tongue driving him mad, while practically all the blood left in his body shot south, hardening his cock to the point of pain.

"Damn it, Sayre." His voice was raw and graveled with need. "You deserve better than this."

She pulled back just far enough that she could smirk at him. "Blood is a part of your life and it always will be. Which means it's a part of mine, too. So I doubt this is the last time we'll go to bed bloody."

"We're not even in a bed," he grunted, coming down over her as he laid her back on the hardwood floor. His right hand fisted in her silky hair, while his left one settled on her waist, his thumb stroking the soft skin on her belly.

With a devilish light in her eyes, she said, "I don't care about that, either." Then she lifted her head, nipped the edge of his jaw with her teeth and asked him, "Are you hungry for me, Cian?"

"Starved," he groaned, ripping at her clothes so that he could get to that soft, bare skin underneath. "And too damn desperate to wait, Sayre."

"Good," she said with a wealth of satisfaction that made him feel like he could level a bloody mountain for her, if that's what she wanted. What she *needed*.

"Tell me you're happy, and mean it," he said in a

rough, breathless rasp, as he shoved her shirt up over her head, then quickly got rid of her lacy bra. "Because I can't let you go, Sayre. I did it once and it killed me inside each day. I can't do it again."

"You won't have to," she told him, running her greedy hands over every part of him she could reach, her delicious scent only getting richer with the rise of her need. "You aren't ever getting rid of me, and happy doesn't even begin to describe how freaking good I feel."

"Thank God," he groaned, pressing his parted lips against the center of her chest.

Lifting his face with her hand cupped under his chin, she waited until his molten gaze had reconnected with hers, before taking a quick breath, and saying, "I want this—want *you*—but I need to tell you…I mean, you probably figured it out…but I never actually fooled around with anyone else. So this is my *first*. My first time."

His breath jammed in his throat, and he blinked as he touched his tongue to his lower lip, letting those husky words work their way into him. It didn't change how he felt about her, or how much he wanted her, because he was in this no matter what. Whether she'd had fifty lovers…or none. But he'd have been lying through his teeth if he'd said he wasn't happy as hell about it.

"Mine, too," he finally managed to choke out, while his blood pounded in his ears, his heart damn near jerking its way through his chest. "It's mine, too, baby."

"Cian!" she gasped with a laugh that felt like pure, white-hot sunshine being injected straight into his veins. Then she smacked him in the shoulder for making what she thought was a joke. But it wasn't. Stripping away the rest of her clothes as quickly as possible, along with his jeans, he lifted his head and looked at her. Watched her luminous eyes go heavy with need as he lowered his hips between her parted thighs and rubbed his hot, granite-hard erection against her slick folds, his own eyes no doubt burning red with the ferocity of his need.

"I mean it," he told her, his deep voice as low and fervent as a vow. "This *is* a first for me, Sayre, because I've never *made love* to any other woman in my life."

"Then do it now," she whispered, slaying him with her beautiful smile as he reached between those slender thighs and pushed a long finger into the tight entrance nestled there, finding her deliciously hot and slick, melting for him like sun-warmed honey. "Make love to me, Cian. Don't make me wait."

"Gotta make sure you're ready," he groaned, squeezing a second finger into that tender, cushiony sheath, the way she clasped him, so tight and hot and wet, shooting a jolt of heat up his spine that had him gritting his teeth, fighting for control.

Then her next words shot it to hell.

Chapter 17

"Please, Cian. We've had freaking days of foreplay. I need you *now*," Sayre begged, thinking that he felt so much harder, pressed against her inner thigh, than he had the other times that they'd done this. Well, not *this*. But the lead-up. The slow build of their lust and love and need that was *finally* going to have its day. Hopefully before they detonated from the heat.

He felt bigger, too, and she knew this was going to be anything but easy. But she didn't care. Nothing worth keeping ever came easily, and she was keeping this man with her for...well, forever.

Suspecting he was worried about hurting her, she was ready to start pleading again, when he pulled his fingers free and notched the thick, heavy tip of him against her opening. Digging her nails into his shoulders, she panted with excitement as he started to carefully push forward, forcing her to stretch open for him, her power bursting free in a glittering array of sparks, letting him know exactly how desperate she was for this moment.

"So bloody tight, Sayre." He muttered the words directly into her ear, his voice so low and sensual it made her shiver even harder, her hands clasping his hips as she tried to pull him closer. "I *knew* you would be like this, lass. So damn perfect it blew my mind."

"Please," she gasped through trembling, tingling lips, not even sure what she was begging for. More? Faster? Deeper? All of them? *Yes!* All of them. She needed *everything*.

As if he heard her silent demands, he put one of his big, hot hands under her ass, tilting her up to him so that he could wedge more of that broad shaft inside her, keeping his rhythm slow and easy, rubbing and stroking all those wickedly sweet spots that were making her slippery and hot and so damn desperate for him she was digging her nails into his hard, gorgeous skin and moaning her head off.

Then he finally bit out a gritty curse, gripped her hips in his strong hands and shoved himself impossibly deep, forcing every single inch of that massive erection inside her. She cried out as he hit the end of her, his cock throbbing against her sensitive tissues, so big she couldn't breathe around the shocking sensation. But who needed air when she was full of this magnificent male, his teeth nipping her tender earlobe as he breathed in a harsh, ragged rhythm, his powerful, bad-ass body buried deep inside hers? Then he started to move, their heat-glazed stomachs and chests sliding against each other, his mouthwatering muscles flexing beneath his tight skin as he rolled his hips against hers, thrusting in a breathtaking rhythm that was getting better each time he pushed inside her.

"How's that feel?" he asked, his husky voice low and intimate at her ear.

"Insanely freaking amazing," she gasped, arching her back so that she could press her swollen breasts harder against his chest.

He breathed a dark, devastatingly sexy laugh into her ear, but she meant every word. He was so big that it kind of felt like she was being split in two, and yeah, that hurt. But there was something beautiful behind the pain—a fullness and need and sense of rightness that overshadowed the discomfort and made her want *more*. Made her need it...*crave it*. She ran her palms up his sleek back, loving the play of powerful muscles beneath his hot skin and the hunger she could feel burning inside him as he used that magnificent body to claim her. Each time that he withdraw, her body fought to hold on to him, and he came back into her even harder, the sounds he made and the way he moved letting her know he needed her just as badly as she needed him. If not more.

"Ah...*fuck*, that's so sweet," he groaned against her temple. He nuzzled her hair with his nose, his right hand curled possessively around her breast as he drove inside her. "So goddamn *perfect*."

"What is?"

Pulling his head back, he locked his scorching, molten gaze with hers. "You're opened up to me, lass. *Completely*. I can feel everything. Everything that's in your heart, and it's... Christ, Sayre, there aren't even words."

Her throat shook, melting with emotion. "Love you so much," she whispered, pushing her fingers into the thick, damp strands of his hair.

Staring down at her as if she were a miracle, something cherished and infinitely precious, he said, "I know, Sayre. God, baby, I know. And you are so bloody beautiful, inside and out. The most beautiful woman in the world."

She couldn't help but smile with pleasure, because even though she knew it wasn't true, he made her feel that way. Because she knew it was how he saw her. Even when she was old and gray, she knew she would be able to see this same devastating level of devotion in his eyes, and *God*, that was so freaking sweet.

"I want it harder," she moaned, curling her hands around the back of his neck, his skin feverishly warm to the touch.

Something hot and wicked moved through his eyes. "Good, because I'm about to take you so hard you won't be able to walk up to bed, and then I'm taking you even harder."

"Do it," she gasped, unable to keep the smile off her face when she noticed his fangs, gleaming and white, drop beneath his upper lip. They definitely weren't his wolf's fangs. They were sharper, deadlier. But she didn't care. If she'd wanted easy, she'd have fallen in love with another man. But she'd chosen *him*, because he was everything she could ever want or need or desire, and she wanted the full experience. Every single scream-inducing thing he could do to her.

"Do *all* of it," she moaned, turning her head so that the tender side of her throat was left vulnerable and exposed, her blood thundering through her veins. "Make the bite, Cian. Make me yours."

"Don't," he grunted, his gaze immediately narrowing to sharp, piercing points of gray beneath his lowered brows. "Don't tempt me."

"But it's time."

Shaking his head, he argued, "I've lost too much fucking blood tonight and you smell too damn good. It's too dangerous right now, Sayre. We need to wait until my control isn't shot to hell and back."

"I don't care about your control. I trust you and it needs to be *now*, when we're finally together like we've been meant to be for so long. This is perfect."

"Sayre," he growled, his hammering thrusts getting rougher...deeper, driving her deliciously close to a powerful release she knew might damn well make her faint, it was going to be *that* intense.

Clutching his hard, slick shoulders, she stared up at his beloved face and said, "You've *died* for me, Cian. Do you really think there's any way any part of you would let me come to harm?"

"No," he grunted, and she figured she'd finally managed to convince him, because his hand was suddenly in her hair, wrenching her head to the side, exposing the tender column so that he could drive those sharp fangs deep into her throat, piercing her tight flesh and making the bond. That unbelievable, tilt-the-world-on-its-axis bond that had her fighting for air, so filled with emotion there wasn't room for anything else. Just love and trust and hope. Joy and happiness and a soul-deep need for this man who was the other half of her heart.

When he tried to pull his head back, she fisted her hands in his thick hair and held him to her, saying, "More. Take more, Cian. Drink from me."

He stiffened at the end of a hard downstroke, packed up thick and deep inside her, his powerful frame shuddering. "No," he snarled against her throat, pulling his fangs back with a wet pop. "I won't use you like that."

"You will," she breathed, keenly aware of the hot blood streaming from the bite he'd made, the two puncture wounds flowing freely. "You promised me everything

I'll ever want, and I want this. I want as deep inside you as you are in me."

"It's wrong," he rasped, his body rigid with tension.

"I belong inside you, Cian, pumping through your veins. Filling your belly." She arched her back, pressing up against him, loving the way their damp bodies rubbed together. "Nothing between us is wrong. Nothing is a sin. I offer this freely, and I'm even begging you for it. I want to be the thing that nourishes you. That gives you what you need."

"Shit," he growled, already lowering his head again, his warm breath rushing against her. "You're too damn perfect to be real."

She screamed in ecstasy only seconds later, holding him to her tighter as a lush, breathtaking orgasm pulsed through her, her hands fisted in his hair as his open mouth closed over the punctures and he started to suck on her. Driving himself inside her with a thick, aggressive rhythm, he devoured the hot blood that flowed through her veins as if it were the most exquisite thing he'd ever tasted. "Oh, God! That's so amazing, Cian."

He gave a low, animalistic growl against her flesh, and she grinned, knowing it was because he'd liked hearing her. When he finally pulled his mouth away, he pressed a gentle kiss to her throat, lapping at the tender skin where he'd bitten her, and she hissed from the pleasure. "Come for me again, lass. Give me one more. *Now*," he growled, dropping his forehead against hers, "'cause I'm about to come for you so bloody hard."

As if her pleasure were his to call and control, they crashed over that dark, devastating edge together, his hips slamming and grinding against hers as he pulsed inside her, his hands gripping her body hard. His raw, guttural curses and her keening cries filled the air, while her power consumed them, fueled by the bond that now flowed so strongly between them. To another's eyes, they would have no doubt looked as if they'd been engulfed in crackling, crimson flames, yet they were thankfully unburned, if not completely shattered when he finally collapsed in her arms. He was still gently thrusting inside her, as if he couldn't bring himself to stop, his hot face resting against the cushion of her breasts as they struggled to catch their breath.

"God, Sayre. I could feel that sweet burn *inside* you," he groaned, sounding drowsy with satisfaction. She let her eyes drift closed as she stroked his head, running her fingers through his hair, and had no idea how much time had passed when he carefully withdrew from her. Then he pushed himself to his feet, lifted her into his arms and carried her upstairs to the bathroom, where he put her in a hot, steaming shower.

Holding her face in his hands, he took her mouth with lush, drugging kisses, while the water sprayed down on them from above, washing them clean.

"It's never been like that for me before," he told her, when they finally had to stop kissing long enough to breathe. Keeping his head bent over hers, he held her face as he stared deep into her eyes, saying, "Nothing ever even came close. And now you own every part of me. *Own* it, Sayre. And I'm so damn sorry. Christ, I'm so sorry, for everything, baby. I told myself for so long that I couldn't love you because I was too much like my father. Because his blood ran through my veins. But the other night, after Aedan came to the Alley, I finally started to figure out that it was just a lie. The truth is that I've been too afraid to let myself love you because I was terrified of ending up like my mother. Of losing…

everything. What if you didn't love me in return? What if I gave you my heart and you broke it?"

Clutching his strong wrists, she blinked the water from her lashes as she said, "I wouldn't. I won't. I'll protect it with my dying breath, Cian."

"I know, baby. I know. I'm just sorry it took me so long to figure it all out. To see that love doesn't make you weak, so long as you're giving it to the right person. When that happens, it only makes you stronger." A wry, lopsided grin started to twitch at the corner of his mouth as he added, "And I'm probably going to have my man card revoked for babbling like this, but even if you didn't love me back, I would still love you like this, Sayre. With everything that I am and will ever be. With every part of me."

"But I do love you. I love you so much. More than anything."

Touching his open mouth to hers, he smiled as he nipped her bottom lip. "I know, lass. I could feel every breathtaking part of it when I was buried deep inside you. So deep I was practically coming out your mouth."

She couldn't help but laugh against those sexy, smiling lips. "Keep talking like that and I think your man card is gonna be just fine."

"Face it, witch. You love my dirty mouth."

"I do," she gasped, already shivering with need for him. "I love everything about you, Cian. And that's why I'd like to come back here. I'd like to split our time between the two countries."

"Why the hell would you want to do that?" And then in a drier tone, he said, "Are you sure you're not just trying to avoid your mother? Because *that* I would actually be okay with."

She shook her head as she laughed. "Don't worry about Mom. She'll come to love you, I promise."

He still looked skeptical, so she leaned closer, pressing her lips to his for another kiss, this one brief and sweet. When she pulled back far enough to see his eyes, she said, "I want to spend time here because I can sense how much you love this country. Maybe not *here*, where your father is, but you love Ireland, Cian. This land, it's in your blood."

"*You're* in my blood."

"And this place is, too. I want to make happy memories here for you. I want the children we'll have one day to know both our countries." She could see the fear that darkened his gaze at her words, and so she said, "Not all wolves and witches are good, and not all vampires are evil. You're proof of that, Cian. It's love that builds a person's heart, and we'll give our children so much they'll glow with it."

He swallowed so hard that she could see the movement in his throat, but he didn't say anything. Just stared down at her with those dark, smoldering eyes.

"Unless you don't want that with me," she murmured, stroking the rigid muscles at the back of his neck.

"God, don't think that," he rasped, the husky words sounding torn out of him. "I want it more than anything. I want to put a baby inside you right now. But...Christ, Sayre. The idea of having all that, everything I want...it still scares the hell out of me."

"Cian, use the bond. *Feel* my love for you. It's okay to be happy," she told him, understanding his fears even better than her own. "It's okay to look forward to the future. To our life together. And I promise I'll help you. I'll be here for you, every step of the way."

* * *

And she was—for every single step—changing Cian's life in ways he'd never even imagined. Each one making it richer, brighter and filled with so much love he knew he was the luckiest son of a bitch on the planet.

After that night, they couldn't keep their hands off each other, and a week went by before they finally left the bachelor's house and headed back home.

Then he had her on the plane, on their way back to Maryland.

And in the car, on their way up to the Alley.

And when they reached his cabin, he took her right back to bed, and kept her there.

In short, he'd become completely insatiable when it came to his woman. Not just for her body, but for every part of her. Those smiles that brought him to his knees and the snark that never failed to make him laugh. They'd talked constantly the past week, when they weren't making love, making plans for the future...sappy and sweet and so filled with hope it was impossible to stop smiling. He would have felt like a lovesick fool if not for the fact that his little witch was the same.

And, damn, did she wear happiness well. As gorgeous as he'd always thought she was before, it was nothing to how stunning he found her now. Cian realized that what he'd thought of as love when he'd first accepted that Sayre meant something to him had only been the beginning. Powerful and strong, but too new to be fully in its own, like the first flake of snow in the world's greatest blizzard. Or the first grain of sand in a never-ending desert.

And what he felt for her now. God, there simply weren't words.

The night was sultry and sweet, the woman in his arms, snuggled against his body, even sweeter. Her heart was pounding, rushing the blood through her veins, and he could feel the darkness in him quickening with awareness, eager for the hot, rich spill as he pierced her flesh. Even his wolf had become addicted to his blood feedings, the intimacy of the act appealing to the beast's primal, possessive nature.

After long discussions on the matter, Sayre had finally convinced him to keep feeding from her until she reached his age, since she wanted them to be able to grow old together. Like the miracle she was, she was teaching him to not only accept that brutal part of his nature, but also to embrace it. And the way she called him her "blood wolf" when she wanted to feel the bite of his fangs made him steel-hard every single time. They indulged often, and he loved how close it made him feel to her, only strengthening their bond.

"Already?" she asked with a soft catch of excitement in her voice, when he rolled back on top of her, pushing his way between her thighs. His cock was hard as a rock as it brushed against her slick, swollen folds.

"I have a lot of time to make up for," he told her, pushing inside her, working his hips in careful nudges until she'd taken every inch. When he was buried deep, her soft little body gripping him like a tight, wet glove, he lowered his head and took her mouth with hot, hungry kisses that curled her toes.

"So this whole making-up-for-lost-time-in-the-sack thing we have going on. Does that mean you'll eventually stop wanting me so much?" she gasped, when she finally had to break away from the ravenous demands of his mouth so that she could catch her breath.

"I should say yes, but I honestly don't see that happening, lass. Each time, I want you even more…and it somehow just keeps getting better." And it was true. Not just on a physical level, though that was unlike anything he could have ever dreamed of. The way she clasped him in her tight body, the way she moved with him and smelled and tasted and felt in his arms—there was simply no comparison. But the emotional aspect was just as intense, if not more so, adding a richer, deeper layer to the act that was impossible to explain. He just knew that he needed it, *needed Sayre*, more than he needed water and air. Hell, he needed her more than he needed blood or the moonlight. His hunger for her had become more a part of him than either his wolf or his "dark" blood could ever be, and he wouldn't have it any other way.

"At this rate, we'll probably kill ourselves with sex," she teased, pushing against his shoulders until he'd rolled to his back and she'd ended up on top, straddling his hips.

"You won't hear me complaining," he growled, mesmerized by the sight of her as she started to move. "More like begging for more."

Eyes gleaming with pleasure, she gave him a beautiful, breathtaking smile. "I love how you do that. How you always tell me how much you want me. You're going to spoil me rotten, aren't you?"

"You bet your sweet little ass I am. Before and *after* I get my ring on your finger." He was ready to pull her down to him so he could take that sweet mouth of hers in another greedy, scalding kiss. But she had other ideas.

"I promise to spoil you back," she whispered, pulling her hair over her shoulder as she turned her head, exposing the vulnerable curve of her throat. It was the signal that she was ready. Ready to give him all that he needed. To nourish his body, as well as his soul.

"Baby," he groaned, his abs flexing as he sat up and buried his face against that warm, tender skin, his mouth watering for the taste of her and his heart thundering like a drum, "you already do."

Then Cian buried his fangs hard and deep, and as he lost himself in the intoxicating taste of his woman, the feel of her reaching into the very heart of him with that burning, blinding light that was pure Sayre, he knew a sense of peace that reached all the way down to his soul. A sense of being *home*, exactly where he belonged.

He no longer feared the present or let the past consume and define him. He didn't have time for that kind of nonsense, because he was too busy looking to the future. To a life that was so much more than anything he could have ever hoped for.

A future he wouldn't give up for anything in the world.

And he couldn't wait to get started.

* * * * *

JUST CAN'T GET ENOUGH?

Join our social communities
and talk to us online.

You will have access to the latest
news on upcoming titles and special
promotions, but most importantly,
you can talk to other fans about your
favorite Harlequin reads.

Harlequin.com/Community

Facebook.com/HarlequinBooks

Twitter.com/HarlequinBooks

Pinterest.com/HarlequinBooks

HSOCIAL

To bring down a serial killer, two detectives must pose
as husband and wife. They infiltrate a community, never
expecting love to intrude on their deadly mission!

Read on for a sneak peek of

UNDERCOVER HUNTER

by *New York Times* bestselling author
Rachel Lee, coming January 2015!

Calvin Sweet knew he was taking some big chances, but
taking risks always invigorated him. Coming back to his
home in Conard County was the first of the new risks. Five
years ago he'd left for the big city because the law was closing in on him.

Returning to the site where he had hung his trophies was
a huge risk, too, although he could claim he was out for a
hike in the spring mountains. There was nothing left, anyway. The law had taken it all, and the sight filled him with
both sorrow and bitterness. Anger, too. They had no right
to take away his hard work, his triumphs, his mementos.

But they had. After five years all that was left were some
remnants of cargo netting rotting in the tree limbs and the
remains of a few sawed-off nooses.

He could close his eyes and remember, and remembering
filled him with joy and a sense of his own huge power, the
power of life and death. The power to take it all away. The
⟨power⟩ to enlighten those whose existence was so shallow.

HRSEXP1214

They took it for granted. Calvin never did.

From earliest childhood he had been fascinated by spider and their webs. He had spent hours watching as insect afte insect fell victim to those silken strands, struggling mightily until they were stung and then wrapped up helplessly to await their fate. Each corpse on the web had been a trophy marking the spider's victory. No one ever escaped.

No one had escaped him, either.

He was chosen, just like a spider, to be exactly what he was

Chosen. He liked that word. It fit both him and his victims. They were all chosen to perform the dance of death together, to plumb the reaches of human endurance. To sacrifice the ordinary for the extraordinary. So he quashed his growing need to act and focused his attention on another part of his life. He had a job now, one he needed to report to every evening. He was whistling now as he walked back down to his small ranch.

A spiderweb was beginning to take shape in his mind, one for his barn loft that no one would see, ever. It was enough that he could admire it and savor the gifts there. The impulse to hunt eased, and soon he was in control again. He liked control. He liked controlling himself and others, even as he fulfilled his purpose.

Like the spider, he was not hasty to act. It would have to be the right person at the right time, and the time was not yet right. First he had to build his web.

Don't miss UNDERCOVER HUNTER by *New York Times* bestselling author Rachel Lee, available January 2015 wherever Harlequin® Romantic Suspense books and ebooks are sold.

HRS

HARLEQUIN®

A *Romance* FOR EVERY MOOD™

**Stay up-to-date on all your
romance-reading news with the
Harlequin Shopping Guide,
featuring bestselling authors, exciting new
miniseries, books to watch and more!**

The newest issue will be delivered right to you
with our compliments! There are 4 each year.

Signing up is easy.

EMAIL

ShoppingGuide@Harlequin.ca

WRITE TO US

HARLEQUIN BOOKS
Attention: Customer Service Department
P.O. Box 9057, Buffalo, NY 14269-9057

OR PHONE

1-800-873-8635 in the United States
1-888-343-9777 in Canada

Please allow 4-6 weeks for delivery of the first issue by mail.

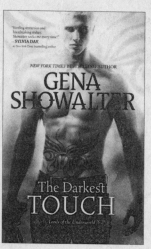